To Hugh

Best Wishes

Leslie McKeown.

Just One More Summer

by
Julie McGowan

Sunpenny
PUBLISHING

Just One More Summer

This work of fiction is completely a product of the author's imagination. Any resemblance to actual characters, dead or alive, is purely coincidental. Likewise, there is no such village as Tremorden, which is created from a gathering together of the author's knowledge and memories of several Cornish experiences.

All Rights Reserved. No part of this publication may be reproduced, stored in a retrieval system, or transmitted in any form or by any means, electronic, graphical, or mechanical, including photocopying or recording, or by any other means known now or to be developed in the future, without the written permission of the publisher.

Sunpenny Publishing
United Kingdom

Copyright © 2008 by Julie McGowan

Cover design copyright © 2008 by Sunpenny Publishing

ISBN 978-0-9555283-2-3

FIRST EDITION: April 2008

Printed in the United Kingdom

ALSO BY JULIE McGOWAN:

The Mountains Between, ISBN 978-0-9555283-3-0

In memory of Sally, a very dear friend.
1953-2008

*

With particular thanks to:

My husband Peter and children Daniel, Catherine, Robert and Elizabeth, for their ever-present love and encouragement.

Rosemary Johnson, for her persistent belief in me.

Barbara Daniels, once again for her professional eye.

Ann and Allan, Debbie and Georgia, Vi and Linda, for their continuing support.

My great publishers, Jo and Andrew Holloway, for their eagle eyes, their friendly approach, and their ability once more to make this process so much fun.

And all the people who've taken the time and trouble to contact me to tell me that they like what I do!

1.

Okay ... Let's get this straight right from the start.
First, this is not yet another story about a nearly thirty-something who is looking for the right man to whisk her down the aisle and spends every working minute agonising over how she'll meet him, or crying because she thinks she's already found and lost him. And spends every non-working hour trowelling on the make-up and propping up a bar in the hope that tonight will be the night, and if it isn't she may as well take the best on offer anyway ... I mean, is this *really* what women have been fighting for, for the last three decades or more?

Second, there won't be any talk of designer labels – except by my mother, perhaps, although she's more into Mondi and Jaeger than Gucci and Chloe. It's all very well if you've got a nifty little job in advertising or the media – which you've somehow obtained by default and miraculously managed to keep, even though you can't use the computer properly and you spend an inordinate amount of time in the ladies' loo. But it's entirely different if you're secretary to a solicitor and the new kitchen units still have to be paid for. The nearest I've ever got to designer clothes is a pashmina of doubtful origin and a pair of Nike trainers in the sales – although at least my underwear's H&M rather than M&S. Even I draw the line somewhere.

Third, I haven't got a tumbling mass of red-gold curls which become engagingly unmanageable at a hint of rain; green eyes, skin that has to be shielded from the sun, or a honed and toned body. Think smallish, darkish, straight hair, trim enough body because I walk a lot, and a complexion that turns dirty brown in the heat. An appearance which my mother, had she been born fifty or more years earlier, would have called 'common', but which she now concedes grudgingly at least allows me to get a tan without staying in the sun long enough to get wrinkles.

Oh yes, and I haven't got the statutory stunningly handsome but gay best friend with whom I can indulge in a bit of mutual shoulder-crying when our respective boyfriends let us down. I'm sure it's all to do with the solicitor's office being on the wrong side of the river – Purley, or at least my bit of it, just doesn't seem to abound with men who have 'come out'.

And while I think of it, there won't be lots of F-words scattered about either, to inject a bit of realism. Yes, I know it's supposed to be everyone's favourite expletive these days, but quite honestly it hasn't infiltrated my part of sedate suburbia to that extent yet. True, Will used it a few times when we were having a mega-row, but that really was in extremis – and I did have one good friend who had a fondness for the word, but I hardly see her these days. Will didn't really like her, you see, so our friendship sort of petered out. And why didn't he approve of her? Because of her foul mouth apparently, which he didn't like in women ... which more or less proves my point, I think. Or else it's the dreary world of solicitors' offices to blame again – I don't mix with people who dare to be so bold.

I haven't even got a handsome but scary boss whose taciturn manner disguises the fact that he is rapidly falling for the darkish looks, straight hair, etc etc, along with my endearing stupidity. Mine is portly and avuncular and breathes heavily from defective sinuses, not passion. Or at least he did up until yesterday, when he ceased to be my boss.

Because as from yesterday I am no longer a solicitor's secretary, just as I am no longer a wife. Now I am an ex-secretary and an ex-wife, soon to be divorced, sitting on the floor of what will soon be my ex-flat, wishing my mother hadn't shown up just at this precise moment.

At this point in my life I really could have done with a mother who wasn't quite so composed, so smart, so *sophisticated,* as mine. Come to think of it, there were lots of times in my life when I would have preferred my mother to be one of those homely bodies who gave out lots of good advice without sounding too much like Claire Rayner and was always there with a comforting bosom to cry on. This was simply another of those times.

She was standing, small – that's the only similarity between us – and elegant in crisp cream linen, with a look of distaste on her face as I crammed a few more T-shirts into my already overstuffed bag.

"But *Cornwall!*" she kept repeating, as horrified as if I had said I was off to war-torn Baghdad. "Why *Cornwall?*"

"'Because I've had enough of London and I need a break – which is exactly what you told me I needed several weeks ago."

"For the *whole* summer? Allie, darling, what on earth will you *do* there?"

I pulled a strap tight on my suitcase and turned back to her. "Very little I hope. At first, anyway. If I do get bored or short of money, I'm sure I can get a job in a pub or something just for the season – or I might decide to stay there forever; I don't know."

"But why not something more exotic? Crete, or somewhere – lots of sun and plenty going on?"

"And plenty of men ready for a short summer fling which will help make me feel wanted again?"

My mother ignored the sarcastic tone in my voice. "Well, it wouldn't be such a bad thing, would it?"

"Yes it would. I've told you, I don't want to meet anyone else – and definitely not some holiday Romeo whose brain is in his trousers and is only interested in a quick wham-bam-thank-you-ma'am."

Juliet (she'd insisted that I call her by her Christian name after she finally divorced my father when I was twelve and was hoping to find a younger man – even going so far as to knock a couple of years off my age as well as hers when necessary) had stayed in a villa in Lindos during her first honeymoon in 1970, high above the little town's only burgeoning disco. So she refused to believe that any of the Greek islands would have changed since then, and winced at my choice of phrase.

"But *Cornwall*," she persisted as I continued to arrange luggage all around her. "It will be full of families and will probably rain for most of the time."

I sighed and stopped what I was doing so that I could face her squarely. She clearly hadn't remembered, and I wasn't going to remind her and get into a conversation which would begin: *Ah, yes, your father ...* and then be full of barbed comments which I didn't want to hear again.

"But it will be *normal*," I said instead. "I don't want a fairy-tale existence for a few months in an artificial setting surrounded by artificial people, because I'd still have to face reality afterwards. And jetting off abroad is no fun on your own, and even if I had someone to go with – which I haven't – I would be lousy company and just spoil their holiday as well. *You* told me I should have a break," I went on quickly before Juliet could say, *but I'll come with you darling if you're going to be lonely,* "and that I should get away from it all, so I'm doing exactly as I'm told." I forced a bright smile. "So you ought to be very pleased that your advice is being taken. Leave me to get on with it, and go back to your Floral Society and all those men who want to make an honest woman of you at the Conservative Club."

It was Juliet's turn to sigh. "Well, if you're sure ..." she began doubtfully.

"Of course I'm sure," I said, more positively than I actually felt because I didn't want Juliet to say *but Cornwall!* again. "And if you really want to help you can keep an eye on this place for me while Sarah is staying here, and remember to leave your answerphone on in case I want to get in touch."

Okay ... So you'll have gathered by now that I'm an almost thirty-something, and I might be broken-hearted, but I'm definitely not looking for anyone else to whisk me down the aisle. Once was enough and I'm not going to spend my waking hours looking for a replacement. What we're talking about here is your everyday marriage, which nevertheless meant everything to me, going to the dogs because my husband, Will, found that he preferred the company (not to mention the bed) of another. It happens all the time – lavish wedding, exotic honeymoon, possibly just enough time for a kid or two (if you haven't had them before the wedding), and then the divorce. Only we hadn't got as far as the kids, just the kitchen units, and those will eventually be paid for by Will as part of the same guilt package which includes letting me have his share of the flat.

Juliet was still hovering uncertainly whilst I moved my bags into the hall, flapping her hands in the 'helpless female' way which has become second nature to her. Nobody would guess at the steely core which has seen off a second husband with an even larger divorce settlement than the first, profited from the substantial gifts of several wealthy admirers in recent years, and even now has a rich Conservative or two panting like overweight pugs at the end of her lead. All of which has led her to view my own predicament as a bit of an occupational hazard best overcome by finding a replacement as soon as possible.

"I'll phone you after the weekend," I promised as I ushered her through the front door. "And don't worry – Newquay isn't far away, and that's the 'new Riviera' – it will be heaving with surfers, so you never know ..."

2.

Why is it that no matter how hard you imagine yourself in a place or a situation, the reality is never what you thought? For instance, I'd selected the guest house because it hadn't imposed a supplement for a single room, but I hadn't quite been prepared for its distance from the sea. The blurb, which had included 'Sea view, B&B, *en-suite* to all rooms' would have been better as 'See view … ', because whatever views the rooms had, they definitely didn't include the sea.

A narrow road, its tarmac disintegrating here and there at the sides, led steeply upwards from the Edwardian villa and was banked by grassy hummocks, which sheltered Tremorden Bay from sight even from the upper windows. I could smell the salt air, though, tantalising enough to fill me with a childish excitement and making me turn back from the window to tackle my luggage.

It was only just after midday; the early morning Western railways service had performed with an uncommon punctuality and there had been a taxi sitting outside the station. Now the rest of the day was before me.

When I'd unpacked my few belongings into the cavernous wardrobe which looked as if it had been installed when the house was built, I went swiftly downstairs in search of the sea, pushing away the unbidden thought that it would have been nice had Will been here to share it with me. Ridiculous thought anyway, because had we still been together we would have been spending our hard-saved money on a much more exotic location, of the type which Juliet would have definitely approved.

In the hallway, on a highly-polished half-table, was a selection of leaflets describing Walks and Excursions and Things To Do, but I ignored them. I certainly didn't need outings and coach trips and people being convivial in sun hats and white sandals. I would find my way about alone.

I couldn't avoid the enquiring figure of the proprietress though, who wasn't going to be put off by my curt nod. Another mental picture shattered, because she was the antithesis of the stereotypical Cornish landlady who had inhabited my imagination. Instead of the buxom farmer's wife with a round rosy face and sturdy outdoor arms, like in custard adverts, Gwen Jarrett had a long narrow face with a large amount of chin, giving her a horse-like expression that made you want to offer her a bag of hay. Her ironing-board figure was encased in a pristine white overall which suggested that the door on the left might be a dentist's clinic, had it not had a metal plate on it stating: *Residents' Lounge*.

She stepped in front of me, blocking the light from the open front door and lifting herself onto the balls of her feet; unnecessarily, as she was already a couple of inches taller than me. She swayed for a moment, but managed to maintain her equilibrium and smiled at me as she murmured, "Everything all right?"

"Yes, thank you," I replied, standing very still and staring at the glimpse of her dress in the 'V' of the overall – a blue silky number etched through busily with swirls of pastel colours like an impressionist's palette – so that the woman would move away.

But she stood her ground. "Off to do some exploring?"

"Hopefully."

"It's still a bit quiet here yet, for young people, being early in the season." Her voice was like Margaret Thatcher's, carefully cultured to hide her origins but not quite succeeding.

"I wanted somewhere quiet."

Her pale eyes surveyed me speculatively, as if weighing up the possibilities as to why I should be here, alone. She stood to one side to let me pass, smiling in what could have been a benign way, but actually looking even more horse-like as the top of her dentures revealed themselves.

"We don't do evening meals of course, but you're welcome to some afternoon tea if you want to come back for a little rest later," she said. Perhaps she was marking me down as recuperating from a long illness and would try to swop anecdotes about her gallstones or somesuch, once I'd been here a few days.

"Thank you," I answered, holding my beach bag in front of me as I squeezed past so that I didn't brush against her rigid form. I could still feel her eyes on me as I went through the door, so it was good to step out into the fresh air. Trust me to choose a place that was probably Cornwall's answer to the Bates Motel! I had a brief flash of Will's face smiling indulgently at my aptitude for such errors, in the days when it was still an endearing quirk, not an irritation.

I didn't follow the steep little road, but strode out across the rough grass, the taller spikes pricking my bare legs, the light sea breeze sending only the smallest of puffball clouds scudding across the sky. The hummocks became sand dunes, occupied here and there by families sheltering from the breeze or an excess of sun, or from the enquiring eyes of other holiday-makers as they changed their clothes. I wound my way between them, the soft loose sand burning my feet as my sandals sank into it. I paused every now and again to scan the horizon and take deep appreciative breaths. This was what I remembered. Momentarily I was eight again.

The tide had gone out a long way and I took off my sandals to walk on the cool compact ridges it had left behind. It was too soon for the school holidays, so there were only a few families with very young children dotted about, building sandcastles and playing beach cricket with arbitrary rules and sponge balls, but I decided I wanted still more isolation. I walked purposefully across the curve of sand to the beginning of the headland where large rocks jutted out almost to the water's edge. Reaching them, I selected a large flat dark grey one, its front, where water had only recently sprayed it, as sleek and shiny as sealskin.

I made it my own. My towel was spread across it, my canvas shoulder-bag dropped by its side, my sandals neatly placed nearby, a paperback (selected impatiently with little real interest in its contents) laid on the towel – all these actions carried out with an economy of movement which I'd developed since I'd been on my own. Many times over the last few months I'd watched myself performing tasks with a precision which was totally alien to the person I'd once been.

Sitting on the rock, feeling its dry heat emanating through the towel, I hugged my knees and squinted out to sea, the midday sun too strong even for my very dark glasses. Everywhere was calm. Some sort of large funnelled boat moved slowly across the horizon, and the voices of the families on the beach, carried in the opposite direction by the breeze, were indistinguishable: faint, high-pitched hummings.

I exhaled very slowly. This is what I'd come for. Time to clear my mind, to think, to plan now that I was free.

Free? The word mocked me, a shallow substitute for *bereft, adrift,* a euphemism for *rejected.*

I hadn't thought it would be as bad as this. When I'd overcome the initial shock of Will's desertion, had absorbed his announced intention of setting up home with Lauren and had finally recognised the futility of clinging on to a marriage that was clearly dead, I'd expected to come to terms with it in as short a time as the split itself had taken.

There'd been well-meaning platitudes from friends and family who thought they understood, but clearly didn't. The words of comfort eventually did nothing but grate on my already shredded nerves, and I'd had to force myself not to voice the hot retorts which remained trapped in my head instead.

"At least you're young enough to start again – it would have been much worse if you were ten years older." *Why? Because I would have a much harder time trying to find a replacement for the obviously defective model I was lumbered with last time? 'This one no good Madam? Well, don't worry, we'll have more in stock shortly.'*

"Thank goodness there are no children involved – it makes everything much simpler to cope with." *And after all, children would have perpetually reminded me that once upon a time I was wallowing in a happiness that must have been built on sand.*

And from my grandmother: "It could have been worse. You could have been widowed like I was and had your heart broken forever." *But why does a divorce imply that your fractured emotional state is only a temporary one?*

At times I wanted to shout that I wished Will *had* died. Because then he would have remained, in my mind and everyone else's, the person I'd been prepared to commit myself to for life, and the virtues I'd loved would have stayed intact and enshrined in the sanctity of the dead. Because then everyone would have accepted my lament for the happy times we'd shared; would have listened to my endless memories of our ecstatic early years; would have allowed me to have a past worth mentioning; would have accepted my grief as a genuine state and not a torrent of bitterness as they supposed and therefore tried to suppress. And would not have implied from what they said, and from what they omitted to say, that the marriage I'd entered into with all the optimism of one truly in love, and at the time loved in return, must have faltered through something lacking in me.

"You need taking out of yourself," declared Jodie, the only girl in the office younger than me, and she had insisted on taking me to wine bars and clubs and introducing me to her friends. But my barbed retorts to the less than inspired chat-up lines of men who had initially found my aloofness beguiling had been seen by Jodie and her friends as ingratitude, so that they had stopped asking me. And when I filled the interminable office hours with a new determination to keep my desk tidy, my filing up-to-date and my in-tray empty, Jodie had retreated even more puzzled, with suggestions that I seek counselling urgently.

But I'd already analysed my actions and didn't need anyone else to identify the reasons behind my altered behaviour. I found comfort in the repetitious tasks, rather like an abandoned child rocking backwards and forwards in its cot. I knew that by concentrating and completing every task in front of me I could push away the unwelcome reflections on what had happened, the hurt of rejection and the ugly pictures of my hopeless pleadings with him not to leave.

The tranquillity of the scene in front of me gradually ebbed the confused thoughts swirling round my head, and I knew that having allowed them their rein they would not intrude again at least for today. Now my head was filled with nothingness, a suspended state where I could think and feel little and which often, lately, came upon me at strange times so that making even the simplest decision, like what to have for supper, became impossible .

Suddenly, out of the corner of my eye, I became aware of a slight movement nearby, but resolutely refused to turn to it.

"It's all right," came a gravelly voice, "I'm not going to bother you. It's just that there are only two flattish rocks around here, and they're close together. And as you're sitting on the one I usually have, I'm going to use this one."

I turned then, ready with a hot retort, in case there was hidden animosity in the words. A tall, thin woman, in her late fifties I guessed, had flung her belongings onto the rock and was unbuttoning a pair of very faded shorts, revealing equally faded bikini bottoms. Her tan was as deeply ingrained in her skin as a fisherman's, so that she had to be a local who spent all summer outdoors. Light brown hair, bleached from the sun in places and showing signs of grey in others, which either had a natural wave in it or had not been brushed for several days, was pushed back from her face with a wide hairband, below which sapphire blue eyes surveyed me for a moment. Then, without any hint of self-consciousness, a T-shirt was pulled over her head to reveal a pair of bare breasts which sagged slightly as they settled back onto her chest, as brown and weathered as the rest of her.

"Don't worry," she flashed a grin at me, "that's as far as I go.

No skinny-dipping – this is Cornwall, after all!"

The grin was infectious and I found myself smiling back. "Would you like your rock?" I asked.

But the woman was already spreadeagling herself on the other one. "No, this one's fine. I'll just have my daily dose of ultra-violet and all those other dreadfully harmful rays which do wonders for my poor joints and then I'll be gone." Her eyes were closed, but as I turned away she went on in a forthright way, "You'd better cover yourself with lashings of cream if you burn easily, though – the breeze hides the strength of the sun."

I lay back on my own rock, feeling ridiculously over-dressed in shorts and top, and returned to my thoughts. My intentions on coming away alone like this had been so varied, depending on the state of my emotions and my hormones, that now I'd arrived I couldn't decide just what I wanted. Solitude, where I could wallow in my grief but kid myself that I was 'recuperating', vied with the pragmatic side of my nature which told me that I should get down to making some concrete decisions about my future.

And despite what I had told Juliet, after months of enforced celibacy there *were* often sudden urges to have a wild fling with an impossibly handsome stranger who would find me irresistible, thus restoring my self-esteem while also exacting revenge on Will's treachery, even if I was the only one who knew about it.

My vacillations became lulled into a torpor by the soothing sounds of the sea and the heat of the sun. I had no idea how long I'd been drowsing when the woman's voice seeped into my consciousness again. "Time to go. The tide has turned, and it moves pretty quickly here. These rocks will be submerged soon."

She was already standing, pulling on her T-shirt, as I, still dragging myself away from the confusion of semi-sleep, sat bolt upright in befuddled alarm.

The woman laughed. "It's all right. You're not about to be engulfed immediately, I just thought I should warn you."

"Thank you," I said, easing myself off her rock and gathering my belongings in an unhurried fashion to show the woman that I was fully aware of the situation. I turned my back as I packed things in the canvas bag, expecting the woman to stroll away, but she stood watching me until I was ready to move off.

"Where are you staying?" She fell in beside me as we played stepping-stones back over the rocks, her long tanned legs and slim hips like those of a twenty-year-old. The wounded side of me hadn't intended to fall into conversation or strike up any sort of rapport with strangers to whom I might have to explain my present sorry state, but it was impossible not to reply.

"The Lansdowne."

The woman stood still and stared at me incredulously. "That dreadful place? On your own?" Then, before I could utter a word in defence of my choice, she went on: "Now you're going to tell me that Gwen Jarrett is a favourite aunt of yours and I will have put my big foot in it once more!"

But the wide grin back in place showed that she didn't really care if she'd offended anyone. Again, I found myself responding. "It sounded nice in the brochure."

"Oh, it undoubtedly is if you're over sixty, can't stand noise or kids and don't really like the seaside but come anyway because that's what you've done all your life."

"I thought I wanted peace and quiet when I booked it," I found myself divulging, in spite of myself.

The woman's eyes narrowed shrewdly as she glanced sideways at me. "And now you're here?"

It was my turn to stand still. "Now I'm not sure," I said.

"Well, at least it's only B&B, so you can get out and about all day. There's lots to do in the bay you know, and plenty of good places to eat and make friends – if that's what you decide you want." She thrust out her hand. "I'm Marsha, by the way. Everybody here knows me. Came here well over thirty years ago with a band of free-loving hippies, but they all eventually drifted back to London and became bank clerks or whatever, and I ..." She gave a short laugh. "Well, I just stayed. Come and search me out if you need a bit of company."

Her grip was strong and dry. If we'd met at a formal gathering, with her straightforward manner and rather eccentric easy confidence I would have put her down as an army officer's wife who in earlier times might have helped shape the sub-continent.

"I'm Allie," I replied. "Thank you; I may take you up on that."

Marsha nodded, and then purposefully moved off, striding along the beach at a quickened pace which indicated that she herself had no further need of my company for the present.

When she was quite some distance away, she turned and called, cupping her hands round her mouth so that I could hear. "A crowd of us will be at the Smugglers' tonight – join us if you like!" She didn't wait for me to call back, but simply waved and went on her way, and I found myself envying the easy ability to be friendly.

It had been a long time since I'd felt part of a crowd.

3.

I hadn't intended taking Marsha up on her offer, of course. She probably issued similar invitations to everyone she met. I spent the afternoon exploring the huddle of mainly white-washed buildings which rose steeply from the sea-front, separated by narrow streets and intriguing steps leading to cool alleyways, which was all there was of the little town known to the locals as 'the bay'. With the sun continuing to beat down it could almost have been mistaken for a Mediterranean village, except for the essentially English appeal of cottage front gardens filled with rambling roses and busy lizzies in crumbling terracotta pots.

I indulged in a huge ice-cream topped with clotted cream to assuage the pangs of a missed lunch as I peered into the various gift and craft shops and skirted round umbrella-topped tables which spilled out from the many cafés and pubs. In several of the shops I spotted bowls and pots and other ornaments, decorated with vivid daubs of colour, bearing cards in front of them saying *Hand-made by local potter Marsha Stubbs,* and found myself wondering anew about the woman I'd met on the beach.

As I mused, my phone rang from the depths of my shoulder bag. Cursing the intrusion, and myself for being too weak-willed to ignore it, I rummaged about in the canvas depths. What is it about a telephone ring that produces such a Pavlovian response in all of us? Except for people in insurance offices and customer complaints departments, of course, who have the ability to ignore it indefinitely built into their training programmes.

It was Juliet. "Darling! Where *are* you?"

"Cornwall. You know that," I replied flatly, hoping that we weren't going to have a repeat of last night's conversation.

"Oh, so you did go then. Darling, are you all right?"

Well, I was up until a minute ago.

"Mother," I said firmly, knowing that to point out our

relationship would irritate her, "I am perfectly all right. I'm only a couple of hundred miles away, the natives are friendly and you can drink the water, so I think I'll survive."

"There's no need to be flippant, Alison," she said, in retaliation, because she didn't actually like my full name either. She'd wanted me to be christened 'Ali' after Ali McGraw, who had died so effortlessly and beautifully in *Love Story,* but my father had argued that it wasn't a proper name and insisted on 'Alison'. But I'd always been 'Allie', except in times of censure.

"Look," I said now, "I told you that I'd call you after the weekend, and I will. Or before, if there's a problem. Which there won't be, because I'm fine. The weather's fine. The guest house is fine, the people are fine, the beach is fine … it's all just *fine*."

"Oh, there's obviously no point talking to you in this mood," she answered, and rang off.

So what did she want me to say? Did she want a saga of missed trains and confused hotel bookings with which to regale the members of the Conservative Club, where I had probably become 'poor Allie' and an excuse for another gin and tonic and some sympathetic murmurings for my long-suffering mother who didn't know how she was going to get me married off again when I had such an attitude?

I headed back towards the guest house, irritated with my mother and irritated with myself for being irritated. *Just when I had been feeling inconsequentially tranquil!*

The phone was still in my hand, and as I looked at it my irritation increased further. Why had I even brought it with me, when I had shaken off every other aspect of my pathetic little life?

There were too many people about for me to give in to the urge to stamp on it until it was broken into pieces – and knowing my luck it would be pretty indestructible and then I'd have to pick it up again, still intact, which would be highly embarrassing. So I chucked it in a large open-topped bin outside a hotel, still switched on, so that should Juliet ring again she could have an interesting conversation with whoever was bound to pick it up.

I immediately felt exhilarated. It was the final link with my old life – with the old me – gone. Nobody knew where I was staying, nobody could contact me; there was nobody to remind me of so much that had gone wrong. I wanted to rush up to the nearest person and grab them and tell them what I'd done, but realised that to anyone else the throwing away of a mobile phone would have no particular significance. Instead, I beamed at everyone I met, so that they would think that behind the dark glasses there was someone they ought to know but couldn't quite place.

Mrs. Jarrett seemed to be in exactly the same position on the hall carpet where I'd left her several hours before, but she must have moved at some point because the white overall was missing, so that returning guests were treated to the full glory of the blue and pink swirls. She appeared almost fluorescent in the dark of the hallway after the bright light outside.

"I'm afraid afternoon tea is finished," she said regretfully, probably pondering on those gallstones.

"That's all right." I decided to be pleasant and magnanimous. "I'll make some in my room. I've only popped back to shower and change before I go out to eat."

"Friends or family?" she asked as I headed for the stairs.

"I'm sorry?"

"Friends or family?" she repeated. "I assumed it must be one or the other to bring you here."

Magnanimity deserted me; mystery seemed a much more alluring option.

"No. Neither." I smiled tightly and strolled up the stairs, leaving her undecided as to whether to offer up another question before I disappeared around the bend in the staircase.

This time I followed the road into the bay, past pebble-dashed bungalows with hydrangeas in the front garden squatting between terraces of bay-fronted B&Bs. Marsha's invitation was still in my mind, but I was determined not to be seduced by it. I had come here purposely to sort myself out, not to lean on a woman old enough to be my mother and her undoubtedly ageing hippy friends. It would be Juliet's Conservative Club all over again, albeit with perhaps more tan and fewer clothes.

Instead I spent a long time sitting on the wall of the bay's small esplanade, staring out to sea in a *French Lieutenant's Woman* sort of way, although without the cloak, obviously. Only for once I wasn't thinking about my lost love, but about my father – which could be construed in a similar vein, I suppose.

Okay; let's get this bit of my past out of the way. My parents split up when I was about nine – nine years and two months, to be precise – and the bit that has always got to me is that I had no idea, right up to the time they told me, that there was anything wrong. Kids are supposed to sense these things, aren't they? Start wetting the bed, or playing up at school, or refusing to go to friends' parties in case their parents have gone when they get back? Not me. I continued to live in this cocoon of well-being, with my fun-loving spontaneous father and my glamorous mother who smiled at everyone and called them 'Darling', including my father right up to the day he left. It was only years later that I realised that smiles could be tight-lipped and unforgiving and 'Darling' could drip sarcasm.

Juliet and I moved to various locations in Surrey afterwards, until she met husband number two – Dan, a big bluff American, who fell for her smallness and her Englishness which always seemed more pronounced when he was around.

Dan was very rich and very kind, but soon bored Juliet immensely. The crunch came when he persisted with plans for us all to move back to the States, whereupon she told him that I'd apparently developed an abhorrence of all things American and a complete resistance to being removed from all my friends. (I was thirteen or so at the time, and had certainly made a lot of new friends, based mainly on the largesse of my rich stepfather and the tales I had woven of the wonderful life I was going to have when we jetted off to the USA, where selected pals could join me for holidays now and then.)

So when Juliet, in full tragic pose, said to Dan: "So you see, darling, I couldn't possibly drag her away from her home, her friends, everything she cares about so very much," the instant pallor this produced as I wondered what on earth I was going to tell my friends now unwittingly colluded in Juliet's scheme, and convinced Dan that he was asking too much of us both. He eventually returned to the States alone, saddened but eternally impressed by the strength of mother-love which could forsake all for a child's well-being.

My father, meanwhile, had settled deep in rural France. He had always been good at languages and quickly immersed himself in the French idyll, initially working as a translator. Not long after he left us he met and married Yvon (whom I always thought of as 'Heave-on'), and devoted himself to renovating an old farmhouse with acres of land for which numerous money-making schemes were begun with much enthusiasm but never quite completed. This was in part due to the time taken up with providing for a brood of dark-haired, olive-skinned children who arrived in quick succession, so that there was always another bedroom needing to be converted from the loft or tagged on to the side of the house.

He kept in touch a lot at first, with letters and funny drawings, and coming over to England to collect me and take me back for holidays in France. But I was shy of Yvon, whose English was as limited as my French, and of her chattering extended family who were more than happy to make a fuss of this quiet little English girl; which made me shrink behind my father even more. And as their own children began to arrive, so I felt more and more of a stranger at each visit, and the father of my early years wasn't the same as this French-speaking, Gauloise-smoking exuberant man who only appeared uncomfortable when he was coaxing his English daughter into becoming one of the family.

It was easier in the end for the visits to peter out and to look forward simply to the ritual exchange of birthday and Christmas gifts whereby I could console myself that my father still thought of me. Juliet, of course, was quite voluble on the subject. "Your father," she would say, "was never reliable. No wonder he's got himself bogged down with all those children. He was never going to make anything of himself."

But when I pressed her for the reason why he had decided to leave us, she was less emphatic. "These things happen," she would say with an elaborate shrug. "People change ... meet other people ... it's the way of the world."

I was still thinking about my father when I left the esplanade in search of somewhere to eat, my stomach reminding me that it had had little in it all day. I wandered through the narrow lanes, seeking out small cafés where eating alone wouldn't look too pathetic, but the *Copper Kettles* and *Harbour Tea Rooms* apparently couldn't stand up to the competition of the pubs and restaurants in the evening, and were all closed.

I emerged from a meandering alleyway only to find that it ended abruptly, directly opposite the Smugglers' Arms, and there was Marsha, sat outside amongst a lively group at wooden tables and benches, glasses of beer in front of them.

Marsha spotted me at once. Damn!

"Well hello! So you decided to join us! Excellent! Come and sit down and meet everyone! And I hope you're going to have something to eat here – it does the best seafood dishes in the bay. Adam, budge up and let Allie sit next to me until she gets to know everyone."

The recently remembered feelings of being a stranger in France as a group of small dark-eyed children watched me solemnly came flooding back as the group at the table turned to look at me. I opened my mouth to make excuses that I had just eaten and was returning to the Lansdowne, but they were already moving round to make a space at the table.

A tanned young man in a dusty vest-top and disreputable shorts flashed a grin at me and obediently moved along the bench so that I could sit next to Marsha. I was struck by his beauty – and I had never considered a man beautiful before. Cropped light-brown hair, streaked blonde in places, emphasised a perfectly-shaped head and bone-structure and his torso, exposed by the ill-fitting vest, looked lean and strong.

You're just sex-starved, I told myself. *And anyway, he'll probably turn out to be the first gay man you've ever met at close quarters.*

I focused my attention on the introductions Marsha was already making. "This is Adam," (the beautiful one) "this is Chris, Marie, Kate, and Simon. Everyone, this is Allie – we met on the beach today."

They were all young and showed no surprise at my inclusion, but welcomed me with a casual warmth.

"Drink, Allie?" asked Chris, getting up.

"White wine, please," I said automatically and then wondered if I should have asked for beer.

"Good idea," said Marsha straight away. "Now that we've slaked our thirst, let's have a couple of bottles with our meal."

There was immediately an animated discussion of which dishes to order for communal consumption, everyone taking pains to tell me what was the best thing on the menu.

"Do you like mussels, Allie? – they're great here."

"Let's have some seafood platters, then she can try a bit of everything."

"And anything that's left, Simon will eat!"

"And chips – we need some chips."

They were the sort of group you always see in a pub when you're having the most boring time of your life, and you spend the evening listening to snatches of their conversation, wondering what it was that made them laugh so and wishing you could be part of it. There were plenty of evenings like that just before Will finally plucked up courage to tell me that he was leaving, when I'd suggest a night out in desperation because I knew something was wrong but felt powerless to cope with it.

So here I was sitting amongst the sort of people I'd always envied, who seemed happy to accept my presence as if they'd known me for years. After all my recent efforts to liberate myself from the rut I had sunk into since Will's defection, here was the golden opportunity to re-invent myself. I could be anyone I wanted to be. *So did I take it? You betcha I didn't!*

I sat there, drinking my wine too quickly, completely overwhelmed by their goldenness, trying too hard to interject a witty comment whenever I could, but even to my own ears I sounded a prat. None of the men tried any chat-up lines – withering put-downs had become a speciality of mine, so I could have coped with that – but then they wouldn't, would they? Who would be interested in smallish, darkish, with a complexion already turning muddy brown after a few hours in the sun, when they themselves were tanned and lustrous?

Marsha was sitting back in her chair at the head of the table, smoking French cigarettes with a small satisfied smile about her lips. I turned to her.

"I saw lots of pottery in the shops this afternoon, made by Marsha Stubbs. Is that you?"

"Yes it is – but no relation to the great George, I'm afraid. Can't paint to save my life – I just mess about with the pottery and a bit of jewellery-making to keep the wolf from the door."

"What she really means," Adam interrupted, with an affectionate smile across at Marsha, "is that she spends the winter, when the weather is absolutely hopeless and there is nothing to do here, in her workshop, beavering away, so that she can devote every summer to total hedonism!"

"Completely right!" Marsha agreed with a laugh. "I decided long ago that a mediocre talent could be best utilised in a place like this, where people are always looking for something a little bit unusual to take home with them, and they don't mind if the rim isn't completely round, or the stones set equally apart."

"She's just being modest for your benefit, of course," Adam said. "You should visit her workshop – there are some beautiful pieces there."

"May I?" As I turned from Adam to Marsha, I intercepted a look between them of such mutual fondness that I almost gasped aloud. Adam had to be almost half Marsha's age; was having a relationship with a man so much younger also part of her freewheeling lifestyle?

Marsha nodded, dragging her eyes back to me. "You may. Contrary to what this young band of layabouts believes, I mess about for at least a couple of hours each morning, sorting out supplies for the different shops and so on – come tomorrow if you like, straight after breakfast." She gave me directions.

"I could fetch you if you want," Adam volunteered.

"No!" Marsha quickly interjected and I found the sapphire eyes scrutinising me sharply. "No – I think it would be better for

Allie to come alone."

The food arrived, which created a diversion as everyone dived in. Simon, as predicted, had his plate piled higher than anyone else's, but also made a point of seeing that I sampled everything on offer.

"Leave her alone, Simon," Kate, next to him, admonished; "not everyone is as much of a glutton as you!" And then proceeded to tuck into a plateful almost as large, which made me wonder how she maintained her stick-thin body.

Marsha, I noticed, ate little, but this was not commented on at all.

The food, which was as good as they had said, soaked up a little of the wine I'd consumed so far, so I tried to make coherent conversation but simply succeeded in sounding like Juliet at a cheese and wine do.

"Do you live in Tremorden too?" was the riveting question I asked of Adam.

"No, London, but I'm here for the summer."

"Ooh, London!" (Too enthusiastic – as if I'd just discovered we were from the same street in a remote Hebridean village) "Where abouts?"

"Crouch End. Do you know it?"

"Er, no. I come from Purley."

He nodded politely, in a *'Yes, I can see that you would'* sort of way, which made me shrink back into my seat.

"You see, Adam?" said Chris, coming smoothly to my rescue. "I keep telling you no-one ever knows anything about Crouch End. 'Dead End' it ought to be called. You should find somewhere a bit trendier, my son."

It was obvious Chris was from the metropolis as well, but I wasn't going to ask him where. Instead I asked if he was here for the summer too.

"Yeah, sort of, off and on." He gave a quick sideways glance towards Marsha, who had her head down listening to something Marie was saying quietly to her. Surely he wasn't involved with Marsha along with Adam? "It's not worth thinking about going back while the weather's so good." He leaned back in his chair and looked up at the sky as if to assess the likelihood of more sunshine tomorrow.

Simon popped his last chip into his mouth and sat back too. "Mmm, that was good, don't you think, Allie? But we need more wine! Chris! You're on wine duty tonight! Let's have a couple more bottles."

I was going to try to make my escape then, but my glass was quickly filled as Simon launched into a funny, convoluted story about a tax inspector and a garage mechanic. At least I think that's what it was about.

As the others laughed and jostled him playfully – whilst he protested, "It's true, I swear!" – I tried to laugh too, but then had to take several big gulps of wine because suddenly I had an overwhelming desire to cry.

Now I should have mentioned, when I was giving out about what you wouldn't find in these pages, that I don't cry. At least, hardly ever. And certainly not when Will left me. Heroines are supposed to these days, aren't they? You know: boyfriend/husband leaves, she tells all to supportive gaggle of best friends who are always available for a chat during office hours, and then she spends the rest of her waking hours bawling her head off, or in bed eating lots of chocolate before crying herself to sleep. For days. And then either piles on the weight according to how much chocolate she's consumed, or loses pounds, according to where the plot is going, and either way ends up crying all over again. Well, sorry. That doesn't sound very heroic to me. Or very realistic – even if a recent Prime Minister was able to conjure up crocodile tears at the drop of a hat. And besides, solicitors' offices in suburbia aren't the sort of places where you can get away with dissolving into floods all over a conveyancing report and expect any degree of sympathy.

I remember crying a lot when it finally sunk in that my parents were splitting up, which in a child is understandable. But not since. Which might be something to do with living with Juliet for so long afterwards. She always used tears to her advantage, you see – especially when she had a male audience who could be guaranteed to come to her rescue – and had developed the art of crying silently, with no hideous facial contortions, puffy eyes or blotchy neck. Just a noble trickle down the cheeks, a dab of the face with a tissue, and a muttered: "I'm sorry – I shouldn't be so foolish ..."

But me bawling my head off in genuine grief, rage, whatever, was a different matter, and another example of when I could have done with Claire Rayner. On these occasions, way back in my childhood, my mother would sigh exasperatedly and exclaim, "Oh, for goodness' sake, Allie, don't do this to me! I have enough to cope with as it is without you carrying on!"

No 'darlings' there, you notice.

So crying simply became something I didn't do. Will's defection brought anger, certainly, and a sense of shame afterwards when I realised how pathetic my pleadings for him to stay must have sounded, but in place of tears there was something wrenching and twisting my insides, causing physical pain and a huge sense of panic. And the only way I could control it was to carry on with my life as normally as possible, and not let anyone see that I couldn't cope with it.

But here I was now, amongst a group of people I didn't know, in danger of bursting into an unrelenting fit of weeping!

I stood up quickly, with a muttered, "I'm sorry, but I must be going now", cutting through Simon in mid-sentence. And then I sat down again just as quickly as the effect of all the wine I'd drunk made my head spin. That was it of course! The wine had gone to my head and produced this overwhelming moroseness.

Marsha put a cool, steady hand over mine. "I expect you're tired – you must have left home very early this morning if you've travelled from London."

There was kindness in her voice, which made the tears threaten again, so I chose to interpret it as patronising, which, in my fuddled state, I extended towards all of them. What did they know, sitting here, laughing and joking, treating me as one of the group when we knew absolutely nothing about each other! It was just a way of sticking two fingers up at me! *See what a great gang we are? Don't you wish you were one of us?*

I snatched my hand away from Marsha. "I'll just settle my part of the bill and I'll be off," I said.

"Oh, there's no need," said Simon, in his impeccable 'jolly chaps' voice. "After all, we invited you to join us."

You see? Patronising.

"And I don't like charity," I said, coldly, pulling my purse out of my bag, alongside a comb with ragged pieces of tissue snarled up in its teeth, a weeks-old Sainsbury's till receipt, and a stubby lipstick, all of which rolled under the bench I was sitting on.

I leaned forward to pick them up, feeling mortified and dizzy, whilst a hasty division of the bill went on around me. As I stretched out for the lipstick I nearly fell off the bench completely, but Adam grabbed my elbow and waited until I'd straightened up.

"It's £11.65 each," Marsha said, but at least she didn't ask me if that was all right.

I paid the money and then stood up again, holding onto the table lightly to get my balance, which I didn't think they noticed.

"Can I walk you back to your hotel?" Adam asked. I looked down at his beautiful, enquiring face and had a surge of longing to lay my head on his tanned muscled shoulder.

"No thanks, I'll be fine. I can take care of myself." I was aware of a sea of faces, none of whom looked as if they believed me.

"We're going that way anyway," said Marie, "we might as well go along together." She and Kate had already stood up, so even in my advanced state of truculence I realised how churlish it would be to refuse.

"Thank you all for a lovely evening," I said to Marsha and the others, with the exaggerated courtesy of one who is trying hard to disguise a growing inebriation.

I can't recall much of the walk back, as the breeze now coming off the sea added to my confused state and I gave walking all my attention. It did cross my mind, though, to wonder how the girls knew where I was staying.

"Marsha told us about meeting you, not long before you turned up this evening," Kate told me.

"And I live just up the road from the Lansdowne – Kate's staying with me for a while," Marie said.

I said goodbye to them outside the guest house. Gwen Jarrett came out into the brightly-lit hall just as I entered the building and my eyes were taking a while to adjust.

"Ah! Just in time before I lock up! You'll need a late key if you're out after eleven, you know!"

"I'm sorry," I said solemnly, "I didn't realise the inmates had a curfew."

And leaving her there with her horse's mouth slightly open, I went up to my room and into the adjoining bathroom where I was heartily sick before sinking to the floor and bursting into tears.

But of course it was the combined effect of being slightly drunk and then vomiting.

Because I never cry.

4.

Fortunately Gwen Jarrett didn't put in an appearance in the small dining room next morning, where I sat in a corner feeling very fragile. A young local girl who looked as if she'd just bounced in after a game of hockey was serving breakfast, bounding in and out of the swing door which led to the kitchen, apparently impervious to the demanding voice of her employer which wafted through along with the smell of frying bacon.

"'Morning! Help yourself to fruit juice and cereals from the sideboard, would you like tea or coffee, and you have a choice of full English – that's eggs, bacon, sausage, mushrooms, tomatoes and fried bread or black pudding – or scrambled, poached, boiled eggs, toast and preserves – or Continental, which is rolls and fresh croissants – and can I have your room number?" she sang out in one breath as she approached my table, making the floorboards creak and the crockery rattle.

I was so entranced by the Cornish twang to her voice that I missed most of what she said, so, with my stomach still inclined to heave, I asked for just toast and tea. She bounced off again, almost colliding with a pale elderly lady in ancient black who was probably there to help her, but kept coming through the swing door with a plate in her hand, looking at it as if she didn't have a clue why it was there and disappearing into the kitchen again. I wondered if perhaps she'd mistaken the place for the residential nursing home where she really should have been. On second thoughts, looking around at the clientele, perhaps this really *was* a nursing home, and I was the one who'd made the mistake.

I had been one of the last down to breakfast, and the room was now emptying. A plump woman with a round tanned face and a shock of white hair standing away from it beamed at me as she left – now why wasn't *she* a Cornish landlady?

"The forecast's good again," she said. "We're off on a trip to

Tintagel. King Arthur's place," she added as if she expected him still to be in residence.

"Have a lovely day," I replied and nodded to her husband, who didn't seem at all enthusiastic about the outing. In fact, apart from the young waitress his wife was the only person with a smile on her face. Marsha had been absolutely right about the guests who stayed here.

Marsha! I cringed inwardly as I recalled my behaviour of the previous evening. My inane trying-too-hard-to-be-liked laughter came back to me, along with my surliness as time went on. Well, that was one prospective friendship well and truly blown. Knowing my luck, though, I would bump into one or other of them throughout the rest of my stay here and would have to say a polite but embarrassed 'Hello' before crossing the road or ducking into a shop.

I poured myself some more tea and picked up a newspaper from a pile next to the sideboard, to take my mind off last night and delay making a decision about what to do today. Scarlett O'Hara's philosophy of 'thinking about that later' was one which I was all in favour of. I was soon engrossed in Jeffrey Archer's latest TV comeback attempt and pondered on the anomaly that, whilst his novels read like a newspaper report, his life read like a novel.

I was still there some time after the room had completely emptied, when Gwen Jarrett put her equine features around the door and said, "Somebody here to see you. *In the Residents' Lounge,*" the emphasis on the latter words obviously indicating that visitors in the rooms were not allowed. How had I ended up staying here?

I went through to the lounge in some trepidation. It could only be Marsha, probably checking to see if I was all right – she was obviously the tenacious sort. Well, I would assure her that I was fine and then tell her that I had all sorts of plans for the next few days. Off to Tintagel, that sort of thing.

Adam was standing in front of the window.

Damn! Despite my insistence that I wasn't interested in finding another man, my mind automatically registered that I was looking just about the worst mess possible, brushing my hair having been the only concession I'd made to having to face the world. Whilst he, of course, was just as golden as last night.

"Hi!" he said, with a dazzling smile. "I've come to take you to Marsha's – she thought you may have forgotten her directions."

"And do you always do what Marsha wants?" I asked in my

best put-down voice to cover my embarrassment.

"No," he said equably. "It was you who said you wanted to see her work."

He'd got me there.

"I – I wasn't going to bother ... after last night ... I didn't think ..." I floundered, feeling my face flush.

"She's really looking forward to seeing you again." This time the smile held a hint of wry sympathy.

"I'm not quite ready ... I'll be a few minutes ..."

"That's okay. I'll wait for you." He went to sit in a busily-chintzed armchair, taking in as he did so the bright floral wallpaper, heavily patterned carpet and array of china animals adorning every surface. "On second thoughts, the sun is beckoning. I'll hang about out on the steps."

He opened the door for me to go through first, so there was just no point in further resistance; and I hadn't even remembered the line about Tintagel.

I quickly changed into a better pair of shorts than the crumpled ones I had flung on earlier, and brushed my hair and teeth. Then I put on just a hint of lip gloss and blusher – simply because I was looking rather hung-over, you understand – before stuffing a swimming costume and towel into my beach bag. If I didn't want to stay long with Marsha I could claim the need for a swim.

Adam turned round as I came out through the front door.

"Wow!" he said as I stepped forward, and my heart lurched a little as I thought he was referring to my appearance. "That's a rarity! A woman who says she's only going to be a few minutes and means it!"

"The sunshine was calling to me as well," I said, in case he thought I'd hurried on his account.

"Good. We can go along the dunes, round to the rocky bit," he said, as I fell into step beside him.

"About last night," I said in a rush, wanting to get it over with. "I don't usually drink so much ... or behave so ungratefully. You must have all thought I was horrible ... I should apologise ..."

"No need," he said airily. "We all get a bit under the influence from time to time. Forget about it. We all have."

So nice. So understanding. I wondered what, if anything, would ever rattle this man. Marsha seemed really laid-back as well; they obviously had that in common. Then I remembered my suspicions of last night that they might be an item. There was definitely something between them.

I stood still as a horrible thought struck me.

"You're a sect, aren't you?" I demanded. "One of those groups who seek out lonely people and brainwash them into never seeing their families again and whisk them off to some strange commune where the men sleep with all the women and things!"

He threw his head back and roared with laughter. "Whatever gave you that idea? Although the bit about sleeping with all the women doesn't sound bad!"

"Well, you'd obviously discussed me before I arrived at the pub last night!" I retorted, feeling annoyed that he was laughing at me.

His face straightened. "Look," he said, his eyes (which weren't quite brown and weren't quite green) fixed on mine, "we were talking over our day and Marsha happened to mention that she'd met you and that you were staying at that god-awful place back there. She also said that she thought you might be a bit lonely here on your own. So when you turned up and she invited you to join us, we were quite happy for you to do so."

His eyes twinkled again. "Believe me?"

"Of course," I said, turning away from him and walking on so that he wouldn't see the lingering doubt on my face. "It's just – well – you all seemed so damned *happy!*"

"That doesn't only come from sleeping with lots of women, you know!" He caught sight of my scowl as he began to laugh at me again and quickly changed his chuckle to a clearing of the throat.

"It's this place, I think." He swept his arm wide to encompass the stretch of beach we were approaching. "It relaxes you – who wouldn't be happy when they've got sea, sun, sand, and good company day after day?"

And Marsha? I wondered. *Does she make you happy?*

"And if it rains?" I said instead. "Are you still happy then?"

"Ah! On those days you catch up with all the boring things you avoid when the sun is shining, like going to the supermarket or getting your hair cut, so that you can make the most of the sunshine when it comes back."

"So Marsha's not the only hedonist?"

"I'm afraid not! Guilty every time!" He held up his hands and this time I was able to laugh with him.

He led me across the beach and over the rocks where I had first met Marsha. Further along we clambered up towards a steep road which swept around to run parallel with the sea front.

"Can you manage?" Adam turned to me just as my left foot slipped and landed in a small rock pool.

"I'm fine," I gasped, wondering if I would look too undignified climbing from rock to rock on all fours.

He reached down and grasped my hand, hauling me up the next few feet, and he kept hold of it until we reached the road. But he let go as soon as we stopped climbing.

"Sorry about that," he said. "I'd forgotten just how steep that last bit is – I don't usually come this way."

"It was fun," I said, trying not to make it too obvious that I was having trouble getting my breath back and vowing to myself that I would have to find some hills to walk up when I got back to Purley. Until now I had thought I was quite fit.

We walked a short way up the road before Adam stopped outside a blue painted gate.

"This is where I leave you," he said, nodding at the gate.

"Marsha's orders again?" I asked, and then regretted that my voice sounded sharp.

He nodded solemnly, before leaning towards me. For a moment I thought – hoped – that he was going to kiss my cheek, but instead he whispered, "Marsha wants you on her own – so that she can start the brainwashing straight away!" He winked as he moved away from me.

And then he was walking swiftly up the road, before I could decide whether to grin or be annoyed with him. So I turned and went through the blue gate.

The house was very white and very tall and narrow, set into a steep cliff face, so that only the front had windows, with frightening views over rocks and pounding waves. Deep, uneven steps led down from the road to a wide terrace in front of the building, and to each side there were terraced flowerbeds planted in a haphazard fashion, with trailing plants in clashing colours which suited the very bright light.

Marsha came out through a sun-scorched wooden door to greet me. "Come in! Come in! Excellent timing, I've just made some coffee."

I moved hesitantly, expected her to make some comment about last night, but she didn't; so I followed her through the door into the basement of the house which turned out to be one large room devoted to her work. At one end were a potter's wheel, a kiln, a stone sink, and rows of shelves and benches with pots and dishes in various stages of completion. At the other end, "the smart side," Marsha explained as she showed me round, were tables and more shelves holding the finished products, including tiny snuff boxes with hinged lids, inlaid with aquamarine and amethyst.

"It's beautiful!" I breathed, holding one up to the light.

"And you shall have one before you end your stay here," Marsha said, handing me a mug of coffee.

"Oh! – I didn't mean – I wasn't hinting! I—"

"I know. Come on, let's have this in the sunshine. The terrace will be in shade later on."

We sat companionably on faded canvas deckchairs sipping the drinks. Marsha downed two large tablets with her coffee. "Hangover!" she said with a grin. "You'd think I'd be used to it by now!"

"I took a couple earlier on," I confessed ruefully. Then I took a deep breath. It was apology time again. "I was a complete pain last night. I'm sorry—"

Marsha waved a hand in the air as she took a deep slug of coffee. "We put you in an impossible position, expecting you to sit amongst a band of total strangers and have a good time immediately. The only way to have made it even passably enjoyable was to attack the wine! Perhaps getting to know one or two of us at a time would be a better idea – if you could still bear us?"

I thought again of their easy intimacy and realised that envy of this was what had made me so resentful and belligerent last night. And this morning Marsha wasn't being patronising, she was being kind and generous.

"I think I could put up with that," I said with a smile, and felt relieved when Marsha smiled back.

"Excellent." She leaned back in the deckchair and closed her eyes. "'Mmm. That sun feels good this morning."

I leaned back too, but kept my eyes open, surveying the scene. Huge frothy waves were breaking over the rocks below in a soporific fashion, whilst the occasional gull circled overhead. Apart from the crashing sea there was no other noise and no other sign of life.

"This is an idyllic spot," I said. "No wonder you stayed."

"I was lucky," she replied without opening her eyes. "I snapped this house up years ago, before Tremorden became quite as popular as it is now. Nobody wanted a place like this then – it wasn't suitable either for young couples with children, or elderly people. But as I didn't have a family and had no intention of ever growing old, it suited me perfectly."

Questions filled my mind. Why was there no family? Where

did Adam and the others fit in? Did he or any of them share the house with her?

But I couldn't probe. Perhaps Marsha was as reluctant to talk about her past as I was.

"Don't you ever get lonely?" I managed instead.

"It's a bit quiet in the winter, when all the holidaymakers have gone," she admitted. She opened her eyes and sat forward in her chair. "But sometimes solitude after a busy summer is quite welcome. I get lots of work done. And there are always friends who visit – or just occasionally I stir myself enough to visit them."

Would this be me in a few decades time, I wondered? On my own and, to all intents and purposes, slightly idiosyncratic but apparently content with my lot? Perhaps Marsha had been an early feminist, determined to survive alone. There was something of Germaine Greer about her, certainly, and Ms. Greer now lived a solitary life in the country but surrounded herself with young students and was apparently fulfilled. But hadn't she recently been quoted as saying that she regretted not having a child?

I was aware of Marsha's intense blue eyes scrutinising me and concentrated on sipping the last of my coffee very slowly, desperately thinking of some light comment which would deflect her gaze. Of course, not having a razor-sharp mentality (especially with a slight hangover), nothing sprang quickly to mind.

"Well?" she asked at last, her voice brisk, "Are you going to tell me what's bothering you? From the look of you, you're in need of sharing it with someone."

I turned sharply to face her, my mouth already shaping defensive phrases. But as our eyes met there was something compelling about Marsha's, as if to rebuff her would be to wound her immeasurably.

I took a deep breath. "My husband left me for another woman, so we're in the process of divorcing. I've left my job, loaned my flat and my car to a friend and come down here for an unspecified length of time to decide what I'm going to do. That's about it."

Marsha nodded her head slowly. "Sometimes it's good to get away on your own. Give yourself time. Especially," she added, the eyes piercing me again, "if family and friends haven't been terribly supportive."

"Ah yes, family! Mine consists of father living rapturously with second wife in rural France – not seen much since my early teens, except briefly at my wedding; mother who is now sitting comfortably having divorced two men and has since dallied with whoever will spoil her most, so what's my problem? – and a grandmother who thinks I should 'get a grip!'

"As for friends," I went on, unable to quell the acid tone in my voice, "the trouble is that after eight years together, my friends are actually *our* friends, and who wants to take sides? There's one old friend, Sarah, who's borrowing my flat to be nearer to Rob, who happens to be an old friend of Will's and with whom she's having a passionate affair, so she's sympathetic enough but mainly busy; and another old friend, Gina, who's produced two children in two years and has just been told that her husband's firm is moving them to Scotland. So not a lot of joy there! I decided I would be better off on my own."

"So why Cornwall?" Marsha asked, but it didn't sound the same as when Juliet said it.

"Oh," I answered, feeling just a bit sheepish, "stupid nostalgia, really. I came here as a child, with my father, not long before my parents split up. I've always remembered it as a sort of sunny time – you know, in a 'Janet and John' way, like you always want to think of your childhood – and then shortly after we were back in London everything exploded between my parents, so the Cornwall time seemed even more magical. I suppose I was just hankering after that again."

Marsha simply nodded once more, thoughtfully.

"So," I said, embarrassment at what I'd disclosed of myself making me prickly, "are you going to tell me now that I should count my blessings, or that I'm young enough to start again, or that he wasn't worth it anyway?"

"No," said Marsha, standing up and stretching her thin body, "I was going to say it's time we headed for the beach. And this time," her voice rose as she took the mugs indoors, "I think we should have a swim."

The water was cold and invigorating, with strong waves that pushed us back to the shore. Marsha swam well, but after a short while stood up, her breath coming in gasps.

"That's about it for me, I'm afraid. Too many cigarettes taking their toll. You stay in, though, if you want."

But I wasn't tough enough to stand the cold water for long and soon joined her back on the beach, wrapping my towel round me until the sun had done its job and warmed me again. Marsha by this time was stretched out, her eyes hidden by dark glasses so that I couldn't tell whether she was awake or asleep.

I lay down beside her, concentrating on the feel of the sun on my skin and the prickling sensation as it dried my wet swimming costume, until I was drifting away into my favourite state of suspended nothingness.

"Do you still love him?"

Marsha's voice cut through my reverie like a scythe.

"Who? Will?" I said, as if she could possibly mean anyone else. "No. Of course not. How could I after the way he treated me?"

I put as much conviction as I could muster into my voice, but she didn't say anything straight away.

"I just wondered," she said eventually, as if it were quite inconsequential, "because sometimes it's difficult to stop – even when they've been complete rats."

I sat up suddenly, all peacefulness evaporated, a torrent of hot denial ready to spill from my lips, but Marsha remained unperturbed, unmoved, and somehow the words just didn't come out. How had this complete stranger, who had only the sketchiest information about me and Will, immediately hit on the one thing that still bothered me?

Because no-one else of my acquaintance had, you see, at least not to my face. Behind my back (which surely, when you come to think of it, is your front, but never mind) there had perhaps been lots of: *'Poor Allie, she'll always carry a torch for him!'* – which is the way members of my family obliquely refer to matters of the heart; but nobody had actually asked me. So I thought they all assumed that I must now hate Will for what he had done to me and that I would much prefer never to set eyes on him again.

Which is how I did feel, most of the time. But there was still this tantalising question: what would I really do if he dumped Lauren and wanted to come back to me?

Many an hour had been wasted spinning fantasies around just this premise. Sometimes I would tell him it was too late because I had found another (unspecified) love; sometimes I would devise ways in which he would have to prove his undying, and this time everlasting, devotion to me; and sometimes I would have become so stunningly attractive and desirable that he would almost be too awed to request the pleasure of my company again. But unfortunately every scenario ended in the same way – me forgiving him, he vowing eternal love mixed with eternal regret for having hurt me so, and the two of us living blissfully together forever.

It was a secret I was reluctant to share with anyone. I mean, how pathetic can you get? My husband cheats on me and then, when confronted, finds all sorts of reasons in our marriage for why he felt the need of pastures new, yet there's this part of me that still loves him!

Perhaps at this point I should say a bit more about Will himself. Picture Pierce Brosnan, or Robbie Williams, or, if you go a bit further back, a very early Sean Connery – but not as far back as Clark Gable, because he was too oily. Anyway, you should get the idea. Tall, very dark and lean, a definite glitter in the eye and an impossibly attractive smile. And very suave.

So why choose a solicitor's secretary from Purley, you may well ask? As indeed I did myself, and even Juliet was pleasantly surprised. Only I wasn't a solicitor's secretary when we met.

We met at university, which should conjure up a story of riotous student life, with each of us having our fair share of lust-driven flings before ending up together after a series of misunderstandings. Only it wasn't like that, of course. Will had taken a gap year, during which he went to drought-hit parts of Africa, so I had finished my degree a year before him and was now working in the university library until something more exciting presented itself. And that 'something more exciting' turned out to be Will.

Apparently he fell for me rather than one of the bevy of leggy, intimidatingly lovely girls I'd seen him surrounded by on campus because I wasn't completely overwhelmed by his charm. Also because I could remember the punch lines of jokes and repeat them sufficiently well to make everyone laugh, preferred Guiness to vodka, and didn't mind sitting through *Match of the Day*.

But some of this came later. Living with Juliet had schooled me to keep my feelings in check, so when Will first leaned over the library counter and said, with his disarming grin, "I wonder if you could help me?" he had no idea that my stomach was flipping over. Or how later, as I helped him find the books he needed for his final dissertation, his nearness in those narrow library aisles made me feel as overcome as the most emotive of Jane Austen characters.

Much later, when we were more sure of each other, and my heart was now firmly on my sleeve and he had convinced me that he wanted me more than anyone else, I asked why me instead of a leggy lovely.

"Because you're real," he'd said. "And you're petite and feminine and you bring out all my primitive male protective urges." And I was thrilled.

Of course, eventually he succumbed to even more primitive

male urges with Lauren – who, guess what, is tall, leggy and lovely – but that was after eight years together, the early ones of which I *know* had been happy.

Will was very ambitious and keen to build up his business, and I was only too happy to help in any way I could. Hence the job in the solicitor's office, which might have been mundane but paid pretty well, and my unlimited access to the photocopier was very handy for Will's business – which only really began to take off just before we split up.

I tried to frame words to explain to Marsha how Will was so damned attractive that it would be impossible for a tiny part of me not to still love him, but then I saw Kate and Marie in the distance and clutched at this instant reprieve.

"I think the two girls are on their way over," I said.

Marsha sat up and peered into the distance before waving energetically at them until they waved back.

"By the way, what does he do, this ex-husband of yours?" she asked as we both watched the girls approach.

I was determined to give nothing more of my feelings away.

"He takes an inordinate amount of money off people for doing something that with a little bit of effort they could do just as easily themselves," I said evenly.

She took off her sunglasses and raised a quizzical eyebrow. "Male prostitute?"

"No. Estate agent," I answered, trying to maintain a straight face.

"Similar", she said, before we both dissolved into giggles just as Kate and Marie threw themselves down beside us. They looked just as lovely as last night. Kate was a tall, slim strawberry blonde – although what that colour has to do with strawberries I've never worked out – with just a smattering of freckles over her lightly tanned skin which gave her a healthy outdoor-girl look. Marie had finer, more delicate features, liquid brown eyes and hair that wasn't fair and wasn't dark, but had too many glossy sun-streaks in it to be described as mousy.

"Hot baguettes for lunch," Marie said, diving into a large carrier bag, "and cold mineral water. Mixed salad all right for you?" She held out a baguette to me.

"Great," I said, "but have you got enough for me as well?"

"We knew you were visiting Marsha this morning and we didn't think she'd let you out of her clutches too quickly," Kate said with a smile as Marsha pulled a face at her.

Marie passed another to Marsha. "They might smell a bit

horsey – I didn't spend too long cleaning up today; I wanted to get down here too much."

She turned back to me as she bit hungrily into her food. "I work every morning at the stables out on the Padstow road – I've been on the go since half-six and I'm starving now." She took another mouthful. "Do you like horses, Allie?" she asked as soon as she could.

"For goodness' sake say yes, or you'll really upset her," Kate said, "'cos she's mad about them."

"I can't say I've ever had much to do with them," I confessed. "What do you do – give lessons to holidaymakers?"

Marie laughed. "Nothing so easy. I'm at the other end of the scale, I'm afraid – or rather the other end of the horse. Humble stable girl, I am, doing all the mucking-out jobs, with the occasional ride thrown in as a reward if we're not too busy."

"Oh." I didn't know what else to say and was trying to hide my surprise that this sleek, elegant girl would be happy doing such a dirty job.

Marsha saw the look on my face and now it was her turn to chuckle. "Surprised because she doesn't look like the back end of a horse as well, aren't you?"

"Well – it's just ..." I decided to be honest. "When I met you both last night I thought you must be models or something equally glamorous because you both looked stunning ... I can't imagine you doing a messy job ..." My voice tailed off, in case it sounded as though I was falsely flattering them, but they didn't seem to take it that way.

"If you knew anything about horses, you'd realise that generally they're a lot nicer to know than most people, so I don't mind the muck," Marie said, "and at least I'm not Bedpan Queen of Ward 19!"

Kate gave her a playful push. "I've just finished my nurse training at Exeter," she told me, "which is why I'm here, waiting to see if I've qualified, and then I'll see if I've any chance of getting a decent post somewhere. And if you saw me in my uniform with my hair scraped back and a plastic pinny on, at the end of a busy night shift, you definitely wouldn't think I was glamorous!"

I wanted to ask about the men, then, especially Adam, but Marie pre-empted me.

"Are you just here for a fortnight's holiday?"

Marsha had lain down again, but I could sense her listening for my answer.

"Not really. I've just packed my job in and ..." I lifted my chin resolutely – "my marriage is over, *definitely over,*" I emphasised for Marsha's benefit, "so I'm here for as long as it takes me to decide what to do with the rest of my life."

"Wow! I can't imagine being married, let alone think about what to do *after* I've been married," Marie said disingenuously.

"That's because you have trouble even deciding what to do next week," Kate told her.

"True," Marie agreed. This was obviously ground they had gone over before. "But what to do with the rest of your life! That's almost too much freedom, isn't it? Like someone telling you that you can have any one item you want from a clothes shop – there'd be so much choice you wouldn't be able to make up your mind. Especially if you haven't got anyone or anything to tie you to a particular place."

"Exactly," I said. "And if you're a ditherer like me, you end up staying in the same rut doing the same things because you can't make up your mind about anything else. So that's why I decided to come away – I thought a bit of distance might help."

Marie nodded thoughtfully. "Well I suppose you can cross getting married again off the list for the immediate future, 'cos I don't expect you'll be wanting to do that for a while, so that narrows it down a little bit."

I spluttered on the bottle of water I'd raised to my lip.

"Oh, gosh! Sorry!" she said, "Have I said the wrong thing again and you've already got another man lined up in the wings and you've come down here to decide whether to keep him?"

"No, nothing like that," I said, smiling at her forthrightness. "You're absolutely right, I don't want another man in my life at all. Been there, done that, and I wouldn't be seen dead in the T-shirt. Just London was too clogged up with bits of my old life and it seemed the right thing to do to get away from it all."

"As long as you don't end up in a rut here instead simply because you still can't decide on what else to do – like I did," came Marsha's muffled voice because she had turned over onto her front.

"You've never been in a rut at any time in your life!" Marie declared stoutly.

"And some of us are very glad you did stay here," Kate said, before tapping Marie on the leg. "Come on. Time we had a swim, before we lose the tide."

Marie groaned, but got up with Kate and simultaneously they stripped off their T-shirts to reveal nothing but bikini bottoms, like Marsha. "Coming in?" Kate invited me.

I shook my head. "Not this time, thanks. I've only just warmed up from earlier."

I watched them both run into the water, thankful that I was wearing my one-piece. I made a mental note always to wear it to the beach, so that I wouldn't be faced with the dilemma of whether to go topless. Or rather, so that I wouldn't feel too odd being the only one in a bikini and not topless.

I've just never been able to do it, you see. Not with other people around, anyway. When it was only me and Will somewhere I didn't mind at all, say on a hotel balcony or something. But I just couldn't imagine being nonchalant about having my boobs on show in a public place. I mean, they'd always *be* there, wouldn't they, between me and whoever I was talking to? (Figuratively speaking of course, because mine aren't really big enough to get in the way of anything.) I wouldn't be able to act naturally like Kate and Marie. I'd always be wondering if I should cross my arms over the top of them when I was speaking to someone – I just wouldn't be able to forget about them.

I mean, it's bad enough on a beach anyway, having to remember to pull your tummy in all the time and wondering if you've got cellulite on the bits of your thighs that you can't really see properly even with a mirror, without agonising over whether other people are thinking that your breasts are a funny shape or your nipples look odd. No, much better to choose a flattering one-piece and make sure you've had a good wax.

Marsha interrupted my mental deliberations. "I suspect Marie has spent too long in my company – she tends to say exactly what she thinks as she thinks it, I'm afraid."

"That's okay," I replied. "It's quite refreshing to be around people who don't automatically suppose you must be desperate to find a replacement to fill the gap left by the earlier model. I mean, if you got rid of a dog because it bit you, you wouldn't feel too keen to go straight out and get another one, would you?"

"But then, if you fell off one of Marie's precious horses, you'd be encouraged to get straight back on and have another go," said Marsha with a humorous lift to the corner of her mouth. "So perhaps all the people you know prefer horses to dogs!"

"Ah! Found you at last!" came Simon's voice from behind us.

"Very clever, Dr. Livingstone," Marsha said dryly. "There wouldn't be many places we'd be, would there?"

He was wearing a pair of shorts in such a loud design I was glad to be wearing sunglasses. "You could have been up in the bay," he pointed out. "Hi, Allie, how are you?"

But before I could answer he was talking again. "Anyway, why I've come to look for you is that I've found your old barbecue – I knew we'd used it last year – in the back of the shed."

"The shed? What were you doing in there? It's full of junk," Marsha said.

"Ah, well, it isn't now – I've tidied it all up for you. Adam needed a screwdriver for that loose window catch in his room and we couldn't find one, so I went to look in the shed, saw what a mess it was and cleared it all out. *And* found the barbecue – so how about I get some sausages and things and we get it going tonight?"

"Sounds good to me," she replied.

The two girls came running up the beach, water dripping from their glistening bodies and hair as they grabbed towels and greeted Simon simultaneously. He told them about the proposed barbecue as they dried themselves and I sat there and envied their unselfconsciousness again.

"We've eaten all the lunch, I'm afraid," said Marie.

"That's okay. You don't think I'd run the risk of going hungry do you?" Simon said, patting his surprisingly firm stomach. "Adam and I had something before I left the house."

Curiouser and curiouser. Last night I'd thought both Adam and Chris might be Marsha's toyboys. Now it seemed that not only did Adam live with her, but Simon had free run of the house too. There were a dozen questions I wanted to ask them, but just as last night, I found myself slightly intimidated by all their closeness – a situation which usually makes me say either too much, or nothing at all. And as they'd seen me at my garrulous and truculent worst last night, I thought that this time I would keep my mouth firmly shut.

So I pretended to be absorbed in looking out to sea, all the while listening to their idle chit-chat whilst wondering uncomfortably whether I should stay (because it would seem rude to leave too soon after they had all arrived), or go (rather than be a bit of a spare part).

Eventually, Kate jumped up, fished her bikini top out of her bag and declared that she was going for a run along the sand.

"Coming?" she asked Marie.

"No, you exercise freak!" she declared, lying down and covering her face with a T-shirt. "I've had enough exertion for one day. The only 'feel the burn' I want is from the sun."

"No problem. See you all later." Kate set off at a steady jog across the beach, a headset clamped over her hair.

"Talking to her boyfriend," Simon commented as we watched her moving effortlessly on the hard sand near the water's edge. "They're joined at the mobile phone."

"I thought it was a Walkman," I said.

Marie chuckled through the T-shirt. "It's certainly music to her ears. She's besotted with Carl."

"Is he far away?" I asked.

"He's back in Exeter," Simon explained. "We always get together here with Marsha in the summer," he went on as if reading my puzzled expression. "Carl will probably join us later when he can get away."

"Are Adam and Chris joining us this afternoon?" Marsha changed the subject as she sat up and lit a cigarette.

"Adam any minute now, and Chris I haven't seen today, only heard singing very badly in the shower before I left the house," Simon reported with a grin.

This was definitely my cue to leave. I didn't want to face Adam's green-brown eyes again today and have all my firm assertions – at least to myself – about never having anything more to do with the male species challenged once more.

I stood up and tied a flimsy sarong around my middle. "Time I was making a move," I said, as if I had a dozen pressing engagements. "Thank you for the coffee and the lunch."

"You're welcome," Marsha said simply, squinting up at me.

"Are you coming along later for the barbecue?" Simon asked. "It won't just be sausages – I do a mean king prawn marinated in peach, date and ginger."

"Sounds good," I said, "but do you have one of those plastic aprons that look as if you're wearing a bra and suspender belt?"

"Er ... no," he answered carefully.

"Then I'll have to turn your kind offer down," I said. "A barbecue just isn't a barbecue unless the chef is wearing one of those."

"So you would have come if I said I had one?"

"Oh no," I grinned. "If you'd answered 'yes' I would have said that I couldn't possibly come to a barbecue that was in such poor taste and an affront to women."

He grinned back. "I take it you've got other plans."

"Sort of. But seriously, thanks for the invitation."

"You know where we are, and you know it's open house," Marsha said. "Call in when you feel like it."

"I will – thanks again."

I strode off along the beach, pleased that I had managed a

light-hearted exchange without embarrassing myself, and wondering if they were watching me go as we had Kate, which made me walk in a stiff way and veer off the beach sooner than I needed to.

5.

Of course I had no other plans at all, and part of me was dying to accept Simon's invitation. But I kept reminding myself that I had come to Cornwall to sort myself out, and to do that I would need time to think, on my own.

So I resolutely kept out of their way, not just that evening, but for the next three days, although it was hard going. I made use of the beach in the opposite direction from Marsha's house, although it had more pebbles and a lot of seaweed, and kept well away from the Smugglers' – even on the evening when they were having the barbecue, in case it went wrong and they decided to eat out after all. I went for vigorous walks along the headland and spent a long time sitting, looking out to sea enigmatically, the breeze rifling through my hair. A bit like Pauline Collins in *Shirley Valentine,* although without the stretch marks, and I didn't find a rock to start talking to. Or a Tom Conti look-alike, come to that.

In fact, I hardly spoke at all, to anyone. A quick interrogation each morning from Gwen Jarrett and a debriefing each evening – although even her interest was beginning to wane when she was continually told 'just walking'; the occasional small exchange of pleasantries with the odd guest, and that was about it.

And boy, I was bored! Not by the beauty of the surroundings, the amazingly good weather or the sounds and smells of the coast, but more with my own company – particularly when quite nearby there was a tantalisingly interesting group of people who were quite happy for me to gatecrash their lives if I so chose.

I really did try hard to think about my future, and tested out a few options in my head. *Return to college and get my teaching certificate,* was one ... Too hard in today's teaching climate, I decided. *Or go back to being a librarian – definitely a soft option, with old-fashioned connotations of floral skirts, sandals and cats ...*

But for this particular Goldilocks there was nothing that seemed just right. I even toyed with the idea, as I sat and gazed out at the Atlantic, of going off to America and exploring the States on a Greyhound bus. But was I really, honestly, tough enough to do that? *Maybe. And Americans are always willing to talk to you, so it wouldn't be too lonely ...*

In between these deliberations, of course, it was impossible not to chew over the disaster zones of my life, and equally, if I'm really truthful, not to ponder on Marsha and her friends. It was obvious that all three men shared her house, but what else did they share? And why was she surrounded by men and women easily half her age, but seemingly so in tune with her? And why did being with her that morning, for such a short time, fill me with a sense of peace and a longing to pour out to her all my fears and anxieties?

When I got fed up with my solitary ponderings I explored more of the byways of Tremorden. Although it wasn't a large town, beyond the more commercialised centre of the bay there were more narrow streets with connecting alleyways than I'd thought. These streets contained rows of terraced cottages, each a different size and shape from its neighbour, as though each person had tacked his favourite design onto the side of one already there, and so on. The end result, because of its very haphazardness, was pleasing to the eye, with brightly-coloured front doors to most of the houses and frothy white net curtains billowing from the open windows of many. Tremorden housewives were obviously a conscientious lot. B&B signs were everywhere, even on the tiniest cottages that looked far too small to hold more than two occupants, but they still looked more cheerful than the Lansdowne with its 'Sea View'.

Every so often I would try to recall the faint images of my childhood holiday here, and occasionally something would seem to evoke a feeling, a fleeting impression which if I tried too hard to recapture would flitter tantalisingly away, just out of reach. But perhaps it was simply the sounds and the smell of the sea and the picture of the bay bathed in sunlight which produced these feelings, which would have been the same at any Cornish holiday town.

There was one street, though, at the top of the bay, climbing steeply away at an angle from the main street, where I definitely experienced a strong sense of *deja vu*. And one house in particular which caught my attention: a tall, narrow, unremarkable house in the middle of the row, with two steps up to its front door. I had a distinct memory of standing at the bottom of those steps, my hand firmly clasped in my father's while he talked to someone stood above us on the doorstep. And somehow the conversation seemed urgent, voices over my head, whilst I waited for my father to finish so that we could go – where? I had no idea.

By the end of the third day of my exclusive company it seemed that Juliet's assertion that it would be no fun on my own was right, but of course I was still determined to prove her wrong. So much so that I decided to phone her and impress upon her just how good it was to be by myself in Cornwall.

I bought a phone card and went straight to a public call box before I could change my mind.

"Darling! They've found you!" she shrieked as soon as she heard my voice. "Are you all right? Are you at the police station?"

"Of course I'm all right. What police station? What are you talking about?" I replied, already regretting my impulsive action.

"Newquay police station. I told them they had to look for you because you were obviously in some sort of trouble."

I wondered if I should put the phone down and ring her again later when the conversation might make more sense. "But I'm not staying in Newquay," I said, resisting the urge.

"You're not? Why did you tell me you were then? It would be 'full of lots of handsome surfers', I think were your very words. But anyway, darling, you do sound fine, and they managed to find you anyway. What happened to you?"

"Mother!" I said as sternly as I could. "I am not with the police and I haven't been in any sort of trouble, so will you please tell me what you are going on about."

"It was after I rang your mobile," she said, her voice a bit harder now that she knew I was okay. "This awful man answered, and when I asked to speak to you, he told me to – well, 'go away' – if you take my meaning."

"Didn't it occur to you that I may have simply lost my mobile?"

"Well, that was what the policeman said at first but I told him that if that was the case you would have got yourself another one and phoned me because you had promised to keep in touch."

"But I've only been away five days!" I exclaimed, making sure that my irritation superseded the little shards of guilt which were trying to stab me.

"Yes, he said that as well, and wasn't going to help at first, but when I said that I was a personal friend of the Chief Constable of Surrey – which I'm not, of course, but one of my bridge partners knows him, so it's almost as good – he said he would see what he could do."

"Well, you'll have to ring Newquay and tell them to call off the sniffer dogs and helicopters because I'm fine and in no imminent danger of being abducted," I said.

"You see, this is what comes of being so secretive and refusing to give me your address in the first place," she said, and I knew she was building up into one of her *'if you only knew the trouble you've caused me'* speeches which had been so well-used in recent months.

"No, it comes of you never believing that I can organise my own life for myself," I countered, reluctant to admit that I could take any of the blame for her over-the-top behaviour.

"Well anyway, darling, I'm very glad to hear you're not in Newquay," she said, neatly sidestepping the potential argument, "because I've been reading about it in the newspapers and all those surfers just want to have a good time with any girl they meet, and then they go off to other parts of the world, and they've absolutely no money. You need to be in Rock."

"But that's full of surfers as well," I said.

"Ah, yes, but the *Princes* go there – in fact it's rumoured that William's on his way now."

"Juliet," I decided to be more magnanimous now and use her preferred name, as she was clearly going through some sort of post-menopausal brainstorm: "I don't think Prince William or Prince Harry is going to be the least bit interested in a typist from Purley who is several years their senior."

"Don't be so silly," she said impatiently. *I was being silly?* "Of course you're too old for them, but they always have people with them don't they – and so many others will be attracted to the place because of its royal connections. It'll be positively humming with people to know."

Now this was an option I hadn't considered during my procrastination. I could be 'in' with the 'in' crowd. Find some upper-class man with lots of money whom I could ensnare with my charms and live a life of indulgence with the *huntin' fishin' shootin'* and now apparently *surfin'* set. Only two problems – one, I didn't want to ensnare *any* sort of man at present, and two, my charms didn't seem up to much if they had already failed to keep the man I'd really wanted, so what sort of upper-class twit would I end up with? Oh, and three, I couldn't actually *do* any of the aforementioned *huntin', fishin',* etc. and wouldn't particularly like anyone who could. I thought I'd explained this often enough to

Juliet, but she was in full flow by this time.

"You'd make such lovely friends amongst these people," she was saying. "And after all, you're very well-connected, you know – well, through my side anyway."

"I've begun to make some good friends here. Including a descendant of Stubbs." *Yes, I know what Marsha said, but I didn't say 'George', did I?* "She has a very exclusive studio," I went on – because there certainly wouldn't be another one quite like it, would there?

"Well good for you, darling," Juliet said, and I must say it was nice to feel that I'd impressed her for once. I decided to go before she asked any searching questions.

"My phone card is going to run out in a minute. How are things with you?"

"Oh, you know," she answered. "Keeping myself busy with this and that, as always. Philip has asked me to go to Cowes with him, so I'm thinking about it."

I nearly said, "Is that *Prince* Philip?" – but I knew she wouldn't find it amusing.

"I haven't heard of Philip before," I said instead.

"Oh, we go way back," she said airily, "but he's a widower now, and we've become friendly again recently. He's very keen on this Cowes trip."

"Sounds like a good idea," I said instead. "You should go – I'm sure you'd enjoy it. Must finish now, Juliet."

"All right darling, but do keep in touch. Where did you say you're staying again?"

But I wasn't going to fall for that one – I didn't want the Tremorden police pestered.

"Just down the coast from Newquay. But don't worry – as I haven't got my mobile any more, I'll call you from time to time to let you know I'm still in one piece."

"I suppose that will have to do," she said grudgingly, "but you still haven't told me what happened to your mobile. If someone's stolen it—"

At this point I cut her off, and hoped she'd blame it on my phonecard. My mother was definitely better in short doses, and this one had been plenty long enough. I wondered if I should present myself at Newquay police station in case Juliet didn't get in touch with them, but decided against it because it could simply create more problems – if in fact the policeman had really intended to act at my mother's behest. Somehow, I didn't think that looking for a grown woman who had declared that she was going to lose herself in Cornwall for an unspecified time would rate very highly on his To Do list.

Instead I decided to treat myself to afternoon tea as a reward for having called Juliet. I chose a café near the top of Tremorden's twisting main street, perched right in the middle of it, so the road had to divide in two to get past, leaving the café with a piece of triangular front garden which was the perfect spot for watching the world go by.

I scanned the people milling about in and out of the shops on both sides, deciding which would be locals and which holidaymakers both by their dress and their behaviour. Locals walked more with their heads down, already sure of their destinations, whilst holidaymakers often looked up at a shop front or spent some time gazing in the windows before entering, and would stop on the pavement for a huddled discussion about where they were going next. I was wistfully reminded of when Will and I had played this game sitting on the steps of the Madelaine in Paris, but on that occasion we were trying to identify nationalities.

It was definitely more fun, I decided, when you were with someone else. Without realising it at first, I began to see if this person was Marie, or that blonde head belonged to Kate … or whether that man was Adam … This was ridiculous! Why keep myself in this solitary confinement when I was obviously craving the company of others? I would meet up with them again and simply enjoy myself.

I began to feel like you do as a teenager when you're hoping a boy you fancy will ask you out, so you elaborately plan lots of opportunities to bump into him, when you can then feign great surprise that he's there. *Perhaps I should go down to the beach now and see if they're there. Or simply walk round to Marsha's and peep over the blue gate in case someone's out on the terrace. Or stroll past the Smugglers' again this evening and hope that a voice will call out to me.* Better still, I could get to the Smugglers' early and sit in a prominent position outside; then when they came along they could be pleasantly surprised to see me and we would take it from there. Yes, definitely, that was it.

You will note that this plan presupposed two things – first that any of Marsha's crowd were intending to be at the Smugglers' that evening, when there were at least a dozen similar venues they might choose, and second, that they would want me to join them again. But my company-deprived mind had not considered anything else – working in a similar way, I have to admit, to Juliet's when she thought she had come up with a perfect plan - and I hurried back to *Stalag 13* to shower and change.

Gwen Jarrett, a vision of biliousness in an acid yellow dress and, would you believe, matching tights, was carrying a plate of shortbread biscuits into the Residents' Lounge as I flew in through the front door. She opened her mouth to speak, but I forestalled her with a: "Sorry, can't stop. I'm in a hurry to get ready to meet some friends."

Of course, Murphy and Sod were apparently working together that evening to ensure that no-one I knew turned up. I parked myself just two tables away from where we had all sat together on that first evening, until twilight became dusk and dusk became dark. Families looking for pizza outlets – fathers and sons freshly attired in matching football shirts, and buggy-pushing mothers in skimpy outfits to show off their tans (wishing or glad, as the case may be, that they had done their post-natal exercises) – gave way to groups of young people, gelled and ear-ringed, all out 'on the pull', and to young couples dawdling along, bodies and minds entwined, or sitting close together, talking low.

And I sat ... And I sat. So convinced had I been that the evening was going to turn out as I'd planned that I didn't even take a book with me for company. At first I was still expectant, so that everything I looked at sparkled and glowed: the late evening sun glinting on the triangle of sea which could be glimpsed down in the bay, before slipping away in a pinky-orange haze over the horizon; the honeysuckle climbing a nearby wall and a clematis grown so tall that it was now entangled in the upper reaches of an evergreen tree. But as the evening wore on and my cloak of aloneness grew thick and heavy, I could only see the ring marks on the battered wooden table before me, the shoddiness of the waitress's black skirt and the dusty layer of sand which the evening breeze deposited all around whilst it toyed with a Cornish Clotted Cream Fudge wrapper, lifting it backwards and forwards across the street.

My first white wine grew warm as I waited, refusing to listen to the little voice in my head that said they weren't coming. My second followed a pasta meal which I didn't even taste, but ordered so that it wouldn't look as if I was waiting for someone. I spent some of the time practising a variety of put-downs in case any of the cheerful *we're-having-a-great-time* men who passed in and out of the pub should say, "Stood you up, love, has he?" – and then I was quite annoyed that none of them did. Probably the look on my face was too much for them.

I argued with myself instead, in a sort of continuous loop. *They're not coming – why not give up and go back to the guest house?* Because Mrs. J. is bound to ask what happened to my evening out with friends if I'm too early. *So take a stroll round the other pubs in case they've gone somewhere else.* But then they might be on their way here and I'll miss them. *Make your way to Marsha's house, then, and maybe you'll meet them on the road.* I'll feel too stupid if they realise that I was coming to find them. *Well you look pretty stupid sitting here all night.* Who asked you, anyway?

And then I got angry. Why, amongst all these happy holiday-makers was I the only one by myself? I hadn't seen one other person walking about or sitting outside a pub like this on their own. (Obviously, all the other sad people stayed at home with a meal-for-one in front of the telly and kept their sadness to themselves, but I wasn't thinking rationally by this time.) And why, when I'd done nothing wrong, did I have to be the one sitting here anyway, whilst Will and Lauren were probably out with friends at some trendy wine bar near the river, impressing everyone with details of the bijou little flat they'd found in Islington (because it was important for Will to have a better address now that he had become so adept at selling pokey apartments to gullible trendies for which they would have demanded compensation from Thomas Cook if they'd been expected to holiday in something similar abroad)? And *why,* when I'd acknowledged that spending hours on my own wasn't going to be the solution I'd thought, didn't the people I wanted to spend some time with have the decency to show up?

Earlier in the evening a harassed couple with a screaming toddler had walked hurriedly by, the dad struggling to hold the child whose arms and legs were thrashing in all directions while her face, a delicate shade of puce, was contorted in utter rage. I wished now that I could be like that child – that I could simply lie down on the floor and kick and scream until I was breathless and too exhausted to even remember what my frustrations had been.

By the time I stomped back to Lansdowne-with-Sea-View I was feeling murderous, in the sort of way that you do when you've reached the point of enjoying your bad-temper and are determined that absolutely nothing on earth is going to mollify you enough to banish it. I thought I had avoided Gwen Jarrett (isn't it strange how some names always have to go together, like

Sven Goran Ericsson, or Farley's Rusks?) but she emerged, still bilious, as I was mounting the stairs.

"You had a phone call this evening," she said in a tone that my temper took to be accusatory, "but I told him that you were out with friends."

Him! Oh no!

My temper dissolved into a deep pool of misery.

"Was there any message?" I asked feebly.

"Just that he hoped you were having a good time. Oh, and to say that Adam called."

6.

There was no prevaricating or pretence next morning. The night had hurtled me from one bad dream to another; dreams where I was standing outside the tall narrow house again, only this time my father had gone in and left me outside and I was beating my small fist on the door and begging to be allowed in, but there was no-one to hear me. Dreams filled with fear, and when I woke up in a panic (made worse by the pitch black room disorientating and suffocating me so that I couldn't remember where I was) I couldn't remember what had frightened me, yet it was strong enough to make me not want to go to sleep again in case it was still there.

Straight after breakfast I went round to Marsha's house. I had been awake since some ungodly hour, watching from my bedroom window as the natural world roused itself, until it was time to go down to eat.

I walked swiftly along the beach, rehearsing what I would say to Marsha, because I had decided that I had to engage her sympathies – although they had seemed pretty engaged on the three occasions we'd met so far. By the time I went through the blue gate and down the crooked steps I was like a coiled spring.

The faded wooden door into her workroom was ajar, and she was inside, packing pieces of pottery into boxes. She looked up as my body in the doorway cast a shadow across the stone floor.

"Well, don't you look tanned and healthy!" she exclaimed, and I warmed to the note of welcome in her voice. "You must have known I was just ready to have a break. Come on in!"

I advanced into the room as she plugged her kettle in.

"Okay. It's like this." I could hardly get inside quickly enough to say my bit. "I came down here to get away from everything and re-think my life, like I told you, but it's not working because I can't think any straighter here than in Purley, although it's far lovelier of course – and hot! – but I can't go back yet because I've promised Sarah my flat for at least a month, and if I do go back I'll be no better off, so I don't really know what to do, and Juliet was obviously right, and I've barely spoken to a soul in three days, and I thought I'd like that but I don't ... and ... and now I feel a complete wimp for marching in here and bleating to you without even saying hello!"

What was I doing? It was like a stopper being pulled from a dam and I'd been jigging from one foot to the other as I spoke like a child desperate for the toilet. She would think I was mad, although to her credit she showed no sign of it, simply picked up the two mugs of coffee and her hangover tablets and motioned me to the chairs on the terrace.

"But Adam called you last night and was told that you were out with friends," she said.

I flushed. "That was to keep Gwen Jarrett quiet."

"Ah," she said, understandingly. Then she was quiet for a few moments.

"I'm sorry," I said, "I shouldn't have come round here like this to heap my troubles on you – I hardly know you."

She smiled. "But that's the benefit, you see. It's often much better to talk things through with someone you don't know. You can get rid of all pretence then. That's why things like the Samaritans work so well. And I invited you to come here whenever you wanted, with or without your troubles."

A thought struck me. "Are you a Samaritan?"

She gave a little laugh. "I don't think they'd have me! Too impatient and too much of a meddler, I suspect. And too likely to suggest to some poor unfortunate that they have a good strong drink, when they're already an alcoholic! But I'm here, I'm on my own, with no ties, and I love company. So it's easy for people to drop by for a chat – I'm much too lazy to go to them as you've probably gathered – and if it helps, that's great. And if it doesn't, well, there's nothing lost and perhaps some friendship gained. That's got to be worth something."

I sipped my coffee, already feeling calmer than when I arrived. Perhaps it was the tranquillity of this house, which felt as if it had always been here, embedded in the cliff face. Or perhaps it was the rhythmic swooshing of the waves on the rocks below.

Or perhaps, I acknowledged, as I watched Marsha covertly over the rim of my mug, it was the sense of peace emanating from this woman opposite me, as unperturbed by my urgent arrival as if it were an everyday occurrence for her.

Which maybe it was.

"And the others?" I said, as my sluggish thought processes stirred. "Have you helped them?"

"Ah, now. Only they could answer that," she said, with a wry shrug. "But we've all known each other for a lot of years, and we've probably all had a few ups and downs during that time when we've needed a bit of support."

I pondered the truth of that.

"So," she said a moment later, "what are we going to do about you?" The briskness of our first meeting was back in her voice as she scrutinised me with narrowed eyes. "You know you're trying too hard, don't you?"

"What?" I said, just as briskly. So far, since Will had left me I had got the impression from everyone I spoke to that I wasn't *trying* hard enough. Trying to get over him, trying to re-build my life, trying to get out and meet other people, trying not to mind people telling me what I should be trying to do next.

Marsha's piercing blue eyes were directed straight at me. "You've come down here apparently 'to forget', or some other similar Foreign Legion cliché – which is nonsense because clearly you're not going to forget a major part of your life, and you're not even going to want to when you still think you're in love with the guy—"

When did I say that? I seem to remember that I hotly denied it on the beach ... obviously not hotly enough!

"—and mooching about on your own isn't going to produce any earth-shattering answers, so why don't you just stop trying?"

"Now you sound like Juliet – she said coming back to Cornwall was ridiculous," I said a shade defensively because I felt under attack. I'd come here for coffee and sympathy, dammit.

"And Juliet is ...?"

"My mother – but she doesn't like to be reminded of the fact because it puts years on her – or possibly just I do," I added.

"Your mother ... oh ..." Marsha seemed lost in thought for a few moments and then bought herself back to the matter in hand.

"I think you did the right thing to get away from London," she said, more gently now. "But you're trying too hard to sort things out on your own when, if you just sit back and relax a bit, they have a habit of working out all by themselves."

"'Chill out', I suppose you mean?"

Marsha grinned. "If you like, yes."

"But I thought that's what I've been doing – lying on the beach, long walks on the clifftops, that sort of thing ..."

"And what have you been thinking about during all that? *Trying* to decide on your future, when I suspect you've steadfastly refused to discuss any of your past in any way that would be helpful so that you could put it behind you in any real sense. *Trying* to do it all by yourself. Perhaps you've been too ..."

"Anally retentive?"

She grinned again. "I was going to say 'uptight'!"

"And I told you last time we met that there's been no-one to talk it over *with!* And anyway, where does talking get you? I tried talking to Will – that was a masochistic waste of time – and otherwise I've been on my own," I said hotly in my defence. Why had I thought being with this woman was peaceful? Although, to be fair, she was still as unruffled as when I'd first walked in.

She waited a moment for me to calm down.

"So how about this deal?" she offered. "You come and spend some time with me in the mornings, when I'm on my own, and we talk a few things through – although not every morning of course, because that will get too awful for both of us – and the rest of the time you mess about with us all, have a good time, treat us all as your friends and learn to enjoy yourself again."

The suspicion that I had stumbled on some weird sect arose again. After all, here I was, emotionally vulnerable, on my own, apparently friendless and insecure – isn't that just the sort of person these types prey on? But the others didn't seem strange or brainwashed in any way – in fact they seemed the most 'together' people I'd met for a long time – and they attracted me enormously. And Marsha, sat opposite me, kindness and patience oozing from her but not in a syrupy sort of way – quite the opposite; she could cut through the crap better than anyone I'd talked to since before Will.

Various people had suggested counselling – including my workmate Jodie, you'll recall – but I had rejected them in a lofty sort of way. Counselling was for wimps and part of our ridiculous dependency culture, which meant that self-styled counsellors, quacks and litigation experts were the only ones who profited. *And I didn't need it.*

Except I obviously needed something – and not just, as one of Jodie's men friends to whom I had been particularly bitchy had suggested, a 'good seeing-to'. I couldn't face going back to Purley in the same state as I'd left it, but at this rate that's what would happen.

I studied the pattern on my coffee mug for some time. A Biblical phrase popped up in my head – a strange occurrence, because I have never considered myself religious and know nothing of the Bible, except from schooldays, and I couldn't even remember it properly. Something about being heavily laden and laying down your burden and finding rest.

"I take it this is a package you're offering?"

"I'm afraid so. You're not going to feel better about yourself and your life until you've shared the burden a bit."

And there was that word, not two minutes after the phrase had come into my head – coincidence, or what?

I tussled with my doubts for a few more moments. I thought again of the last few days and how alone I'd been. Come to think about it, I'd been alone and lonely for the past ten months since Will had left me. But I still had my suspicions.

"No group therapy? I won't have to stand up and say, 'Hello, I'm Allie and I'm a failure,' or anything?"

"No. Just me and you, chatting over coffee – like we're doing now."

"No New Age mysticism or psychobabble?" I persisted.

"Absolutely none," she confirmed. "And no energy crystals, sitting under glass pyramids, exposing of your inner self (which always sounds vaguely disgusting), or analysis of your face, feet, or any other part of your anatomy. Oh, and definitely no Tantric sex."

"What exactly *is* Tantric sex?" I asked, in spite of myself. "I keep seeing it mentioned in the papers."

"I'm not absolutely sure," she said in conspiratorial tones, "but I think you have to keep very still, which must spoil the fun completely."

We both laughed, which eased the tension.

"Look," she said, "how long have you booked in to stay at Gwen Jarrett's?"

"Two weeks," I said, at which she winced.

"Well, how about you give my suggestion a try until your time with her is up? With a bit of luck you will have realised by then that our sort of hedonism is the best medicine of all, and if not, there'll be nothing lost and you can slope off back to Purley or wherever."

"And the others really won't mind me tagging along?"

"Whoever is my friend is their friend," she said firmly. "How do you think they all got to know each other in the first place? And you must have noticed that they're very easy to get along with."

I looked directly at the periwinkle eyes and saw complete frankness in their depths.

I took a deep breath. "Okay," I said.

"Good. Now why don't you come and help me with the rest of these wretched boxes, and then we can have some lunch and decide what to do with the rest of the day?"

We went back indoors, but before we tackled the boxes Marsha said, "Come and see the proper part of the house – you'll feel more at home then."

We went through a door at the back of the workshop and up a narrow staircase, which opened out into a large living room, dominated by superb views from the windows which stretched along one side.

"Kitchen through there," Marsha nodded her head to a door at the far end, "and a loo on this floor, bedrooms and bathrooms on the two floors above. Far too many stairs when your bones start to creak like mine, but I'm too hooked on the place now."

Noises of plates and dishes being rattled were coming from the kitchen and the next moment Adam appeared in boxer shorts and a T-shirt, clutching a mug and a plate piled high with toast.

"Oh, hi Allie!" he said casually as he tucked in. "I thought I heard voices downstairs, but Marsha's always talking to herself. Would you like some toast? I called you last night, did you know? Did you have a good time?"

I said *no, yes, no* to each of his questions.

"Gwen Jarrett's been giving her a hard time, so she's been fobbing her off with different stories," Marsha explained for me. (You see how she always used Gwen Jarrett's full name as well?) Then she asked him to help with the boxes.

"Sure," he said through buttery mouthfuls. "Just give me five minutes to shower and change and I'll be down. Simon's dragged Chris off to look at a motorbike or something – he's got too much energy, that lad, you know. He's just like Tigger."

He headed for the door, licking his fingers. "Don't you lift anything till I get there," he warned Marsha, grinned at me and was gone.

"Having three men staying in your house must keep you busy," I said as we waited in the workroom for Adam to join us. "With having to cook meals and cleaning and everything, I mean," I added hastily, in case she should think I meant anything else. Which of course I did, and this was my clumsy way of extracting more information about the set-up I had just allied myself to.

The eyes twinkled – at my discomfiture, I suspected.

"Ah," she said, "the longer you know me, the more you'll come to realise that I don't do anything that doesn't have some benefit for me. Come to think of it," she went on, speculatively, "none of us do anything we don't really want to – there's always a payback, even if it appears to be self-sacrifice. Even martyrs must enjoy their martyrdom, I've always thought, because there's invariably an easier route which they refuse to take ...

"I'm digressing – a terrible habit I'm afraid. What I was going to say was that providing a holiday home for those three," she jerked her head upwards, "means that I do less than when I'm here on my own, because free board is paid for in other ways. One of them is always happy to cook a meal, or do some shopping, and Simon, as you saw the other day, just has to potter about with something – so things get mended, whether they need it or not, or cleaned out or whatever, and it all works to my advantage.

"*But,*" she went on with a grin, "that's as far as their gratitude extends!"

"Oh! Of course! I didn't think for a minute ..." I lied, wishing for the millionth time that I didn't colour up so easily.

"Well you'd be the only one within about a ten mile radius of Tremorden who *hasn't* thought," she said. "Which also suits me well, because it enhances my reputation no end, which ultimately means I sell more pots.

"And," she continued mischievously, "who wouldn't feel flattered to be linked with any of them, especially at my age?"

Before I could answer Adam joined us, standing beside me so that I caught a faint whiff of aftershave (which I didn't recognise except to realise that it wasn't the same as Will used), although he didn't actually appear to have shaved. His beauty was only enhanced by the faint line of stubble around his chin – making me wonder what it would feel like rasping against the delicate skin of my breast. Well, I hadn't even stood next to a man – any man – for four days, remember!

Come to think of it, apart from Adam holding my hand to help me over the rocks the other day, I hadn't been touched by a man since Will left (except for the occasional clumsy pat on the arm from my erstwhile boss when I had been looking particularly woebegone). Is this what happens to widows or divorcées if they have no inclination or opportunity to settle down with someone else, I wondered? Spending years and years never feeling the touch of a man's hand ever again ... Was that what it was like for

Marsha? Did she ever seek the comfort of simply leaning her head against Adam's shoulder, as I had yearned to do the other evening? My insides flipped at the thought.

"How much are we packing away?" he was asking Marsha as I fantasised.

"All of it."

"All of it?" The harsh note in his voice brought me back to reality in time to catch an almost imperceptible glance between him and Marsha which I knew had something to do with me being there before he went on, in his usual carefree way, "Oh ... oh, all right ... Let's get cracking then."

"I'm following Simon's lead and having a good clear-out," Marsha explained to me. "Everything must go, as they say, and then I intend to have a complete break for a few weeks before deciding what to do next."

We worked side by side for the next hour or more, wrapping everything carefully in bubble-wrap and sticking delivery labels on the containers.

"I've got a van coming round tomorrow to take them all away," Marsha said as I was packing the last of the little snuff boxes. "That will please the driver, when he realises how many steps he has to carry them up! *No, not that one—*" her hand shot out as I was putting in the aquamarine and amethyst box I had admired the other day. "That one's for you."

"Are you sure? It's beautiful – thank you." I already knew better than to protest again.

She smiled. "I like your taste – it is one of the best ones I've produced. It can be a keepsake of your time here."

There was the merest hint of wistfulness in her voice, but before I could be sure, she turned away from me and surveyed the empty shelves.

"I suppose it could all do with a thorough clean now," she said, but with little enthusiasm.

"Not today," Adam said firmly. "That's definitely a rainy day job and then we'll all chip in and get it done – it won't take long if we have a crack at it together."

"You see?" she said to me, cocking her head towards Adam, and I felt ridiculously warmed to have a shared moment with her.

"You're right," she said to him. "That's the most I've done in days – I'm jiggered. Let's have some lunch."

We sat outside, eating in comparative but companionable silence, watching the sea with the gulls swirling overhead, obviously sending messages to each other that there was food about.

Then Marsha put her plate down on the ground and leaned back in her chair with her eyes closed, and suddenly she looked older.

"That's me finished," she said. "Time for a very long siesta – here, in this chair, because I can't be bothered to move – *and*," she opened her eyes briefly and encompassed both of us, *"on my own."*

"Okay," Adam said. "Come on Allie, we can take a hint. Let's clear off and leave this grumpy old lady on her own."

She kept her eyes shut but pulled a face at him while he pulled me to my feet and we tiptoed up the steps and out onto the road.

"So what would you like to do now?" he asked me, and of course I immediately floundered.

"I don't know – I don't mind – you don't have to nanny me, you know ... if you've got other plans ..."

"The only other plan I have today is to get back here this evening because we're saying goodbye to Chris – he's going back up to his family in London for a while – and I sincerely hope you're going to come to that because, frankly, we're all getting a bit bored with one another and it's good to have a new face amongst us."

I quelled the immediate retort that if they were looking for scintillating wit and entertainment they had come to the wrong person, and squashed the image that came into my mind of me in a Bonnie Langford-style tap-dancing outfit performing, for their gratification, the routine I learned when I was about six.

"That would be good," I said instead, pleased that I managed to sound cool, until he said: "So what do you fancy?" and I wanted to shout out, *"You!"*

What was wrong with me? Yes, he was the best-looking man I'd seen for ages – well, probably since I'd met Will, I'd have to say – but I hardly knew him; he might have horrible personal habits for all I knew, not to mention a steady girl or two tucked away somewhere; and anyway, I wasn't here for that sort of thing.

I quickly calculated where I was in my monthly cycle. That was it! I was at the bit where my body thought it would be a great idea to be ravished quickly and as thoroughly as possible by anyone reasonably presentable so that I could assuage my procreational-intent hormones (exacting revenge on Will only being a satisfactory by-product at this time).

I became aware of Adam standing there, still waiting for an

answer.

"Not a long walk," I said eventually, which was a little bit better than the *'I don't mind'* routine over again, "because I've done lots of that lately; and not sunbathing. Something active."

"Right. Then it's a pedal boat out in the bay," he said, "which is relatively cheap, great exercise for the legs as Kate is always pointing out, and only any fun at all if there's two or more of you. What do you think?"

My hormones would have been happy whether he had suggested we swept a few chimneys together or sat in a motorway lay-by, but the rest of me thought a pedal boat was the best idea.

"Come on then," he said, and moved off slightly ahead of me, so that there wasn't any chance for our arms to brush and our fingers entwine – not that I was even considering that for a moment, of course.

His earlier remark about Chris returning to his family came back to me as we powered our way around the coastline, and when we paused to look back at the bay I gathered enough breath to ask Adam about it.

"He lives with his wife and two little girls in West London – not far from Heathrow. He has a car showroom there."

"So why did he come down here on his own?" I didn't ask the more obvious question – *Is he the only one who is married?* – but naturally it was the one I really wanted answered, just as anyone would, to get a complete picture.

"Marsha had been a bit unwell earlier in the year, so we all came down a little sooner to check that she was okay. Chris could only manage a week or so, but had to come alone because the girls are still at school – and he couldn't leave the job for too long. But the whole family will be down later on."

"Another piece of the jig-saw sorted," I said. "Which only leaves the mysteries of you and Simon."

He raised an eyebrow at me.

"Well," I provided, "you know why I'm here for the summer, and I know now what Kate, Marie and Chris do. But what about you two – do you have to rush back soon to earn your crust?"

He chuckled. "Not us! We've got it all sorted. Simon runs a very successful recruitment agency – well, when I say 'runs' it, I mean in a nominal sense. He's inherited lots of family money and the family business, but he has an extremely able and ambitious manager who is only too pleased for Simon to take extended holidays. As for me, I'm a snapper.

"Freelance photographer," he explained when he saw my

puzzled look. "So I'm a bit like Marsha – work like stink for nine or ten months of the year so that I can bum around for the summer. By the time I return to London I'm literally hungry enough to chase the work again."

"And is it always Cornwall, for the whole summer?"

For the first time in our brief acquaintance I saw his face take on a closed expression.

"This year, definitely," he said. Then he quickly changed the subject. "The tide's turning, so we'd better go back in or we'll have to pedal twice as hard to get back."

But at least he hadn't said that he was married.

Not that it would have mattered if he had. He just hadn't *seemed* married, and I always like it if my intuition is right.

And if my sex-starved body was insisting that I fantasise about someone, I preferred it if I didn't have to think of them with a wife in the background.

7.

You will have guessed the rest by now, no doubt. The summer passed by idyllically in Cornwall as Adam and I drew closer and I was able to deal with all the pain left by Will. After a few false starts, we eventually proclaimed our love for each other, my divorce came through, Marie and Kate were bridesmaids at the wedding (where my mother wore the biggest hat imaginable and tried to get off with the best man, Simon, because he had a public school accent and was too polite to point out the age difference; and if he had, she would have just brought up Joan Collins to show it didn't matter), and after an appropriate passage of time Marsha was godmother at the christening. And we all lived happily ever after in fewer than eighty pages.

Except it wasn't quite like that. In fact, it wasn't like that at all. For a start, the sessions with Marsha were anything but cosy, and I began to see that she would have made a good interrogator for British Intelligence. Actually, I wouldn't have been surprised if the whole hippy thing was just a front and really she had been rigorously trained by MI5.

No matter how determined I was to present myself to her in a particular light, she always managed to make a deft, clean incision straight to the root of whatever canker we were currently trying to excise. And I never saw it coming. One minute we would be talking about something quite innocuous and the next we would be deep into the strange convolutions of my psyche.

"Doesn't this bore you?" I asked her one day, when I had rambled on about some aspect of Will's treatment of me so that even to my ears I was sounding whiny.

"Why would someone you care about bore you?" she answered.

"But you've only just met me. Why should you care?"

"Have you anyone else to care for you?" she countered.

Clever, you see. She nearly always answered such a question with another question, so that I would have to work out the answer for myself. On this occasion I opened my mouth to cite each of my parents as a matter of course; but then I closed it again. Did Juliet *really* care about what happened to me? I know she loved me in that inextricable way that mothers and daughters seem to have, even if they think they don't get on very well, which meant that probably after bickering with her for most of my adult life I would end up caring for her in her old age. But then would that be because *she* loved *me* or *I* loved *her*, or because I would still be trying to get her to admire and approve of me and having her dependent on me would be the last opportunity and, even if she never specifically demonstrated her love for me, I could kid myself that her gratitude was love? And by that time she would be too bound up in the selfish demands of old age to be able to *care* for me.

And all of this from one simple question from Marsha.

Then there was my father, and I've explained that one already. I remembered the strength of his love, but his caring ended when he took off for France and the delectable Yvon.

"No it didn't," said Marsha. "It ended when you tailed off your visits to France and showed him that you didn't need him to care."

"But he didn't even make an effort when my marriage broke up!" I declared hotly.

"Did you expect him to?" she asked.

"No ... not really ... I thought he wouldn't understand how I felt."

"So he lived up to your expectations, then."

"So you're saying it's my fault that my father doesn't see me any more!" I was angry now, and resorted to attack as the best form of defence.

But Marsha remained her imperturbable self. "Of course not," she answered. "I'm just pointing out that in every relationship there are two people and each has the ability to influence that relationship."

Basic stuff, I know, but I had spent ten months or more building up this *'the world is against me when I've done nothing wrong, and who cares anyway, I'll cope on my own'* defence system, and could no longer see the blatantly obvious.

She was the same with my relationship with Will. Every occurrence we discussed was turned around to see how I had influenced the outcome. Even his treachery with Lauren wasn't exempt, although the act itself was deplored.

Sometimes I would get so angry and confused that I would leave the house and spend the rest of the day on my own, doing the Pauline Collins bit again, but I always went back. Partly because there was something inexplicably hypnotic about the whole set-up, which I still can't really explain, and sometimes because I would have thought of some clever response to an earlier altercation that I was bursting to tell her so that I could wrong-foot her – but, needless to say, I never succeeded.

One of the hardest times was when we got round to the topic of marriage as an institution. Marsha, never having been married as it transpired, had a fairly caustic attitude towards the whole thing as far as she herself was concerned, but she could see that it was a desirable state for many others.

"It was the one thing I was sure I was going to be good at," I admitted, "and the one thing I was more determined to succeed in than any other. I suppose I'd seen my parents make such a hash of it that, with all the brashness of youth, I was convinced that I wouldn't let the same thing happen to me."

It was a whole life plan I'd had, you see. To meet someone I was capable of loving so much that I'd never get bored with him like my mother did with her men, and I would love him so well that he wouldn't want to leave me in the way that my father had. And after an appropriate amount of time we would have an agreed number of children, for whom we would provide a stable environment in which they would blossom and look up to me as the best mother in the world.

Yes, I know, I know, we were back to 'Janet and John' again, but don't tell me that there is any woman alive who, having met the man of her dreams, hasn't soon been weaving new dreams of a rosy future to whatever arrangement she personally aspires.

If I'm really honest (and I'd reached the point here of being more honest with myself, and Marsha, than I'd been for a long time), I'd have to admit that the shattering of my dreams regarding the future – namely the children and the security, i.e. the destruction of my long-held life plan – was almost as hard to bear as losing Will himself, and it was one of the hardest things to talk to Marsha about.

"I really thought I'd cracked it," I told her as all the earlier sensations of inadequacy and failure came flooding back, "and I'd wanted it to work so much ... and babies ... I wanted babies ... And don't say that I'm still young enough to have those babies because I've heard all that before *and it doesn't help!* ... And no-

one seems to remember that I need to meet a man I can trust before the babies come into it ... and I'm never going to trust a man again, so the babies will never happen, and that's not fair, because Will and Lauren can have babies whenever they want ... and I ... I ..." The pain had reached my voice, which had risen throughout this anguished speech and was now almost incoherent.

"I wasn't going to say any of that," Marsha said softly. "I was thinking that you might like a hug."

And moving to where I was hunched over in the chair, she put her arms around me and held me very tightly whilst I sobbed like the babies I wanted so badly. She may not have been as well-padded as Claire Rayner, but I couldn't recall ever having felt such unspoken sympathy and understanding pouring out from another person before. But then, I couldn't recall ever having broken down in front of anyone like this before.

As I've said: I never cry.

Except, it seems, when on holiday in Cornwall.

There was an up-side to all of this, however, because every down has an up. Yes, I know that sounds terribly clichéd in an 'every cloud has a silver lining' sort of way – as if I'm about to do a Julie Andrews in *The Sound of Music,* or go on about spoonfuls of sugar, but every cliché is based on truth. And I was rapidly beginning to see what Marsha meant about everything we do having a payback. Each occasion we talked, no matter how traumatic it seemed at the time, left me feeling more of a human being again; it was becoming a truly cathartic exercise and I could see how vulnerable people can become hooked on therapy. So my cup was definitely looking half-full rather than half-empty.

And the payback was my being able to develop a friendship with Adam on equal terms. Please note the use of the word 'friendship' here, because that's what it was.

I was getting on well with all of them by now, and beginning to see their individual personalities rather than just an indistinguishable group of exceedingly happy people, and I spent time with each of them on their own when the others were doing their own thing. But it was Adam who sought me out more often than anyone else, and it was Adam, I have to confess, whose company I manoeuvred to be in whenever I could.

And, hormones notwithstanding, I was quite happy for it to be just friendship. The fact that he obviously didn't fancy me but seemed to like me as a person was enormously refreshing, and made me see that throughout my life my view of the male species had been coloured by my mother. Thus my rather limited dealings with them had been with an eye to whether they were marriageable material, within which their 'fanciable' rating was important. But now for the first time in my life I had a friend who was male, and I was able to enjoy this phenomenon without over-thinking it.

Okay, so if you believe that, you'll believe anything. Truth was that the more time I spent in his company, the more (against all my better judgement) I longed for him to show me some partiality. It was hard to ignore the butterflies that his perfect smile produced, or the frisson of excitement when he put his arms round my shoulders to help me train his binoculars in the right direction.

I reminded myself (repeatedly) of my assertion that I had not come to Cornwall seeking any sort of romantic idyll. I chivvied myself (constantly) about what sort of a fool I would be if I allowed myself to fall head over heels with a man who was Mr. Nice-Guy to everyone. I told myself (continually) that he only invited me to join him because he was bored with the others, or was determined to be friendly to Marsha's protégé. And sometimes I would manage to convince myself.

You see? my inner voice would shriek when he showed affection to Marie, or flung his arm casually around Kate's shoulder and allowed it to rest there.

How sad are you? it would ask, when I was so aware of his presence next to me that I was sure everyone else would notice my ragged breathing and the difficulty I had focusing on what was being said.

Ridiculous really, when I knew for sure what happened when you, or at least I, fell for a man who oozed charm and good looks.

It's just good to have a friend, I told the inner voice when I jumped at the chance to spend time with him, and ignored the voice's reaction which translated into something which sounded like *'Phuh!'*

We quickly discovered likes and dislikes so similar that at first I was suspicious again.

"Has Marsha had a word with you, to be extra nice to me and boost me up?" I asked him when we had just finished a round of naff miniature golf, for which we'd both admitted a secret love.

"No she hasn't!" he exclaimed indignantly.

"Okay, okay," I said quickly. "I was just checking." And

feeling just a mite edgy on this particular occasion because I'd come from quite a tough morning with her.

"Has she been giving you a bit of a hard time?" Adam asked, with an admiring chuckle in his voice.

"How do you know?" I said quickly, all hackles and suspicion again. "I thought she never discussed anyone with anyone else."

"Nor does she. But we've all been through it at one time or another – that's why we're all here."

I stared at him, saying nothing so that he would say more.

"She's helped all of us, Allie, just like she's helping you now. And not just us – every now and again someone else will turn up to see her – but we all were around at more or less the same time, so the bonds we forged then have stayed pretty strong. We've all got our stories."

I thought back to that first evening at the Smugglers' when I had seen them as such perfect people, and had envied and resented them.

"So what's your story?" I asked gently.

He was quiet for a while.

"I'm sorry – I shouldn't have pried – you don't have to ..." I faltered.

"No – it's all right – it's no secret anymore. I was just trying to put it all in a nutshell ... so here goes:

"I never knew my father – I don't think my mother really did, either. She was just a teenager when she became pregnant with me, couldn't cope, and I ended up in care for most of my life. The trouble was, she felt guilty about it all and kept trying to make things work, so she'd have me back. Then she'd meet another boyfriend – usually some low-life who didn't want another man's kid hanging around – and I'd be back in a home again. Well, I couldn't cope with that too well and was a right little tearaway. Did too many things to even begin to tell you about."

"But ... but," I interrupted, "you seem too—" I stopped. Whatever I said would sound patronising and middle-class.

"Intelligent, well-spoken, successful, to have come from a run-down council estate?" he said grimly, and then softened it with, "not to mention so good-looking, of course!"

"Well-educated ... I was going to say well-educated ... yet you must have missed a lot of education ..." I faltered, because of course I had meant all the things he'd said.

"Ah. Well, you see, I've had two strokes of luck in my life," he said, overlooking my embarrassment. "The first was when the social workers decided I should be fostered. I think they'd run out of Children's Homes for me by then, so they decided to foist me onto some unsuspecting couple, because I still looked pretty angelic. And they found the perfect couple as far as I was concerned. He was a teacher and she wanted to be nothing more than a housewife and a loving mother to this considerably unlovable twelve-year-old."

We'd wandered down to the shore by this time and were sitting on the rocks below Marsha's house, watching a boat pulling a water-skier backwards and forwards across the bay. Unconsciously Adam took my hand and held it very tightly as we watched the water-skier tip over into the water for the umpteenth time.

"They were so good to me – even wanted to adopt me, but the powers that be, in their mighty wisdom, decreed that whilst they could lavish all their time and energy upon me, they were too old to be adoptive parents."

"Anyway, I did a lot of growing up with them. I discovered that I had a brain I could use and started reading voraciously, under Uncle Ted's watchful eye – and that's when I became interested in photography too; they bought me my first camera."

He gave a harsh laugh. "I really thought I had it made. Whichever idiot decreed that kids in care should be placed with families from similar backgrounds so they can 'relate' wants his head examining. This was heaven as far as I was concerned and I quickly picked up everything I could from them – table manners, social behaviour, how to speak properly – and I didn't want any reminder of where I'd come from."

He smiled at me, but the smile didn't reach his eyes. "I was like a twentieth-century version of 'Oliver' – and I definitely wanted more."

"So what went wrong?" I asked, stroking the hand that was still grasping mine, too engrossed in his story to even notice what I was doing.

"Auntie Maureen died. Suddenly one day, completely out of the blue. Neither Uncle Ted nor I could believe it ... Perhaps if we'd stayed together we would've come through it eventually – which, if I'd really been his son, we'd have been left alone to do. But no – along came another social worker we hadn't met before, who decided that Ted was 'unable to cope with the reality of the situation', and I was taken away from him. Not without a fight, of course – and I'm talking literally here – which just reinforced the social worker's conviction that she knew best. God, how I hated her!"

His lips were drawn tightly together as he stared at the horizon, and he seemed to have gone away from me completely. Back to the teenager pretending to be tough.

"Was that when you met Marsha?" I asked carefully after a few minutes. I had to hear the rest of the story by then – I was like the wedding guest held in thrall by the Ancient Mariner.

He shook his head. "Not straight away. My mother came back into the picture then, and persuaded them that I should try living at home again – after all, I was nearing the age when I could begin to earn something, and she was older and finding it harder to get a man. So back I went – and hated it more than I'd ever done before.

"I didn't fit in, you see. I spoke differently now and wanted to do other things – my head was full of everything Uncle Ted and Auntie Maureen had shown me. My Mum was horrified – thought I'd turned into a right little snob and made no bones about saying so to the neighbours and all her friends. So I became a tearaway again, bunking off school, even though I desperately wanted to learn ... making out I didn't care about anything ...

"And when I was sixteen I cleared off completely. I'd wanted to go back to Ted and look after him, but he was in residential care himself by this time; pre-senile dementia, they called it. I had nothing to speak of – oh, except that I was pretty, so I could have been a rent boy if I'd had the right inclinations. But even I could see the dangers of going down that road, so I left London and came down here with a girlfriend who was as screwed up as I was, to just bum around. That's when I met Marsha. The girlfriend had cleared off with someone who was marginally less of a loser than me, and I was sleeping rough on the beach."

"And she took you in?"

He chuckled again; but it still held no amusement. "I thought I'd taken her in at the time. You know, she seemed like a soft touch to me – another do-gooder who had no idea what life was really like. But of course she wasn't. I treated her appallingly at first, throwing all her hospitality back in her face – and throwing up once or twice, I seem to remember, when I'd tried to blot everything out with cheap booze. But she never gave up on me ... she got me back on course eventually, made me learn, gave me the confidence to think seriously about photography ... she was my second stroke of luck."

He turned to face me, his eyes the darkest I'd ever seen them. "I owe her everything, Allie – and so do the others, although they'll have to tell you their stories themselves. But that's why we all come back."

Our hands were still entwined. Slowly I leaned forward and kissed his cheek.

"What was that?" he asked with a wry smile. "The sympathy vote?"

"Definitely not," I said solemnly. "It was hero-worship for the intelligent, well-spoken, successful person you've become!"

"Not to mention so good-looking," he murmured.

"Oh, that most of all!" I declared with a grin.

He grinned back and, bringing both hands up to hold the sides of my face, slowly and deliberately pressed his lips against mine.

What can I tell you? That he tasted as good as he looked and my mouth – nay, my whole body – responded with an urgency that made me hot with embarrassment when I thought about it afterwards? That my insides were rapidly turning to liquid and I didn't want him to stop? That at first I ran my hands over his springy hair and wallowed in the sensation of a man – a man I fancied like mad, to boot – kissing me, wanting me, after all these long, lonely months?

All true. But as we came up for air, in the moment before Adam gave me just a little smile and began to kiss me again and my body felt as if it could lurch dangerously out of control, my mind began to work just as furiously.

What was I doing? Adam wasn't the right person to have a restorative holiday fling with; he was beginning to mean too much to me for that sort of brief encounter. So what was the alternative? The development of a deep and meaningful relationship with commitment on both sides, leading eventually to an assumption that we'd be together forever?

Oh, no. No. Too scary. I couldn't go down that road again.

I gently, reluctantly pulled away from him.

"What was that?" I asked, forcing the wobble out of my voice and sounding lighthearted. "The gratitude vote, for all the compliments?"

He smoothed the hair back from my face where his hands had messed it up.

"I'm certainly grateful for the opportunity," he said. "I've been wanting to kiss you ever since that first morning when you accused me of being a kidnapper."

Well, that was something to think about. All the time I'd been so aware of his presence I hadn't realised those feelings were reciprocated. I packed the thought into a recess to take out again and consider when I was alone that night.

His eyes searched my face. "And now you're wishing that I hadn't done that, aren't you?"

"Oh, so Marsha's taught you her mindreading tricks as well, has she?" I answered, aware that I too was doing one of Marsha's tricks, answering a question with a question.

"She didn't need to," he said. "I can see it in your face. I'm sorry – I didn't mean to make you do something you didn't want to."

"Oh no, you didn't – I do – I mean … it's not that I don't fancy you … well, you should have been able to tell that from the way I nearly ate you just now … it's just …"

I floundered about as he surveyed me steadily. "You're scared."

I nodded.

"Frightened you might get hurt."

I nodded again. "You understand?"

"Why do you think I'm still single?" he asked wryly. "Tell you what, why don't we do the old AA thing? You know – one day at a time. I won't put any pressure on you, and as long as you promise not to ravish me when I'm being vulnerable, we can take things slowly until we've really learned to trust each other."

I smiled. "The not ravishing you might prove a bit difficult, but I'll do my best."

"A bit of good old-fashioned courting," he said, smiling back, before putting his arms around me. "Which, you understand, does not preclude some genteel embracing and a few chaste kisses."

I nestled into his arms as we leaned back against the rocks, feeling safer by the minute.

"Of course," he whispered in my ear, "this is only until I've learned enough about hypnotism from Marsha to get my evil way with you!"

We sat in silence for a few minutes, relishing our new closeness.

"Are all the stories as bad?" I asked at length.

"Oh, some have had a lot more to cope with than me," he said.

I nodded. "It makes all my whingeing to Marsha seem trivial. Lots of people get divorced and cope with it."

He shook his head. "If you're close to cracking up, it doesn't matter what the cause of it is – pain is pain. But I tell you something –" his voice took on a fierce note that I'd not heard before –

"in lots of instances it's bloody parents who've a lot to answer for. When – *if* – I have kids, they're not going to get screwed up because of me!"

It was my turn to laugh harshly. "That's what I said, having watched the mess my parents made of themselves and me, but if I'd had my way when I still thought my marriage was going to be for ever, there would have been a couple of them by now, hanging round my skirts and asking where their Daddy is."

"Yes, but I bet you would have loved them, come what may!"

"Oh yes," I said softly, thinking of the babies in my life plan. "I would have loved them."

We both stared out to sea, and to some far distant glimpse of dreams to come and dreams gone by.

"So why has Marsha spent her life helping everyone else?" I asked then. "Why hasn't she got a family of her own?"

Adam shrugged. "She doesn't say very much on that score. I think there was a man many years ago, and a child who died, but she won't be drawn on the subject and none of us have pressed her."

"It's funny," I said after we'd sat for another couple of minutes; "I thought you were such 'shiny happy people' when I first met you, like in the REM song."

"And so we are *now*," he said, jumping down from the rock with a return to his usual exuberance, "because we've exorcised the demons. And fancy you liking REM! – another coincidence," he went on as we walked rather aimlessly along the beach.

"*Out of time*, or *Automatic for the People?*"

It was a game we had begun when we first realized how close many of our preferences were.

"*Automatic for the People*," I said promptly, "because of —"

"—*Everybody Hurts* and *Nightswimming?*"

"Exactly!" And we both laughed, glad to expunge the sombreness of the last few minutes.

"Noddy or Big Ears?" I asked.

"Neither, because Noddy is a little wimp and Big Ears is a pompous know-all."

"Agreed. Well, what about *Wind in the Willows* or *Winnie the Pooh?*"

"Hmm. A close one. I think it has to be *Winnie the Pooh* because he sings such awful little songs, and Eeyore is such a depressive."

"And Piglet is such a coward!" I exclaimed happily, because that was my choice too.

I found myself watching them all closely that evening as we gathered at Marsha's house – a cool evening following an afternoon of unexpected rain, so we sat in the large sitting room, looking out on a sea that had become grey and misty, and laughing at Simon's inexpert attempts to play a battered guitar he had found in Marsha's shed along with the barbecue.

It was hard to believe that they all had difficult pasts – what on earth could have happened to Simon, for example, when he seemed to have everything *but* unwanted baggage from an earlier life? He was strumming earnestly and making strangled noises that could have been singing, not caring a hoot about the derogatory remarks coming his way.

"No, listen, listen!" he protested. "I've got it now. Listen!"

"Oh, *no!* I can actually recognize that – it's *Kum Bah Yah!*" Marie shrieked, throwing toffee wrappers at him. "Stop him, someone, please! I can't bear it!"

"It's the only one I can remember," he said. "We used to sing it in the Boy Scouts."

"Right," said Adam, snatching the guitar away from him, "you're definitely stopping now, or you'll start going on about gangling goolies next, and that will be even worse!"

"I think it would help if you tuned it properly first, Simon," Marsha said, laughing with everyone else, "I don't think it's been touched since the days when I thought I was Joan Baez and tried out my protest songs on it."

"Were you any good?" Kate asked.

"Well ... there were certainly a few protests raised," she answered, "but not the sort I wanted to hear. I think my playing was on a par with Simon's."

"Huh! You realise you've all hurt my feelings so much I'm going to have to drown my sorrows with a very good bottle of Chablis, don't you?" he said, looking not the least bit forlorn as he headed for the kitchen in search of glasses.

This was all some time after my initial two weeks were up, of course – by which time I had decided to stay on longer, even though at that point I wasn't entirely sure that Marsha's plan was working, but I couldn't think where else to go. Also, I couldn't face the thought of starting again in a new place.

Now that Chris had left there was a spare room in Marsha's house, which she immediately offered me.

"Even if Chris comes back later on he'll stay in the bay, because he'll have the family with him," she told me.

But I declined the offer with as good a grace as I could. It was exceedingly tempting, but I still felt the need to hang back now and again, and my reluctance to be too beholden to anyone was still very strong.

In the end I was able to negotiate a long-term deal with Gwen Jarrett. The Lansdowne was still the pits as far as guesthouses went, but it was spotlessly clean (even the hardiest germ would have quailed when faced with Gwen Jarrett in glorious technicolor) and the season was moving on, so it would have been difficult to find anywhere better that still had vacancies.

Besides, I wasn't there very much at all. On the days when I was seeing Marsha I would leave immediately after breakfast and rarely return before nightfall, and on the days when I wasn't seeing her there was always something to do with Adam or one of the others.

One morning there was the frantic tooting of a high-pitched horn outside the guesthouse just as I was finishing my breakfast. I guessed it must be for me – the other residents, who I swear were all octogenarians, were going on a coach trip to St. Ives, and it didn't sound like a coach. One of them thought it was the fire alarm, though, whilst another thought it was the battery on his hearing aid indicating it was running out, and this resulted in an interestingly surreal conversation.

"Is that the fire bell? Perhaps we should leave."

"Damned battery, I only changed it a while ago."

"Well, really, I think Mrs. Jarrett could have got someone other than a paying guest to do that."

"Why? Has she got a hearing aid as well?"

"She may have – she doesn't seem to have heard that awful din – the place could go up in flames for all she knew. Then where would we all be."

"I'll take it out for now."

"Well if you're going out, so am I. I'm not staying here to sizzle."

It was the sort of conversation I could have had at any time with Juliet – and she wasn't even sixty yet; a worrying thought.

I reached the front entrance at the same time as Gwen Jarrett, whose elongated features were bunched into an expression of disapproval. On the gravel drive were Simon, Adam and Kate, sitting in a strange contraption which looked like a miniature Land Rover, painted in fading psychedelia. Simon was sounding the rubber horn attached to the side with such alacrity that he should have been wearing a checked waistcoat and shouting 'Poop poop!'

"Come on, we're off to Padstow for the day!" he bellowed as soon as he saw me. "Get your things!"

"What on earth is this?" I asked as I climbed into the back seat alongside Kate a couple of minutes later.

"Don't you know anything about history?" Adam swivelled round in his seat and gave me one of his devastating smiles as Simon drove us over every little rut in the road. "It's a Mini Moke – one of the most sought-after accessories of the Swinging Sixties."

"Ah! It must be Marsha's then! You didn't find this in the shed as well, did you Simon?"

"No," he laughed. "It's kept in great comfort in a garage near Marie's house and given an outing once or twice each summer if it's lucky. Good fun, though, don't you think?"

I wondered if Simon had ever sat in the back seat, which seemed to have slightly less suspension than Marsha's deckchairs.

"So why isn't Marsha with us? Or Marie for that matter? Am I taking up one of their places?" I was still at that stage of feeling as if I were gatecrashing, you'll notice. Not all the time, just when there were things organised like this.

"Marsha hardly ever leaves Tremorden in the summer," Kate explained. "She says that the summer months are what she moved there for, so she doesn't see why she should go anywhere else while there are lots of visitors to battle with. She saves up excursions for other times in the year when she says you can really get to know what a place is like.

"And Marie's working this morning, but she's going to keep Marsha company this afternoon," she went on.

"So we have the whole day to ourselves in this little beauty," Simon said, smacking the side of the car with affection. I had a horrible feeling he would be calling it 'she' and 'old girl' by the end of the day. I didn't like to say that I would have preferred the comfort of his BMW, which was parked just up the road from Marsha's house.

"And why Padstow?" I asked.

"Because we thought you should get to know a bit more of the area, and what better place to start than Padstow?" Kate said. "And anyway, I don't think this thing will go much further than that."

"And we can get a little chuggy boat across the harbour to

Rock," Adam added.

"Well that will please my mother," I said. I told them about the recent telephone call, and felt inordinately pleased when they laughed.

Padstow was bustling and quaint, and Rock was full of gleaming youngsters who made even Kate feel jaded. "And I'm only twenty-three!" she wailed. We stopped there for lunch though, because Simon ran into an old friend who insisted on buying us all a drink.

"This happens all the time when we're out with Simon," Adam explained. "His family have always owned property down here, so there are lots of people he knows – and look at him! I think networking is built into his genes!"

"But he doesn't stay with his family?" I asked, to be met with a raised eyebrow and a grimace which said: *Don't go any further down that road.* "Oh. Okay." So Simon had family problems – I felt even more that I had joined a club.

Which made me think of Juliet, so I bought a postcard of Rock which I thought would please her, but couldn't resist adding, "Wills and entourage not arrived yet, but will keep looking."

Back in Padstow Kate decided that we must all go for a bike ride.

"Come on, it's good for you," she insisted when Simon groaned. "And Allie will love it – we can hire bikes at the waterfront, and follow the old railway tracks to Wadebridge."

"That's miles!" he protested, as Kate dragged him along.

"It's not that far, and it's all on the flat," she persisted.

"What do you think, Allie?" Adam asked.

I hadn't ridden a bike for years, but all of a sudden it seemed like a great idea. "Sounds good to me. I don't know whether my legs will agree in the morning, though."

"It's not your legs you have to worry about," Simon said. "It's those two little bones underneath your bottom rubbing on the seat all the time. By tomorrow you'll be begging Kate to get you one of those air-rings they use in hospitals."

"Not any more we don't. When were you last in hospital?" Kate laughed.

"I've avoided the place since hearing all your horror stories. All right, all right, I'm coming!" And he marched on ahead with Kate, far less reluctantly than he was making out.

"Is Kate really besotted with her Carl?" I asked Adam as we followed on behind. "She and Simon look pretty good together." I may have forsworn men in the long-term myself, but I wasn't above matchmaking for others.

"No chance. Kate and Carl are definitely an item – you'll probably meet him soon, he's a nice bloke – and besides, Marie's the one Simon has always hankered after."

Which says a lot about my female intuition or whatever, because I hadn't picked up on that one at all. I said as much to Adam.

"He doesn't make a big thing of it," he answered. "Marie still finds it difficult to trust a man – any man – enough to have a proper relationship, even though she knows that Simon would be more trustworthy than anyone else."

"Part of her story?" I asked.

Adam nodded. "'Fraid so. Perhaps you weren't so wrong after all when you accused me that first morning of being part of a sect. We're certainly a strange bunch. 'Applicants must show evidence of severe dysfunction to be eligible for membership.'"

"But you're all so *happy*," I insisted, desperate for them to remain the golden, carefree people I'd envied from the start.

"Yes, we are," he said. "We are. But just every now and again those little demons will come and sit on our shoulders and have to be pushed away again. That's when we usually go running back to Marsha for reassurance – works every time."

"Perhaps Simon is being too considerate," I said. "Perhaps it would be better if he just swept Marie off her feet – you know, didn't give her time to think about it ... it might do the trick. Sometimes ... well, sometimes that's what women want ..." My voice tailed off.

Listen to me! A few weeks with Marsha and 'move over Claire Rayner'! As if I knew the answers to anyone's problems – if only!

But Adam was nodding thoughtfully as he looked at me. "'Mmm. Swept off her feet ... That's a thought. I'll have to bear that in mind."

I looked down at my feet, because I knew he wasn't talking about Simon and Marie any more.

"Seen the film?" he said suddenly and then grinned at my puzzled expression. "*What Women Want?*"

"Oh, yes, yes. Not bad," I answered, relieved that he hadn't scoffed at my amateurish attempt at agony-aunting.

"So – Mel Gibson or Bruce Willis?"

"Umm – would have been Bruce Willis a few years ago, before he lost so much hair and started taking himself too seriously. Now it must be Mel Gibson."

We were at the waterfront by this time, and for the next few hours there was little chance of proper conversation as I pedalled purposefully to Wadebridge, usually trailing a bit behind the others, because as I said, it had been a long time since I'd ridden a bike. But it gave me a chance to admire the bunched muscles of Adam's back and put a new slant on my response when he called over his shoulder, "What do you think of the view?"

Simon was right about the bones in the bottom, which travelling back in the Mini Moke did nothing to ease, but it didn't matter. I felt wonderfully warm and relaxed inside, like I used to as a child when we returned from the beach in the evening with salted hair and wind-stung skin and the ending of a perfect day made you want to cry just a little bit because it was such a shame it was dying.

Which is probably why I had the dream again, of standing outside the house with my father. But this time there was a tall, willowy figure standing on the step above us, and I should have known who it was, but I couldn't quite see the face.

8.

"Darling! You sound wonderful! How are all your new artist friends? I got your card – I knew you'd like Rock!"

As you may have realised, I was calling my mother, which I now did on a roughly weekly basis.

"Do you look as good as you sound, with all that sea air?" she went on. "You were very clever to choose Cornwall, you know, with all this good weather we've been having. There's a terrible heat-wave in Greece, so you'd never have been able to go out in the sun, and there are thunderstorms all over France ..."

Philip must be treating her very well, I decided, because it always put her in a magnanimous mood. If it continued she would soon be persuading herself and everyone else that it was her idea to pack me off to Cornwall to 'recuperate'. But that was fine by me – I liked her more when she was buoyant like this.

"... especially over the part where your father lives," she was saying now with a certain smugness, which spoilt things a bit. "I've seen Sarah, and she's looking after the flat well, but wants to know how much longer you want her to stay. When *are* you coming home, darling?"

"I'll phone Sarah," I told her, neatly side-stepping her question and turning the subject round to what had been happening to her, which with Juliet was never difficult. Because, in truth, I didn't know when I would be home.

Home. I'd been in Tremorden for over seven weeks, and Purley seemed like another world. It didn't seem like home.

We were now well into August and, as Juliet said, the weather had been superb. As had everything else. It was as if by wishing to revive the times of my childhood hard enough, it had actually happened. Every day was like an Enid Blyton story – we only needed a dog called Timmy. And looking back, it was hard to remember what we did, and when; the days simply merged into one another.

Sometimes it was shopping with Kate, or more often Marie, after Carl had joined them in the little house they shared a few streets away from the Lansdowne. Sometimes it was big gatherings on the beach with Chris and his young family who, as predicted, had returned to Tremorden and were staying on a caravan site just outside the town. Always there was laughter and fun, and always there was Marsha in the middle of everything; playing fondly with the little girls on the sand or letting them have a go on her potter's wheel and praising their misshapen efforts, which were nevertheless fired and painted; joining in the silly games which evolve when a lot of people, mellowed by a glass of wine and affable company, have what sound like good ideas at the time; or, increasingly it seemed, simply sitting back, as on that first night, smoking her French cigarettes which made her cough horrendously and watching us all through narrowed eyes, a benign smile playing on her lips.

Sometimes there would still be a snatched hour of just the two of us, flat out on the rocks where I'd first met her. No inhibitions now, and she probably found out more about me then than anyone else had ever done.

Except for Adam. With him I could talk about all the silly things that make us what we are. We discovered a shared love of films; you'll probably have realised by now that I have a penchant for the soppy romantic ones. Well – *I* don't think they're soppy, but Will always did. I usually watched them on my own when he was out – playing squash, I think. He liked macho action films, which I did too sometimes, because who could resist Arnie's *'I'll be back!'* – but it would have been nice occasionally to have had my choice for both of us to watch.

And books – modern and literary. Adam liked Shakespeare, I liked Dickens, but we both liked the Brontës and Austen, with a smattering of Hardy. Not that Will wasn't well-read – but he liked sci-fi, which I didn't, and authors like Salman Rushdie, who I couldn't get into, and not just because I didn't like his photo in the papers.

Okay ... So you'll be wondering by now why I ever married Will in the first place, as we had so little in common. Well, you have to remember the Pierce Brosnan/Robbie Williams effect and the wonderful boost to the ego that such a man can have on a fairly mousy librarian.

In return, Will loved the boost to his own ego that my ever-adoring eyes gave him. At the time, you see, he was still struggling to make it in the big world out there, and desirable though the leggy lovelies were, they were also high-maintenance, and he didn't have the time for all that. And when we first met I did the whole *'I'm not impressed with your face or your reputation'* bit, which for him represented an irresistible challenge. The trouble was that once I'd fallen for the sultry good looks I couldn't keep the act up, and reverted to: *'Doormat – please wipe your feet all over me'* instead.

I could see all that now, though of course I couldn't then. But the months spent on my own and the weeks I'd now had with Marsha and Co. had changed my perceptions.

'Character building', my grandmother would have called it. 'Bloody-mindedness', my mother said.

It was undoubtedly a bit of both. By the time I arrived in Cornwall I no longer particularly cared what anyone thought about me; and Marsha and Adam had since shown me that I could really get to like myself if I tried long enough.

It felt like I'd grown up. Part of me wished Will could see me now – so that I could show him how I'd changed, and how he didn't matter to me any more (except just occasionally during a sleepless night when I could have done with his arms around me, but I was working on that).

Gradually I'd learned the gist of everyone else's stories, which together read like a social worker's dossier.

There was Marie, who'd been habitually assaulted by her father over many years before she found the courage – via Marsha – to report him, which had ultimately led to his prosecution and the end of her parents' sham marriage. Despite Marsha's help, poor Simon had his work cut out trying to convince her that not all men were going to imprint the same emotional scars on her.

Simon, as I'd thought, was an ex-public schoolboy – who'd been expelled for drug problems, when what he'd probably needed was a shoulder to cry on because his parents were going through a messy divorce. He'd been sent to their home in Cornwall until a new school could be arranged, and it was there Marsha had found him, trying to steal from a shop to fund his drug habit. He never went back to boarding school.

Kate had also moved to Cornwall in her teens, this time for treatment of her severe anorexia – hence the still rather obsessive need to exercise, in a Princess Diana way of controlling her body.

Marsha had come across Chris when she'd been asked to give pottery lessons at a Youth Detention Centre. The job hadn't lasted long because she had made too many unfavourable comments about how the centre was run, but she'd been there long enough to take Chris under her wing and offer him a home when he was released.

"And after the cheerless place I'd called home all my life in London, it was like being in heaven," was how he described it to me. "Four kids, with four different fathers and a mother who found it difficult to come home from the pub when she had to climb nine flights of stairs to our flat because the lift was out of order again, and so were her legs. I tell you, I never laugh at *Only Fools and Horses*."

I began to see why Adam had spoken so vehemently about parenthood.

It was after the trip to Padstow that Gwen Jarrett had cornered me as I was leaving the dining room.

"I couldn't help but notice, my dear," she began, her voice devoid of the Cornish twang which would have made it 'middear', "that you've made friends with those young people who hang around Marsha Stubbs all the time."

I said nothing, but simply waited, so that she became a little uncomfortable.

"It's just that I thought I should warn you – as you're here on your own – well, they're not the sort of people those of us who've lived here a while would recommend you consort with ..." She moved closer to me and lowered her voice conspiratorially, although there was no-one left in the room. "There are all sorts of rumours about what they get up to – *drugs* probably, and other *illicit goings-on* ... she's a very bad influence ..."

My instinctive reaction was to defend Marsha hotly, but then I remembered her glee at having a bad reputation.

"That's very interesting," I said, lowering my voice too, so that Gwen Jarrett leaned forward, her eyes glistening with expectation. "In fact, did you know that they're under investigation as we speak? Members of certain ... shall we say, *organisations* – are studying their activities very closely. *That's why I'm here*," I whispered and then winked deliberately.

"Ah!" she said in mistaken understanding, straightening up and nodding her head knowingly. She looked at me with new respect before solemnly returning my wink, so that I had to flee the room in case I broke down in giggles.

Marsha laughed heartily when I told her, until her smoker's hack took over, and then made me tell it all over again when Carl and Kate turned up because she liked the way I imitated Gwen Jarrett's voice.

Adam laughed too, and after that made a point of walking back with me to the guest house at night and spending a long time talking to me outside, when we knew Mrs. J. would be watching – and sharing goodnight kisses which were growing longer and more lingering as time went on, when we knew she wasn't.

She never said anything when I went into the building, so I would just give a little knowing smile and a slight lift to one eyebrow (I'd practised that for ages in front of a mirror when I was in my teens because I thought it made me look cool) before bidding her goodnight.

One night, when we were strolling back from Marsha's, I confessed to Adam my inhibition about being topless on the beach – or not, in my case.

"Ah! There's a simple remedy for that," he said. "You go to the beach late at night, with someone you trust not to make you feel foolish, and you fling all your clothes off together and go running into the sea. After that, your inhibitions disappear."

I had to respond to his crooked grin. "You mean – a night like tonight – with someone like yourself, perhaps?"

"Well, now you come to mention it – why not?"

"Skinny dipping – you and me – now?"

"You trust me by now, don't you?" he asked.

"Y-e-e-s."

"*Really* trust me – about everything?"

I took a deep breath. He had never given me a moment's doubt of his sincerity and we'd grown closer with every day that passed.

"*Really* trust you," I affirmed.

"It's a beautiful night – they won't stay as warm as this for much longer."

"And you reckon that afterwards I'll be happy to brazen it out on the beach with the rest of them?"

"'Mmm – that's the theory ..." I could see his white teeth flashing in the moonlight ... "And even if it doesn't work, you shouldn't leave Cornwall without trying it once ..."

"What about when we come out? We'll be wringing wet ..." The thought of being in the sea with a naked Adam was becoming unbearably tantalising.

"We dry ourselves quickly with a T-shirt or something, then run across the beach until we're warm."

I have to admit I'd been hoping he'd suggest a more romantic way of warming up, but then he'd always been so careful not to frighten me off. Suddenly, though, I wanted him to see that I could be impulsive and devil-may-care.

"Okay. You're on!"

He laughed, grabbed my hand, and we ran down to the beach.

"Last one in's a coward!" he said, already stripping off his top and tugging at his shorts.

I concentrated on flinging my own clothes onto the sand so that he ran slightly ahead of me into the water.

"Straight in and dive under the waves," he shouted.

The water took my breath away, but I did as he said, plunging into the next wave and coming up a few yards away, spluttering and shaking the water from my eyes.

Adam was standing in the water right next to me. Amazingly, I stood up too, not minding that my breasts were on display, with the nipples rigid from the cold water.

"What do you think?" he asked.

"I think you were right!" I answered, and then shyness overtook me, not about my body, but because I wanted to tell him that he was beautiful. "Let's do it again!" And I plunged back under the water.

We swam about for ages, until my teeth were chattering so much I could hardly speak.

"Come on," he said, taking my hand again, "we've had enough."

We ran back up the beach together and frantically rubbed our bodies down with our thin cotton shirts. But by this time I was shivering with cold so much that I was getting nowhere.

"Come here," he said, and, reaching over, pulled me down into the sand, his body covering mine whilst his lips covered my face with kisses. I closed my eyes, drinking in the feel of his skin against mine and the scent of his hair.

"I thought we were meant to run," I whispered.

"Don't you prefer this?" he asked, covering my mouth with his so that I couldn't answer.

"'Mmm. Much better," I murmured when I could find my breath.

And oh, I wanted him so badly then. And I knew that he wanted me too – well, let's face it, it wasn't difficult to tell when we were both lying there buck naked. I moved my hips against the hardness of his body and he gave a small groan.

"Oh, Allie," he murmured, burying his face in my neck whilst his hand caressed my breast before moving expertly down my thigh, with my hands set to do a little exploring of their own. And then ...

And then a dog barked a little way along the beach. Wouldn't you know it?

Adam swore softly. "Where there's a dog there's bound to be an owner – we'd better go."

He sat up, quickly pulling on his shorts before gently dressing me.

"Next time," he said, "next time, I'm going to make love to you very slowly in just the right surroundings."

His voice was so full of sensuous promise that I shuddered deliciously and this time *I* felt beautiful.

We stood up and he took me in his arms again. "Still trust me?" he asked.

"Still trust you," I said.

We walked arm-in-arm to the guest house, but this time we didn't let Gwen Jarrett see us saying goodnight.

As you'd expect, the evening marked a watershed in our relationship. It was impossible to fight against the attraction I felt for Adam any more, even though at times I still wondered if it was wise to get involved so quickly and, it seemed, so soon. Like bereavement, there didn't seem to be any clues with a divorce as to how soon you should be 'over it'.

We didn't say anything to the others about our new-found closeness and, even though they must have noticed something different about us – my body found new meaning for the word 'hot' every time we were together – they made no comment. Occasionally I thought I detected a little satisfied smile lurking about Marsha's lips, which, unless it was my heightened emotions imagining it, was as if this was what she had planned all along; but she, too, said nothing.

Adam began pressing me to take up the offer of Chris's old room which was still empty – apart from anything else because it was impossible to be alone indoors at any other time, so his promise to me on the beach remained unfulfilled. But I still desisted, partly because I would have been embarrassed if Marsha and Simon were to be truly aware of the extent of my lust for this man and partly because I was enjoying the tantalising anticipation of our relationship.

(Note: the skinny dipping experience hadn't had its intended effect of me going blithely topless on the beach. When Adam was there I couldn't do it because I would have caught his eye and blushed at my memories of that night, and when he wasn't there I couldn't do it because I was sure everyone else would somehow know how I'd managed to pluck up the courage. So, still some hang-ups there to work on.)

Okay ... So you'll have figured out by now that this idyllic situation wasn't going to last. It couldn't really, could it? Nobody actually lives that happily ever after because all the everyday things like the mundane aspects of earning a living and being grumpy for that first hour in the morning, or bickering about cleaning out the bath, get in the way.

But Tremorden had become my Camelot, suspended in time and place, where none of these things mattered and everyone loved everyone else, and especially loved Marsha. She was the benign queen bee around whom the rest of us buzzed and without whom we had no purpose. And I wanted it to stay like that forever, because, after Will, I deserved my happy ending, and after what they'd each been through, so did the others.

Only I'd forgotten, when I was going on about every down having an upside, that it worked the other way round too. I'd been going around for the last few weeks on a different planet, a living example of every romantic cliché to be found. So when it all collapsed, 'coming down to earth with a bang' didn't even begin to describe it.

9.

Looking back, there had been a feeling of the end of the summer in the air that morning. Chris and his family had returned to London and I'd gone to meet Kate after she'd seen Carl off back to Exeter, where she was going to join him at the end of the week. My bank balance was telling me that it was almost time for me to make some financial decisions, but I kept putting it off. Like I said, I wanted Camelot to go on for ever.

There was a stiff breeze coming off the sea, and Kate and I were laughing at our dishevelled state as we pushed open the old wooden door into Marsha's house, looking forward to a warm drink.

"Kate! Is that you?" Simon's anxious voice shouted down the stairs. "Up here, quickly!"

He was standing in the doorway, a bloodstained towel in his hands.

"Marsha's having a nosebleed – I can't get it to stop!"

I was about to tell him to calm down. After all, it was only a nosebleed and perhaps he was one of those men who panicked at the sight of a bit of blood. But thank goodness I didn't.

Kate had already pushed past him into the room, so it wasn't until I followed that I saw Marsha, slumped in the chair, pale and breathless and at least ten years older, with blood seemingly everywhere.

"Call an ambulance, she'll need to be admitted," Kate told Simon.

"I've got the car outside," he said. "Couldn't we ...?"

"We won't get her up the steps properly and that might make things worse," Kate said. "Do it – now!"

"Allie!" she went on, "get me something cold from the freezer – frozen peas or whatever, and then the first aid kit from the workroom."

She didn't need to tell me twice. Her voice had the sort of command to it that brooked no argument, but as she turned back to Marsha, so it changed to a gentle reassurance.

"It's all right. We'll soon sort this out. Try to take some slow breaths – that's it ... nice and calm ... you'll be fine ..."

Marsha herself was concentrating too hard on breathing to do much more than gasp a few words which I couldn't make out.

By the time the ambulance arrived Kate appeared to have the situation under control. She'd packed both of Marsha's nostrils with gauze, which had already turned bright red, and, with me holding the frozen peas over the bridge of Marsha's nose, had cut her bloody vest top away and managed to help her into a clean blouse. Meanwhile, Simon had kept a look-out for the ambulance and I hadn't dared ask about what was going on.

"Where's Adam?" I asked him instead whilst Kate was giving information to the ambulance crew using unintelligible medical-speak.

"He's just popped out to get a few things – he was supposed to be back by now." His face was almost as ashen as Marsha's. "He'll need to know what's happened ..."

"Simon, it's all right – they can fix nosebleeds. They'll soon sort it out at the hospital," I said, soothingly.

The expression on his face as he turned to me made me take back the hand which had been about to pat him sympathetically on the shoulder.

"You still don't know ...?" he began.

"Don't know what?" I asked, increasingly alarmed now. "Simon, what's all this about?"

But the ambulance men were ready to leave then, with Marsha strapped to a stretcher, her tall lean frame looking shrunken, wrapped in a red blanket.

"Look," I said to Simon, "leave me your car keys and you go with Kate and Marsha. I'll wait here for Adam – and Marie if you want – and we'll follow you in as soon as we can. You never know, by that time she might be all sorted out and ready to come home again."

My voice sounded too hearty; I knew it did, because there was obviously something going on here that was much more serious than a simple nosebleed, but Simon wasn't going to tell me and Kate was too bound up in caring for Marsha to stop for a conversation.

Simon handed me his keys and hugged me. "Thanks Allie. See you in a while," he said, and followed the little entourage as they negotiated the stairs down and the steps back up to the gate.

I'd only just cleared up the mess in the sitting room and put the bloodstained towels in the sink to soak when Adam arrived, bounding up the stairs, whistling, his arms full of carrier bags.

"What's up?" he asked, stopping in mid-whistle when he saw my face. "Where is everyone?"

I briefly told him what had happened.

"How bad?" he questioned, with uncharacteristic urgency.

"It looked like a very bad nosebleed," I answered. "But I don't know how bad *bad* is, when I don't know why everyone is taking it so seriously! I heard Kate say something about medication. What's *wrong*, Adam?"

He pulled me down on the sofa beside him and slowly ran his hands over his face before turning to look at me. His expression was the bleakest I'd ever seen as he struggled to find the words.

"She's got cancer, Allie. Everywhere. Nothing can be done – it's too far gone for a cure—"

"*Cancer?* You mean she's *dying?* Marsha's dying?"

He nodded. "That's why we're all here. She's known for a while and, when she told us, we agreed that we would come down again this year but stay for as long as we could – for just one last summer. It was the only thing she wanted – for everything to be like it had always been – and it was the only thing we could do for her." His voice was a ragged whisper.

It was as if scales dropped from my eyes. Just like when my parents told me they were divorcing. Why did it always take me so long to see these things?

Because, a little voice in my head told me, *in this instance you were only interested in your own salvation, not anyone else's.*

It was all obvious now – the pills for the 'hangovers', although I never saw her drink very much; the hacking smoker's cough that no-one ever commented on; the sallowness sometimes glimpsed in the evenings under the perpetual tan, which I'd thought was probably the colour you went when you reached a certain age and had spent years in the sunshine; the growing reluctance to leave Tremorden, and, at times, to leave the house; the way that there was always someone with her ...

"That's why she's packed her workshop away," I stated rather than questioned. "She's never going to do any work again."

Adam nodded. "It had spread from her lungs, where it started, and she was told it was in her brain. She knew that eventually she might find movement difficult, so she decided to quit while she was ahead."

I became angry then, scared-angry. "None of you told me. Why didn't you *tell* me?"

I thought of everything we'd shared, Adam and I. All those trivial but vital bits of information that bring two people close together. I'd thought there was nothing we couldn't talk about.

"I trusted you. I thought we trusted each other," I cried as I jumped to my feet. "We were supposed to be honest with each other. Why weren't you honest about this?"

"She didn't want you to know," he said. "She asked us not to tell you. She knew you needed help, and she thought that if you knew she was dying you wouldn't have talked to her so freely. I mean, let's face it, until you get used to the situation, it's what we all do, isn't it?"

I said nothing, holding on to my anger, because it encompassed everything – anger with Adam for not telling me, anger with myself for being so blind, and anger at Marsha for making me need her – yes, and love her too – when she wouldn't be here for much longer. All mixed up with gratitude for what she'd given me, horror at the thought of what she was facing, and fear that my new, happy, safe little world was going to be rent asunder.

"She was right, Allie," Adam persisted. "Think about it. Would you have got to know us all – would you and I have discovered each other if, at the beginning, she'd said, 'Do drop in at any time and share your troubles with me. Oh, and by the way, I'm dying of cancer, but don't let that bother you at all – it's nothing'?"

I shook my head, acknowledging he was right.

"But you could have me told since – or at least mentioned that she was ill," I cried, my voice sounding harsh and ugly, "*Marsha's dying* – and you couldn't tell me!"

I was hopping from one foot to the other, as I tend to do when agitated, my arms flailing about.

He put his arms around me and held me tightly, "I was going to, so many times," he confessed. "But we were having such a good time, you were so happy, Marsha seemed to be doing all right and summer was nearly over. I thought we'd both be going back to London soon, so I'd tell you then – or perhaps, if I'm honest, I half hoped Marsha would tell you herself before you said goodbye."

"But you've all been so carefree, so cheerful," I said. "How could you, when you knew she was dying?" The Cornwall effect was happening again; I was close to tears.

"Like I said, we've all had longer to get used to it, and it was the only thing we could do for her that meant anything. And even when you know someone's dying, you can't be doom and gloom all the time – Marsha certainly hasn't been, so we all took our cue from her.

"Look, I don't want to rush you," he went on, "because I know this is a hell of a shock, but I think we ought to make our way to the hospital."

"Oh – oh yes, of course – I'm sorry," I tried to gather my scattered wits. "What about Marie?"

"We'll pick her up on the way. Those bloody horses can stew for one day."

I sat in the back of the BMW as Adam drove the three of us to Wadebridge, the events of the past two months kaleidoscoping through my brain, my emotions in a whirl. Disbelief and denial sparred in my head. I wanted it to be yesterday still, when everything was hunkydory, God was in His heaven and all was right with the world. I didn't want this sadness, this knowledge that the others had been carrying around with them for all this time. What about this laying down of burdens and finding rest? Did it always have to be replaced by another big load?

Kate and Simon were waiting in Accident & Emergency.

"She's okay at the moment," Kate said immediately to our unspoken questions. "They've put a cocaine pack in her nose which will stop the bleeding, but she's got to stay in for a couple of days to make sure it doesn't start again and because they'll probably want to take some fluid off her lungs, to make her more comfortable."

"Can we see her?" Marie asked.

"We can go up to the ward and pop in for a few minutes, apparently. We were waiting for you to get here first."

But when we reached the ward we were told that only one or two could go in, briefly, because there were lots of things they still wanted to do to Marsha.

"We've already had a little chat with her in Casualty," Simon said. "You three go in."

But I hung back on the pretext that three would be too many. In truth, I couldn't face her just yet. Adam was right, damn him. I didn't know, at the moment, how to be. What did you say? 'Feeling better?' 'Hope you'll get well soon?' I could imagine Marsha's straightforward gaze and honest response to either of those gambits.

But Adam and Marie actually came out smiling.

"We've got a list," Marie said, "of things she wants while she's in here, books and things – but no grapes because she can't stand them."

"And we've not to come over all together, because she doesn't want to have to make polite conversation with us all around her bed," Adam added. "She says she preferred it in the old days when it was strictly two visitors only between seven and eight o'clock, children only on Sundays and Sister played war if you perched on the edge of the bed. I'm beginning to feel sorry for the nurses already!"

We all gave relieved smiles then and on the way home there was lots of determined chat about who would do what whilst she was in hospital and who would visit when, but equally determinedly there was no chat about what the longer term held. We all hung around the house for the afternoon, so I volunteered to cook a meal and shooed everyone else out of the kitchen, even Adam. I needed to be on my own, but, perversely, I didn't want to go away from the house just yet.

I was battling with so many emotions, none of which I felt were noble enough to share with anybody else. Also, there was a creeping feeling of apartness. Whereas the others had so much more shared history, I had come into Marsha's life so recently that I felt I should no longer be there; that I should quietly depart and let them care for Marsha until she could no longer be cared for, and then grieve for her together. *Sans* intruders.

I would like to be able to say that these thoughts were honourable ones – that I was only considering Marsha's and everybody else's feelings, but that wouldn't be true. Most of what I was feeling in that kitchen was self-pity. That the exclusive club which they had formed really had no room for me – I had only ever been an honorary member, and now that membership seemed tenuous.

But, on the other hand, I couldn't simply walk away. The thought of not having Marsha around for too much longer was hard enough. The thought of not seeing Adam either was intolerable. It seemed that I was back where I had started all those weeks ago; my future was still as uncertain, and my ability to cope with it just as questionable.

So much for Marsha's assertion that if I just stopped trying so hard, everything would sort itself out. And so much for my assertion that I had grown up during these past few weeks, and was now truly independent. Another part of my life that seemed to be built on shifting sand.

I didn't begin to think of any of this properly from Marsha's perspective until I was back in my cheerless room in Sea Viewless. Simon and Kate had been to visit Marsha in the evening, and once I knew that Marsha was still all right for the time being I decided on an early night.

"I'll walk you back," Adam said immediately.

I nearly declined, until I pulled myself out of my own misery sufficiently to catch a glimpse of his. I called myself all sorts of an unfeeling cow then, because Marsha had been so much to him for so many years. It would be like facing up to losing a parent – or worse, because Marsha hadn't been an obligation inflicted on him by birth.

As soon as we'd left the house we both began to speak.

"I'm sorry—"

"I shouldn't have—"

We laughed, for the first time that day.

"Me first, because I'm bigger than you," he said, in an attempt to keep the smile on my face. "I shouldn't have left you in the dark like that."

I stretched up and kissed him very gently on the lips.

"It's okay," I said. "I do understand why – I think. It was just a hell of a shock, that's all. I still can't quite take it in – and I have this strong feeling that I shouldn't be here – that I'm intruding ..." There, I'd said it. "I feel I should leave – you said yourself we'd both be heading back to London soon ..."

His beautiful greeny-brown eyes held mine intently.

"Allie, please don't think that. Marsha wanted you here – at least wait until she comes home and then talk to her – about all of it; she'll understand. And I need you here, Allie. I don't think I've ever needed anyone in my life as much as I need you now."

Which was totally irresistible of course. So I promised to wait until Marsha came out of hospital and we strolled along the sea front arm-in-arm all the way back to the guest house.

For once Gwen Jarrett was nowhere to be seen, which I was relieved about, because I'm not sure how I would have reacted had she made some caustic comment about Marsha.

Up in my room I couldn't settle. Having felt a bit of a spare part at Marsha's house, I now wished that I'd asked to stay over and sought comfort from Adam's body. Now that I was truly alone for the first time that day, I couldn't get the image of Marsha out of my head and thinking of what it must be like for her. How had she managed to stay so serene and focused? How had she managed to calmly begin to pack her life away and not crack up over the unfairness of it all? How, that day when we boxed up her workroom, had she been able to dwell on my problems instead of agonising over saying farewell to a lifetime's work? What did she think of in the early hours of the morning, when perhaps pain or anxiety had brought her awake?

She was home from hospital after a few days, looking thinner than ever, but otherwise not admitting to any frailties, but it was several more days before I was able to talk to her alone. This was partly due to the natural protectiveness of Marie and Kate who hovered over her constantly, but also to me keeping my distance because I felt uncomfortable now that everything had changed.

Kate was stoutly declaring that she wouldn't return to Exeter for the autumn, intending instead to stay with Marsha for as long as she was needed, but Marsha persuaded her to visit Carl for a few days to think things through before making any definite decisions. Marie was also persuaded to return to work by the basic need to earn money.

So it was that I found myself one morning alone on the terrace with Marsha, drinking in the warmth of a late summer sun, just as we had when I first arrived, except that Marsha had succumbed to the greater comfort of a sun lounger to relax upon rather than a battered deckchair.

The two men had been summarily dismissed with the directive to go and find something useful to do, because Marsha wanted time with me on her own.

"The other day must have scared you," she said without preamble as soon as they had left. "It was the wrong way for you to find out."

"I wasn't scared," I replied straight away, to show her that I was made of sterner stuff. "I just wish I'd known what was going on."

If I'd expected an apology, I wasn't going to get one.

"And now you're feeling that you've been left out – or rather never really admitted to our little world," she said.

"Have you been talking to Adam?" I asked defensively.

She gave a short laugh. "No need. It's just how I would have felt if our situations had been reversed."

She sighed. "It was my master plan going awry, I'm afraid. I'd been feeling pretty well and it was nearly the end of the summer – I was hoping to last out until everyone went away again. And I wanted it to be a special summer for you – not one overcast with a sense of doom and gloom – especially when you've been getting on so well with Adam."

It was my turn to laugh. "I didn't think that would have passed you by. Is that part of your master plan too?"

"Oh no, because there can never be any certainties where people's feelings are concerned." The old twinkle was back in her eyes. "I'm always pleased, though, to see a little romance developing – and if it becomes something bigger and long-lasting, then I shall definitely take the credit!"

Her face became more serious. "So. Now you are trying to decide whether to stay and watch me die – although I must warn you that it is probably going to take quite a while yet – or return to pick up the threads of your old life."

"I would have to be thinking along those lines anyway – I haven't got an unlimited source of income like Simon, unfortunately."

She nodded. "I can't tell you what to do – except to say that you are welcome to stay here – in this house, if money's getting tight, you know that – for as long as you want. But if you decide to return to London, will you *please* persuade Adam to go too? – or that lad isn't going to have a bean to bless himself with through the winter."

"I don't think my influence is that strong," I pointed out.

"I think you're underestimating yourself. Haven't I taught you anything?" she said in a gently mocking tone. Then: "Oh! Listen to me! The prospect of imminent death really makes us control freaks even worse, you know – wanting to tie up everyone else's loose ends just because ours are already firmly knotted."

She grinned at me, but I couldn't smile back.

"Aren't you scared?" I blurted out.

"Of what? Dying?" Marsha wasn't bothered by my question, but seemed to consider it for a few moments, so that I was about to apologise and tell her to ignore my nosiness.

"No-o. I'm not scared of dying itself. I've come to realise that it's harder to *watch* a loved one die than to actually go through the process oneself."

I remembered what Adam had said about there once being a child, and also that Marsha didn't like to discuss it. I sought frantically for something to change the subject, but she began to speak again.

"I am scared of having a *bad* death, though. The control freak again, I suppose."

"*Is* that something you can control?" I asked, suddenly aware of how totally ignorant I was about such matters.

"I think so, up to a point," she said. "For instance, I want to make sure the right drugs are there when I need them, so that I'm not in lots of pain – that would be horrible for me and for anyone looking after me. And, as you know, I would prefer to be here, rather than in hospital, which is why I'm seriously considering taking up Kate's offer – except that it seems awfully selfish."

"Perhaps it would be more selfish to turn her down," I said softly. "Perhaps it would give her a bit of that 'payback' you've often talked about."

She looked at me for a moment. "Do you know, I think you may be right! That's just what I would have advised someone else, isn't it?"

Her winning smile was back in place, "Come on, let's talk about something other than my prospective departure to the after-life – which I'm not quite sure about, by the way. On the one hand the thought of being reunited with those I've loved is immensely attractive, but not if I also have to share eternity with all those people I actually detested when they were down here!"

But I couldn't laugh, or finish it there – I had too many questions going round in my head.

"How can you sit there and make jokes about it – so coolly?" I persisted, feeling ready to howl on her behalf.

"Ah! You mean I should be ranting and raving at the unfairness of it all. *'Do not go gentle into that good night,'* and all that? Well, you're seeing me over two years later, of course, when all the wailing and gnashing of teeth has been done. I did get terribly angry at first – we all think it's never going to happen to us, don't we? But in the end all that anger and resentment is terribly tiring, you know. There were quite a lot of regrets – I'd been looking forward to becoming an utterly disgraceful old lady! – but in the end I decided that if I only had a limited amount of time left, I was going to do lots of things I wanted to do and not waste it crying over what might have been. I think it's what your grandmother would have called 'getting a grip'."

"And have you done all the things you wanted?" I asked, trying to imagine how long my own list would have been.

"Most of them," she said. "In the end it really concentrates your mind and you realise that what you actually want to do most is to be with the people you love, in the places that mean the most to you. There are one or two people from my past whom I would have liked to see again, but, realistically, if I'd lived to be a hundred that might never have happened."

We were both lost in our own thoughts for a moment or two,

until Marsha looked directly at me, and I could see the determination in her face.

"Now then," she said brightly, "are you going to take pity on this poor invalid and get her another cup of coffee?"

I really tried, after that conversation, to behave as normally as possible, but somehow I couldn't treat it all as naturally as the others did – presumably because they'd had time to grow used to the idea that this would be their last summer with Marsha. Whereas I could only dwell on how lovely it had all been, how tragic it was going to be pretty soon, and how unfair it seemed that someone as essentially good as Marsha should have her life cut short in this way.

All the things I hadn't noticed before now seemed magnified. The suggestion that we spend an evening indoors because the air was chilly was a euphemism for Marsha being too weak to face a livelier evening elsewhere. Simon's latest enthusiasm for taking over the kitchen to prepare exotically delicious soups, whilst served amongst lots of tomfoolery and derogatory comments admittedly, was an excuse to tempt Marsha's flagging appetite.

There was celebration when Kate received the news that she'd passed her finals, with a meal that everyone took a hand in preparing whilst becoming very drunk and silly so that it tasted abominable but nobody cared anyway. At least, as Simon pointed out, by eating in we could all become pie-eyed without having to negotiate the treacherous steps to and from the house. We all agreed vigorously so that we could ignore the fact that Marsha wouldn't have managed the walk to anywhere else.

It was wonderful to have the excuse to forget about recent events and have a reason instead to revel in high spirits. Even Marsha looked better than she had in days, with some colour in her cheeks and a return of her lively wit. By midnight we had reached the stage of finding a game of 'Twister' hilarious, where wit turned into derogatory comments about everyone's inability to follow instructions.

"Stay – just for tonight – both the girls are," Adam whispered to me as we untangled ourselves midst much giggling from yet another collapsed heap on the floor.

His eyes were bright, not just with wine, but with longing and my insides did their familiar lurch as I looked at him.

"Okay," I whispered back.

We waited until everyone else had taken themselves off to bed, like two naughty children who didn't want the grown-ups to know what they were up to. Eventually, there were no more footsteps or creaking doors to be heard overhead.

Adam stretched out his hand to mine. "Come on."

Like all the others, his room overlooked the sea, and was simply furnished with oddments which, given Marsha's artistic eye, somehow looked perfect together. The curtains weren't drawn, and a sliver of moon could be seen in the sky, casting a shaft of eerie light onto the floor.

Tenderly Adam drew his finger down the side of my face; a simple movement filled with such eroticism that I shivered with delight. Then he took my face between his hands and kissed me until my head was spinning, from wine and from want. My own hands fumbled with the urgency of needing to undo his shirt, but he stopped me.

"I promised you that this would be very slow," he said.

And it was. I relaxed in his arms and gradually we peeled off the few layers of clothing that separated our bodies. Then he lifted me onto the bed and began to explore my body, rapturously, with little kisses and flicks of his tongue, until nerve endings in previously undiscovered places were tingling with desire, and the delight of being desired.

It was easy to respond with an abandon I hadn't known I possessed. I wanted to know every inch of his body and claim it as mine.

"Wow!" I exclaimed a long time later. "Where did you learn all of that?"

He lifted his head from my breast and chuckled wickedly. "There are occasional benefits from having had such a misspent youth." He shifted his weight until his lips were on the little crevice of my collarbone. "I can show you a lot more," he whispered enticingly, "like this ... and this ..."

In true good friends style, no-one commented on my presence in the house next morning still in the clothes of the night before. Adam walked me back to the guest house some time before lunch so that I could change, teasing me because I was shy of Gwen Jarrett knowing that I had spent the night with a man.

"It's the disapproving look on her face that will mark me down as 'that type of girl' from now on that I don't fancy," I said. "Mind you, I don't think she's a 'Mrs.' at all – I think it's just a courtesy title, like housekeepers always had years ago." I giggled wickedly. "I certainly can't see her ever having done what we spent most of last night doing."

Adam pulled me to him. "We could do it again tonight if you moved into the house."

But I still resisted. I wanted to hug this new stage of our relationship to me for a while. Savour it during those few hours I spent on my own; revel in the different person I was becoming.

Kate went off for a long-weekend with Carl and her family to celebrate her success, leaving us with a hundred and one instructions for any eventuality which might befall Marsha in her absence.

"For goodness sake don't die on us this weekend," Adam told Marsha severely, "or she'll never forgive us."

Kate had finally persuaded Marsha to let her return to take care of her and had arranged to do some agency nursing at Wadebridge for the foreseeable future. Simon seemed content to run his business by having lengthy conversations on his mobile phone with his managers, when his plummy voice would come out with lots of business-speak about being proactive and achieving closure – but at least he never suggested running something up the flagpole to see who saluted it. The rest of the time he was content to read the broadsheet newspapers, tut over the Labour government and wait on his two special ladies, Marsha and Marie. When he got bored he would have one of his Tigger days and fix something in the house, whether it needed it or not, or suggest a special outing which, thank goodness, would be in the BMW, not the Mini Moke, as a concession to the cooler weather.

I think Marie was finding it difficult to cope with the evidence of Marsha's slow decline almost as much as I was, as she spent increasing amounts of time at the stables, despite the fact that visitors were beginning to tail off. Or it could have been that she was finding Simon's dog-like devotion too much to handle. I never did find out, because she was always friendly towards me but never as open as the others.

Which left Adam and me still prevaricating about our immediate futures, neither of us wanting to be the first to make a decision. Although we were close and happy, neither of us was certain that our relationship would flourish under the demands and strains of living in London. At least, that was our excuse. In reality, neither of us wanted to admit that a perfect summer was drawing to a close. So we tried to put it off for as long as possible, until Marsha became impatient with us.

"For goodness' sake, go out for a good long walk, the pair of you," she said one afternoon in early September. "Take a look at the leaves starting to turn colour, and make up your minds what you're going to do to get through a long wet winter. Gwen Jarrett will be closing at the end of the season, which is always the third week in September according to her calendar," she warned me, "so you'll have to make a move by then. Go on – and don't come back until you've made some decisions!"

10.

We did as we were told and set off for a stroll around the town. The beach had a forlorn look after a few days of storms and bluster, and there was still a strong breeze, which made conversation difficult. So we made our way up through the winding streets towards the top of the town, where the houses eventually petered out and gave way to fields bounded by hedges and occasional trees which all leaned inland, away from the prevailing winds.

"See that?" Adam said as we turned off the main road into the street that often dominated my dreams. "That house over there is where Marsha used to live years ago."

I grabbed his arm. "Which house?"

He stared at me for a moment, surprised by the urgency in my voice. "The tall narrow one in the middle, with the steps going up."

It was the only tall house in the higgledy-piggledy row; but I hadn't really needed him to identify it for me to know it was the same house.

A flush of heat crept up my spine as realisation dawned. The hazy willowy figure at the top of the steps in all my dreams was Marsha. I closed my eyes and I could hear my father's voice again, and this time I could hear Marsha's in reply. Only the words themselves were indistinct.

I shook my head. Perhaps I'd got it wrong. It was my imagination that Marsha was standing in the doorway – I was superimposing her image onto someone else ...

But I wasn't. As the seconds ticked by and the image became stronger, without a doubt I knew it was Marsha.

"Allie! Allie! What's the matter? You look terrible! What is it?"

I opened my eyes and stared into Adam's concerned ones. But I wasn't seeing him. I was still seeing two adults, facing each other, debating something of which the small child beside them understood nothing.

He gave my arm a shake. "Allie?"

I pulled away from him and turned back the way we'd come.

"I have to see Marsha," I said, already beginning to hurry along the street. "I need to talk to her."

"But why?" he asked, taking long strides to keep up with my dogged footsteps. "Why has showing you the house where she used to live upset you so much?"

I didn't answer, too wrapped up in the torrent of unanswered questions that were filling my head even to heed his presence beside me very much. In the end he stepped in front of me and held me firmly by the shoulders, his expression as determined as mine doubtless was.

"Allie! Stop! You're obviously very shaken about something. Tell me about it! Perhaps I can help."

I shook my head. "You can't help. Only Marsha can. It's in my past. And hers. She knows about it. I must see her."

But he refused to move. "Her past? But you've only just met! And she doesn't like talking about her early life, you know that. Tell me first, see if I can do anything – she's so weak now, she shouldn't be upset about anything."

"Who says I'm going to do that?" My voice rose defensively a couple of tones. "I just need to ask her some questions – important ones, at least to me. But I'll do it carefully. I can do that, you know."

"Of course you can – when you're calm, which you're not at the moment." His voice was developing a hardness I hadn't previously heard. "We're supposed to trust one another – take your anger, or whatever it is, out on me!"

I thrust his arms away. "I need to talk to her," I persisted mulishly and tried to push past him. But he stayed where he was, barring my way, so I stepped off the pavement, right in the path of a car which had just turned the corner.

"Allie! Look out!" Adam grabbed me just in time as the car brakes squealed and the wheels swerved to avoid me. A man's furious face glared at me through the windscreen and he mouthed an obscenity before driving off.

Adam held me pinned against the wall of a house, his face almost as furious as the driver's. "What the hell are you playing at? You nearly got yourself killed – you're in no fit state to go anywhere, least of all back to Marsha's! Now, *what is this all about?*"

At any other time his body pressed so close to mine and his masterfulness would have left me weak at the knees, but on this occasion his superior strength merely angered me even more.

A mild-looking middle-aged man carrying a leather shopping bag who had witnessed my dice with death was hovering nearby, clearly trying to pluck up courage to ask me whether this man was bothering me.

"We're fine. Really. Thank you." I said to him, my mouth stretched into a grimace that I hoped would pass as a reassuring smile. The man muttered something and moved off reluctantly, taking a good look at Adam as he went past in case he was spot-lighted in a future edition of *Crimewatch*.

"You know I came down here with my father, when I was a little girl," I hissed at Adam, "and the one thing that keeps coming back to me is that we stood outside that house – *Marsha's house* – and she and my father were arguing. Only I didn't realise until now that it was Marsha – but she must have known! From all the things I've told her, she must have realised! All this time, she's known my father, and never told me!

"And what makes it worse," I went on, straightening my clothes as Adam loosened his hold on me, "is that soon after that holiday my father left – for good. So I'm sure Marsha has something to do with it. Otherwise, why would we come down here, without my mother, and see Marsha at all? And if it was purely coincidence, why hasn't Marsha mentioned it?"

Adam opened his mouth to speak, but I held up my hand to silence him.

"I don't want your voice of sweet reason. Marsha's made me confront lots of things during our little heart-to-hearts, but the one thing we've never really touched on is my parents' divorce. I need to know Marsha's part in it."

"Aren't you over-reacting just a little bit here? Your father might just have been asking for a room to stay or something. What are you going to do if Marsha claims to know nothing about you, him, or whatever did or didn't happen?"

"They weren't just passing the time of day. I can remember their voices – they were angry, emotional, it meant something, I know it did."

"So at most they may have had a holiday fling – it could be as simple as that."

"Then it won't matter if Marsha tells me about it, will it? Presumably even in her hippy 'all you need is love' days she wouldn't have had so many partners that she can't remember them. I just have a horrible feeling that she's something to do with my father leaving us when we returned to London."

We'd been walking quickly along the road as we spoke and we were now back near the tea rooms, where the main street divided into two. Adam grabbed my arm and propelled me into the front garden.

"Come and have a drink and let's talk about this a bit more, before you do anything hasty."

I shrugged his hand away again, but he plopped me down onto a seat.

"Two teas," he said to the waitress, sufficiently tersely for her not to question why we should want to sit outside when the wind was whipping itself up for a gale.

"What's *with* you?" I demanded angrily. "You go on about trust and being open with each other – well, I've trusted you, and Marsha, and been as honest as I can, and then I find, for the second time, that Marsha hasn't been honest with me ... and you seem to think that's okay."

"That's not true! I just think you might be getting a bit too emotional about all this to be reasonable, and that won't do Marsha any good. And besides, if she does remember your visit as a child, she may prefer not to talk about it – it may be private."

I glared at him suspiciously. "Do you know something about this? Is that why you're being so protective towards her?"

"No I don't know anything about it! There are lots of things in Marsha's life that none of us know about – we've always respected her right not to tell us."

"But it's never affected any of you, has it?"

"True. And I can understand your need to sort out your own past, up to a point."

"And what is that *point,* exactly?" I demanded.

"That it's just that – the *past.* And presumably it's not a very happy one, or Marsha would have talked about it readily. Sometimes it's better to let things be. After all—"

He stopped and looked away.

"After all, *what?*"

"Well ..." He looked uncomfortable for a moment, then set his mouth in a grim line: "You haven't made too much effort to have these burning questions answered up till now, have you? Why haven't you asked either of your parents for more details of why and how they divorced, if it bothered you that much?"

"You don't know what they're like!" I cried. "I've tried to talk to them, but it's not easy."

"Then go and try again. Pester *them,* instead of a dying woman." His face was near mine now, across the table, and, oh, I ached to reach out to him and cross the chasm that was opening up between us. Instead we glared at each other implacably.

"You're accusing *me* of over-reacting, but I think it may be the other way about," I said.

"I'm not over-reacting. I just care about Marsha, that's all. You have to understand – Marsha's been the only family I've had for years – it's instinctive to want to protect her, especially now."

"So it's just as well, then, that we haven't played the game, isn't it?" My voice seemed to have acquired an ability to spout words all by itself, with no reference to my brain, which was wrestling with the thought that perhaps all I was seen as was a 'pest'. Perhaps I'd read wrong things into our relationship. Perhaps this was only meant to be a holiday fling. It seemed I'd got so many things wrong.

"What do you mean?" Adam's voice cut into the turmoil and I heard my voice replying.

"The choosing game. Which would it be, Marsha – or me?"

I couldn't believe it as soon as the words were out. My brain re-connected with my mouth in total horror! What had I said? How could I have expected him to choose, or even wanted him to?

"I'm – I'm sorry," I stammered, "I didn't mean – please forget I said that – I wasn't thinking straight – it was so stupid ..."

Our eyes held for several seconds, mine brimming with the love I felt for him, his dark and unfathomable. The seconds ticked on, but he said nothing. With those few stupid words I'd blown it all. I fished in my pocket for some loose change.

"That's for my tea," I said, getting up and placing the coins quietly on the table as the waitress tottered towards us with a tray.

I left the garden rapidly and began to run down the hill, part of me listening for Adam's footsteps behind me, but they didn't come.

Marsha was in the living room, curled up in a large comfy arm-chair by the tall windows, watching the waves far below froth over the rocks to the mournful cry of the gulls overhead. She turned as I burst into the room.

"You're back early ..." Her smile of welcome faded when she saw my face. "Oh my dear, whatever is the matter? Where's Adam? Is he all right?"

She stood up, her pitifully thin body outlined against the

window, which stopped me in my tracks, reinforcing Adam's doubts that I could do this without upsetting her.

I took a deep breath. "I need to talk to you. Now, while you're alone."

"But of course. Here." She sat down again and patted the chair beside her. "What's wrong? Have you two had a row?"

"Not exactly." I threw myself down in the chair and turned so that I could watch her face. I paused, seeking the right words. I really didn't want to hurt her but I had to know.

"It's about something way back. You might not want to talk about it, and I don't want to upset you, but ..." I trailed off, uncertain suddenly.

"It's all right. Carry on," she said with that quiet serenity.

"We went past a house today. A house I've recognised since I first came here – I remember it from when I was a child. Adam said it was your old house. And then I remembered more – you and my father, arguing, on the doorstep, with me there beside him. I'm right, aren't I?"

"Ah!" She cast her eyes down at her hands entwined in her lap.

"Marsha?"

She leaned back in the chair. She didn't speak for many moments, till I thought she wasn't going to answer at all, but then she took several long, deep breaths as if summoning up all her energy.

"I wasn't sure it was you, at first," she said at last. "Then, as we talked, as I got to know you more, I realised without a doubt that you were Ian's child." She gave an apologetic little smile in my direction. "You don't look much like you did when you were – what – eight years old?"

"Nine," I said. Then: "Why didn't you say?"

"Because there was too much to tell. Because I didn't think you were in a fit state to appreciate any of it. Because I wanted to keep it to myself. I don't know – lots of reasons ..."

And suddenly I felt the mantle of her calm about my shoulders; our roles reversed, very gently.

"Tell me now. Please? If you can? I want to hear."

"All of it?"

"All of it."

"All right, then ..."

She began to speak as if I were no longer in the room. "Ian was one of our original gang – we all came down to Cornwall one summer, over thirty years ago. It was a summer a bit like this one – at least it seems so, through rose coloured specs – full of sunshine and blue skies. We had a wonderful time. We rented a house, all of us, in Morwenna Terrace – the house you saw today. We'd wanted one nearer the beach so that we could sleep out under the stars on clear nights, but that was all we could afford. Ian and I became lovers."

"You had an affair with my father – and you never thought to mention it?" I interrupted incredulously, the mantle scrunching slightly.

"Because there's more to it than that. After a few months we were all flat broke and had to turn our attention to doing boring things like bar work to pay the rent. The idyll began to fray at the seams a little. Several of the others, including Ian, thought we should go back to London and return again the following year. But I'd already begun to make small pieces of jewellery and they were selling well, so I wanted to stay.

"Ian didn't fancy staying here through the winter when everything was quiet – he was very lively in those days – and he didn't want to live off me, which I could understand. He said we should go back to London and find somewhere to live together there, where I could set up a proper business and he could teach. I was tempted, very tempted. I'd fallen in love with Ian, and I knew he was in love with me, but I'd also fallen in love with our Bohemian lifestyle and with this place – I wanted it to go on for ever."

Camelot, Marsha's Camelot, all those years ago.

"We argued a lot and the more we quarrelled, the more I dug my heels in – I was very stubborn in those days." She gave a mirthless laugh. "Still am, I suppose. Anyway, I told him to go in the end – but I was testing him, really. I thought our love was strong enough to make him come back. But in the end he went – and he didn't return."

A fit of coughing overtook her and I went to the kitchen to fetch her some water. My hands moved automatically as I tried to imagine Marsha and my father together. Somehow it seemed to fit better than my father and Juliet.

"So why couldn't you have told me that you and my father were old flames?" I asked her when the coughing subsided and she was getting her breath back. "I'm a big girl now, I could have handled it."

She shook her head. "It's more complicated than that. Do you want to hear the rest?"

"Of course!"

This time she closed her eyes as she spoke.

"After Ian went I stayed in the house, making my jewellery and helping out at a local pottery because I couldn't afford to set up on my own. All the time I was sure he would come back. But I didn't hear from him. Then I found out that I was pregnant – quite a shock, despite all my protestations of free love and so on."

A shiver ran through my body. The child that she lost! *My father's child!*

"What did he say – my father – when you told him?"

She shook her head. "I didn't tell him. I was too proud. He hadn't come back to me, so I wasn't going to force him to because I was expecting his child."

I threw aside the mantle completely. "But it was his child too!" I cried. "He had a right to know."

"Perhaps. But I wasn't thinking like that then. I nobly persuaded myself that he was better off not knowing – I was releasing him from obligations so that he could live his own life."

"So did you tell him, later – is that what you were arguing about?"

She shook her head again, her face a weary shade of grey.

"It gets worse. I had my baby – a beautiful baby girl I named Anna, and I loved her so much I chose to keep her all to myself. I didn't want to share her with a father who didn't know of her existence and hadn't been in touch since he left. But when she was a year old she contracted meningitis and died. There was no need to tell him then – as far as I was concerned it was solely my loss and I grieved alone."

Everything outside was monochrome. Storm clouds were gathering, so that the sea and the sky fused into steel grey. Inside, we sat in the gloom of this murky September afternoon, she thinking about the baby she had loved so dearly and lost, me thinking about the half-sister who had entered and departed this world unknown to any of my family.

"So why – why did we come back again, that summer?" I croaked at last.

"Apparently your parents' marriage was going to pot and Ian, so he said, had never forgotten me. He was on a nostalgia trip really –" she smiled wanly at me, "it seems to run in the family – and he wanted us to try again. He just walked back into my life after the better part of a decade and hoped to find me just the same."

She sighed. "No. That's not entirely fair. He looked me up, half expecting that I would have set up home with someone else and be surrounded by a horde of children. When he found that wasn't the case he became terribly excited. Said that he was fed up with his false life in London and wanted to settle down here – he intended bringing you too, by the way, although I don't know how he was going to square that with your mother – and we could re-establish our relationship ..."

"And did you explain, then, what had happened – about Anna ...?"

She made a sharp movement of the head before being overtaken by another fit of coughing, so prolonged this time that I was scared she was never going to stop. I made some tea for both of us whilst she recovered her strength, part of my mind listening for the banging of a door downstairs. Adam hadn't returned yet and I felt a wave of panic at what had happened to us, but then Marsha began to speak again and all thought of him left me.

"I'm sorry," she said. "Where were we? Oh yes, you were asking if I'd told Ian ... about Anna ...."

She smiled sadly at me. "It was you being there, with him, you see. Part of me longed to take him back again – even after all this time – and tell him what had happened. Just as I hadn't shared Anna's life with anyone, I hadn't shared the loss of her either. There'd been some achingly lonely times after she died but I'd told myself that I was coping – getting over it. It was a long time before I recognised that you never get over the death of a child – you just learn to get on with your life, and your loss becomes part of it.

"Ian would have been the only other person in the world to whom my baby's brief existence would have meant anything at all. But there he was, with this beautiful dark-haired little girl by his side – Allie, who should have been Anna – and, to my eternal shame, I was overcome with jealousy.

"You could have been her; you *should* have been her – the child we'd had together. But instead you were the child he'd had with someone else. He had everything – and was unhappy with a good part of it, although not with you – and I had nothing – and I was eaten up with the unfairness of it all. So I told him that he meant nothing to me any more and that I didn't want to see him ever again – and to this day he hasn't known that he fathered *two* daughters here in England."

"So that's what happened on the doorstep?"

She nodded. "We'd met before, one evening in the hotel where you were staying, but I hadn't seen you then and I told him I needed time to think. Then he brought you to the house that morning, and tried to persuade me, and I couldn't bear it."

We sat.

"Your tea's going cold," was all I could think of to say through the maelstrom of emotion in my head.

Dutifully, she sipped.

"You were never going to tell me, either?" I managed some moments later.

She gave an almost imperceptible shrug. "I decided it would serve no purpose. You were in a pretty fragile state when you first arrived here, and I was trying to ease your burden, not add to it. Then you would have been racked with the question of whether to tell your father, and I suspect you would have done so, which would rake up all sorts of memories and emotions – for what? It would change nothing, achieve nothing, except cause a lot of upheaval."

"And you never felt he had a right to know – about his daughter?"

"I felt *I* had a right to take whatever secrets to the grave with me that I chose." The blue eyes, still bright despite her weakening condition, looked at me levelly. "It takes a long time to build up the sort of serenity that I've achieved – I was selfish enough not to want to disturb it."

I could hear the rebuke in her voice and had to look away. God knows, if I was banging on about 'rights', that she had the right to be selfish at this stage in her life.

I stood up, feeling the need to get away, but reluctant to end it there.

"Were you always so sure?" I asked. "All these years, so sure that you'd done the right thing – no doubts ...?"

"Oh! There were plenty of those, believe me! Especially after your visit. I agonised over whether I should have told Ian, and whether I should have contacted him afterwards and explained. But, even if I'd wanted to, I had no idea where you were living in London – there was no way I could have found him."

"The hotel where we were staying would have known!"

She nodded. "Yes, I expect it would." She gazed out of the window. "I thought about you both so much. In a way, your visit acted as a sort of catalyst – it tore away at the cocoon I'd built around myself in the mistaken belief that I was 'getting on with my life'. The jealousy which I felt was the first honest emotion I'd acknowledged for years ...

"I left that house soon after and moved here – I'd been clinging onto the place where I'd been happy, with Ian and then with Anna. I decided that I would never settle down with a man and have more children because I couldn't face that sort of pain again. And then I met Chris when I started teaching at the Remand Centre, and began to help him, and I sort of realised that perhaps this was something I could do well. It was my way of sublimating my lingering maternal feelings, I suppose. And there were so many kids whose parents had let them down in one way or another ..."

She swung round to face me. "It seemed like fate, too, when you turned up here this summer. Giving me a chance to make up for sending Ian away all those years ago, by helping his daughter ... it was the next best thing to making my peace with him."

My grandmother, who for years has been prophesying that her own demise is just round the corner, has a habit, whenever she buys new clothes or whatever, of saying, "These will do me till I go." Her words came into my mind then, as Marsha referred to doing things in obvious preparation for the time when she would 'go'. But the pathos of the words was belied by her delivery, in which there was no self-pity or supplication. Her voice was as strong and forthright as ever. Neither was she seeking reassurance from me that she had indeed helped me. She was simply relating the facts and her actions and expecting no knee-jerk sympathetic response because she was a dying woman.

It struck me that she had greater issues to dwell on than whether I approved or not of her actions all those years ago.

Which was just as well, because my mind was in a complete turmoil and I couldn't have identified any one feeling clearly at that point. And through the turmoil, like train lights in a tunnel, were Adam's eyes, full of remorse that I should have asked him the unaskable. I couldn't face that look again.

"I must go," I said at last.

She stood up. "Back home?"

Home? I didn't know where that was any more. My flat in Purley seemed alien in my imagination, and Juliet had moved house so many times that there was nowhere in my memory I could regard as 'home'.

But I simply said, "Yes."

She nodded, her eyes searching my face so that I had to look away and move towards the door. But as I turned the handle I stopped. I couldn't leave her just like that. I turned and ran back across the room to where she remained motionless and put my arms around her. She held me tight, my head clasped to her meagre shoulder. Part of me wanted to stay there for ever.

"I wish you had been ... *my* daughter," she whispered softly into my hair.

I stepped back out of her embrace, not trusting myself to speak.

This time I made it through the door and, as I closed it behind me, I saw that she had returned to her chair and was once again gazing out at the sea.

11.

You'd probably expect me to say at this point that I spent a sleepless night tossing and turning trying to make sense of everything I'd been told – but I didn't.

When I left Marsha that afternoon I hurried first to the railway station, my head down, intent on every step so that I wouldn't notice anyone I knew, although I couldn't stop my ears straining for the sound of Adam's voice. I booked an early morning ticket back to London and a taxi for twenty minutes before that with a calm that surprised me, followed by the purchase of a pay-as-you-go mobile phone and two bottles of white wine from the nearby sell-everything shop.

Then I headed back to the guest house to tell Gwen Jarrett I would be leaving the next day. Her response was stony at first, until I mentioned that there was a problem with my father – an ironic reference to the truth if ever there was one – and insisted on paying for my room until the end of the week, when she relented sufficiently to offer me a belated afternoon tea. Her eyes had taken on the same beadiness as when we first met and she'd thought there was a juicy story to be heard. How she would have enjoyed this one!

"Thank you, but no," I said, more graciously than I had ever been to her since my arrival. I waved the mobile at her, without disclosing the wine bottles. "I have quite a few calls I must make."

"I understand my dear." Understanding nothing, she patted my arm with a hand that felt reptilian in its chilliness and gave me the sort of sympathetic smile reserved for the bereaved.

Once in my room I phoned Sarah, still calm and collected, told her that I felt it was time for me to return to the flat, and apologised that it was such short notice.

"Is anything wrong?" she asked.

"Of course not – except that my money is running out faster

than I thought – and the guest house is closing for the winter."

"Oh, well, that's all right – then I can tell you my good news," she said, a note of suppressed excitement creeping into her voice. "Rob and I have decided to get engaged, he wants us to move in together, so we've been looking at a flat, and we think we've found one, so if you want to come back straight away that should be all right because I could be gone very soon anyway." She spoke in a breathless rush, her happiness seeping down the 'phone connection.

"That's wonderful!" I exclaimed, even more impressed by my hitherto undiscovered acting ability than by her news. "I'm really pleased for you both. And you must stay at my place as long as you want to; you've been so good to look after the flat for me."

"Actually," she confessed, "I haven't been here all that much – I've stayed round at Rob's quite a lot – that's one of the reasons we decided to find somewhere together; his place isn't that big, and I knew you'd be back sometime. But I'll be here tomorrow evening when you arrive, so we can catch up properly on each other's news."

Well you won't be hearing much of mine, I decided as I finished the call and refilled my wine glass. I toyed with the idea of calling Juliet to tell her I was returning, but couldn't face it, so persuaded myself it would be nice to surprise her instead.

Before I became completely numbed by alcohol I packed my bags ready for the morning, concentrating intently on the job in hand and shutting out thoughts of anything else, in much the same way as I'd done when Will left me. Then I sat on the only chair in the room, purposefully making my way through the wine, thanking providence that I'd bought the type that had screw tops, and waited for Adam to come round.

It was like a repeat of that night at the Smugglers'. At first I was convinced he would turn up. I imagined scenes between him and Marsha where she told him what had passed between us, and, full of sympathy, knowing I hadn't meant those dreadful words, he would hurry round – even, I conceded as the evening progressed, if it had to be with a bit of urging on Marsha's part. But he didn't come.

As I poured more and more wine down my throat – after which, having encountered my empty stomach, it passed into my bloodstream very quickly – I became increasingly angry. As rain hammered down on the roof above me and darkness fell unusually early – whether due to the weather or to my developing blurred and tunnelled vision, I'm not sure – I dwelt solely on the fact that once again I had been let down by those I trusted and loved, and I was no better off than when I first came to Cornwall.

After a confusing and complicated attempt to use the bathroom and to undress, I passed out on the bed.

As if to mock me, next morning dawned bright and sunny and the tang of the sea air through the open front door even overrode the smell of frying bacon. I staggered into breakfast, eager only to down as much water and as many cups of tea as possible, and suddenly everything which had grated about the guest house took on a poignancy because I was leaving. Rosie, the aptly-named bouncy young waitress, smiled at everyone, taking their orders with a flourish as the floorboards protested under her tread, and even the elderly Martha brought my tea at the first attempt without having to return to the kitchen to check who it was for.

I was going home, yet at that moment Gwen Jarrett's guest house seemed more like home than anywhere I'd ever been, and I didn't want to leave it. What I really wanted to do was run across the beach until I reached the blue gate – across that golden sand and feel its wet compact ridges under my feet, with the occasional soft squelch of worm casts between my toes and the splatter of water on my calves where little puddles had remained from the outgoing tide; with the sun on my back and the cool morning breeze on my face, to clamber over the rocks to where lay the two I always thought of as Marsha's and mine; and then to fling myself into the arms of Adam and tell him that I was sorry, that it didn't matter, nothing mattered as long as we could still love each other and be together.

But I was never going to do that. I had begged a man once before not to leave me and I wasn't going to do it again. I'd messed up big-time and Adam obviously wasn't going to forget it, so I was going to have to live with that.

As I settled my bill Gwen Jarrett noticed my bloodshot, puffy eyes, and found her face for the bereaved again – which, given her features, in truth meant that she pulled a long face. Today I found it neither funny nor tiresome, but could view her with some affection. And when, with an awesome display of gums, she said: "It's rare that we have a guest who stays so long – almost one of the family – I do hope you'll visit us again," the swirls of her vivid dress began to blur and I had to hurry out to the waiting mini-cab.

It was on the train that I really fell apart. I chose a window seat with a table and glared so ferociously at the other passengers that none of them dared to sit next to, or opposite, me. In the back of my mind I still expected – hoped – that Adam would come running onto the platform just as the train began to leave, in the best tradition of romantic films, and beg me to re-consider, and we'd have a disjointed conversation through the glass until either I jumped off the train and left all my luggage to go where it wanted, or he jumped on and explained everything to a sympathetic ticket collector.

What kind of a fool was I? He wouldn't even know that I was getting this train.

My stomach lurched as the engine pulled us away from an empty platform, so that I thought I was going to be sick. I closed my eyes. How could it have all gone so wrong?

Hurt like I'd never felt before washed over me. I couldn't remember even the break-up with Will feeling as bad as this – probably because it hadn't been so sudden. Part of me had mistrusted and doubted him long before he had found the guts to tell me what was going on, so there had been been a strange element of relief when he finally left.

But this – so many people and so many emotions were involved. I wondered what Marsha would tell the others about my sudden departure – what would she ultimately tell Adam? Would it have been better if she hadn't told me the truth? If she'd just pretended that she and my father had had some sort of brief romance, and left it at that? But then, I'd demanded the truth, and Marsha wasn't one to shirk what she considered right.

Perhaps she would tell them all everything she'd told me. I imagined their collective anger as they sympathised with Marsha for having to disclose secrets she'd preferred to keep buried just because some interloper from the Home Counties had insisted on knowing of the past. Or perhaps she'd keep her own counsel, but Adam would let them know there had been discord between all three of us, and they would form their own conclusions as to who was at fault. Whatever, I knew for certain that they would close ranks around Marsha in their avowed determination to protect and care for her, and I would never be allowed into their charmed circle again.

I hurt. I hurt all over, as the mental anguish transformed itself into physical pain. My body ached; the burden I had been so pleased to unload onto Marsha seemed to have returned at least threefold.

I dwelt on the relationship between Marsha and my father, and those harsh words which had been bandied back and forth over my head all those years ago. I realised that throughout my growing up I'd had a sneaking sympathy for my father for leaving us. Juliet could be so trying and he was always so much fun that had I been given the choice (as children seem to be given these days), I would probably have opted to go with him.

Flashes of those rebellious teenage years went through my head, taking me back to times I'd almost forgotten as surely as the train was carrying me back to places I wasn't sure I wanted to be. Arguments with Juliet over everything and nothing, with me storming off to my room to smoulderingly plot how I could flee to my father – who, seeing my distress at my mother's unreasonableness, would put aside all notions of Francophilia and take me to his fun-loving heart once more. Because he would understand; because he had been there too – had *had* to leave, as a result of my mother's vituperation. Even when the physical distance between my father and me had become an emotional one as well, I'd maintained the belief that, whatever else, we shared a bond in the way we had suffered at the hands of Juliet.

But now, of course, there was a different picture to consider: perhaps it had been my father's philandering ways which had broken up the marriage. He must have met and married Juliet pretty soon after leaving Marsha, so that relationship can't have mattered all that much to him. Then, when he found that Juliet was too much to handle, he had fled to Cornwall with me – as bargaining material? the sympathy vote? – to try and re-establish a relationship he'd abandoned a decade before. Who knows how many dalliances may have come and gone in the interim? He was a charmer, there was no doubt about that, and Juliet had always branded him unreliable; and he hadn't wasted much time in setting up home with the exotic Yvon once he'd gone to France.

The case was mounting against him, shattering all the previous conceptions with which I'd been reasonably comfortable. I longed to unravel it with someone, but ironically the only person I could have done that with I had left, dwarfed by the chair which encompassed her, gazing out across the sea, possibly at a distant shore which she would soon be visiting, and which would be invisible to the rest of us.

'I wish you had been ... my daughter.'

A little chink in the maelstrom of my thoughts allowed through a glimpse of what life would have been like had Marsha and Ian really been my parents. Enid Blyton wouldn't have had a look in. I saw images of a rapturous childhood bathed in perpetual sunshine and high spirits, perhaps with a sibling or two to complete the cosy scene, but still with me at its heart, loved and cherished by two loving, cherishing parents.

And at this point I resented them both – Marsha and my father – for not fulfilling that dream, and for making me wish that Juliet had not been my mother. The fact that I'd wished the same thing so many times as I grew up mattered not at all, because on those occasions my feelings hadn't been tinged with the pity I now felt for the woman who'd been let down by her husband.

Okay ... So you'll have gathered by now that I was all over the place emotionally, and this was reflected in my physical behaviour as I shifted restlessly in my seat with each new wave of thought and counter-thought, now gazing unseeingly at the landscape rushing by, now changing my position and passing a vacant eye over the other inhabitants of the carriage.

I became aware of a mother and her two children, who must have boarded the train somewhere in the West Country and were now positioned across the aisle from me. The mother had one of those obvious, patient voices which declared to the world her maternal efficiency and ability. She spoke to her children in calm, measured tones and they, a boy and girl of about eight, responded in such an intelligent manner that I wouldn't have been surprised if they'd swept away the educational games and puzzles she produced for them at regular intervals and whipped out the Times crossword instead. There were probably other mothers in the carriage who could hear them and were at that moment bathed in guilt at their own inadequacy, resolving to bin all videos and strictly limit television watching the moment they got home.

I suddenly realised that part of the physical pain I was experiencing was coming from my stomach, which had had nothing substantial in it for many hours. The mother across the aisle had thrown a few covert glances my way when I'd twisted abruptly in my seat, so now, when I stood up equally abruptly and asked her if she'd watch my things while I went to the buffet car, she flinched momentarily and glanced protectively at her chicks before smiling brightly.

"Of course we will."

"Is there anything you'd like?" I asked with more graciousness than I felt. A token question anyway, as there were neatly packed lunch boxes in front of them containing Scotch eggs on a bed of lettuce and tomatoes, and organic juice cartons by their sides.

"I don't think so, thank you," she beamed. "We're fine, aren't we children?"

The children nodded dutifully, mindful of not talking with their mouths full, and their complacent mother beamed at me again before I stomped off, wondering whether she had experienced, in their conception, the sort of ecstasy I'd had with Adam. She reminded me of an early infant school teacher I'd had, whose carefully-pronounced statements had been full of 'Mrs. Humphries doesn't like this,' or 'Mrs. Humphries wants you all to do that', and it had taken many weeks of puzzling over who this mighty unseen Mrs. Humphries was before I'd realised that the teacher had been talking about herself. Once the penny had dropped, it became apparent that most of the teachers spoke to little ones in this strange way. Perhaps there used to be a teachers' manual which forbade the use of the first person pronoun until children reached a certain age ...

I bought a strong coffee and a large cheeseburger and chips to feed my hangover, but when I got back to my seat I caught the little boy giving me – or rather my bag of chips – covert glances. I leaned across the aisle.

"I've bought these and now found that I don't want them after all. Perhaps the children would like them?"

I placed the chips squarely on the table, at which the children, with polite thank yous, fell on them immediately, so that the mother could do no more than echo their thanks.

A hint of a conspiratorial smile from the boy warmed my heart for a moment, until chirpy references from the mother about 'Daddy' indicated that, conceptual ecstasy or no, she still had her man, whereas I'd just managed to lose mine – again.

Why, I berated myself, in between grease-laden munches of burger (which may as well have been cardboard), had I allowed myself to become so emotionally charged when Adam pointed to the house? Why couldn't I have bided my time and spoken to Marsha as soon as the opportunity arose, and thus avoided the painful argument with the man – it now hurt to admit – I had fallen in love with? I hadn't been aware of the truth for over twenty years; another few hours wouldn't have hurt ...

Even then, if I had simply fallen out with Adam over whether or when to talk to Marsha, the situation would have been redeemable. But no, I'd had to go for broke and ask him to choose, and his refusal had told me everything. Now there was no going back; and as I faced this fact I pushed the remnants of my meal away from me and groaned, so that Mrs. Perfect Mother looked up in alarm lest I was sick over her side of the carriage.

    I turned away, towards the window, wrapped my arms around myself and, with my eyes tight shut, flayed myself with what might have been until I thought my heart would break.

12.

"Darling! You look wonderful! Why didn't you tell me you were coming back? What a lovely surprise! Have you eaten? You look so well! Doesn't she look well, Philip? All that sea air has really suited you! Or perhaps it's a bit more than the air! What do you think, Philip? *Doesn't* she look marvellous? And what have you done to your hair? – It looks so much better like that!"

Philip opened his mouth twice to respond to Juliet's urgent demands for his opinion, but in the end settled for a beaming smile and nod of agreement.

Okay ... you're probably wondering why Juliet would think how healthy, well, wonderful etcetera I was looking, when I was such a complete wreck on the journey back from Cornwall?

Well, it was now several days later and I was ensconced once more in my flat – alone, I'm happy to say, because Sarah had moved out the day before – and I had only just phoned Juliet to tell her I was back.

In the intervening few days I had reassessed my position – my whole life, in fact – and come to several conclusions, the most startling of these being that, after years of longing for my mother to become Claire Rayner and all those times I had scoffed at her materialistic self-centred approach to life, I'd had a complete change of heart. Juliet, I now saw, had it dead right. It's called Looking After Number One. And instead of railing against her self-centredness and persisting in striving for some 'happy-ever-after' ending which just never happens in real life, I should have been using her as my role model.

Just look at the evidence. She divorced husband number one after he let her down. Did she ever shed a genuine tear of remorse? No, she didn't. (Those shed for dramatic effect in the presence of male comforters don't count – except to illustrate my point.) Instead, she set about finding a replacement to her liking as soon as possible, selecting prospective candidates at will, with a cool detachment and single-mindedness that was really quite breath-taking. Dan she married for just as long as it suited her, and then she moved on – heart and mind intact, bank balance larger, and many more men to pick up and discard as she fancied. Q.E.D.

You may have noticed a certain cynicism of tone when I've mentioned Juliet's way of life before, but not any more. It's all to do with attitude of mind. She was right all along and if there was one thing the Cornwall experience had taught me it was that taking out one's emotional baggage and rummaging through it *ad nauseam* really didn't do one any good. Packing it away and depositing it permanently in 'Left Luggage' was the only way to move forward.

Obviously I had a lot to thank the people I met in Cornwall for. I firmly believed that Marsha had helped me to feel better about myself, and she'd also taught me that it doesn't pay to put your trust in someone because in the end they only let you down – Juliet had sort of been saying this for years, but which of us ever listens to our mothers until it's too late? Anyway, I would always remember Marsha with great affection, and the wonderful summer in Cornwall – at least up until the day it all went wrong.

And Adam – well, he was part of the reinforcement as well, I suppose. He showed me that unless one was extremely vigilant, and if one allowed one's heart to always rule one's head, one – you – I – could just make the same mistake over and over again. In this case, falling for another good-looking man who fools you at first into believing you are the special force in his life.

So Adam was packed away in the same box as Marsha, and I was sure that in a very short space of time I would stop seeing his beautiful face and wide grin and appealing green-brown eyes every time I closed my own ... it was just an imprint that would fade, like the rings of bright light you still see when you close your eyes after looking at the sun ... and it was just habit to keep thinking that I could hear his voice calling me when I walked along a street; and habits, like love, eventually die.

Where was I? Oh yes, Juliet had just turned up with Philip in tow and I was wowing them both with the vibrant, energised, new me.

"It was wonderful!" I gushed. "I never expected the weather to be so good – and those surfers! The beaches looked like something off *Baywatch* most of the time! I feel like a completely new person. Fitter too – all that exercise!" I gave an almost imperceptible wink in Philip's direction.

My mother threw me a strange look as she arranged herself carefully on the sofa – probably because I sounded a lot like her, so she would be thinking I was taking the mickey, but not quite sure why.

"I'm so pleased for you, darling. Did you take many photos? – I'd love to see all those arty friends you made."

I gave a light-hearted laugh. "Do you know, I completely forgot to take my camera with me? You remember what a dither I was in when I left – and then I kept meaning to buy a little camera when I was there, but you know how it is!"

This was easy. You just brushed everything away with a carefree comment here, a skim of the facts there. *The six rolls of film currently sitting in my bedroom* – brush, brush – *forgotten. The smiling face of Adam, his hair tousled in the wind, in most of them* – sweep, sweep – *consigned to history. Easy.*

"What a pity!" Juliet was saying now. "They must have been fascinating people if you spent so much time with them."

"Oh, you know. Holiday friendships. They were nice enough." *Marsha, sitting in a deckchair, watching me with her piercing blue eyes as I unravelled my life. Her arms about me on the day I left.* Brush, sweep.

I wouldn't have been surprised if a cock had crowed.

Philip cleared his throat. "And what," he asked, looking faintly surprised at the sound of his own voice, which was understandable as he'd been spending a lot of time in Juliet's company, "do you intend doing now that you're home?"

I looked around the small sitting room. Had it always been this dark and airless?

"Well, first of all I'm going to redecorate this place," I announced to all three of us. "Lots of white, I think. I read somewhere that it's the best colour to do everything in if you're thinking of selling eventually. And I might – when the divorce is finalised. And if I don't sell I'll like the white anyway – it reflects the light so well doesn't it? – sort of a Mediterranean feel. Perhaps the odd bit of pale yellow as well—"

"That reminds me," Juliet interrupted: "Will called the other day." (Was it the mention of the divorce that triggered her memory, or the word 'yellow'?) "He wanted to talk to you about ... something or other."

Previously I would have bristled at the mention of his name and anxiously pressed Juliet for details of what he said, what he wanted, which was always futile because she was hopeless at remembering those sort of things unless they directly affected her. Now though, the mention of his name brought nothing. *Thank you, Cornwall.*

"There are some papers here in all the post I've been wading through – it's probably about those." I dismissed him with a shrug. "I'm changing my number and going ex-directory, by the way – I want to get rid of those nuisance calls – but I'll contact Will if I find anything important."

The calls I really wanted to be rid of were those from Will himself, as well as from his business contacts who would call from time to time after we split up, unaware of the situation. And, sad clinging person that I was, on some occasions I omitted to tell them the true state of affairs. But no more. From now on, any contact with my ex-husband would be strictly on my terms.

Philip geared himself up to speak again. "And apart from redecorating ... have you thought ... a job, you know ... what you'll do ... if you've not enough money, that sort of thing ... be happy to help ... if you needed ..."

It was obviously agony for him to mention such a crass subject. I smiled at him, genuinely this time. The edges of his eyes crinkled in response, evidently relieved to have got it out. He was a dapper man, possibly a well-preserved sixty, in a light-weight summer suit with a glimpse of expensive wristwatch peeping out from his impeccably tailored shirt. His face was lean and kind. The sort of man who would look wonderful modelling for 'Saga' adverts. Perhaps he did, for all I knew.

"Isn't he a sweetie?" Juliet chirruped beside him. "And he means it, you know," she went on as if he were no longer beside her. "He doesn't like anyone to worry about silly things like money."

My smile widened. I suspected Juliet would drop her 'treat 'em mean, keep 'em keen' routine for quite a while for this one.

"That's very good of you," I told him, "but I'm going to join a temping agency tomorrow, which should keep me going fine until I find something permanent."

As they were leaving, Juliet said, "You must keep those high-lights in your hair, you know darling – they help get rid of that mousy air you always had."

I wondered if a hairdresser could precisely simulate the 'Cornish Sea and Sunshine' shade.

I smiled to myself in the hall mirror as I closed the door. It was a mirror I'd brought with me from my mother's house when Will and I had married. It was the same mirror I'd practised my teenage enigmatic raised-eyebrow look in front of, and during the last few days I'd practised one at length entitled 'Radiant, Carefree Young Woman'. This afternoon I'd used it until my cheeks ached, and it seemed to have worked.

Juliet was right – I did look different. My skin glowed with health, and my hair, longer and more casual and with the afore-mentioned sun streaks, framed my face, ridding it of its earlier rather prim demeanour.

I piled my hair up on top of my head and struck a provocative pose, head tilting back, glancing slightly over one shoulder. Adam had taught me how to do it when we were messing around one day and I was asking whether he photographed lots of sexy models ...

I bit down hard on my lip and let my hair fall.

"You can do this!" I hissed at my reflection.

Now at this point I rather fancied the idea of the temping agency finding me a nifty little job in the middle of London, where I could meet the type of people I vilified when I first started on about all this. I'd been thinking, you see, that if I was going to be more like my mother, then I should start mixing with the same sort of crowd. You know, get used to the heady thrall of office politics and romance gleaned from within the confines of the ladies' loo. I even went to Whistles and spent the last of my savings on a new efficient-but-sexy suit and a couple of tops which would never have done for the solicitor's office. I was looking for Agnes B, but couldn't find her. Which was a shame, because I would like to have found out what the 'B' stands for – presumably something either unpronounceable, or of which Agnes herself is embarrassed. But then, if you're going to be coy about your surname, why stick with a Christian name like Agnes? Definitely one of life's little mysteries.

Anyway, within days the agency came up with 'covering for maternity leave at the head offices of a housing company' which, they said, was near Westminster, thus fitting in with my mental pictures of after-work vodka and Red Bull evenings in trendy wine bars, and lunchtimes spent indulging in retail therapy that would probably cost a good deal more than psychotherapy.

In the event, the company was housed in a building on the south side of Westminster Bridge, next to what looked like the only remaining bomb site from the second World War – now grandly advertised as the 'Waterloo Eurostar Car Park'. But it was only a quick walk over the bridge to the hub of British government, where lots of men in dark suits mingled with camera-laden tourists.

My Whistles suit really wasn't needed (although I wore it anyway), because the female staff consisted primarily of young girls with pert bottoms and fourteen inch waists which they showed off with hip-skimming trousers and skimpy jumpers from Top Shop and River Island. I shared an office with three of them: Stacey, Donna and Emma (or 'Stace', 'Don' and 'Em' as they affectionately referred to each other), who were all terribly impressed when they discovered that I could do real shorthand.

"That means she'll get to do David's letters when his secretary's away," Donna moaned.

"Well, he's not going to ask you again, let's face it," Stace said. "Not after the balls-up you made of it last time."

David was one of the directors – a tall, well-built young man with a swarthy complexion and a penchant for pin-striped suits lined with red silk.

"Don's dead keen on him, but we've told her she doesn't stand a chance – they'll want him to marry one of their own," Emma told me. "It's a family-run business, see – all Jewish – so don't go saying something's 'kosher' unless you really mean it."

"Anyway, who said I wanted to marry him?" Donna defended herself. "It's just he's one of the few worth fancying who ever comes into our office."

Our department was ostensibly under the jurisdiction of a sales manager called Derek, a short stocky man whose suits were baggy in all the wrong places – or perhaps it was his body that was baggy, it was difficult to tell. He didn't really bother us too much, but drifted about the building with a permanently distracted air, brought about apparently by his uncertainty over whether his wife was suffering from post-natal depression or having an affair with his best friend.

It was quite a cheery place, though, when Derek wasn't there. We were supposed to answer people's queries regarding a number of property developments throughout the south-east, and send them glossy brochures which featured houses with apparently acres more garden than the actual ones on the developments. There never seemed to be any great rush to get these out, though, and the rest of the time was spent in dealing with the myriad problems encountered in the other departments (we were supposed to be the General Management Office as well), and putting small change into various collection boxes which came round for a number of celebratory 'dos' for people and events neither I nor the three girls had ever heard of.

There were several unattached men in the Accounts Department (as well as one or two who thought they were), whom Stace & Co. spent considerable time discussing, in a detached objective way, whether or not the subject was within hearing range. They did the same with me on my first day.

"Do you think we ought to tell all the others that she's started here, and take her out to the Goat?"

"Well ... she's only a temp ..."

"Yeah, but she might stay the whole time Vic's off, if she likes it here."

"And that's longer than a lot of people stay when they've come here permanent."

"All right then. I'll tell the other offices we've got a new girl."

Stace eventually turned to me after firing off several e-mails to people who were only a few feet down the corridor. "We always go to the Goat and Bicycle when someone starts or finishes – they do good sandwiches and panini. It's a sort of tradition, except the architects and directors don't come."

She was right about the sandwiches, which were deftly made to order and delicious. Quite a number of people turned up to view the new addition to the sales office, even if she was only a 'temp', and I quickly discovered that Fergus, one of the publishing team who put together the astonishingly misleading sales brochures, always honed in on new females but shouldn't be taken seriously: "He keeps his brain in his trousers, because there's not much else worth considering down there" (Donna).

Then there was Miles, who lived up to his name - once he started talking he could go on for miles and miles and miles ... In the end, Stacey just grabbed me by the arm while he was in full flow and took me off to meet someone else, and I don't think Miles even noticed.

As more and more people piled into the pub I heard someone shout, "Adam! Over here!" to a chap apparently standing just behind my left shoulder.

I froze, my sandwich mid-way to my mouth, a hot flush flooding my body from head to toe as if I were starting an early menopause. I forced myself to turn round and lift my head to those greeny-brown eyes. Get it over with straight away, that was best ...

A small pleasant-looking guy with dark curly hair smiled at me before squeezing past and calling for a bottle of Bud. No greeny-brown eyes, no beautiful face. Just as well.

I slapped a smile back on my own face and gave my attention to an earnest woman from Accounts who was asking what I had done before.

I learned a lot of things in my first few days. Like how you get and maintain a fourteen-inch waist. The trick is only to eat at lunchtimes when someone's arrival or leaving necessitates a gathering at the aforementioned Goat; otherwise you spend your lunchtime in the shopping areas, well away from the eating areas, and then dash back to the office because you're late, which gives you your daily exercise.

Then there was the retail therapy. I'd often wondered how girls managed to go shopping so often in central London and still afford to eat, or at least drink, and pay for all the other things necessary to survive. Here, the trick is to spend a lot of time looking at things in the shops and buying just one small item to justify the excursion. Preferably you buy something that can be shared around the office, like nail varnish, because it helps to while away those long afternoons.

The girls were actually good fun, taking me out in turn for the lunch hour, with patronising good humour, to their favourite haunts and a great little market down a side-street just past Westminster Abbey. At first they were reticent about saying too much about their private lives in front of someone so much older who patently hadn't racketed about as much (despite the new, looser, vibrant image), but gradually they forgot about this and chatted uninhibitedly, only putting the boot in occasionally with comments such as, 'Was it like that when you were young?'

They were frankly curious about my past, and, having been given the bare bones of my marriage and divorce, spent inordinate amounts of time chewing over what I could have done or should have done and what I needed to do next, from the highly experienced vantage point of their nineteen or so years. Emma, who'd been engaged once but had broken it off (the catalyst being that he refused to change his hairstyle because it was the way his last girlfriend liked it), was considered more of an authority on scumbags than the other two. She would suddenly break off from adding names to the database on her computer, to say things like, "Mind you, I think I'd have confronted him sooner – and her, come to that."

At which the other two would also stop work, and give serious thought to the issue; but they were so up-front in their questions and comments that I didn't mind. (The summer in Cornwall, though, was not disclosed. No need, of course, because it had been safely swept away.)

I think they had only persuaded Derek to replace the pregnant Vic so that the lunch-hour could be fairly split, with two going off together in turn – there certainly didn't seem enough work for four of us. Sometimes, though, I'd volunteer to take lunch on my own and then let the three of them troop off together, which was like school being let out early.

"Are you sure you don't mind?" Stacey asked the second time I offered. "What will you do all by yourself?"

They were stunned when I told them that I liked to wander around Westminster Abbey and look at the tombs of dead kings, or go into the lobby of the House of Commons and watch the Members and staff bustling about with little darting glances out of the sides of their eyes as they made sure visitors recognised their importance. Or I went to the Army and Navy stores to look for things for my flat.

I didn't tell them that sometimes I just liked to stand on Westminster Bridge and feel the autumn breeze from the river rifling through my hair, and allow myself just a few moments to be back in that magical summer, before I got the sweeping brush out again.

"Meet anyone interesting?" Emma asked, as Donna twitched her lips when I came back from one such jaunt. As Donna had predicted, I had indeed done some work for David, the director, just the day before, and it seemed that today he had been seen leaving the building on his own just a minute after me. And, according to the girls, going to places like the Abbey was only ever a smokescreen for an assignation. Of such, apparently, are office rumours made.

So while my working life wasn't exactly staggeringly exciting, it was bearable, and a change from what I'd done before. It filled my days adequately, and with the journey by tube and train back to Purley taking quite a time, the early part of the evening was usually accounted for.

Which only left a few hours each day and the weekends to fill. I decided to forge ahead with the re-decorating of my flat and then throw my own 'welcome home' party and invite all my friends. Yes, I know I'd been bleating on all these months about not having any friends, but you don't need lots of *close* friends for a party – just make sure you tell everyone you invite to bring a few people. As well as my new colleagues, Sarah and Rob would be willing to do that, and I could ring up Jodie at my old office, to show her that I wasn't such a miserable bag after all. And then there were the other flat-dwellers in my building who may be wondering what had happened since the days of the plate-throwing rows Will and I had had.

The party would have to be soon, before my tan faded and I stopped looking so interesting. So each evening after work and straight after the necessary trip-for-one round Sainsbury's on a Saturday, I flung myself into covering every square inch with white emulsion. Which, with the flat being small, didn't take very long.

"Darling, don't you think it's going to look just a tiny bit stark?" Juliet asked, peeping round the door of the half-finished sitting room from the safety of the hall, where she stayed in case she got any paint on her Jacqueline Kennedy-inspired two-piece.

"Nonsense! Everything in here is far too dingy. It needs lots of light. I'm going to clear out all the clutter, too. I'll add colour with just a few bright pieces of this and that." A picture sprang up in my mind of a large room with long windows, the sun reflecting masses of light off its pale walls, and a few beautifully shaped pieces of pottery adding shades of warmth and fire; they fused into the bright swirls of Gwen Jarrett's dresses ...

"Are you all right? You've turned terribly pale!"

Juliet's voice wafted into my consciousness as I felt an overwhelming urge to be sick.

"I think it's the fumes from the paint!" I gasped.

"I don't expect you're eating properly," she said, so I assured her I was fine but agreed to have dinner with her and Philip that evening. A few hours away from the flat and my own company sounded like a good idea.

Most of the time, though, I didn't mind being on my own as I redecorated. It was vital, I discovered, to play very loud music at the same time as I wielded the roller, and to sing along with it. I found some old *Take That* CDs which had languished at the back of a cupboard for some time, as Will had always turned his nose up at them. Now they took me back a decade, to a time when I was brimful of optimism. I fast-forwarded *A Million Love Songs,* though – not for any reasons of sentimentality, you understand, but because the rhythm was wrong for painting.

My bedtime reading had changed since my return. Instead of a romantic novel, which I'd got a bit sick of as so many of them seemed the same – and the classics such as Austen and Hardy now bored me, I decided – I pored over the latest interior style magazines, choosing which colours I would add to which rooms.

"A bit daft having a party after you've made it all lovely," Em pointed out when I came staggering into the office with a deep blue rug for the bedroom. "I wouldn't want people puking all over my stuff when it was brand new."

I hadn't thought of that. I'd simply wanted everyone to see what a different person I'd become and I wanted my surroundings to reflect that. I also didn't want to admit that I'd envisaged a much more sedate affair than Em was imagining – but there could still be the danger of spilt wine.

"Okay. I'll have the party first, before I change the furniture and things, then it won't matter."

"Much better," Donna nodded sagely. "At least if your walls are all white you can soon put a bit more emulsion on if anyone throws up over your paintwork."

13.

You could tell how long it was since I'd thrown a party by the length of time it took to get me, the flat and the food ready – in reverse order; the amount of agonising that went into preparing all three; and the fact that there I was, twenty minutes before I'd invited everyone, all done up like a dog's dinner and absolutely certain that no-one was going to show.

I was taking a final, final look at myself in the hall mirror and making a mental note to get an even larger one for the bedroom. Now that my hair was longer I had spent ages putting it up in such a way that it looked artlessly spontaneous, and I was wearing a new dress. A flimsy, strappy little number in cream with bold red splashes, which matched the bold red of my finger-nails and toenails – the latter on show tonight because I was wearing ridiculously high, almost-not-there shoes, which Stacey had persuaded me to buy. She'd insisted they would look perfect against the handkerchief hem of my dress and she'd been right, quelling my incredulity at their price, which seemed to be in inverse proportion to the amount of leather used.

But the mirror told me that while I might not be the fairest of them all, I could certainly hold my own amongst this evening's crowd – assuming anyone actually turned up, I thought, anxiously checking my watch again. To my relief the doorbell rang at that moment, so, fixing the 'I'm having a great time' smile on my face, I flung the door open.

"Allie? Wow! Don't you look fantastic!"

"*Will!* What are you doing here?"

"Come to see you, of course! But you must be going out – I'm sorry, I've obviously timed it badly."

My head was spinning. *Will. Here. Party in twenty minutes.* He'd just said 'I'm sorry' – only about turning up unannounced admittedly, but it was never a word in his vocabulary before.

Thank goodness I was wearing my new dress. Keep the smile in place. Think of water under bridges.

"Why didn't you phone?" was the wittiest thing I could think of saying.

"I did. Lots of times. Sarah told me you were away, but she didn't know where, or when you'd be back. So I phoned Juliet and she said you'd gone away on a brilliant holiday – she didn't say where either – and didn't know when you'd be back. And now you've apparently changed your number, so I was passing and thought I'd call in ... just on the off-chance. Not the right time, I can see ..."

I'd forgotten how dark he was, and how his hair curled over the back of his collar if he let it grow too long. I'd forgotten the way he moved with an almost cat-like grace that could be sexy or menacing, depending on the mood. I'd forgotten the way he could stand, like he was doing now, in that self-deprecating way that made him look so damned attractive. *No, you hadn't forgotten,* I chided myself, *you've just been determined not to remember.*

"If it's those papers, I've sent them back to my solicitor – he was supposed to send them on to yours and—"

"No!" he cut in. "Well, yes, it is about them, but not in that way. Look, I can see you're going out – you look terrific by the way – can we get together some time? I need to talk to you ..."

"I'm not going out; I've got lots of people turning up any minute now – a bit of a party. What do we need to talk about?"

"A party?" There was a glint I didn't recognise in his charcoal eyes. "Celebrating your freedom – or something else?"

"Neither – not that it's any of your business." I thought fast. So much for the brand new, ex-directory me. "Look, if you want to talk, you can call me at work – tomorrow, or one evening next week. I'm really very busy right now. I'll get you the number."

Of course, as soon as I stepped away to find paper and pen, he followed me into the flat. Damn! Now I couldn't even shut the door on him.

"You've done the place up," he said, surveying the sitting room, then coolly appraising me from head to toe. "And not just the flat's changed ... It must have been some holiday – the tan looks brilliant!"

(Okay, so I'd had to top the tan up in the end, because we were now into October, but he didn't need to know that.)

"It's called *moving on.* Fresh beginnings," I said waspishly. "Isn't that what you recommended for both of us? And when everything is finalised I shall probably move away."

There was a clatter of footsteps outside, making me wish that I hadn't propped the building's main door open so that everyone could get in more easily.

It was Sarah and Rob.

"I know we're a bit early," Sarah said breathlessly, "but we thought you might need a last-minute hand – Oh! Will! I didn't know you'd been invited!"

"He hasn't!" I hissed, "He's just leaving!"

But Rob had already pushed past the two of us.

"Will! Great to see you!" He pumped his old friend's hand enthusiastically. "How are things going?"

What is it with men? If you had asked Sarah to name her beloved's best qualities, she'd have put thoughtfulness and understanding way up high on the list. But put two men together who've shared the soap after a game of rugby and they become oblivious to any social nuances or emotional situations that normally they'd pick up on straight away.

Rob had already moved into the sitting room with Will and was waving the bottle of wine about that he'd brought along.

"Glad we came early after all!" he was saying. "Time for a quick one together before everyone else turns up." I assumed he meant a drink, as he was now heading for the kitchen, but I was almost too bemused to be sure.

"I'll find the corkscrew," Sarah said, pushing him in front of her and mouthing 'sorry' to me as they went.

I turned to Will. "I don't think this is a good idea. There'll be lots of new friends turning up in a minute – I don't want to have to explain your presence."

Will raised a sardonic eyebrow. "Ashamed of me?"

"I just want you to go. If there's anything we need to talk about – and I can't think that there is – then we'll have to do it some other time."

He smiled easily. "You're right, of course. I was just hanging on to tease you – like I used to. You'd rise to the bait so prettily!"

Now that's not how I remember it. What I remember is Will being deliberately awkward and provocative so that I'd become testy and high-pitched and he could then accuse me of starting a row.

He moved towards the door, to my great relief. "Perhaps we could have a meal together – I really do need to talk to you. Maybe dinner one evening next week?"

I opened my mouth to ask whether this would be with or without Lauren, but before I could speak he laid his hand on my arm and regarded me soulfully. "Please, Allie."

"Not dinner – lunch. I'll meet you one lunch-time, if it's really so important. Phone me."

"All right. That would be good. Thanks, Allie. Say goodbye to Rob for me, will you?" He grinned in that wicked Robbie Williams way he had. "Sarah's obviously keeping him in the kitchen until you've got rid of me!"

The old Allie would have felt sorry for him then, as if she were depriving a small boy of a special treat. But this was the new, super-improved version, and I bundled him out of the door unceremoniously before turning back to Sarah and Rob – who, as Will had predicted, now emerged from the kitchen.

"Sorry Allie," Rob said sheepishly. "I didn't think – it was just so natural to see you two together – Allie and Will, like old times."

Sarah slapped his arm. "And you're not thinking much now! I'd stop there, if I were you and pour the girl a drink – she looks as if she could do with one."

Before I could tell the hapless Rob that he was forgiven there was a commotion in the hall as Stace & Co. burst into the flat with a few others I didn't recognise.

"Who was that dishy bloke we met on the stairs?" Donna demanded immediately.

"That," I said with a wry smile, "was my ex-husband. Would you all like a drink?"

The three girls' eyes were like saucers and there was a new respect in their eyes.

"But he's lush!" Stace exclaimed. "You didn't tell us he was so good-looking! What a pity he wasn't staying!"

"You've heard of a wolf in sheep's clothing, haven't you?" I said grimly. "Well, he's a wolf in wolf's clothing. And he's already spoken for – my replacement, remember? Now, introduce me to your friends, and I'll introduce you to mine, and then we can all start enjoying ourselves!"

If the test of a good party is how many people stay until the early hours, how much booze is consumed, the decibel level of the music and how many people dance until they can no longer stay on their feet, then mine was a success. Best of all, *I* felt a success. I didn't want to think about my reaction to seeing Will after all these months, so, with some initial fortification from Rob (who followed me around contritely, replenishing my glass, until I finally told him to go away), I threw myself into playing the vibrant hostess.

And it worked. Friends and acquaintances I hadn't seen for

months showered me with compliments about how good I was looking, and I danced until my legs ached. One of my most constant partners was Elliott, a friend of Jodie's, whom I had put down in a big way during my *'I hate all men for ever'* phase, but thankfully he didn't appear to remember this.

"You're shenshashunal," he slurred at about 2 a.m., his eyes firmly fixed on my Wonderbra-enhanced cleavage, even while the rest of him swayed a little. "I must shee you again!"

"Why don't you call me in the week?" I suggested, intrigued to see whether he would remember anything the next day. "Jodie has my number."

"Great party!" everyone said as they spilled out onto the slumbering street some time later, and I knew there'd be lots of *'hasn't she changed?'* comments on the way home.

Sarah offered to stay and help clear up, but I shooed her away because she'd only want to speculate on what had brought Will to my door and I was too tired even to care. It was time to peel the fixed smile off my face.

She turned up again at noon, though, which I had to admit was a relief, because the harsh light of day showed up just what a mess the flat was in. By this time we both felt too fragile to utter anything more than brief comments on what needed doing next, and it was late afternoon before we were sat at the kitchen table with a mug of coffee, contemplating a purple 36D bra that regrettably neither of us could lay claim to.

Anti-climax had settled in for me. It was that sort of autumn afternoon of subdued light and melancholy stillness that I hated. Not for me the exclamations of delight over trees turning copper and burnished gold – it did nothing to disguise the fact that the year was dying and the drabness of winter was just around the corner. The party now seemed a pointless waste of time. Faces of those who had been there swirled around my brain as I swirled the remnants of my coffee around the bottom of the mug. None of the faces had that profile, that amused but tender gaze ...

"He hasn't called yet then?" Sarah's voice wafted into my thoughts.

"He hasn't got my number."

"Will? But you said you'd given him your new one."

"Oh! Er ... sorry. I thought you were talking about someone else ..." I cast about wildly under Sarah's all-knowing stare. "Umm ... Elliott ... the chap I was dancing with last night ... he said he would call ..."

Sarah raised her eyebrows expressively. "I didn't think he

looked much like your type."

"You mean he didn't look like Will." I shrugged. "But then, Will turned out not to be 'my type' either, didn't he? So I don't know, really, what my type is." *Greeny-brown eyes in a tanned face. Cropped hair and even white teeth.*

Stop it!

"And if Will does call me, it'll only be because he wants to renegotiate the divorce terms because of Lauren's latest must-have – you know, a new BMW to match Will's, or whatever," I went on with asperity.

Sarah got up to go. "Well, if he does contact you and you want to talk it over give me a shout." She thrust a packet of paracetamol purposefully across the table at me.

I grinned ruefully. "I know. I'm being a crabby cow, and I shouldn't be when you've come over to give me a hand." I stood up and gave her a hug. "I'm sorry. Hangover talking. I'll call you, promise – give you a full break-down on every male who comes hammering at my door after last night!"

By mid-week Stace & Co. had just about exhausted the party inquests. Every fanciable male had been dissected, every female's attire had been analysed, and numerous theories put forward as to the the reasons behind the two girls having a slanging match in the bathroom, which nearly came to blows but was the crowning glory as far as it being a good party went.

Each morning one or other had asked, "Anyone call?"

By Wednesday morning I was able to report that Elliott had phoned and that I'd arranged to meet him for a drink on Friday night – just to see if either of us could remember what the other was like when we were both stone cold sober.

On Thursday morning there were raised eyebrows when I entered the office in the Whistles suit but with a crisp new shirt they hadn't seen before and my hair up.

"Oh, my—! You're meeting someone aren't you? Today!" Donna exclaimed. "I bet it's David, isn't it? I haven't seen his secretary arrive yet. I bet she's off on a course or something, which you already know about, and he's going to call you in to his office to help out, and then he'll see you looking like that and ask you out to lunch and—"

"—And then he'll whisk me off to Tiffany's and I'll come back with a huge diamond engagement ring and a copy of *The Christian's Way to Convert to Judaism*," I said bitingly. My head ached and I wasn't at all sure about the hair. "Now if you'll excuse me, I've got some work to do."

I could feel them making eyes at each other behind my back, but nothing more was said for a while. Then Emma piped up: "I suppose you'll be wanting to take your lunch break on your own?"

I swivelled my chair round to face them. "Er ... yes, I would ... if that's all right?"

She shrugged and looked at Donna before saying, "Depends. What time do you want to go? – it might clash with what we want to do."

"Yeah," Donna agreed. "Like, if it's a special time and we might be wanting –" (sudden inspiration) "to get our nails done, for instance. It could be difficult."

"Oh, all right, I'll tell you," I said, caving in because I needed to talk to someone about it and Sarah had been out last night. "Will phoned yesterday, just before I left the office. He wants to meet me for lunch – remember he turned up before the party 'cos he wanted to talk to me about something?"

"How could we forget?" Stace said, "What do you think he wants?"

"I've no idea," I said firmly, "and I don't particularly care as long as it doesn't hold the divorce up."

"So what are we going for today, then?"

I looked blankly at Stace.

"You know – the image. 'Successful Career Woman who Scares Men Away'? 'Seductress Who'll Make Him Wish He'd Never Left' – or what?"

"It's obvious, isn't it – she's got to be a mixture of 'Look How Well I'm Doing Without You', and 'I've Got Lots of Other Men Falling at my Feet'," Emma said.

"That's about it," I agreed. "Even if there aren't any men." But they weren't listening to me now; they were busy scrutinising me from head to toe and talking about me as if I were a tailor's dummy.

"The clothes are fine – what about the make-up, Don?"

"I think she could do with a bit of lip gloss – it'll show her tan up more – I've got some in my bag."

"And some body lotion on her legs – they'll look smoother when she sits down and crosses them in front of him."

"What about the hair – a bit looser around the edges, do you think? Just a few tendrils?"

Derek chose to come out of the little cubby-hole which was his office at that moment. "Have any of those brochures on the new development at Chorley gone out yet? I need to start correlating the response …"

He was met by the blank stares of the three girls as if he were speaking in an alien language (despite the pile of glossy brochures sitting prominently on Donna's desk), followed by a grimace from Stacey which clearly said, *'Can't you see you're interrupting something very important?'* So he shrugged defeatedly and retreated to his cubby hole, while the girls returned to the real business in hand.

By one o' clock I was being shepherded out of the building in a waft of *Miracle,* kindly donated by Emma, to trip over Westminster Bridge to a trendy little fish restaurant, which I'd deliberately chosen so that I could pretend I'd forgotten that Will wasn't very fond of seafood.

Will was already there, suave in a dark suit. I remembered just in time to quell the apology for keeping him waiting that sprang automatically to my lips.

"How was the party?" he asked, to cover up the awkward moment when he didn't know whether or not to kiss me on the cheek.

"Good. Friends brought friends, you know the sort of thing – I met lots of interesting people. It went on for hours, so everyone must have been having a good time."

We each turned our attention to the drinks which had just arrived. I sat quietly, determined to make him lead the conversation.

"So, what are you up to these days? – You're looking very business-like," he said after we'd ordered and I'd had the small satisfaction of watching him struggle to find something he'd like on the menu. Eventually he'd asked the waiter if he could have a plain omelette.

"PA to the sales director of a speculative housing corporation just over the river," I answered, tripping off the sentence I'd practised with the girls that morning. "Just for a short time, though – I'm keen to keep my options open at the moment."

"And then? Your plans for the future – what are they?"

I began to realise that under the affable manner he was adopting (similar to the one he used with clients) there was a tenseness about him that was unfamiliar.

I shrugged. "I think I mentioned – when everything is sorted out I'll probably move on. Pastures new, and all that."

"Anywhere in particular?"

Iridescent early-morning sunlight playing on the water; the relentless pounding of waves on rock; the soothing rhythm of water being sucked back over pebbles; cliff-tops with, at their edges, long harsh tufts of sea grass bowing in the breeze ...

I shook my head to clear the vision. "I haven't decided yet. Probably away from London, though – possibly abroad. I've a few job options I'm following up." I was beginning to feel proud of my nonchalance.

"I'm sure whatever you choose will go well. You have that look of success about you." His voice was soft with admiration.

I inclined my head graciously at this rare compliment, whilst wondering what on earth this was leading up to. Lauren must have some outrageous demands to be met, for him to hedge around me so cautiously.

Will concentrated hard on his omelette, taking so long to dissect it into equal portions that it began to look rubbery enough to bounce.

My own dish of mussels and clams in a creamy sauce was too good to waste, but as soon as I'd finished I pushed the plate away from me.

"Okay Will. What's this all about? You said you wanted to talk to me, but it can't just have been about my future – my game plan as a soon-to-be divorced woman has never bothered you up till now. But I'm warning you that the settlement is not open to re-negotiation. I'm happy that it's a fair deal and, if that doesn't suit you and Lauren, it's too bad."

How was that for firm? I wished Stace & Co. had been sitting at the next table.

He looked up at me with the soulful expression that had captivated me all those years ago, and had always won me over in the past. He was so damned handsome I could see anew what had kept me attached to him for so long.

He pushed his own plate aside and leaned towards me. "It's nothing like that ... This is really difficult. You've changed so much – I don't quite know how to tell you what's on my mind."

"Experiences change everyone, Will. And change was what you wanted, I seem to recall."

"And I was wrong. Lauren and me – we're finished. Not together any more. I couldn't go on with it; I just kept thinking about you and how I treated you before I went. It was unforgivable of me, but, perhaps, when you see I've changed too, you might be able to forgive me after all."

Will and Lauren finished! I couldn't believe it. He'd been totally besotted.

"Forgiving isn't too difficult, eventually," I replied tartly, my voice more shrill than I'd have liked. "It's forgetting that's more of a problem."

"I quite agree," he said, throwing me even more off balance. "It was forgetting which was my problem during all those months! I couldn't forget you at all, you see ... no matter how hard I tried to, and ... well, once we were apart it was easy to see how dreadfully I'd treated you."

"You mean you ran out of excuses for yourself!" I cried, and then realised my raised voice had attracted the attention of several people. "You'd used up all the best ones on me for the past two years," I hissed instead.

He shook his head. "No excuses. All I'd like now is the chance to make it up to you." He held up his hand as I opened my mouth to protest. "I know I can't ever expect you to love me the way you did, and I'll never stop calling myself all sorts of a fool for not appreciating what we had, but if you give me one small chance, I'll show you how much I've changed ... with no strings attached, I promise."

I stared at him, wide-eyed. That sort of second-rate B-Movie speech would have been bad enough on the big screen, but coming from Will it had a compelling fascination.

"Let me get this straight. *You've* finished with Lauren because you couldn't stop thinking about *me,* after leaving *me* because you couldn't stop thinking about *Lauren*? Have you considered therapy?"

He looked so appealingly hang-dog that, despite myself, I found my heart doing a little flip.

"I know, I know!" he said. "I've made a complete balls-up of everything and I don't deserve you even to be sitting here with me! But all I'm asking, really, is that you put a brake on the divorce proceedings, and give me time to prove to you that I'll never treat you so badly again."

I took a deep breath and tried to resurrect my calm exterior.

"With what final intent?" I asked as coolly as I could.

"What do you mean?"

"I mean that it's all very well to say let's halt the proceedings so that you can do your gallant bit and impress me all over again, but we can't go on like that indefinitely. I'm assuming that your intention is, having done your penance for as long as I deem necessary, for us to live together again."

He was watching me intently, his dark eyes unfathomable. I bet he was dying to comment on the hardness of my response.

But he held himself in check commendably.

"Ultimately, that *is* what I would like – more than anything else in the world."

I thought of what *I* would like more than anything else in the world. The lid began to jiggle on the box into which I had so resolutely packed my summer experiences. The contents began to spill out.

I want Marsha not to be dying. I want to tell her I understand about her and my father, and her decision not to tell me. I want to be back in Cornwall with her and Adam, and the foolish words between us never to have taken place. I want to be in love with a man who loves me in return; to have his children ...

I seemed to spend my life hankering after things that had gone and could not be reclaimed: my childhood when I still had two parents; my idyllic summer with Marsha and Adam ... my marriage.

Now I was being offered a chance to redeem one of those things. A few months ago I would still have leapt at the chance to have Will back, and crowed with delight at Lauren being vanquished. But now? Now ... I didn't know.

"Allie?"

Will's voice broke into my thoughts. He was watching me carefully and I could see the anxiety in his eyes. Did he *really* want to try again? Did I even want to give him the chance to prove himself? I recalled the various scenarios I had dreamed about where Will would come back to me, and how I would react. Now one of those scenes was being played out, and I wasn't at all sure of my lines. Part of me wanted to hurt him as badly as he'd hurt me, to shout at him, to lash out physically, to let him know just what his leaving had done to me; not have it glossed over with glib words and sexy smiles.

But I just sat there. Very still.

"Isn't there anything you can say?"

I shook my head. "It's all too sudden. What do you expect me to say? I've got a life of my own now – I don't intend to give it up, just like that."

"And I'm not asking you to," he said quickly. "I'm just asking whether I can start seeing you again – take you out to dinner, that sort of thing. Step by step get to know each other once more. See if that old spark can be resurrected."

"When you say you've 'finished' with Lauren – how finished is it, exactly? Finished as in 'we're not living together any more', or finished as in 'I've changed my mind but I haven't got round to telling her yet'?"

He looked immensely wounded, but had the sense not to say too much, given that I would soon remind him of how he had treated me.

"Lauren's moved out," he said. "When I explained to her how I felt, she realised that our situation was hopeless. So ... I'm on my own again, and missing you – *because* I was missing you – and you're on your own ..."

"I had an affair – during the summer," I told him, feeling a certain satisfaction when the intensity of his gaze flickered for a second. "It's over now, but I'm seeing someone else."

Okay, so I hadn't actually gone out with Elliott yet, but Will didn't know that.

"Well, you look so stunning I'm not surprised men are falling over each other to go out with you," he said gallantly, conveniently forgetting that a cheap jibe during one of our many rows before he left was about how drab I had become.

I looked at my watch. "I need to get back, I've a lot of work to do." If I didn't go soon there would barely be time to let the three girls know what this was all about.

He stood up to help me with my jacket. "Could you give me some idea – of whether I stand any chance at all?"

He smelt of an aftershave which I didn't recognise – Lauren's choice, presumably. Minus one point, Will, for not remembering that *Davidoff* was my favourite. But his nearness was unnerving all the same. In our early days he would help me on with my coat and then kiss my neck, making me melt.

I stepped away from him. "Why don't you call after the weekend? I've got a lot on over the next few days and I need a bit of time to think things over."

He nodded and then his brow creased in anxiety. "But the divorce papers and so on – will you put those on hold, just for now?"

"I've already sent the last lot back – there's nothing more to be done, is there?" I asked innocently and enjoyed seeing the discomfort on his face. Could he *honestly* be having a change of heart?

"All right," I relented after a few moments. "I'll tell my chap that I want a short delay – but I mean only a *short* one – while I think about what you've said today. But quite honestly Will, I can't see a lot of point in all this. It's probably much better that we draw a line under that part of our lives and get on with the next bit."

He shook his head. "I can't contemplate the next bit any more – not without you. I'm determined to win you back, you know."

Impressive, if just a teensy bit sickly.

"That makes me sound like a 'trophy wife'," I quipped. "Not my cup of tea at all. Let's leave it there, Will, and speak after the weekend."

I leaned forward and gave him the tiniest peck on the cheek, for provocation's sake, moving away again before he could so much as catch my arm. "Thanks for lunch."

14.

I left work early in the end, the 'Oohing' and 'Aahing' of the three girls proving too much for me. For all my flippancy when I told them that Will wanted me back, my head was aching and I needed time on my own to think things through.

I thought of phoning Sarah, but if Rob got so much as an inkling that Will could be back on the scene he'd do his utmost to persuade Sarah to make me agree. Juliet had been whisked off by Philip on a cruise, 'because the Med is so beautiful at this time of year, darling'. Actually, it's beautiful at any time of year when someone else is paying.

Juliet wouldn't have been a lot of use anyway. Whilst I was still determined to admire her finer qualities, her ability to advise me regarding my former husband wouldn't be very high on the list. He was really much more her type than mine, I suppose – a handsome ladies' man who strove for the good life and could make whoever he was with the envy of other females. She would urge me to give it a go, while reminding me that I didn't have too many years left to find such a quality replacement. After all, she'd been just as surprised as me when I'd managed to hook him in the first place.

And his infidelity? "Oh, you know what men are like, darling, you just have to keep them on a very tight leash."

Juliet had obviously done a lot of sweeping under the carpet herself over the years. Interesting to note that I'd inherited at least one trait from her.

I curled up on my sofa in my beautifully stylish sitting room, alone but not alone. I had two unseen companions bickering either side of me. On my left was Old Me; the one who remembered what life had been like in those early days when Will and I had first been together. Memories, hopes and aspirations were dragged out and replayed to a nostalgic background of *Happiness*

– which owed nothing to Ken Dodd, by the way.

And don't forget, Old Me whispered, *how your ultimate dream was to be happily married and have children – think how quickly that could be within your grasp if you patch things up with Will.*

On my other side was New Me, urging me not to lose sight of my hard-won independence and all I'd gone through to achieve it.

He could let you down again, New Me insisted. *And anyway, you're not so taken in by those dark good looks any more, are you? Your passions have changed direction somewhat lately.*

—*Forget about the summer,* Old Me said. *It was an aberration, and it didn't work anyway. You can't have loved this man for eight years and not have any feelings left for him – at least give him a chance.*

It'll just hold you back, New Me insisted. *More tears at bedtime and nothing to show for it. You're different now – you could have a new life opening up for you, cut loose from the old one now.*

—*Like Cornwall, you mean,* Old Me mocked. *That got you a long way didn't it? You could still start again – with Will. Sell the flat, buy a little house somewhere, be what you always wanted to be ...*

... With you worrying every time Will came home late, New Me shouted, *in case there was another pair of long legs and mane of blonde hair that had taken his fancy ... have you no self-respect?*

—*Have you no sense?* Old Me shrieked. *You hoped for months and months for exactly this – he wants you again!*

"I'll give him a few weeks – that's all! Let him run around me for a bit while I think how I feel about him. But I'll keep any other options open as well," I said out loud in the end.

My two companions faded, each wringing their hands at my prevarication.

I was pleased to be meeting Elliott the next evening, if only to take my mind off things. He took me to a trendy wine bar in Croydon, which was interesting in itself because I didn't know Croydon had any trendy wine bars.

"You're so much happier than when I met you last year," he told me after I'd sparkled my way through the first drink. Oh, so he had remembered. I looked down at my glass, embarrassed.

"I think I was extremely unpleasant to you then," I said, "I'm surprised you've even bothered to ask me out."

He shrugged. "It was okay. I knew what you were going through. I went through it when I split up with my ex, Karen – I didn't have a civil word for anyone."

I felt even worse then. He'd probably tried his best with me all those months ago, and I'd thrown it all back at him, convinced at the time that nobody could or ever would suffer the way I was suffering.

I smiled at him. "I was sure then that I would never get over my marriage breaking up."

"Well, you look pretty much over it to me, now. A different girl."

He was nice. Not the best-looking guy in the world, and there wasn't even the hint of a spark on my part, but I felt comfortable with him.

He ordered another drink for us both and we fell to talking about what we were each doing now – I have to confess that, having put him down on the first occasion we met and having been the worse for wear on the second, I couldn't remember much about him at all.

"I'm a marketing co-ordinator for an electronics firm," he told me. I smiled brightly, remembering the *Little Book of Dating*'s first rule: ask your date about himself, and look interested.

"And what does that mean, exactly?" I queried.

Perhaps I shouldn't have included the word 'exactly' because he took me literally and gave me an intricate run-down on his job, the promotion he really wanted and deserved (but no-one had recognised his true brilliance yet), and the strain that the cut and thrust of office politics had put on his marriage.

I managed to keep my 'interested' face in place, and murmured a few 'fascinatings' in mainly the right places, but it was difficult because I kept getting distracted – first by his habit of clearing his throat and stretching his neck every few moments, and then by the realisation that somehow we were now onto a bottle of wine and most of it was going into his glass. My sparkle began to fizzle out.

From then on it went from bad to worse. Somehow we had drifted into the break-up of his marriage. "Of course, it's not until you're completely over the whole damned mess that you're able to look back and see just what went wrong," he told me, and then proceeded to itemise everything that had gone wrong in his mess with Karen. I must have forgotten – had dating always been this boring?

Despite all my good intentions, or perhaps because out of desperation I'd also begun to attack the wine a bit, my thoughts kept straying to the summer. There hadn't really been any proper 'dates' with Adam – but there had been all that spine-tingling excitement every time we were together as our feelings for each other deepened ... that wonderful voyage of discovery that made each day a tantalising experience ...

Stop!

I got the brush out and swept vigorously, making a new effort to turn my attention to Elliott. But then Will loomed into my slightly unfocused mind's eye. If I went back to Will there'd be no more bothering with this dating lark – and babies, there could be babies ...

"Oh, I don't know!" I said aloud, fed up with Will, with Elliott, and with myself.

"I'm sorry?" Elliott said, cut off in mid-sentence.

"Umm ... I don't know ... whether I agree with what you've just said ... er ... it all depends ..."

"But you never met Karen; how could you agree or disagree?"

"Exactly! It would be unfair of me to comment, wouldn't it?" I groped wildly for some fragment of what Elliott had been saying. "I mean, I couldn't put the blame on Karen when I don't even know her ..."

"But it isn't her fault she's got polycystic ovaries, and I wasn't suggesting otherwise!" There was a hint of belligerence in his voice as well as a puzzled look on his face.

"Of course it isn't – and you're not ... Oh, look, Elliott. This is hopeless. This is my first date in years, and I don't think I can remember how it's supposed to go – I think I should go home. I'm sorry ..."

He insisted gallantly on accompanying me back in the taxi, despite my assurances that I would be fine on my own, but it was a very quiet journey.

He coughed and stretched his neck as we turned into my road. "I don't suppose you'll be inviting me in for coffee?"

"I don't think there'd be much point, do you?"

He looked down at his knees. "That's a pity – 'cos I fancy you like mad, you know."

I tried to smile sympathetically in the dark of the cab. "But neither of us is really ready for anything else, are we? You obviously still feel very deeply about Karen –" he opened his mouth to contradict me, but I wouldn't let him – "and I don't honestly think I've got myself properly sorted out yet."

The taxi had come to a halt. "Thank you for a nice evening," I said, leaning forward to kiss him on the cheek. But he grabbed me round the neck in a sort of rugby hold and kissed me full on, his mouth hard and very wet on mine. When I pulled away I just about managed not to wipe my mouth with the back of my hand.

"I'm sorry," he gasped, "but it's been so long for me too – since I've been out with anyone—".

"Goodnight Elliott." I got out of the taxi without saying anything more, and bolted into the building.

So altogether the weekend ended up a bit flat. Up until then my homecoming had been quite busy: new job, decorating the flat, getting to know my new workmates, arranging my party ... And the past week had been exciting, I had to admit, with the prospect of meeting Will again and going out on a new date – even if both events had been nerve-wracking as well. But now all that had been and gone; I was in a state of confusion regarding Will, and had nothing to look forward to.

I mooched about all day Saturday feeling sorry for myself and hating anyone I encountered in the street or in the shops who looked cheerful, especially if they were with someone else. I tried to write to my old friend Gina, the one who had decamped to Scotland some months back, as I'd been feeling guilty about not keeping in touch. But what could I write? If I started to tell her about the summer I would get to thinking about Marsha and everyone again, which I was determined not to do, and if I didn't mention the summer there wasn't much else to say.

So I sat by the window chewing my pen, for a long time, wondering idly whether Lauren was as heartbroken over her split with Will as I'd been, and whether now was the time for me to get a cat. I don't actually like cats, by the way, but the getting of a dog has always been associated in my mind with people who are optimistic about their future. The acquiring of a cat, on the other hand, would be a declaration that my future looked bleak and empty.

The ringing of my doorbell on Sunday morning was such a welcome relief that I ran to answer it. Glancing out of the window I could see Sarah's blue Polo in the street below. *Great! Rob must be playing rugby, and she'd come over for a good gossip.*

"Come on up!" I sang into the door entry before pressing the buzzer, and then hurried into the kitchen to put the kettle on, already forming sentences in my head to describe my dreary night out with Elliott.

There was a light tap on the flat door just as I threw it open.

"Hi! I'm so glad I found you in!"

"*Will!* I thought you were Sarah!" I looked out into the hall, in case she might be lurking behind him. Will looked over his shoulder too.

"No," he said with a grin, "it's definitely just me. Sorry to disappoint you."

"Oh. What do you want? You were supposed to be calling me."

Yes, I did sound very curt, but you should have seen what I looked like! I tried to tell myself it didn't matter, because I wasn't intending to impress Will anyway, and he'd seen me in varying degrees of awfulness over the years, but I couldn't convince myself. Looking good had given me the upper hand in this tentative bid at restoring some sort of relationship, and now I felt at a distinct disadvantage.

"I know I was supposed to phone after the weekend," he was saying, "but I couldn't stop thinking about you, and it's such a beautiful day that I just got in my car on impulse and came over. Thought you might like to go out somewhere – but if you've already got plans ... or if Sarah's on her way round ...?"

Was that a smirk on his face? He must have known by the state of me that I had nothing arranged.

"Umm ... well, I'm not sure ... you'd better come in ... Sarah hadn't said definitely ..."

I led him into the sitting room, glancing through the window again as I did so. Just past the not-Sarah's Polo was Will's BMW. Damn! Why hadn't I seen it? And he was right, it was a beautiful morning. Bright blue sky, with sunlight flashing through the golds and reds – the sort of autumn day that even I had to concede was stunning.

"I thought perhaps brunch somewhere on the river?" Will said to my back. "Or we could drive to the coast, if you like ..."

"No! Not the coast!" I turned sharply. Okay, Brighton wasn't the same as Cornwall, but I still didn't want to stand on the beach and watch the waves with Will. "It wouldn't be worth it, with it getting dark so much earlier now," I said in a softer tone, "and anyway, I'm not sure ... I wasn't expecting to ... there were things around the flat I meant to do today ..." I waved a hand inefffectually around my immaculate sitting room.

In bygone days my indecision would have irritated Will enormously, as he much preferred me to be swept up in his enthusiasms. But now, hearing the kettle ping in the kitchen, he simply said, "Why don't we have a coffee while you're deciding? If that would be all right?"

"I suppose so." I was more annoyed with myself than with him, because the prospect of going out for the day, even with my ex-husband, was infinitely more appealing than staying in alone, but I didn't want to seem needy in any way. "But I have decided," I went on after a pause during which Will continued to look hopefully at me. "I could do with some fresh air, so you have a coffee while I go and change."

I made him his coffee – white with one sugar, I remembered automatically – and then took myself off to the bedroom, carefully closing the door.

It all felt surreal. My husband sitting in his old place, waiting for me to get ready. Me, in the bedroom, with the door closed so that he wouldn't catch a glimpse of me in a state of undress, as if he were a stranger. Weird.

I decided on fairly new jeans and a brand new top bought in a recent foray to River Island with Em. I didn't want to wear anything that might smack of sentimental reminders of earlier days, but also didn't want to look as if I was making much effort. I had to add a bit of make-up, though, because I was looking a bit tired around the eyes – no other reason.

"I like what you've done to the flat," Will said when I returned to the sitting room. "It's much lighter and seems bigger. Was it all your own work, or did you have someone else in mind?"

"What?" I could feel my colour rising under the make-up. How did he know about Adam? How could he know where my inspiration came from?

"You said you were seeing someone else – I thought you might have changed everything together, you know."

Oh. He meant Elliott, I suppose.

"Strangely enough, I'm quite capable of making decisions about my surroundings all by myself," I said haughtily. "I don't need anyone else's influence."

"I'm sorry," he said. (Note: second spontaneous apology in just over a week – was he going for some sort of record?) "It's just that I'm so anxious about the chances of us getting back together again that it was my clumsy way of finding out how much this other bloke figures in your life."

He must have mistaken my look of total surprise at this hitherto unknown backing down for further hauteur, and held up his hands. "I'm making a mess of this. I have no right to know anything more about your private life. Let's start again – where would you like to go?"

We settled for brunch by the river in the end, and he took me to a little place not far from Hampton Court, where we'd never been together before, and I decided not to enquire how he knew about it. It was too cool to sit outside, but we chose a table overlooking the Thames, which gave us something to comment on when the conversation threatened to come to a halt.

Not that talking was so difficult. I'd decided to be as waspish as possible so Will wouldn't think that all he had to do was turn up and I'd go out with him – just as I had today (but wouldn't have if I hadn't been feeling terminally bored by my own company) – but it was difficult to maintain any sort of attitude when he consistently refused to rise to the bait. He'd already pledged to be as nice as ninepence to me, so we had an exceedingly polite conversation that could have been taken straight out of some *Etiquette for Conversing with an Ex-Spouse* handbook. In fact, a few more occasions like this and I could have written it.

There were several no-go areas; Lauren was an obvious one, and I refused to be drawn on how I'd spent my summer. Then there was my supposed relationship with A. N. Other, which, although I had no wish to see Elliott ever again, I felt was a myth worth preserving for the meantime.

Which left jobs and family. We skirted nicely round both of those, Juliet and Philip providing a bit of light relief, and I caught up on news of his sister Annabel's latest off-spring. I hadn't mentioned that he had a sister, had I? Well there'd been no need, really, especially as she and her family hadn't figured much in our marriage. It seemed that Will had been seeing a lot more of her since our break-up, though.

"Annabel's so contented," he said. "Never thought I'd see my little sister so settled. I suppose that's what children do for you. And her two are great little fellows – I've grown very fond of them. They're enormous fun."

Excuse me? Will, who had been ready to bolt from the room if Annabel's firstborn had so much as stirred in his sleep, in case he was about to produce something unpleasant from either end of his body, now eulogising the joys of children?

"I've discovered that I can relate to the little monsters much better once they become more active," he went on, as if reading my scepticism. "I think a lot of men are the same."

'Hmm.

See? Old Me was whispering in my ear. *You play this right and you could be hearing the patter of tiny feet yourself in no time.*

See? New Me whispered back. *In no time at all you could be not just a deserted wife, but a deserted mother as well.*

"That was lovely," I said out loud as I finished the last of my eggs. "I hadn't realised how hungry I was."

"It's not easy to eat properly when you're just cooking for one, is it?" Will answered. "And you know what my cooking's like – it hasn't improved."

'Hmm.

"Do you fancy a stroll?" he went on when I didn't answer. "We've never been to Hampton Court Gardens, have we? At least, I still haven't – I don't suppose you ...?"

"No, I haven't. Great idea."

The gardens were lovely, even so late in the year, and I did my best to be excited about the maze, even though there were so many gaps in the hedges that you couldn't help but see which way you had to go; but as the afternoon wore on and the sun disappeared, I felt the old dislike of this season creeping over me. Perhaps it could only be enjoyed when you were very young, with all the anticipation of celebrations: Hallowe'en, followed by Bonfire Night, followed by Christmas. Perhaps you only truly enjoyed it again once you had children of your own.

Suddenly Hampton Court seemed a sad place to be. After all, it was a monument to one of the greatest loves that went tragically wrong. How smitten Henry the Eighth had been with Ann Boleyn, if the history books were to be believed, and how swiftly had his love faded!

And here I was, on a late Sunday afternoon with the chill beginning to seep into my bones, making polite conversation with a man who had appeared at first to love me completely, but had managed to betray me utterly and who now claimed he wanted to make amends. Did Henry, I wondered, have any fleeting desire to change his mind before the blade fell – quickly quenched because he was King and could not confess to error - and then it was too late?

I turned to Will to say I wanted to go home, catching him off guard for a fraction of a second. For once the suave confident facade was missing. His face was pinched and cold in the gathering October gloom, and for a moment I felt sorry for him.

Sorry for him? – In the time it took for me to feel aghast at my reaction – *sorry for him* wasn't an emotion I'd ever expected to experience as far as Will was concerned, and seemed much too tender – the facade was back. He smiled brightly at me, so that I wondered if I'd imagined it just because my own mood was darkening.

"I think I'd like to go home now," I said as if I were an invalid who had been taken on a little outing as a pick-me-up but had worn out my strength.

"Of course," he replied, with the solicitousness of a carer.

I don't know whether he expected me to invite him up to the flat, but he didn't suggest it and neither did I.

"Can we do something similar again?" was all he asked.

"Perhaps," I answered. "But I really would like a few days to think about things – can we leave it for now?"

He grimaced. "I told you I wouldn't give up without a fight, but I don't want to rush you." Out came the disarming smile. "I hope I haven't spoilt my chances by turning up unannounced today?"

I managed a tired smile back. "I've had a very pleasant day, Will. Let's leave it at that, shall we?"

Once in the flat my spirits plummeted even further. It all seemed so pointless, somehow. Looking for love, wanting to be loved, needing to produce children – for what? There were no tears (remember? – I never cry ... except in Cornwall); just an overwhelming sense of the futility of life itself. Pathetic, really.

I resisted the urge to call Will on his mobile and tell him to turn his car round and come back for the evening, just to keep me company; that would have given out all the wrong sort of signals.

Marsha's voice wouldn't leave my head, the one simple question she had asked when we discussed Will playing over and over like a damaged CD: *'Do you still love him?'*

I hadn't answered her clearly then, and I couldn't now, but oh, how I longed to be with her again and be cocooned in her special brand of caring! I didn't even have her telephone number, although doubtless Directory Enquiries could supply it. But I couldn't do it. I couldn't ring up a dying woman to foist more of my pathetic problems on her.

Just as I couldn't bear to ring up and hear someone tell me that she'd died.

Totally fed up with myself, I did the only thing I could do: put *Take That* on loud enough to sing along to, and got the ironing board out. Because who ever wants to do ironing when they're happy?

15.

Somehow it's okay when you admit to PMT yourself, isn't it? It's only exceedingly irritating when it's suggested by somebody else – especially if that somebody is male – and always in a patronising manner as being the cause of your bad temper, your lapse in efficient functioning, or your omitting to give that (male) person his due quota of subservience or respect. Anyhow, I'm happy to confess to PMT being at least a contributory factor to my bad humour on that Sunday, because after that things started to look up a bit.

One of Juliet's intermittent postcards arrived on Monday morning. We seemed to have spent most of the past few months communicating in this way, and it seemed a very satisfactory arrangement. This one informed me that, the cruise completed, she and Philip were now heading off to the Algarve, where some of Philip's chums had a villa.

"We've made lots of wonderful new friends," she chirruped. "I hope you have too, darling!" I could almost the picture the look on her face if she knew that my social life currently consisted of carefully orchestrated dates with my ex-husband, and nights out with Stace, Em and Don. Thank goodness she was going to be away for a bit longer.

Work took on a new aspect that week with the demise of Derek, whose anxiety over the behaviour of his wife had caused him to lose the plot completely and take extended sick leave. In his place appeared Merrill, an import from one of the branch offices who had jumped at the chance of making her mark at Head Office. She soon had us jumping too, clearing out the rubbish from the office, until our surroundings acquired a minimalist air of which the most rigorous interior designer would have approved. The brochures on the development at Chorley were dusted down and distributed, now several weeks late, to their intended destinations, and in no time at all a hitherto unknown 'work ethic' had entered the precincts of the General Office.

At first the three girls rallied against the regime imposed by this (it has to be said) extremely chic boss.

"If I were you, I'd be asking the agency to find me something else," Donna said in grumbling tones, "now that all the fun has gone out of this place. She'll have her eye on David next, you wait and see."

But, goody-two-shoes that I was, I rather liked Merrill's business-like approach, and it felt good to get my teeth into some real work again. The girls then mounted a rearguard action to wear down Merrill's resistance so she'd become as work-shy and shopaholic as they were, which made for an entertaining time as I watched her steeliness pitted against the combined ingenuity of Emma et al.

Meanwhile I was being wooed (but not yet won) by Will, who kept up a regular campaign of invitations to dinner, films and shows. Sometimes I went, sometimes I didn't, and sometimes I cancelled almost at the last minute. Sometimes I was free to chat to him on the telephone and sometimes I wasn't, and I never called him. On one occasion I turned him down for a night out with a crowd from the office at a karaoke bar, where I surprised them and myself by belting out an old Aretha Franklin number, *Say A Little Prayer,* and generally having a great time.

In short, I was as capricious with Will as I possibly could be, and as I'd never been in the past. But I didn't manage to catch him out. His good humour was scarily consistent no matter how I treated him, and he didn't try to force the pace. He would pick me up from the flat, but never insisted on coming in at the end of an evening, and he never invited me to his place.

"Obvious reasons," he said with a rueful smile. "I don't think you'd be comfortable there ... you know. But I'm moving to a different place soon, one with no associations, and perhaps then you'll come round to supper?"

Now that was tempting, if only to see what sort of 'supper' Will was capable of producing.

He'd made small attempts to introduce a physical element into our tentative relationship, kissing me tenderly when he dropped me off after an evening out, and once more passionately as we walked along a secluded street after a candlelit dinner. I'd almost found myself responding, recalling earlier times when Will's touch alone would thrill me – until bells clanged in my head, warning me that this was my cheating ex-husband who'd probably romanced Lauren in just the same way.

"I'm sorry," he'd said on that occasion, when he felt me pull back. "But I couldn't resist it – you've looked so lovely all night."

Just the right amount of flattery at the right time, which left me wondering why on earth I didn't throw in the towel of my resistance and call off the divorce proceedings completely.

"I think he's really changed," Sarah said when she called me at the office one day. "He's been out for a drink with Rob a couple of times, and all he's done is sing your praises and damn himself for being all kinds of fool. Anyway," she went on before I could comment, "can I use your washing machine? Mine's gone on the blink and I can't get it fixed until the end of the week."

"No problem," I said, "except I won't be there until late this evening – Merrill's asked us, or rather told us, that we have to stay for as long as it takes to clear a backlog of sales enquiries. Then I might go and have something to eat with the others."

"Er ... that's okay, I've still got a key." Her voice became rather sheepish. "It's one I had cut for Rob and I forgot to give it back to you ... do you mind?"

"Of course not. Help yourself. Must go – I'm being watched."

It was nearly ten by the time I got home, but the phone was ringing as I entered the flat. Will, I suspected, with a feeling of irritation, checking up to see where I'd been all evening.

But it was Sarah again.

"See? I told you he'd changed!"

"What are you talking about?"

"The flowers," Sarah said. "They were magnificent! And when was he ever in the habit of sending you flowers just for the hell of it?"

"I haven't got any flowers," I said, looking around in case I'd missed something. "Start at the beginning."

"It was when I was leaving the flat," she explained. "This delivery guy turned up – you know, the sort who arrives on a motorbike in black leather – with this huge bouquet and asking for you. I told him that you weren't home yet, and offered to take them for you, but he said they had to be delivered in person. So I told him where you worked – perhaps that wasn't such a good idea in retrospect, but he seemed a genuine bloke – and off he went. Didn't you get them?"

"No, I didn't. He probably missed me at the office as well. Perhaps they'll turn up tomorrow."

But there were no flowers next day, and Will, calling me to

ask whether I fancied a 'quiet night in with a take-away and a bottle of wine, so that we can talk' made no mention of them.

"What do you want to talk about?"

"Umm ... I've got some ideas ... about the future ... I wanted to run them past you, to see what you thought ..."

Diffidence? Will?

You see, it just wasn't him, and it didn't feel right. Not yet anyway, but I couldn't quite put my finger on why.

"Not tonight, Will. I've been working late this week, and I think an evening curled up with a bottle of wine would just have me snoring on the sofa in no time. Perhaps Friday?"

There was a pause. "All right. Friday it will have to be. But I do want to talk to you then – it's important."

Which made me feel a bit mean. I really was giving him quite a run-around. But I stuck to my guns; I didn't feel ready to hear about plans for the future – I was still much too confused about the present.

Lunchtime found me standing on Westminster Bridge, staring into the gloomy depths of the Thames which a pale sun struggling through low clouds had failed to brighten. Merrill had insisted that we took our lunch breaks two by two, but today Stace had gone to have a quick manicure and facial ready for a heavy date, and it felt good to be on my own for a while as I hadn't yet tired of soaking up the atmosphere of the city.

I thought of Wordsworth standing here nearly two centuries ago, and wished for a little of the 'calm so deep' that he had felt. What would he make of it now?

Lost in thought, I didn't hear the person who came to stand beside me, was unaware even of a presence until a voice said, "*Earth has not anything to show more fair* – and I can't remember the next line!"

It was the same poem though! Just as I'd been thinking of it! And the voice – so familiar! I turned quickly to a leather-clad figure, helmet tucked under his arm.

"Adam!"

"Hi, Allie."

We stood there, grinning inanely. Just looking at each other. None of the cross words we'd had in Cornwall mattered any more. The feelings of hurt had disappeared. He was here.

"Blake or Wordsworth?" he said at last.

"Wordsworth," I said promptly. "More accessible, and I can't stand that tiger."

"'Mmm. Shame about all those daffodils though."

We stood for more moments, until I managed, "How did you know I was here?"

"I tried your home address first – Gwen Jarrett supplied that information – and a friend of yours told me where you worked. So I've been loitering about for hours, hoping I'd catch you."

"You're the leather *Milk Tray* man!"

"Well, it was flowers actually, but I didn't fancy bringing them to your office. I thought you might ... well ... anyway, they're languishing in my flat at the moment."

There was another pause. So much I wanted to ask him. Why now? Was it Marsha? What had happened since September? Questions whirled around my head. And all the time I was aware of his body, his face, his eyes, his nearness.

"How are you, Allie?" he said eventually, meaning it.

And that was it! A blinding flash of comprehension! That was what had been missing from all of Will's blandishments and attention. That's what had kept me so unsure! How could I have failed to see it?

Never once had he asked, *'How are you, Allie?'* Never once a desire to understand or even hear about the pain he'd inflicted upon me. Only promises of change, of a different future – *his* plans, *his* changes, sweeping away all the agony and damage of the last two years with a bigger brush than I'd ever used! Why was I so stupid as not to have seen that underneath all the superficial gloss of caring and flattery was the same ruthless Will, wanting me and the rest of his world to bend to his whim? Even today, when he'd said he wanted to talk, it was to outline *his* thoughts, *his* ideas for the future.

It felt like a revelation of Damascene proportions. Adam, with those four precious words, had made me see the light.

"Allie?" The beautiful eyes, even more noticeable now that his face was less tanned, focused anxiously on me. "Perhaps this wasn't such a good idea ... I should have phoned ... written you a note ...."

"No!" I almost shouted, grabbing his arm in case he should move away. "No, I'm fine, really I am, and pleased to see you – it's just such a surprise – there's so much to say ..."

We were beaming again. Standing there beaming, on a cold November day, getting in the way of all the people who were rushing hither and thither.

"Can we go somewhere for a coffee?" he asked as Big Ben struck the hour.

"Oh Adam, I can't, not right now, my lunch break is over."

But I knew I wouldn't go back, not if it meant that we had to say goodbye.

"Later then – as soon as you've finished – I can be here ... or anywhere ..."

"Promise?"

He nodded. "Promise."

We'd begun to walk along the bridge when I stopped suddenly. "Marsha? Is she ...?"

"Still with us. But very weak. She wants to see you – but that's not why I'm here," he added quickly and I knew he was remembering my previous barbs about being Marsha's errand boy. "I'm here because *I* needed to see you – it's just taken me this long to pluck up courage."

"Am I that formidable?"

"Terrifying," he grinned.

We'd reached the office block.

"This is where I work," I told him.

"I know. Fourth floor. Shall I be here when you finish?"

I nodded. "5.30."

I turned towards the building, wondering how on earth I was going to get through the next few hours without giving anything away to the others. The events of the summer were too complex and too personal – much more personal than a potential divorce, I realised – to be mulled and mauled over.

At the revolving plate glass doors I stopped. This was ridiculous. On impulse I turned and ran back down the paved approach.

"Adam!" I was breathless as I caught up with him, but not, I think, due to being unfit.

"I just wondered – if you're free all afternoon? I don't think I can go back in there –" I jerked my head towards the building – "and I'm only a temp, they wouldn't miss me, I could call in sick ..."

He smiled. "I'm between assignments at the moment – whatever the photographer's equivalent of 'resting' is. I've got all the time in the world – well, at least until tomorrow."

"I could be getting a migraine," I said. "They come on very quickly."

"Best you phone them, then, isn't it?" he said gravely.

I looked about hurriedly, but why would there be a phone box between an office block and a derelict car park site? Adam rummaged in a pocket before producing a mobile.

"I assume you still haven't got one?"

"Got the mobile, just no top-up credit," I confessed.

I moved away from him to tell my lies to Merrill so that I could sound ill without him making me smile. Merrill was full of sympathy, but even that didn't make me feel guilty.

"Do you want someone to go home with you?" she asked solicitously.

"No, no, if I get away now I should make it to Purley before it gets really bad. Thanks, Merrill."

"I can't take you anywhere on my bike, I'm afraid," Adam said, as we hurried away before we bumped into Stace or anyone else returning from lunch, "I don't have a spare helmet."

We walked through to the anonymity of Waterloo station instead, and settled for the station coffee bar.

"Are you really okay?" he asked as soon as we were settled at a table. "You look different."

There it was again, the caring tone, the concerned eyes. I grimaced. "Paler – the tan's faded. Back to being mousy."

"More fragile – but definitely not mousy."

I looked away, suddenly shy. There was so much to say, and yet now here we were and there didn't seem any way to say it.

"Did Marsha tell you—?"

"That afternoon—"

We both started at the same time and then laughed and relaxed a little.

"Please," I said.

"No, you first," he answered, inclining his head.

"I just wondered – did Marsha tell you about our conversation, when I got back to the house? Did she explain why I left so suddenly?"

He nodded. "She told me everything she'd told you, I think. About her affair with your father, and about the baby."

"Was she very upset, afterwards?"

"I think she was glad to have talked about it in the end. But she was sorry that she'd driven you away. That's why she'd like to see you again, to make amends."

"There aren't any to make as far as I'm concerned. I've had time to think about it all now and I understand – I do. It was wrong of me to sit in judgement – I don't know what I'd have done in her situation. It was just all a bit of a shock."

"Allie, that afternoon, when you left – when we argued ..."

"Oh, that was stupid as well –" In my eagerness to be friends again I swept my hand across the table and narrowly missed sending my coffee flying, "I shouldn't have flounced off like that and—"

"Hey, just a minute!" He grabbed my flailing hand and held it firmly on the table. "You'll be taking responsibility for Third World Debt as well at this rate! ... What *I* wanted to explain," he went on, "was that I should have followed you and told you why I hesitated the way I did. The thing is, when you asked me to choose between you and Marsha ..." I was shaking my head, embarrassed to even think about those stupid words, but he was looking down now and didn't see. "I suddenly realised that if I truly had to choose, then it was you, Allie. It would always be you. And after all these years of having Marsha in the background, rooting for me, giving me everything my own mother failed to provide, I felt so ashamed that someone I'd only recently met had the power to wrench me away at a time when Marsha needed me most."

Shame washed over me again, for the umpteenth time since that awful day. What had I been thinking of, even *asking* him to choose, when I would never really want him to? My choice would have been to still have him *and* Marsha in my life – and his choice apparently would be always to have both me and Marsha in his life, so why had it all gone so stupidly wrong?

"It was such a revelation, to know just how strongly I felt about you, that I spent ages in that café, thinking through what I should do about the immediate future," Adam went on. "Believing, of course, that I could catch up with you later at Marsha's, when you'd have had time to talk to her, which was obviously so important to you – and then you might have had a clearer idea of your future, as well."

So he had loved me all along. What a stupid, insecure, self-centred fool I'd been! His talk was all in the past tense though. What had I thrown away?

"I thought you might have come to Gwen Jarrett's that evening," I said, remembering the hours I'd sat at the window, waiting for him. "I was too proud to come back to the house to find you – and later on, I'm afraid, I was too drunk to even try!"

"I ended up getting furious about the whole thing," he admitted. "I felt bad that Marsha was clearly distressed at having hurt you, so I turned it into anger against you for making all this happen. By the time I'd calmed down the next day, you'd already gone."

I nodded. A sort of lull descended on us, and we sat for a few moments sipping our coffee, each dealing with private thoughts. My own ran along the lines of what might have happened if I'd delayed my departure by just a few more hours – but who would ever know?

Adam began to speak again. "I came back to London a week or so later, armed with your address and promises to Marsha that I would get in touch with you – but somehow ... well, it never seemed like the right time. The longer I left it, the more I convinced myself that you wouldn't want anything more to do with me, and I told myself that it was better to draw a line under the whole summer thing and explore pastures new ..."

Now didn't that sound familiar?

"I suppose in the end my courage deserted me," he went on, "and I was trying to get back into the whole work thing, and going backwards and forwards to Cornwall in the meantime, and ... that's about the sum total of my pathetic excuses, I'm afraid."

"But you've plucked up courage this week. Was that down to Marsha nagging you?"

"No, it was Marie of all people."

"Marie?" She was the one who'd seemed the least interested in our relationship.

"Yes. She took me to one side when I was down there last week and said that she was sick of me turning up looking so dreadful, and when was I going to do something about it? And I said that I wasn't going to do anything, because it was too late – even Marsha had stopped talking about you, so I assumed she was content to let things be. But Marie said that was just Marsha not wishing to interfere, and that she often said to the girls how worried she was about me, and about you, and that she wished she could do something to make things right again. And then Marie told me that if there was one thing I could do for Marsha before she died, it was to sort myself out, find you and make it up with you, and get you to come back down to Cornwall."

"Wow! Marie said all that!"

"And some! She was a right little spitfire when she got going, I can tell you." He grinned. "I'm only here now because finding you and hoping you wouldn't blast me away was marginally less frightening than having to confess to Marie that I hadn't tried."

"Is she still busy at the stables? And is Kate still down there? And Simon?"

Suddenly there was so much I wanted to know about all of them and I bombarded him with questions, which also helped to fend off the main one: if I went back to Cornwall for a visit, would it be as a single, or as one of a couple?

We talked our way through two more cups of coffee and a

couple of Danish pastries, explaining our lives to one another. Around us waitresses collected dirty crockery, cleaners swept floors, and travellers came and went, met each other or said goodbye – all oblivious to the fact that they'd been in the presence of the happiest girl in the world that afternoon, chatting animatedly to the person she hoped was the happiest man in the world.

There was so much to say that we jumped from subject to subject, then hauled ourselves back to an earlier topic not completed. My descriptions of Stace, Em and Don made him laugh, which sent a gratifying glow up my spine, and he filled me in with everything that had been happening in Cornwall. Soon, it was late afternoon.

"I'll need to be getting back," I said, "before everyone leaves the office – someone's bound to see me otherwise, and although it's not the most exciting job in the world, it pays the bills."

"When can I see you again? There still seems to be so much to say – and we haven't touched on you coming down to see Marsha."

I hesitated. Would suggesting we meet tonight seem too pushy? Too desperate?

"I'm free tonight," Adam said at the exact moment I was thinking of it. "But perhaps you're busy ...?"

"No – no, that would be fine. Why don't you come round to my place? We could eat and talk at more or less the same time – and you know where it is. Unless it's too far? I don't even know where you live."

"I took Chris's advice and moved – I've now got a glorified broom cupboard in Shepherd's Bush," he said. "But I'd much rather come to you, it's no problem."

"Will you still be in your leather outfit? It's very ... er ... becoming!" And it was. Leather trousers and a soft, tight jacket clung to the contours of his body, giving him a lean, mean look.

He laughed. "I was thinking of driving my car. I usually only use the bike in inner London so that I can get from one assignment to another easily – but I can still wear the leather if you want!"

His face took on such a suggestive air that I giggled, and felt myself flushing at the same time. "It's up to you," I said in the end.

"And do you want the *Milk Tray* this time?"

"Definitely – they're my favourites."

16.

I sat on the tube to Victoria, and then the main line train, in a trance. Everything had changed in just a few hours. The only thing we hadn't touched on was my divorce, and I hadn't told him anything about Will being back on the scene. There was no need. I knew now exactly what I was going to do: tell Will I didn't want to get back with him, and that our divorce would have to proceed. Will hadn't changed, I was certain of that now; he was still a wolf in wolf's clothing. For all his assiduous attention over the last few weeks, I'd had a deeper, more meaningful conversation and a more honest, caring exchange of views with Adam in just one afternoon. Even if our relationship went no further, I couldn't go back to Will knowing that I could feel so strongly about someone else.

I was so busy thinking all this through that I nearly missed my stop, but once home I went into overdrive. I whipped up a quick *bolognese* sauce which could be added to some pasta later on, popped a bottle of white wine in the fridge, and took some crusty bread out of the freezer to defrost while I turned my attention to my appearance. A perfumed bath and thorough hair wash was definitely in order, followed by the agonising decisions of whether the hair should be up or down, how casual the clothes should be, and wondering what sort of statement the flat would make about me. After all, this was the first time Adam would be seeing me on home ground.

If ever there was a time I needed the worldly-wise advice of the three girls it was now.

By ten minutes to seven I was pacing up and down, having decided on fairly casual black trousers and a scarlet funnel-necked jumper, with my hair loosely pinned on top of my head.

Adam turned up promptly at seven, with chocolates and flowers, but not the leather gear. "It gets too hot indoors," he confessed. Instead he was casually dressed too, in cords and a shirt, his hair – not as cropped as in the summer – just brushing the collar.

He followed me through to the kitchen and uncorked the wine while I put the flowers in water. Sarah was right; they were magnificent, filling every vase I possessed.

"This flat's a lot nicer than I thought it would be, from how you described it in the summer," he said, looking round approvingly.

"That's because I changed everything when I came back – fresh start and all that, plus it gave me something to do."

We walked back into the sitting room with our glasses, but drinking wasn't on either of our minds. Gently, Adam took my glass and put it aside with his. Then he took me tenderly in his arms and pressed his lips to mine. *Heaven!*

My arms had just reached up around his neck to pull him closer when there was an urgent knocking at the door.

Reluctantly I pulled myself away from him. "Stay right there," I said, huskily.

My heart sank when I opened the door and found Will on the landing.

"Sorry, I didn't ring the entryphone – I came in with Dave from upstairs, and I know you want a quiet night in, so I won't keep you, but I just wanted you to have a look at these …"

Before I could say a word he'd walked straight into the sitting room, stopping abruptly when he saw Adam, now with glass in hand.

"Oh, I'm sorry," Will said, "I didn't think you were expecting company."

"I wasn't," I said, but not before I'd noticed a dangerous glint in Will's eye. "Will, this is Adam, a friend I made on holiday in the summer. We bumped into each other today. Adam, this is my ex-husband, Will."

"Well, actually, still her husband – we haven't got as far as becoming exes yet," Will said, putting down a pile of stuff he was carrying onto the coffee table and extending his hand to Adam, and I could tell that he knew Adam was the 'affair' I'd mentioned. "Pleased to meet you."

"Hello. Allie's told me a lot about you," Adam said, his voice level, not looking at me.

Will's eyes scanned the room, taking in the flowers, the chocolates and the wine, but I was determined not to offer him a drink.

"I thought we were going to talk on Friday," I said pointedly.

"So we are," he agreed, turning his most devastating smile on me, "but I've come across a couple of lovely properties today that I thought you might be interested in, so, as you were intending to put your feet up, I thought you could take a look."

He placed a hand lightly on my shoulder before turning back to Adam. "I expect Allie's told you that we're getting back together again."

"We're doing no such thing!" I said hotly, before Adam could reply, as I shrugged off Will's hand.

"Oh, come on now darling, we can surely let good friends in on our hopes and aspirations, can't we? And after the way we've been getting on these past weeks, you're not going to let me down now, are you?"

"Will, this is neither the time nor the place!" I said through gritted teeth, my mind seething. Why, oh why hadn't I explained some of this to Adam this afternoon?

"No, you're right," Will said, his charcoal eyes darker than ever and completely unfathomable. "Forgive me. I'm sure you two have got lots of holiday snaps to swap, or whatever. I'll leave you to it. Nice to meet you – Adam, wasn't it?"

How patronising could you get! Before I could even follow him out to the hall and give him a piece of my mind, he strode out of the flat on his long, pinstripe-clad legs.

I shut the sitting room door after him and leaned against it, closing my eyes and taking a large gulp of wine before I opened them again to look at Adam.

"It's not like he made it sound at all," I began. "He and Lauren split up – well, he left her apparently. He's been angling for us to get back together again for weeks, but I wasn't convinced – I told him I'd think about it. But I'd already decided, *before* we met today, that I would tell him on Friday it really wouldn't work ..." I was aware that I was gabbling, but I couldn't stop myself; while Adam, as inscrutable as Will had been, gave no reaction.

"It's really none of my business," he said at last, "but if he's got as far as househunting for the two of you, he hasn't got the message yet, has he? He's left his mobile here, by the way."

It was sitting on the coffee table, on top of the apartment details. As his mobile was almost permanently attached to Will's left hand, he must have been more agitated than he appeared, to have left it behind. Just as I went to pick it up with an impatient gesture, the entryphone buzzer went.

"That'll be him back for it," I said. "I didn't think it would be long before he missed it."

I was tempted simply to throw it out of the window and hope it hit a tender part of his anatomy, but I managed to retain my composure and simply pressed the button to let him in.

"I'm sorry about this," I said to Adam as I left the room, to the sound of Will already knocking on the door.

But it wasn't Will standing on the step. It was a grey-haired man with a short but shaggy beard, probably in his late fifties – honestly, this was getting to be like *Noel's House Party!* You remember – where he used to be 'surprised' week after week as different celebrities turned up at his door. It would probably be Mr. Blobby next.

"Allie?" the man said.

I peered closer in the rather dim hall light, and then reeled back in shock.

"*Dad?*"

I couldn't believe it! My father – here, on my doorstep, completely out of the blue, after – how long?

I was so stunned I could only repeat myself: "*Dad?*"

His hair was a lot greyer than the last time I'd seen him, but then, it *had* been several years – I couldn't even think how many. His hair had been longer then, too, and he hadn't had the beard (which I'm not sure was an improvement), which had made it harder to recognise him immediately. His face was leaner, tighter, with many more creases around the eyes. But, even under the beard, his tentative smile was still the same.

He held his head on one side and diffidently held his arms out to me. "I know it's been a long time, but have you got a hug for the old man?"

I went towards him in a daze, uncertain whether I really wanted to hug this man who was so closely related to me, but felt like such a stranger. We kissed on each cheek, in the French way, before I pulled away from him.

"What's wrong? Are you in trouble? Has something happened?"

Various scenarios ran through my mind at the speed of light. Something must be terribly wrong for him to be here – perhaps the beard was an attempt to be incognito; after all, it had almost worked on me!

"Nothing's wrong, nothing at all," he said quickly. "I just wanted to see you – one of those impulsive things, you know."

"But why didn't you let me know you were on your way? – I

could have missed you altogether ..."

"I did try to call, last night, but apparently you've become ex-directory," he pointed out. "And I was too busy travelling today to try again, so I just trusted to luck."

I suddenly became aware that we were still on the doorstep.

"Come in, come in, I'll put some coffee on, get you something to eat," I said, ushering him through, sounding as if he'd trekked here from the Himalayas. My mind was in a whirl. I'd almost forgotten that Adam was still in the sitting room.

"Adam, this is my father. Dad, this is Adam, a friend I met in Cornwall in the summer," I said in almost perfect imitation of the earlier introductions. It seemed Adam was destined to meet all the people tonight with whom I had difficult relationships. We just needed Juliet to turn up now with Philip in tow to complete the happy line-up.

"Dad's just come over from France to see me," I explained as they shook hands, trying to make it sound as if he did it all the time, while also trying to remember exactly how much of my family background I'd revealed to Adam during our time together. Probably most of it.

Adam had stood up to greet my father. Now he said, "Perhaps I'd better go. You two will have a lot of catching up to do."

'Hmm. I'd obviously told him all of it.

"Oh! There's no need!" I cried. "You've only just got here, and we haven't eaten yet – there's enough for three ..."

"No, really. You might have Will back here any minute, looking for this, and there'll definitely be too many of us then." He picked up the mobile as he spoke. "Tell you what," he went on, "why don't I deliver this to him – save him coming back, or save you having to return it to him. What's his address?"

I groaned inwardly. This was going from bad to worse. What had happened to my hoped-for romantic evening with Adam, where the plan had been that all our earlier passion for each other would be rekindled? (I'll confess here that I'd even changed the sheets on the bed. Okay, I know at the start of all this I was looking down my nose at the idea of jumping straight into bed with someone you've just met, but this was rekindling, as I've already said. Completely different.)

What was worse, if Adam went round to Will's flat they might fall into further conversation about Will's and my supposed intention of getting back together again. But if I refused it would look as if I wasn't telling the truth when I said Will meant nothing to me.

"I'm sorry if I've intruded on your evening," my father was saying now to Adam.

Of course you've intruded on our evening! I wanted to shout at him. *Why couldn't you have turned up during all that time when I was on my own and desperate for a shoulder to cry on? Not now, just when I believed the tide was turning in my favour!*

"Not at all," Adam replied to him. "We were only going to swap holiday snaps, as I understand. We can do that some other time."

Ouch! ... I gave in, scribbled Will's address down on a piece of paper, and handed it to Adam. "It might be a bit out of your way."

"That's all right. I've got plenty of time."

Was that another dig? He wasn't given to making them, but I wasn't sure any more. I didn't feel sure about anything.

I followed him out into the hall.

"It would be all right if you stayed, you know. My father might only be here for a short while – you can never tell with him. We haven't even sorted out about seeing Marsha yet ... And I meant what I said about Will – it's all in his imagination ..." God, I sounded needy! But I just wanted him to kiss me again and tell me that it was all right, that he trusted me.

He shook his head. "As I recall, you've a lot of ground to cover with your father. He's not going to want to talk to you in front of a complete stranger."

His voice was firm, but kind – I think, I hoped. He waved the mobile at me.

"I'd better deliver this, or you'll have your ... er ... Will, back on your doorstep again. I'll be in touch."

And he was off down the stairs and out through the door before I could summon up the courage to shout after him for his phone number, or his address, or anything.

I went slowly back into the flat. How could one day have lifted me up so much, and set me down again with so many problems? I'd found Adam once more, or he'd found me, but I had no way of contacting him again. And now I had to face whatever problem my father had decided to present me with – because problem it would certainly be; I had no doubt about that. Impetuous though he was, I was under no illusions that he'd come all this way on a whim because he hadn't seen me for so long. Probably Yvon had fallen for the Builder's Bum of one of the myriad Gallic workmen that were always in and out of their house. Or, given his history, more likely my father had become bored with his French idyll, and done a bunk.

He was standing uncertainly in the sitting room, and my heart melted a little at the sight of him. This was the father, after all, who had given me most of the happy memories of my childhood, even if he'd also been the one ultimately who'd shattered them. And Marsha had made me see that I'd had a considerable part to play in our estrangement in recent years.

"I should have contacted you first," he said straight away. "I've messed things up for you."

I shook my head. "You didn't spoil anything. Will had already turned up and done that."

He raised a quizzical eyebrow, but said nothing.

"Coffee, wine, food first, or all three?" I asked him.

"Wine and a chat first," he said. "And then I thought we might go out for a bite to eat – my treat, of course."

I didn't reply to that directly, but poured him a glass of wine and we sat down opposite each other. I'd see how the 'chat' went first, before agreeing to a meal in public.

"So, how are things with you, Dad?"

He smiled. "I can see by the look on your face you really mean, *'why are you here?'* But everything's fine with me, you can rest assured. Yvon and the kids are great. Send you their love. I'm here because of you."

"Because of *me?* Why?"

He took a mouthful of wine and sat back. "Your mother called me when you went missing in Cornwall – she seemed genuinely worried."

"I hadn't gone missing! I just hadn't called her for a while because I wanted to have some time to myself!" I said hotly. "Juliet can't stand it if my ideas don't fit into some sort of game plan she thinks I should follow!"

"I know, I know," he said soothingly. "And I wasn't too bothered at first, until she phoned me again to tell me that she'd 'found' you and you were having a great time with the friends of an artistic lady descended from the great Stubbs."

"Oh," I said. "I didn't know she'd done that. She didn't tell me."

My father leaned forward, cradling his glass between his hands and staring at his feet.

"I realised then where exactly in Cornwall you must be, and that the 'Stubbs descendant' you'd met was likely to be … Marsha?"

He looked up at me, but I was silent.

He sighed. "And I figured if that was so, there was a high chance that at least one of you might remember things from the past which would lead to a realisation of who you each were. Which also might mean that you'd understood some of what went on many years ago – and I couldn't get it out of my mind."

He took a long slug of wine.

"Correct on all counts so far," I said softly.

"So then I kept thinking and thinking about both of you," he went on as if he hadn't heard me, "and how I'd let you both down. Marsha all those years ago, and then you, my precious daughter. I'd let this chasm develop between the two of us, and told myself that that was how you wanted it. But *I* was the adult. I should have made more effort to keep in touch with you, to find out what you *really* wanted."

He looked up, ruefully shamefaced. "Bit late in the day for all the guilt trips, I know. Bit late to blame it on a sort of 'male menopause' as well, I suppose, but then I always was an emotional late developer. Anyway, the guilt, anxiety, call it what you will, kept gnawing away at me over the weeks. I just had this feeling that I needed to see you.

"I would have come over when things went wrong with Will," he went on, "if I'd thought that was what you wanted. But the letter you wrote, saying that your marriage was over, well – it was a bit ... dismissive, I suppose."

He had a point there. The tight little letter I'd sent him had resembled the sort of formal notice you'd put in a newspaper.

But when I was younger and didn't cry when I hurt myself, you still recognised my need, I wanted to tell him, *and you still hugged me for being brave.*

Instead I said, "But you decided to come now."

He swallowed more wine before answering. "It dawned on me that if you had gone back to Tremorden, without telling Juliet, you were probably searching for something – some answers, some nostalgic reassurance, I don't know what – but it's what I'd done when I felt desperate all those years ago, and I suppose it struck a chord. So in the end I told Yvon all about it – I'd never really confessed to her how much I'd missed you before – and she said I should come over at once and tell you what was in my heart." He laughed shortly. "It sounded good in the French! ... So, here I am ..."

I nodded. So many questions were teeming in my head!

"And my mother?" was the one I started with. "Did you feel

bad about her, too?"

His head shot up. "What do you mean?"

"Well, as I see it, you walked away from Marsha, and you feel guilty about that. Your relationship with me has become distant, to say the least, which you now also feel guilty about, although I don't think that has been altogether your fault ... but when you couldn't get back together with Marsha, you walked away from Juliet as well. Do you feel sorry about that?"

I was surprised to hear my voice sounding so angry. So much for thinking I'd got my emotions under control.

"I wasn't the one who ended our marriage," he said quietly.

"But you were the one who left!" I cried.

"I know, I know. But it wasn't that clear-cut. Have you spoken to Juliet about any of this?"

I shook my head. "She doesn't know about Marsha. And all she's ever said about you leaving was, 'People change,' or something like that. So," I went on, with a hard smile, "you can get your version of events in first."

He took charge of the wine bottle and poured us both some more. "And you can decide what you want to believe," he said equally grimly. "But I haven't come all this way to fill you up with some cock-and-bull story. I could have just kept quiet and let you believe whatever your mother or anyone else told you."

I was silent, a trick I'd finally learned from Marsha.

He took a deep breath. "Marsha was the love of my life. The time we spent in Cornwall together was extraordinary. But I couldn't see how it could last forever – there must have been some fragments of the male provider underneath my hippy exterior, and I wanted to return to London to make a solid future for us. I didn't have Marsha's artistic talent, and I didn't want to spend the rest of my life living off her. So we argued, and I left. As soon as I got back to London, I met Juliet. She was the complete opposite of Marsha – petite, sharp, funny, materialistic, totally wrapped up in the London social scene. It was so easy to get caught up in the whirl as a way of forgetting Marsha."

What could I say? Hadn't I tried to do exactly the same thing since returning from Cornwall?

"Then, before we knew it," he went on, "you were on the way. We got on well enough – loved each other after a fashion – and Juliet was frantic that she'd be left on her own with a baby. So we married and, when you arrived, we were certainly happy for a time. We were both besotted with you, but I think eventually it just wasn't enough. Juliet hankered after the life she'd had when she was single, and she discovered that I wasn't as exciting or as ambitious as she'd thought I was. Can't say I blame her either – once you were here, my old feelings of wanting to be free of the rat race, free of the city, began to resurrect themselves and I didn't want the hectic socialising any more."

"But I don't remember any rows," I said. "That's why I felt so shocked when you left – I had no idea."

"No, there weren't many rows – not in your hearing, anyway. I suppose the best way to describe it is that we went our separate ways. Juliet went out more and more, busying herself with friends, while I resurrected my Bohemian tendencies – which drove her to despair."

"But you said she was the one who ended the marriage?" I queried.

He looked rather discomfited. "Your mother had lots of ... well, several anyway ... close friendships ..."

"You mean affairs?" I interrupted. "It's okay. You can be honest about it. I've played a lot of truth games since the beginning of the summer. I'm getting used to it now – I can handle it."

"Well, yes, there were one or two that went beyond the bounds of friendship," he admitted. "Then, eventually, Juliet said that she wanted a divorce – that I was holding her back from being truly happy ... that she'd found someone else ... etcetera, etcetera. I'd thought, when I stopped to think about it at all, that we'd continue to jog along together until you were older and then maybe we'd drift into some sort of separation. So her demands that we called it a day came as a bit of a surprise – stupid really, when I think how un-together we were."

I gave a short laugh. "Well, at least it's some consolation to know that I wasn't the only one it had taken by surprise! And was this why you fled with me to Cornwall?"

"I suppose it was – yes. Juliet was forcing me to confront my future, and I hadn't properly resolved my past. I took you down to Cornwall with some madcap idea that Marsha and I could get back together again and that I could have you with me if she was prepared to mother you. I didn't think Juliet was too knocked out by motherhood to mind."

"But it didn't happen that way – I discovered that from Marsha."

He smiled ruefully. "No it didn't. I did my usual bull-in-a-china-shop bit of expecting Marsha to be as fired up with the idea as I was, but she didn't want to know. I felt quite devastated. And then, when we got back, Juliet insisted that you should stay with her. She rattled on about how you shouldn't be uprooted from everything you knew ..."

"Hmm," I said, "I think she used much the same speech when she was divorcing Dan." I frowned. "But he can't have been on the scene when she wanted to divorce you?"

"No. This was a guy called Philip – but it all fizzled out after we'd separated. I think perhaps his wife found out, or something. I'm not sure, because I'd cut loose completely by then and gone to France."

Philip? Wow! So that's what she'd meant when she said they went way back!

It was time to readjust my thinking all over again. Since the summer my father had replaced my mother as the villain of my damaged childhood, but now I knew that Juliet was the bigger culprit – which I had been convinced of during my teenage years, but for the wrong reasons. Then, it had simply been my adolescent disdain and the sheer difficulty of living with her which had fuelled my conviction, but now I knew differently. I also knew now that there *were* no villains, just people making each other unhappy.

"The truth is," my father said, breaking into my thoughts, "that we should never have married in the first place – we were never truly suited. The only good thing that came out of it was you, and I even managed to mess that up."

I sighed, suddenly tired of all these Jerry Springer-type confessions of angst and error. I wasn't too sure about this touchy-feely discussion with my father, either, when the man I recalled – admittedly from a few years ago – would brush aside any navel-gazing with exuberance and stir everyone into doing something active to take their minds off whatever it was.

I was reminded of a TV jingle of my childhood that began: *'There are two men in my life ...'* Well, currently there were three in mine, all of whom were capable of reducing me to emotional turmoil. I made a vow to reduce that to two by the end of the week.

"Why don't we have something to eat?" I said brightly, "and catch up on other news – this is all too much at the moment."

He stood up, evidently relieved at my suggestion. "Where shall we go?"

But I shook my head. "I'd rather stay here, if you don't mind – I've only got to put some pasta on."

He seemed happy with that, and prowled around the kitchen and sitting room as I prepared the food, commenting on my choice of books and music, firing off questions about my life and answering my polite enquiries about my half-siblings in France. I did my best to be interested in the oldest boy's start at university and the prowess of the four following behind him, but it was difficult not to dwell on the fact that this was supposed to be a romantic evening with Adam. There was a contraction in my chest every time I thought that I might not see him again – especially if Will filled him up with more rubbish about us.

Unceremoniously plonking two plates of *bolognese* down on the table, another thought suddenly struck me.

"Have you made arrangements for staying anywhere?"

My father tried to look nonchalant, but there was a definite underlying sheepishness.

"Oh, I thought I'd find somewhere once I got here," he said airily. "There can't be too many hotels bursting at the seams in Purley."

"There aren't too many hotels in Purley, full stop," I said. I carried on eating for a while before making the obvious invitation. "I have a spare room here – you're welcome to stay."

Part of me would have liked to have stressed that his sudden arrival was too much of an imposition for him to be able to stay, to let him know of my indignation at his turning up after such a long time, but another part of me was tired of currently falling out with every man who crossed my threshold – and, after all, he was my father.

"That's very kind of you," he said, almost formally. "I don't want to be any trouble – I wasn't taking it for granted that you would put me up, you know."

I smiled, deciding after all that I didn't want there to be any more barriers. "You would have put me up if I'd suddenly turned up in France. Although, I might not have been so generous if I had some hot live-in lover!"

He smiled back. 'So ... Adam? Is he ...?"

"Just someone I met through Marsha," I said quickly, regretting my light-hearted remark.

There was a pause before he said, "And Marsha – how is she?"

I'd been dreading this question. In the end the only way to deal with it, I decided, was to be as open as Marsha herself would have been.

"She's still in Tremorden, obviously, surrounded by a band of people who love her to bits because she's mothered them all. Selling lots of pottery through the local shops, which visitors snap up because it's original and colourful – but the local people, or some of them anyway, are still a bit wary of her, even after all these years. Probably because she doesn't mince her words, and she's stayed a sort of 'free spirit' all her life – and she quite enjoys her acquired notoriety."

He grinned. "Yes, that sounds like Marsha."

I sighed. "But she's ill, Dad, very ill. She's not going to get better."

The grin disappeared. "What's wrong with her?"

I told him everything then. All about Marsha's illness and how I'd found out, and how Kate and everyone was determined to look after her. I told him how I'd first met her, how she'd helped me and what she had come to mean to me. I told him that she'd never married and how she'd sublimated all her emotions into helping so many damaged people.

But I didn't tell him about Anna. That was Marsha's secret, and it wasn't for me to divulge it.

He interrupted with lots of questions as my tale unfolded, but when I'd finished he sat, shaking his head wistfully.

"We parted very acrimoniously that summer," he said. "I always thought that one day we'd meet again and I could make things up with her."

"Well, if it's any consolation, I did exactly the same thing," I told him. "The reason for Adam being here earlier was to tell me that she's been asking to see me again."

The next words were out of my mouth before I'd even finished thinking them. "Why don't we go down together – both make our peace, while we still have the chance?"

He clutched at the idea eagerly. "Do you think we could? Would she want to see me after all this time, especially if she's very sick?"

I could remember her saying something about a list of people she would have liked to have seen again before she died. Surely my father would be on that list. Perhaps, ultimately, this was the only thing I could do for her.

"I'm certain of it," I said emphatically.

"When?" he asked, his old impulsiveness emerging. "Tomorrow? Could you come with me tomorrow?"

"Why not?" I said, catching his energy. "I'm only a temp. I've been off sick this afternoon. I can take a few days – they can only sack me!"

17.

We left in my little car straight after breakfast, despite the fact that we'd stayed up late talking. And, once in bed, I hadn't been able to stop all the events of the day from whirling round in my brain. I'd switch from incredulity that my father was here and we were reconstructing our relationship, to even greater incredulity that Adam had also turned up, to longing for him to be here right now with his arms around me, to anxiety that Will would have succeeded in persuading Adam that my future lay back with my ex-husband. And then I'd go back to the beginning and agonise about everything all over again, until sleep finally caught up with me and I did it all in my dreams instead.

Having left a brief message for Merrill, I cursed for the first time my lack of an answering machine. If Adam were to phone I wouldn't know about it, and he might not try too many times. On the other hand, of course, he may also be intending to visit Tremorden at the weekend ... it would be the perfect place to explain away any misconceptions Will had planted.

I pinned all my hopes determinedly on this outcome and gave my attention to my father, who had made a quick call to Yvon in impressively rapid French, with associated Gallic hand gestures even though she couldn't see him, to tell her of our plans – which, he reported, she was delighted about. My own French was nowhere near good enough to understand all that he had said, but if he really had told Yvon everything about Marsha, then she went up several notches in my estimation for giving our trip her blessing.

The first hour or so of our journey, as we battled our way round the M25 to join the M3, was taken up with my father's exclamations of how far the tentacles of outer London had infiltrated the Home Counties and how congested everything was. But once we'd left the worst of the traffic behind us he relaxed and began to tell me of his life in France in greater detail. This time I listened more closely and more receptively than I had the night before, because I was genuinely interested in promoting our new-found closeness, and also because I wasn't so worried about Adam. Cornwall was going to exert its magic and sort all that out.

"I wish, now you've got your own life a bit more sorted out, you'd come and stay with us again," my father said. "We'd both really like you to become part of the family."

"Perhaps," I replied, remembering afresh the adolescent feeling of being the odd one out amongst so much French-ness. "I'd have to brush up on the language, though – I know less of it now than when I was fourteen."

"Well, if you stayed long enough you'd soon pick it up again – or have lots of short stays, if you'd be more comfortable with that. It would be good for our lot, too, to get to know their English sister better."

The long talks I'd had with Marsha came into my head; I'd eventually come to recognise that I'd played at least an equal part in the estrangement from my father. What a lot of wasted time there'd been! ... And still would be, if he hadn't had a bad attack of conscience and I hadn't learned something about accepting olive branches.

"It's funny," my father mused, "but the life I've got now is just what I'd imagined I would have with Marsha. I've been very lucky to have found it with someone else."

Which got us to talking about Marsha again.

The nearer we were to Cornwall, the more she was on both our minds. It was only a few months since I'd seen her, yet I was still apprehensive about a reunion. She had looked so frail when I left – how would she be now? And would I be able to cope well enough not to let any shock at her appearance be apparent to her acute powers of observation?

I was also becoming almost as nervous as my father about their meeting. What if I'd got it wrong, and she didn't want to see him after all?

It was early evening when we finally reached Tremorden. Gwen Jarrett, of course, was closed for the winter, so we couldn't stay there – which was a pity, because Dad would have enjoyed her idiosyncracies. On the other hand it was just as well, because my hasty exit had been based on the assumed decline and possible demise of my parent. It would have been difficult to have turned up with one who was so obviously hale and hearty.

Instead, we booked into the Tremorden House Hotel, a much

grander affair whose lofty portals hadn't welcomed summer visitors in tatty shorts and T-shirts. Now, though, it seemed to be the only place offering rooms, and we were quickly allocated adjoining singles and offered a table for dinner.

"Excellent! This is on me!" my father exclaimed, signing up for a three-night stay. He'd already said that no matter how things went with Marsha, he'd like to look round for a day or two. I wondered if I could point out the difference in price between English and French establishments without offending him – he'd said that he was still doing translating work and some teaching, but I didn't know how much of a drain on resources his large family was. But I mentally shrugged it off. If he couldn't settle all of the bill after all, I'd be happy to chip in when the time came.

As soon as I was in my room I found Marsha's number and dialled it quickly, before the mixture of nerves and anticipation became too much. Marie answered on the second ring.

"Hello. It's Allie here – from the summer? I'm back in Tremorden for a few days and I wondered if I could call in and see Marsha? If it would be convenient?" I sounded horribly formal, as if I wanted to see her about an insurance policy.

"Allie? You've come!" Marie shrieked down the line. "That's great! Yes, of course she'll want to see you, you idiot, we all will!"

A wave of relief swept over me at her friendly tone and I acknowledged that my growing apprehension throughout the journey had been as much to do with facing the others as it had to do with facing Marsha. I should have remembered how non-judgemental they all were.

Marie was still speaking: "She can't hear me at the moment – I'm taking this downstairs, but she'll be so pleased when I tell her. Did Adam find you, then?"

"Er ... yes ..."

"So is he here with you?"

"Er ... no ... the thing is, Marie, that I've come down here with my father – he arrived suddenly from France. Umm ... I don't know how much you know about the circumstances ..."

"It's okay. We all know what happened. Does he want to see Marsha, is that it?"

"Yes. And I suggested he came down with me because of something Marsha said once about wanting to meet people from her past again – but I don't really know if that included him. How is she, Marie?"

It was her turn to hesitate.

"She's still fine mentally, apart from getting very tired, and then her words slur a little bit. Physically ... well, I think you'll notice that she's a lot weaker than in the summer. And there are good days and bad days, as you'd expect ..." She paused and I could imagine her biting her bottom lip, as she tended to when she was thinking hard about something. "Tell you what, why don't you both come over tomorrow – late morning, say, to give Marsha time to wake up and so on – and you see her first. We'll know then what sort of day she's having and you can sort of test the ground out – tell her you've seen your father again, or something – and then she might say how she'd like to see him. What do you think?"

It sounded like a good idea. "Who else is here?" I asked next.

"Just Kate and me at the moment, but Simon will probably be down at the weekend. And, I hope, Adam. Did you two sort yourselves out after all?"

I gave a dry laugh. I'd forgotten how forthright this lot could be. "We were starting to, Marie, but then my Dad turned up ... and other things ... it got a bit complicated. I don't know what he's doing now – I'll tell you about it tomorrow, if I may."

I relayed all this to my father over dinner in the hotel dining room, where we were the only diners, apart from a bunch of raucous middle-aged women who turned out to be the receptionists and clerks from the local health centre enjoying a pre-Christmas night out.

"Do you think Marsha will have as much difficulty recognising you as I did – because of the beard?" I asked.

He laughed and stroked the straggly growth. "You forget – this was part of the uniform for all self-respecting male hippies, along with Biblical locks of course. I only shaved it all off to become more respectable for your mother. Mind you," he went on ruefully, "it grew a bit more thickly in those days and it didn't look as if I'd spilt white paint in it."

We didn't linger too long over coffee in the lounge afterwards, the cosy wing armchairs in front of a genuine log fire making us both too drowsy. As we went to our rooms I gave him an instinctive peck on the cheek. "Goodnight, Dad."

He hugged me in return and I know for both of us the simple gestures marked a return to the old relationship we'd enjoyed. This time my night wasn't spent reflecting on what might have been, or even on what was yet round the corner. Instead I soon drifted off to sleep, thankful that at least one broken relationship had been salvaged.

The early part of the next morning was spent in a tour of the town, a bitter wind keeping us away from the sea-front, but we were both mindful of the time, and it was with a sense of relief that I eventually led the way to the house amongst the rocks.

Marie was waiting for us, greeting my father as if she already knew him rather than just of him, and flinging her arms around me with no hint of recrimination for leaving with no goodbyes.

"Kate's still upstairs with Marsha, but she won't be long."

The basement room which had been Marsha's workroom had been turned into a comfortable living area with sofas and battered armchairs, television and a hi-fi. There was a makeshift kitchen at the end where her kiln and wheel had been.

"It's given us a second living room when we're all together and we get a bit much for Marsha at times," Marie explained. "Her bed is in the main sitting-room now, you see, so she can't get away from us that easily."

Kate clattered down the stairs then, bursting into the room looking as lithe and gorgeous as she had in the summer.

"Oh, it's so good to see you," she said as we embraced. "And Marsha can't wait, so you'd better go straight up and we'll talk later. And don't worry about your Dad," she went on; "I'm going to pick his brains about how much nurses earn in France."

"Do you want me to come with you?" Marie asked, but I shook my head and started up the stairs.

My courage deserted me a bit as I tentatively pushed open the door, but then Marsha's voice came, almost as strong as I remembered it.

"I'm not coming to meet you – takes me too long to get settled again, so you'd better come straight in."

She was sitting just where I'd left her, but in a different armchair, by the window. This time, however, she was surrounded by the accoutrements of sickness, including an oxygen cylinder. Further back in the room her bed was partially hidden by a rattan screen. There was nothing gloomy about the room, though, despite the wintery day. Her bright pieces of pottery were still scattered about, there was a colourful rug over her knees and a log fire burned in the hearth.

As soon as she saw me, she simply opened her arms as I scuttled across the room towards her. There was a surprising strength in the hug that she gave me, but I couldn't hold her as tightly as I wanted to. There was no substance to her body at all. My hands covered the bony knobs of her spine below the sharp protrusions of her shoulder blades and, when she relaxed back in her chair and I took the seat beside her I could see that the skin on her forearms was almost translucent. It was like one of those children's books on the human body, where you lift up the first page and, underneath, all the system of blood vessels, in bright red and blue, are revealed.

But although the flesh was definitely weak, it was clear from her penetrating gaze that the light of her spirit was still shining.

"I'm so glad you've come," she said, her one hand, sinewy and mottled, still holding on to mine.

"I haven't brought you anything," I faltered; "... flowers ... I didn't think ..."

"Good!' she exclaimed, "You'd only have got chrysanthemums at this time of year, which I can't bear. They're funeral flowers – and I'm not ready for them just yet!"

"How are you?" I asked. "You look ..." Oh God, this was awful, floundering around for words that could sound positive.

"Terrible!" she said for me. "I know I look terrible, so it's just as well that I gave up on my looks long ago and don't have too many mirrors in the house! But I'm not too bad otherwise – all the drugs keep me pretty cheerful.

"And they've given me this wonderful chair," she went on. "Look!" Pressing some buttons on a handset made the chair tilt back, then forward again, and the footrest also moved up and down. "I call it my 'Thora Hird'!" she said, with something resembling her old alacrity.

She leaned forward conspiratorially. "The worst of it is not being able to smoke just when I want to – because of this thing." She indicated the oxygen cylinder. "They're afraid I might blow us all up, so I only have a cigarette under Kate's watchful eye when she's moved the thing out into the hall."

There was no point in denying the assessment of her appearance. Marsha wouldn't have stood for that sort of flannel.

"I wanted to get in touch ... after I left ... once I'd had time to think things through ... but I couldn't ..."

Her other hand covered both of mine. "I know, I know," she said soothingly, and it wasn't just a platitude. As soon as I was with this woman, I knew that she understood everything, spoken or unspoken. "It was a difficult day for us both – and for Adam. But you're here now – tell me what you've been doing. I've become such a recluse that the only excitement I get is demanding to know what other people are up to – and as I'm an invalid you have to humour me, you know!"

Her voice was still strong, but each sentence was punctuated by a sharp intake of breath which made the hollows in her collarbones tense and pulsate. It was obviously easier for me to do the talking, and I needed no further bidding. For the third time in as many days I chronicled my recent past, adapting it each time to suit the person I was talking to. I hadn't told Adam about Will, and I hadn't told my father about Marsha's lost child. This time, I stopped short before mentioning the arrival of my father on my doorstep.

Marsha was quiet for a moment after I'd finished, staring ahead.

"Are you tired?" I asked. "Do you want to rest?"

She shook her head. "I was just thinking, listening to you now, how different you sound from the first day we had a chat like this. You were so wounded and defensive then, but look at you now. You're working things out for yourself and starting to take charge of your life.

"But," she went on, turning her head so that I had the full force of her penetrating gaze, "there are still two things you haven't dealt with."

I might have known I wasn't going to get too long to bask in her approbation.

"What," she asked, "are you going to do about Will?"

I lifted my chin resolutely. "That's easy. As soon as I return to London I'm going to tell him there's no chance we can get back together again. I've realised I just don't love him any more – all the time I was in Cornwall I thought perhaps I did. And when he turned up again, there was the fleeting feeling that we might be able to reclaim what we once had. But now I know that wasn't really enough in the first place."

Putting it into words like that for Marsha made it more crystal clear than it had ever been before, and again I experienced a tremendous rush of release. I was free of Will, and of everything that had happened between us.

There was quiet for a moment, broken only by Marsha's laboured breathing.

"And the second thing," she said at last. "What about Adam?"

I didn't want to talk to her about him. If seeing us make something of our relationship was so dear to her, I didn't want to dash her hopes, at least until I'd had a chance to see him again and put him straight about Will.

"We didn't really get much time together. I think he'll be coming here for the weekend." My fingers were all mentally crossed. I took a deep breath.

"But there's something else I need to tell you about."

She raised a quizzical eyebrow but didn't speak.

"My father turned up yesterday at my flat. He got an attack of the guilts about me after talking to my mother, and decided he wanted to sort things out between us. That's why I didn't have much time to talk to Adam." I was rushing my words, wanting to get it all out quickly.

"*Ian?* Ian's back in England?"

I nodded, watching her face closely for any reaction. Had a faint trace of colour seeped into her gaunt cheeks?

I continued more carefully: "He worked out, from something my mother said, that you and I had met during the summer, and it made him want to put things straight between us all."

"You've brought him with you." It was more of a statement than a question. I nodded again.

"You mentioned once that there were some people you'd like to see again, before you ... while you still had the chance ... and I thought he might be one of them. But it's your call," I went on hastily, "you don't have to do anything you don't want to."

Her lips twitched into a wry smile that would once have been a guffaw. "Since when have I ever done anything I didn't want to?" she asked.

She was quiet for a moment, as if concentrating on getting more air into her congested lungs.

"Have you made your peace with him?" she asked eventually.

"Yes," I answered. "We talked a lot last night, and on the way down here. We both realised that things could have been very different if we'd tried a bit harder. And we agreed that we would in the future, so yes, I've made my peace with him."

She made an enormous effort to take a deep breath and exhaled it as slowly as she could. "Then I'd better do the same," she said.

"Does he know about me? How I am now?" she asked next, and I could see the anguish in her eyes.

"I've told him everything," I assured her. "Everything except about Anna. I didn't think it was right for me to explain about her."

Her head was bent, her eyes focusing now on her interlocked hands resting on the rug over her knees. "But he should know about his daughter. I've been thinking about this a lot since you left. It was one of the reasons I wanted to see you again." She raised her eyes to me. Their sapphire intensity had darkened and dulled with pain, but I didn't know if it was physical or emotional. "I was going to ask you to tell him about Anna after I'd gone – so that her little life would still mean something to someone ..."

"I'll do that for you, if that's what you'd prefer," I said quickly. "I didn't want to come back here and cause you any pain—"

She reached for my hand again and grasped it tightly. "You haven't, you haven't," she assured me. "And I want to see Ian again – you were right, he was on my list. It's just now ... with all this ..." Her other hand gestured at the oxygen, the inhalers and pills on a side table, and finally swept across her own wasted body. She gave a grim little smile, "I'm obviously more vain than I've always claimed to be!"

"He told me that you were the love of his life," I said quietly, because the old Cornwall tears were pricking the back of my eyes, "so he'll always think you beautiful. Besides," I leaned forward and covered her hand with my other, "he's grown a beard because he thinks that's how you'll remember him best, but it's very grey, and if his hair was a bit longer he'd make a wonderful Fagin!"

"Now I can't wait," she said with a hint of her old dryness.

"It doesn't have to be now, though – or even today. We're here until Sunday at least. You've plenty of time to think about it."

"No," she said, doing her best to square her shoulders, "it's time to grasp the nettle. Practise a bit of what I've preached to you lot over the years. And believe it or not, this is my best time of day. So send him up, but tell him to bring some tea with him – we're likely to talk ourselves dry once we get going."

I relayed the message to the three of them waiting downstairs, and my father was duly dispatched with a tray of tea and a brief squeeze of the arm from me. Kate insisted on going with him to check on her patient, but was soon back down again with instructions for us all to go out for a walk or else prepare something for lunch.

Marie had taken one look at my face once my father had gone upstairs and silently handed me a mug of tea.

"It's difficult if you haven't seen her for some time," she said after I'd taken a few sips. "When you're with her every day like we are you don't notice the changes so much."

"How much longer has she got?" I asked hoarsely, grateful for the warmth of the drink.

"The doctors can't say. It seems to be a race as to whether

the tumours in her lungs or her brain will get her first. Or whether, even though she's always been as tough as old boots, her heart will give up under the strain. And being Marsha, of course, she doesn't often admit to feeling worse."

Kate had rejoined us by this time and we set to, companionably preparing a thick vegetable soup for lunch, sticking to the downstairs kitchen area by mutual consent so that it wouldn't seem as if we were eavesdropping.

"Your father's a nice man," Kate told me.

"Yes," I said, "he is. The trouble is, I've spent most of the last decade unable to tell who was a nice man and who wasn't."

"Adam is," Marie said pointedly.

"I know," I replied. They both waited, just as Marsha would have done, until I was forced to fill the silence with an explanation of Will and the tale of what had happened last night – was it only last night?

"So Adam probably thinks I had every intention of going back to Will but was just having a little dalliance for the evening with him before I did so, and if he saw Will again when he took his mobile back, Will would have done his utmost to reinforce that idea. And I had no way of getting in touch with Adam, except to hope that he would be coming down here this weekend."

"Oh, for goodness' sake, what are you two like!" Marie exclaimed, throwing down the knife she was attacking a pile of carrots with, and snatching a piece of paper from the noticeboard on the side of a cupboard. "This is his mobile number. Ring him now and tell him that you're here and anything else you think he ought to know. Take the phone out into the hall, or the loo or somewhere, if you don't want us to hear."

I meekly did as I was told, sitting on the bottom of the narrow stairs, my heart pounding as I dialled the number, so that when I heard *'Welcome to the Orange answerphone service'* in a voice that sounded more plummy than orangey, it was a bit of an anticlimax.

"Oh. Hi, Adam, it's Allie," I said, in those strangled tones we all seem to adopt when leaving a message – as if the plummy woman is listening, and smirking at our ineptitude. "Umm, I just wanted to let you know that I've come down to see Marsha – with my father – they're talking now, which is good, I think – well, obviously better than if they weren't talking ... so ... er ... perhaps I'll see you over the weekend, or ... Anyway, thanks, 'bye."

Thanks? What was I thanking him for? The word was as instinctive and meaningless as always saying *sorry* when it's the other person's fault for whacking you with a shopping trolley.

Marie was scraping vegetable peelings into the bin when I went back into the room, whilst Kate was piling all the ingredients into an old-fashioned pressure cooker.

"Well," Marie said, "Did you speak to him?"

"He wasn't answering," I told her, "so I left a message. Shall I make some more tea?"

I saw a quick glance, which clearly said: *'Lay off for now'*, pass from Kate to Marie, and we fell to catching up on news about Simon and Chris and his family instead as we waited for my father to return.

After what seemed an age he appeared in the doorway, his face inscrutable.

"Everything all right?" I asked quickly.

"Fine," he said with a brief smile. "I think Marsha's ready for some lunch now."

We all joined her, making purposefully light-hearted conversation over the hot soup and rolls and pretending not to notice that she simply toyed with most of hers. Once or twice I intercepted a fond glance or a more unreadable locking of eyes between her and my father, and there were lots of sentences which began, 'Do you remember when ...?' But it was obvious afterwards that Marsha was tired. We promised to come back again later as Kate began to shoo us out of the room so that she could have a sleep.

There'd been no reference made to Marsha and my father's reunion but, after we had helped Marie to clear away, he said quietly to me: "Will you come for a walk?" – and I knew where we were going.

18.

In the shelter of a stone wall surrounding the squat old church that crouched, as if flattened somewhat by the persistent sea breeze which had attacked it over the centuries, at the top of the hill above Marsha's house, we found the tiny grave of my half-sister.

The baby's resting place was well-chosen, though, away from the wind, where it would be constantly warmed by the sun instead. A simple white marble cross marked the spot, with the words 'Anna Stubbs' and the dates of her birth and death inscribed in a circle in the middle of the cross. No sentimental words about gone to be an angel, or of the loss to the woman who had borne her; for what words could have said enough?

My father had said little on the way to the church, and now he stood there, shaking his head and repeating, "I had no idea ... no idea ..."

After a while we sat on a bench opposite the grave, tucked into the side of the church wall.

"If only I'd known, before I left, that she was pregnant, I'd never have gone. It was a silly way to split up anyway; we could probably have found a compromise if we hadn't both been so strong-willed. And if she'd explained ... when we came down here that summer ... things might have been so different. I should have picked it up, *somehow,* that she was feeling so hurt ... but I was only concerned about how *I* was feeling ..."

"And if it had worked out differently then, if we had stayed here in Tremorden with Marsha that summer, look how many other things wouldn't have happened. You wouldn't have had any of your beautiful French children for a start – and you can't wish that they'd never happened," I pointed out, suddenly feeling years older than my hapless, impetuous father. "It's easy to look back with the wisdom of thirty-odd years later, and think how differently we might have done things."

"Would you ever have told me?" he asked.

"Probably. But not while Marsha was still alive. I didn't consider it right to divulge something she'd kept to herself for so long," I replied. "I know finding out about the baby has been a shock for you, but are you glad you came here with me?"

"Of course," he said emphatically. "We were able to talk almost straight off – after the first few awkward minutes when we skirted round each other a bit. It's like all the years in between had fallen away. I just wish she wasn't so ill – we could have come here together ..." He stared again at the miniature grave.

"I wonder," I said a few minutes later, when we had talked a bit more about Marsha's health, "whether she will want to be laid to rest here, with little Anna."

He shook his head. "No, she doesn't. She wants to be cremated and her ashes scattered from the rocks outside the house. She doesn't really believe in burial, but when it came to the baby she couldn't bear to be parted from her in such a final way."

I raised an eyebrow at him, making him grin sheepishly. "We were always good at cutting straight to the chase, and that aspect of our relationship hasn't changed a bit. And, believe it or not, it was the sort of thing we'd discuss when we were rather earnest hippies – freedom of the spirit, and so on."

We left the church to wander up to Morwenna Terrace and the tall, narrow house, where my father told me tales of what had happened there during the days when he and Marsha had lived together with their little band. It had obviously been exciting and innovative at the time, but, compared to raves and Ecstasy and the sort of sexual shenanagins that are now commonplace, it seemed a time of innocence and naivety.

It was growing dark by the time we retraced our steps to Marsha's.

"Adam rang," Kate said as we were taking off our coats and scarves. "He's stuck on a job or something at the moment, but he'd got your message and said that he won't be able to come down until Saturday afternoon."

"Oh," I said, trying not to let my feelings show one way or the other. "Did he say ... was there any other message?"

"The mobile signal was bad," she replied, "I kept losing him. I did hear something about 'damned difficult to get hold of', but I don't know whether he was referring to himself or you!"

Simon and Chris had also been in touch – apparently

Thursday afternoons were always the time for touching base and letting the girls know who to expect for the weekend. Simon had been planning to come down on Friday anyway, but gratifyingly Chris, on hearing that I had returned, made swift arrangements to snatch a couple of days too.

I was pleased that they'd both be arriving the next day; it would help to make the waiting until Saturday afternoon a bit more bearable.

We spent a cosy evening all together in what was now Marsha's bed-sitting-room, initially poring over photographs of my father's family, which I didn't know he'd brought with him. Yvon appeared dumpier and plainer than I remembered her, which I'm sure Marsha was gratified to see, while the children ranged from gawky adolescence to healthy youth.

"You can tell they're all French, can't you?" Marie said in her straightforward way.

"How?" Kate asked.

"The haircuts," Marie replied promptly, "and the olive skin – you know, I bet they never get sunburned like we do, they just go a deeper shade – and their shorts and T-shirts never look quite as disreputable as ours."

My father laughed. "Do you know, it's years since I moved to France, and all the children were born there, of course, to a French mother – yet all the villagers still refer to them as 'the Englishman's family', so they would be delighted at your endorsement of how French they look!"

Marsha dispatched Kate to her bedroom then, for a large box stowed away at the back of a cupboard. It turned out to contain several photograph albums of the early years of Marsha and my father in their 'way out' youth. My father exclaimed in delight over them and then exchanged wry glances with Marsha as we three girls chuckled and made rude comments about the outrageous clothes and hairstyles.

"I'll have you know we were the height of trendiness," Marsha said, holding the box on her lap and trying to sound hurt as we giggled over the flared 'loon' trousers, the tie-dyed grandad vests, the wild hair and the men's droopy moustaches and Biblical beards.

Although there were moments when she was quite animated, I couldn't stop myself from casting surreptitious glances when she wasn't looking my way, because she was with us but at the same time not with us. Occasionally Kate would murmur, "All right?" – to which she would respond with a quick nod and a little smile, as if they shared a secret.

Eventually I realised it was loneliness that hung over her like a mantle. The loneliness of having to do battle with something none of us could be truly part of, no matter how willingly we poured our love and care over her. I'd never known anyone who was dying before, and hadn't appreciated that when it comes down to it, we all face our mortality in absolute isolation.

"Any more in there, Marsha?" I said loudly in a rallying tone to mask my despair.

"There's just one," she said, lifting out a small silvery-white book, like a wedding album, and putting the box to one side. For a moment she hesitated, a faint flush of colour appearing on the skin stretched tightly over her cheek-bones.

"I've never shown these to anyone before – but it would seem appropriate tonight. They're all the photos – fewer than I would have liked – of my ..." she smiled faintly at my father; "of *our* daughter."

She held the book out to him, which he took slowly. Marie stood up.

"This is a time for just the three of you. We'll look at them later, if we may. Come on, Kate, let's get some drinks made."

We huddled close to Marsha's chair as my father turned the pages. It wasn't necessary to say words simply to flatter Marsha; Anna had really been a pretty baby. Each picture was accompanied by brief details and dates and comments on her progress.

"I wanted to keep a record," Marsha explained to my father, "not just because she was my first child and I was besotted, but because I think I've known all along that somehow, at sometime, I would be able to show them to you."

He studied each photo intently. "She was so much like you, Allie, when you were a baby; it's like looking at the same child." He turned to Marsha. "I can see now how it must have knocked you – when we turned up all those years later."

Marsha nodded. "All I could see was Anna, not Allie – it hurt so much at the time."

She turned to me with a smile; the same smile as when she had first offered me her friendship: "But I'm very glad I've had the chance to see how she would have been as a young woman."

The girls came in with hot drinks for everyone, but the album wasn't opened again that night. We all knew there was too much emotion flying around, and we left soon after, so that Marsha and Kate could begin the arduous preparations necessary to settle Marsha down for the night.

There seemed to be no-one about when we returned to the house on Friday morning. The door from the terrace was unlocked, as it always was in daytime, but the workroom was empty, although there were breakfast dishes and trays still on the draining board.

"Hello!" I called up the stairs, reluctant to go up in case I was encroaching on a private time. After a few seconds Kate's head appeared at the top of the stairs.

"Hi!" she said. "We're a bit at sixes and sevens this morning – Marsha hasn't been feeling too well and Marie's popped out to the chemist. I'll be up here for a while, so just make yourselves at home."

"Is there anything I can do? Do you want a hand?" I asked, fully aware of just how useless I would be at bedside nursing if it were asked of me.

"No, we're fine, thanks. But you could put the kettle on," came the reply, much to my relief.

We washed and dried all the crockery and tidied everything away with little conversation passing between us, both glad of something to do while we chewed inwardly at our anxieties. Eventually Kate joined us, her professional, calming smile in place, but there was a strained look around her eyes as she took the cup of coffee I proffered.

"Does Marsha want one?" I asked, but she shook her head.

"I'll take her something up shortly," she said. "The morning ablutions have tired her today, so I'll let her doze for a little while."

She told us then that the doctor had been called out earlier in the morning because Marsha had woken feeling distinctly unwell.

My father and I exchanged guilty looks. "Do you think this has all been too much for her?" he asked.

Kate shook her head emphatically. "How can you say something is too much for someone who is dying anyway? Seeing you both again will have brought her more inward satisfaction than any number of 'extra' days of sitting in her chair feeling that there was still unfinished business needing attention.

"Anyway," she went on, "she wanted to see the doctor because she finally admitted to the pain having become worse. He wanted to put her on a morphine pump, but you know what she's like! She told him that she just wanted stronger tablets for now, because she was having a houseful of guests this weekend and a pump would get in the way! I'm not sure of what, but neither I nor the doctor dared ask! She said he could come back on Monday and she would reconsider!"

We shared a weak smile of relief that Marsha was still essentially herself.

"What did he think of her condition generally?" I asked.

"Well, she also admitted to a weakness down her left side, which she's had for days, but made out to him that it was something completely new. He thinks she's either had a slight stroke, or it's from the brain tumour. He's increased her steroid drugs, which help to reduce the pressure in the brain. Other than that," she shrugged, "she could have a massive stroke at any time, or simply fade away from us over a period of time ..."

We spent the rest of the day taking it in turns to sit with her, my father and me taking longer turns, to give Kate and Marie a break. When I was with her we'd spend a lot of time just gazing out at the sea, remarking on the antics of the seagulls now and again, and a couple of times Marsha fell into a light doze. I was struck once again by the solitariness of the battle she was waging against this assault on her body.

"Oh dear, I've done it again," she said as she emerged from one of her sleeps. "Was I dribbling?"

I assured her she wasn't. "That's good," she said, "because I've drifted off once or twice when Ian's been here, and I'd hate to dribble in front of him.

"It's funny, you know," she went on, "I've never been one for sleeping much – it always seemed such a waste of time, but now it sort of creeps up on me when I'm not expecting it, and it's completely welcome because my body gets so tired. I think one of these days it will just engulf me completely – I'll simply sink into one enormous sleep with a great sense of relief and I'll be too, too tired to wake up again. And that will be it."

"That doesn't sound too scary," I said, reaching for her hand, because *I* needed the comfort.

"No," she said, "it's not." Her face became more animated. "But I'm looking forward to this weekend enormously. I want to see you and Adam happy together, and I'm going to ask Simon to make sure he looks after Marie and lets her know how he feels. Then you'll each have someone, you see, and I can stop meddling in all your lives!"

I couldn't tell her, then, that it might not be as easy as that. Before I could say anything we heard new voices downstairs.

"That will be Simon or Chris arriving," Marsha said. "Go down and tell them that they can come up and see me whenever they're ready."

I don't know whether it was their welcome presence or the impact of the new painkillers, but she seemed to perk up during the rest of the day and managed an early dinner with the rest of us.

"Tomorrow," she declared, "should be a celebration! Adam will be here, which means it will be the first time we've all been together since the summer. And as Ian is here as well, it's going to be an even more special evening."

"Excellent idea!" Simon agreed in his usual enthusiastic way. "A pity it's not barbecue weather, because then I could do one of my specials! Tell you what though, Chris and I will prepare the food – give you girls a break – what do you say, Chris?"

Chris gave a mock moan. "As long as you're not badgering me to go to the shops at the crack of dawn! The only chance I get of a lie-in on a Saturday is when I'm down here."

"That's settled then," Marsha said with a little nod of satisfaction. "Now, if Kate will just help me to get back into bed, I'm going to be very rude and say that I only want Ian's company tonight. He'll be leaving on Sunday, so I want to be greedy and have as much of him to myself as possible. Is that all right, Ian?"

He smiled at her. "Your wish is my command."

"Good. And you youngsters can clear off and have a night out together while I've got someone else to take care of me. Make the most of it while you can."

"She's right, you know," Simon said, when Kate joined us after settling Marsha in bed with my father sat by her side. "We should go out and have a change of scene – especially you and Marie."

"I don't know," Kate said reluctantly. "What if something happens? She wasn't at all well this morning ..."

"Then Ian can call us," Chris said, as firmly as Simon. "If we only go to the Smugglers' we can be back in five minutes. Marsha will be very disappointed if we don't."

She was eventually persuaded, so that a short time later we were ensconced with pints of beer in the fuggy atmosphere of the Smugglers' Arms.

It was a different place from the bustling summertime bar, when the doors would be open so that sunlight could stream in and the air would be full of the pungent smells of oily rope and fish. Now, with the stout oak doors firmly closed against the elements, there was instead the smell of woodsmoke from the fire, with occasional accompanying gusts into the room when the wind blew down the chimney, mingled with the aroma drifting through from the kitchen where the famous bar snacks were prepared.

Now that the two girls had been persuaded to leave the house they visibly relaxed, and there was a determination on everyone's part not to talk about illness or sickrooms. I wondered if any of them was missing Adam's presence as much as I was.

With Marsha's words about seeing us happily together still ringing in my ears, I made more effort than anyone to keep the conversation light-hearted and irreverent and, to my own surprise and theirs, became the life and soul of the party.

Eventually, though, Kate began to get twitchy and it was time to go. They walked me round to the Tremorden House Hotel, with plenty of jibes about having come up in the world, but I didn't wait for my father to join me. I went straight to my room so that I could work out what I was going to say to Adam that would convince him, no matter what lay unresolved between us, that it was important to play the part for Marsha's sake.

19.

I spent a weary night full of Technicolor dreams, in which I was begging Adam to stay with me but he was determined to push me into Will's arms, whilst Marsha was in the background saying, "Don't they make a wonderful couple?" – but I didn't know who she was referring to. It was a relief in the end to get up, shower, and head for breakfast.

My father, though, who was already half-way through his meal, was in little mood for talking this morning, other than to tell me that he hadn't been very late getting back last night – as if he'd been out on a risqué date – and that Marsha had been fine when he left. It was a further relief to hear, or rather feel, the reverberations of a heavy tread that even the high-quality Wilton couldn't muffle and, on looking up, to see the amiable face of Rosie, erstwhile waitress for Mrs. Jarrett.

"Rosie!" I exclaimed, with sufficient vigour to have been addressing a long-lost school pal, "How lovely to see you! I didn't realise you work here as well."

"Only at weekends through the winter, on account of Mrs. Jarrett being closed until the spring, but even then I'll only be working weekends for her, 'cos I'm at college now," she announced proudly.

"That's great," I said. "What are you studying?"

"Nursery nursing. I've always loved little ones and babies, and you can make good money as a nanny these days, you know."

I had a fleeting image of Rosie's sturdy arms flinging a tiny baby over her shoulder enthusiastically and patting it soundly to bring its wind up, at which it would probably oblige simply from surprise at being handled so robustly. On the other hand, it would be a lucky baby to have such an unfailingly cheerful girl looking after it.

She was waiting for me to order – at the same time, I noticed, casting meaningful glances at my companion.

"Ah! Let me introduce you to my father," I said at once.

"Oh, but I thought he was ... but it was obviously wrong, wasn't it, 'cos he's here with you, so he can't have been, or he wouldn't be, would he? Here with you, I mean ... like he is ... now ... if he was ... and would you like tea or coffee with your breakfast?" she ended in a rush, her look of embarrassed perplexity matched only by my father's look of complete confusion at this garbled speech.

"I'll have tea and poached eggs with brown toast," I answered, before leaning towards her slightly. "Mrs. Jarrett may have thought I was leaving in the summer because something had happened to my father – but as you can see, she'd got it wrong, because he's fine."

She scribbled furiously on her notepad, before leaning towards me a little in return and saying, in a stage whisper, "I understand. And I think your ... Dad ... looks very nice."

And with a solemn wink that she'd probably learnt from Mrs. J. herself, she bounced off through the swing door into the kitchens.

"What on earth was all that about?" my father asked, so I told him about Lansdowne-Without-Sea-View, and Mrs. Jarrett and her funny ways, which brought us both back into a more talkative mood.

"Rosie, who has obviously been well-trained in the art of deduction by Mrs. J., seems to have decided that you must be my sugar-daddy instead of my real one, and that bit of news will probably be all round the bay by lunch-time," I finished.

"I'm more flattered than I can say," he said gallantly, turning the full charm of his smile on poor Rosie as she returned with my tea.

It was the sort of story we knew Marsha would appreciate, and the telling of it when we went to see her helped to set a cheery tone for the day as she happily regaled my father with more tales of how she had bolstered her own reputation for loose living throughout her years in Tremorden.

There was an air of bustle about the whole house that day, mainly instigated by Marsha's desire for a mini-party that evening, and Simon's Tigger-style approach to carrying out her wishes. It was good, though. It infected everyone with a sense of fun and purpose, when there had been a tendency to do the hushed voice and meaningful glances routine that seems to creep in around a person as sick as Marsha was.

Or perhaps my own heightened sense of expectancy over Adam's imminent arrival simply made me think that everyone else was as full of suppressed excitement as I was. It was excitement mixed with a dreadful feeling of apprehension, though. I couldn't rid myself of the notion that Will would have done his damnedest to convince Adam that our marriage was back on again and that Adam, however reluctantly, would believe that I was nothing but a shallow two-timer. I couldn't get out of my head what he'd said in the summer, about still being single because he found it hard to trust anyone. Would he trust me now? His other words were also reverberating through my mind – "It was always you, Allie."

He didn't arrive until late afternoon, when the curtains had finally been drawn against the inky blackness of the sea and I had begun to think that he wasn't going to show up at all. Simon and Chris, fortified by a couple of glasses of wine already, were making noisy preparations in the kitchen; my father was glued to Marsha's side, as he had been for most of the day; and the two girls and I were putting up novelty balloons around the room, on Marsha's direction. They'd been found in the back of a drawer and many of them had slogans like *Happy 18th Birthday* or *Congratulations,* but it didn't matter.

Marsha had undergone a two-hour rest, insisted upon by Kate, followed by lengthy inhalation of various drugs through a nebuliser and a dose of painkillers, and was already dressed in her best and in pretty good form.

"You didn't need to do all this for me!" Adam said theatrically when he appeared in the sitting room doorway, striding over immediately to kiss Marsha.

"We didn't – and I was beginning to think you'd miss it anyway," she said with a smile as he bent over her. "This is a 'welcome and farewell' to Ian here, who I think you've already met and you know all about anyway. He arrived with Allie on Thursday but he's going back to France tomorrow."

The two men shook hands before Adam advanced on the girls, saying something jokey which didn't register with me because of the drumming in my ears, before kissing them and then turning to me.

"I've brought you something," he said, fishing in his pocket.

"Oh?" The drumming was my heart thudding in my chest now. His very nearness was making me want to swoon into his arms like some Victorian maiden. He'd brought me something – a present, a love token, it didn't matter what, or whether I would like it, it was surely a romantic gesture which would signify that everything was all right between us ...

He handed me a top-up phonecard. "For your mobile. You've got to be the most infuriating person to try to get in touch with."

I didn't know whether to laugh or to cry. Infuriating! This didn't say anything I'd wanted to hear.

"I've left my mobile in London," was all I could think of in reply.

"Oh, well." He shrugged and them leaned forward to kiss me on the cheek as he had done with the others, but, aware of Marsha's eyes on us, I flung my arms around him and kissed him on the mouth. Which surprised both of us.

He drew back, his face never having been more unfathomable, his eyes questioning. But before either of us could say anything, Chris burst into the room.

"Put that man down, Allie, and give the poor devil a drink. He's got a bit of catching up to do. How y'doing, mate?"

He was carrying a tray of glasses, and was followed by Simon with a bottle of champagne.

"I know it's quite early," he said, "but the food will be ready by about six, as I figured Adam here would be starving, and I'm always peckish by then anyway, so let's get started on the pre-dinner drinks."

We all grabbed glasses enthusiastically and pretended that eating early was an excellent idea rather than acknowledge the fact that by nine-thirty Marsha would be too tired to continue.

When our glasses were filled, my father stood up.

"I'd like to propose a toast," he said solemnly. "To old friendships which last forever," he gave a little bow to Marsha, "and to new friendships which should do the same. Thank you all for making Allie and me so welcome this year, and, I hope, for many years to come." He raised his glass high. "To friendship!"

"To friendship!" we all repeated.

"That was a lovely toast," Marsha said into the slight silence which followed. "But now for goodness' sake, someone change the subject or Simon will get that dreadful guitar out and threaten us with *Auld Lang Syne!*"

"What a brilliant idea!" he exclaimed. "I must look for it later on, but I'm afraid I can't oblige now because kitchen duties call! Adam, perhaps after you've taken your things upstairs you and Ian could drag the dining table into the middle of the room, and bring in a couple of extra chairs from the hall. This isn't going to be a suitable meal – nay, *feast!* – to be eaten from our laps."

He bustled out to the kitchen, but was soon back to claim Chris, who was chatting to Adam and Marsha.

"Honestly!" he said, "If I don't watch him all the time he downs tools and expects me to do it all! I bet Fanny Cradock never had this trouble with her Johnny!" And with a camp toss of his head he shoo'ed Chris out in front of him.

"*Who* is Fanny Cradock?" asked Marie.

"I've no idea," Kate answered.

"Babies!" Marsha laughed.

"Think Delia Smith – or Jamie Oliver," added my father, and a soft 'ahhhh!' filled the air.

I moved over to a corner of the room to carry on with the balloons, and soon felt, rather than saw, Adam standing beside me.

"We need to talk," he said quietly as I stood on a chair to pin a bunch of balloons to the picture rail.

"I know," I replied, stepping down but keeping my eyes to the floor. I couldn't bear to see any condemnation in his face. And it could take some time to convince him, if I could at all, that I had no intention of going back to Will, no matter what. "I need to explain everything ... about Will and me ... but not now. Marsha is hanging her hopes on we two getting together and I don't want to disillusion her in any way ... not this weekend, when she's so happy to have my father here, and us all together, like the summer ... could we just go along with it ... please? Just for the weekend?"

"I think I can manage that," he said levelly, but, without looking at him, I couldn't read anything into his voice.

"Thank you," I said quietly, then more loudly and cheerfully: "Just a few more over here – come on."

Moving the chair towards the opposite corner of the room, I just managed to hear him say: "But as soon as we're back in London, we talk." This time there was no mistaking the steeliness, which made the thudding return to my chest.

He was as good as his word, though, staying close to me throughout the evening, smiling winningly in the way he had in the summer when I'd first marvelled at his good looks, or casually putting his arm round me, or catching hold of my hand, or standing very close and whispering to me. Mundane words every time, as it happened, but I'm sure we put on a sufficiently good show to fool everyone that this was real. Occasionally I even relaxed enough in his arms to fool myself.

Marsha was dressed for the occasion in a long crushed velvet dress in midnight blue, with a beautiful fringed shawl around her shoulders.

"*Biba,* circa 1965," she told us, fingering the dress. "I've kept it all these years because it was the only dressy dress I possessed then that looked classy, and I've never found one I liked more. Of course, I had more bosom to fill it in those days, and I used to wear it with my hair up and a thin black velvet choker round my neck. Do you remember, Ian?"

It was clear how painfully thin she was, because the dress hung on her, even though it was probably only a size ten; but you could still see how it brought out the colour of her eyes.

The table was finally ready, and the food brought in with much ribbing of Simon and Chris, but it was in fact remarkably good. Marsha stood up with the intention of walking to the table, but after a few seconds to steady herself she said, "Oh dear, it suddenly seems a long way away."

Her words created one of those moments of stillness, like when the band stops playing when you weren't expecting it and your lone voice suddenly fills the air. As if a director had shouted 'Cut!' we all stood there, shocked into immobility as the true extent of her frailty was brought home to us. The Marsha who had strode purposefully across the beach that first day I met her with such *joie de vivre* was now struggling to will her legs to cover a yard of carpet.

My father broke the spell. With one swift movement he scooped her up in his arms and carried her, not to the head of the table, but to the centre, so that we could all cluster round.

"I told you to go easy on that champagne," he said. I'd never loved him more.

"Isn't he masterful?" Marsha murmured, as he lowered her onto the chair, her eyes, still full of such determination, challenging us not to feel sorry for her.

We all began to talk at once then, of course, piling food onto our plates and replenishing our glasses, laughing at any witticism, no matter how weak, until we were comfortable again. The table was groaning under a variety of dishes from simple pastas to more complicated things wrapped in vine leaves.

"You have to try a little from each plate," Simon instructed everyone, placing tiny morsels himself on a plate for Marsha, who managed quite a few mouthfuls before pushing the rest around like a child trying to hide her peas under the mashed potato.

"My compliments to Fanny and Johnny," Adam declared

after his second plateful, raising his glass to them as his other hand, resting on my shoulder, burned through the fabric of my dress. "And we must just be thankful that Simon didn't decide to be the Naked Chef!"

Afterwards, in the general hubbub of plates being carried out to the kitchen and Simon being allowed to find his guitar as reward for his culinary efforts, I managed a few moments alone with Marsha.

"So," she said, "everything is going well between the two of you."

I didn't know if it was a question or a statement, but I forced myself to face her searching gaze and, for the first and only time, I lied to her.

"We're fine." I smiled. "Absolutely fine."

Our eyes held for a few moments before she nodded towards my father. "It's been a wonderful few days. Thank you for bringing Ian to me."

"I'm glad it's worked out so well. I did wonder on the way here whether it might have resulted in some verbal fisticuffs."

She grinned, almost like the old Marsha. "There were times when we would literally throw things at one another – although I always tried to make sure we only used pots which were flawed!

"The days have gone quickly," she went on, "you'd think, sitting here all the time, they'd go slowly, but they don't. Sometimes the nights are interminable, but not the days. I'm going to miss—"

She bit her lip and didn't continue.

I wanted to tell her that everything would be all right, to erase the stricken look that one could glimpse when her guard dropped momentarily. I wanted to say that we'd be back – me, my father, Adam, maybe in a few weeks, before Christmas, whatever. But there was no point. We both knew that it was doubtful whether she would see another Christmas and we both knew that nothing and no-one could influence the inevitability of her decline.

She took a few gasping breaths and gathered composure.

"I still haven't spoken to Simon properly – you know, about Marie. It's on my mind that I should – while there's still time. So I want you to do it for me."

"*Me?*"

"Yes. I want you to have a word with Marie, not Simon. Simon will devote the rest of his life to her, I know that. But she needs help to accept him. Please – try to talk to her – *tonight.* I think it needs to be done tonight." She spoke urgently; her breathing was becoming more laboured and there was a blueish tinge to her lips.

"Let me get Kate," I said, half rising in my chair, "I think you need some of your inhaler stuff ..."

But she stayed me with her, hand grasping my wrist, her eyes demanding what her breath could not.

"I'll do the best I can," I promised, to which she finally nodded before relinquishing her grip to let me fetch Kate.

The inhalation revived her sufficiently to be able to enjoy the rest of the evening, albeit with delicate oxygen 'nasal specs', as Kate called them, lodged in her nostrils to aid her breathing. But, as we'd all known, within a few hours she'd had enough. We tactfully withdrew to leave her to Kate's ministrations, but she insisted that we each return once she was propped up in bed, to say a proper goodnight.

It was my opportunity to speak to Marie, which in some ways I was relieved to do as it gave me something else to think about other than Adam's nearness. Part of me felt proud that Marsha had asked me to act on her behalf. I had a cosy vision of Marie and I having a girly heart-to-heart, after which she would be so convinced of her and Simon's future together that she would immediately declare her undying love for him. The violins were already playing in the background. When she went up to her room to fetch a cardigan I followed her, rehearsing a dozen different ways of opening the conversation, but in the end I knew that only straightforwardness would do.

"Can I come in?" I asked from the doorway. "Marsha's asked me to talk to you."

"Marsha has?" She swung round from her wardrobe, a wariness immediately in her expression. "What about?"

I advanced into the room and plonked myself firmly on the edge of the bed whilst she perched on a wicker chair.

"Simon." I said simply. "You know what Marsha's like, ill or not, she misses nothing. She's watched Simon caring for you, caring *about* you, and she thinks that deep down you feel the same, but won't admit it ... or something like that ..." My confidence was ebbing as Marie's face hardened, her eyes boring into mine.

"Marsha doesn't always get it right, you know."

"Maybe. But she asked me to talk to you, so I promised I would, although –" I tried a weak smile – "I'm not really sure what I'm supposed to say."

"You're supposed to tell me that it's time I rid myself of my antipathy to sex; to being touched by men in any but the most brotherly fashion; to realise that not all men are bastards like my father; and that if I relax enough with the right man, I will get to enjoy it." Her voice was as hard as her face. "Sometimes Marsha doesn't know when to stop interfering – and I don't think it's any of your business. It's for me to deal with."

Okay ... So maybe the girly chat would be a bit harder than I thought. Hold the violins.

To be fair, if I'd been as brutalised as Marie had, I don't think that I would have wanted any truck with men either ... except this was Simon we were talking about, and you couldn't meet a gentler soul ... and I'd promised Marsha I would try.

"You weren't above interfering between me and Adam," I persisted, my voice rising indignantly, "and technically that was none of *your* business – but you were anxious to stop Marsha fretting. I'm just trying to do the same thing. And you're plainly *not* dealing with it, or Simon wouldn't still be living in hope and you wouldn't still prefer to be without a man in your life ... and using horses as a substitute!"

Nice one, Allie. Start to sound angry within two minutes, and hint at a bit of bestiality while you're at it. It was at this point that I decided to cross counselling off my list of possible future careers.

"Do you think I haven't heard all this before? From people who've known me a lot longer than you have. Look, I appreciate your concern, and I know you're trying to do right by Marsha, but things are fine as they are. They probably don't seem it when you're just visiting, but with all due respect, you really don't know what you're talking about!"

Her voice was angry too, but all I could hear was the patronising *'you don't know what you're talking about'* – which was probably true, but who ever cared about truth when they felt patronised? Besides, I was getting fed up with all this relationship stuff; me and Will, me and Adam, Simon and Marie, me and my father, Marsha and my father – it was all too much, especially when I'd consumed more white wine than was good for me. And Marsha was dying.

Suddenly I was spoiling for a fight.

"What *you* don't realise," I said, standing up and jabbing my finger at Marie, "is that sometimes those of us who are merely *visitors* can see things a bit more clearly than you lot who are here all the time! The only thing Marsha has done wrong, as far as I can see, is to give you all too much support – there's a sort of invisible umbilical cord still attached to each of you that keeps you dependent on her. But at least all the others have seen the need to move away, move on, make that cord as thin as possible, learn how to cope with life on their own, but where have you strayed beyond the safe confines of Marsha and Tremorden?"

"I don't need to go anywhere else! I'm happy as I am!"

"Are you? Are you *really?*" I queried. "Happy to live out the best years of your life without ever experiencing the highs and lows of a proper relationship? Without the prospect of having children one day?

She didn't answer me, merely stared at my vehemence.

"So what," I asked savagely, "are you going to do when Marsha's dead? Are you still going to expect Simon to be here for you, whenever you want?"

She'd turned white at these words, upon which I spun round, intending to make a grand exit. But she stopped me with a quiet, "I do care about him, you know – I care about him a lot."

I turned back. "Then either do something about it, or put him out of his misery and send him on his way so that he can meet someone who can give him a proper life!"

I left quickly, too charged up to take much notice of her stricken face, running down all the flights of stairs until I reached the basement. I didn't want to go in to Marsha, or see any of the others – including Adam – until my anger left me.

It evaporated pretty quickly when I let myself out of the house onto the cold terrace. Coming in off the sea whooshing below, the whip of the wind carried faint tangy spits of salt water that stung my burning cheeks. All of a sudden the awfulness of what I'd just said swept over me.

I'd done it again. Turned up here, made the most of everyone's hospitality, including this time their kindness to my father, and ended up having a row with one of them. And how could I do that to Marie, who'd made so much effort this week to befriend me and grow closer to me than she ever had in the summer? How could I presume to tell someone else how to run their life, when I continued to make such a botch of running mine? Talk about seeing a splinter in another's eye and ignoring the plank in one's own!

I began to shiver, but it wasn't just from the cold night. I forced myself to stay where I was and think about my motives for becoming so unreasonably cross with Marie.

It didn't take me long to find the reason – I was jealous!

Jealous of Marie because, seemingly with little effort on her part, and certainly no encouragement, she had the unstinting love of a good man who seemed prepared to wait for her forever. I dug deeper and saw that I was also jealous of the quiet unassuming life she led here under Marsha's wing, whilst I had returned to London and struggled, for the most part unsuccessfully if you looked at it closely, to make a new life for myself.

I wrapped my arms around myself and buried my head on my chest in shame. Shame that I could feel jealousy for a girl who had experienced more violence and degradation than I would encounter in a lifetime ...

The door opened behind me, throwing a shaft of yellow light across the terrace onto my back. I felt a presence beside me, but even Adam would be no comfort to me at the moment – I couldn't even turn to face him.

But it was Marie. We stood side by side, staring unseeingly into the night.

"Are you all right?" she asked eventually.

"I should be saying that to you," I mumbled. "I don't know why I let rip like that – it was unforgivable ... I'm sorry ... truly sorry ... I—"

She interrupted my miserable apology. "You were right. About everything. I know that. I've known it for ages, although," there was a glimpse of white teeth in the darkness, indicating a smile, "no-one has ever said it to me so vehemently before! I've usually gone all defensive – even with Marsha – and they've backed off, or trodden gently around me, 'remembering my past', and all that."

I cast a swift glance across at her, but she was looking out towards the skyline again. "I don't seem able to do 'treading gently' very well," I said.

"You were right about the umbilical cord, too. It's a bit of blather really that we all gather so assiduously to make things good for Marsha – we all need to be here for ourselves just as much."

"So would anyone who'd been cared for in the way Marsha's cared for you," I pointed out. "It's what anyone would feel about their own mother –" the thought of Juliet and what a terribly demanding invalid she'd be intruded here – "well, unless you had a mother like mine, that is. But you would if Claire Rayner was your mother ... or Marsha."

"I still see my mother from time to time," she said, with perhaps just a hint of wistfulness. "But there's no feeling between us. I think she just sees me as the troublesome child who caused her marriage to break up."

"I'm sorry."

She shrugged. "It's probably easier for her to believe that, than confront the fact that she knew what was going on and did nothing about it."

"I meant about everything. Truly."

"It's all right – really. I just don't think I can change, not now." She turned to me with a smile. "But you and Adam seem to have sorted things out?"

I smiled back ruefully. "We're simply both good actors. For Marsha's benefit, again. He wanted us to have a heart-to-heart, but I chickened out. It's still threatened for when we're back in London, though – and I don't have a good feeling about the outcome."

I could see her smile widening. "Then we're both hopeless cases aren't we?"

I nodded.

She caught my arm, "Come on, let's go and say goodnight to Marsha together."

Marsha was already quite sleepy, so that when I said I'd see her tomorrow, before we left for London, she closed her eyes and just gave a brief nod. "It was a lovely party," she murmured. She still wanted my father by her side though. "It's the closest I can get to persuading him into bed with me, now that he's a respectable married man," she managed to joke feebly, in a voice which was more slurred than usual.

I waited for him downstairs with the rest of the gang, but I gave up continuing the pretence with Adam and he made no move towards me. The others seemed to sense my reluctance to join in, too, leaving me to sit cradling a cup of tea whilst they talked idly, and argued gently about which video to watch.

Despite Marsha having seemed so tired it felt an age until my father joined us. "She's fast asleep," he told Kate, looking pretty washed out himself. "I don't think you'll need to go in to her until the early hours at least."

20.

It was raining heavily as we made our way back to the hotel, where my father insisted that we have a nightcap. "Stop you catching a chill," he said. "You're soaking – and I'm not much better."

The rain seemed to have woken him up, imbuing him with a restlessness that had him watching the people coming through into the lounge from the dining room, dressed restrainedly but definitely in their best for dinner on a Saturday night. His eyes flitted from one to the other as he swirled the brandy around in its balloon, but he didn't appear to want any riveting conversation from me.

"What time do you want to leave tomorrow?" I asked in the end, realising that now was not the time to embark on *The Origin of the Species,* or similar intellectual repartées.

"Umm ... whenever it seems right ... or when you want to ... presumably you'll be going into work on Monday?"

"I think I'd better, or I won't have a job left to go to. When will you go back to France?"

"Sometime on Monday ... yes, Monday," he said, as if he'd only just decided. He gulped at his brandy, which I hadn't known was a drink he liked, but then there were still lots of things I hadn't learned about him by my teenage years.

I finished my Bailey's and decided to head for my room. "Too much wine and good food," I said, raising an enquiring eye at him.

"I think I'll stay and have one more of these – I don't feel quite ready for sleep yet."

"Oh! Do you want me to stay a bit longer?" I asked dutifully, although my body was yearning for bed.

"No, no. I'm going to sit here and do a quiet bit of reminiscing – and work out how I'm going to explain it all to the children when I get home!"

I was in a deep sleep when the knocking came on my door, so that it took me some moments to emerge from the layers of slumber before realising what it was. I thought it must be the middle of the night, but I noticed as I staggered towards the door that it was 8 a.m.

My father was there, already dressed.

"Chris has been on the telephone," he said. "He thinks we should go over."

"Oh." The sleep-dryness in my mouth suddenly spread to my throat. "Did he say why?"

He came into the room, taking my hand as he did so and drawing me down onto the side of the bed.

"Marsha died. Last night. In her sleep. It was – would have been – very peaceful."

It didn't matter that we'd all known it was going to happen. Shock-waves ran through my body at his words, flooding me with heat before leaving me cold, very cold.

"How? – was she—?"

"Kate found her apparently, when she went in to check on her a few hours ago. They didn't think it was worth getting us up in the middle of the night."

I nodded, several times, and swallowed hard, before darting ineffectually about the room, trying to concentrate on finding clothes, thinking what to do. "Right. Okay. I'll be ready in a minute. I'll just … um …"

My father stood up and grasped my hands again. "Take it steady. There really isn't any need to rush."

But there was. There was a great need to be there, at the house, to be where something of Marsha might still linger, and be with everyone else who was affected by her death.

"I'll wait for you downstairs," my father said.

I was half-way to the bathroom with a bundle of clothes in my arms. "No – no, please stay here! Wait for me – please."

I stumbled towards the bathroom again, then stopped and turned back to him once more. "Are you – all right?"

He nodded. And then I was in his arms and we were holding each other tightly, so tightly. "Go on," he said after a few minutes. "Get dressed. I'll stay here."

We drove round to the house through empty Sunday-morning streets whose hush seemed appropriate to the situation. There was the same hush within the house, despite there being so many of us. We all hugged each other quietly and, when Adam's arms came round me, as two friends who shared a great sorrow, it was all I could do not to break down.

Marie's eyes were red from tears but Kate was pale and composed, relying, I guessed, on her professional response to death. Mugs of something – I don't know if it was tea or coffee – were thrust into our hands as we asked the inevitable questions of what had happened during the night and what would happen next.

"The doctor's been," Kate told us. "He's signed the death certificate because he'd only seen her the day before and he'd felt she could go at any time. The undertakers are coming later, and the vicar's going to call round after morning service."

"The vicar?" my father said in surprise. "I didn't know Marsha had anything to do with the church – she had very little time for it when she was younger."

Simon gave a hint of a smile. "Apparently she wanted to hedge her bets. She still wasn't sure that there was anything in religion, but she'd opt for it, just in case!"

"Umm ... she's still upstairs, obviously ... do you ... would you like to see her ... before the undertakers come?" Kate looked from me to my father. I looked to him too. I'd never seen a dead body before.

Adam must have read my expression. "She looks very peaceful," he said quietly. "Kate's care again. There's nothing to be upset about."

Kate bit her lip. "I just wish I'd been with her – I can't get the thought out of my head that she was on her own ... she might have needed something ... someone ... she might not have been able to call out ... I don't know ..."

Adam broke in again, more harshly this time. "You mustn't beat yourself up with that idea. The doctor said that she'd either had a stroke or her heart had stopped. She wouldn't have been aware of what was happening."

"I'm sure Adam's right," my father said. "I'd like to see her, please."

"I'll come with you," I said, remembering what Marsha had said about sinking into 'one enormous sleep'.

As soon as I saw her I realised why Adam had said there was nothing to fear in seeing death. Marsha simply wasn't there. Her body was, her face so calm and free of the furrows of pain that you could see how striking she would have been in her youth.

But that was all. Wherever Marsha was now, she wasn't here, in the room that had been her whole world for the past few months.

Someone had found some winter-flowering pansies and placed them on her pillow, their colours deep and vibrant against the pallor of her face. I leaned over to kiss her cold brow, whispering words of farewell, even though she wasn't there, before moving away to make room for my father.

On the other side of the rattan screen the room was just as we'd left it the night before. The dining table still dominated, with a half-empty bottle of wine and some used glasses still in its centre, and crumbs on the carpet beneath. The chairs and sofas still had the indentations of our bodies, and beside one was a crumpled napkin. It was a harrowing, mocking reminder that the party was now truly over.

I dragged a chair across the room and began to take down the balloons, with their incongruous festive messages. I could almost hear my mother saying, "What will the vicar think if he sees the room in this state?" Marsha would have found such a concern amusing and probably left everything deliberately, but I couldn't stop myself from tidying up.

Deep in thought, I wasn't aware that Adam had joined me until he spoke.

"Are you okay?"

I nodded. "You were right. There was nothing to fear. Thank you."

I handed him the balloons as I took them down, but said nothing more. I was worried that if I began to tell him I was discovering bereavement gave you a permanent feeling of having been kicked in the stomach, and a sense that the feeling would never go away, I might fling myself at him and beg him never to leave me, which wouldn't have been appropriate at that time at all. I concentrated hard on my self-imposed tidying task instead, and when my father joined us Adam went downstairs.

"I think we should still leave this afternoon," my father said. "There'll be nothing more we can do here by then."

I nodded my agreement. The house already felt altered from Marsha's death – I had been wrong to think there would still be something of her here.

For the rest of the morning things happened in sporadic bursts. There would be conversations about how thankful we were that we'd all been together, and what a great weekend it had been, how happy Marsha was before she died, and thank goodness she had seen Ian again, but these would peter out as one or other became upset, to be replaced by more desultory comments or yet more cups of tea or coffee.

Then there were the painful minutes which we'd all been secretly dreading, when the undertakers arrived to remove Marsha's body – which, although it was agreed that her spirit had gone and the body that remained wasn't really her, still had us clutching each other as the men struggled with stairs and steps. The arrival of the vicar, who seemed as surprised to have been called as we were, was less traumatic but marked out the need for plans to be made, which was a bit of welcome relief in a way.

By early afternoon the funeral had been provisionally arranged for the following Friday, providing the crematorium could be booked for the same time, and Simon and Chris were set to wade through Marsha's bulging address book of friends and acquaintances.

"Are there really no relatives?" I asked.

"She was the only child of only children," my father said, "and I think her parents were quite elderly when they had her because they were already dead when we met – probably another reason why she so readily built up a 'family' of her own."

He turned to everyone gathered in the downstairs room.

"I hope that later on – in the Spring, maybe – you'll all come over to France for a holiday. I'd love to see you all again, and we have plenty of room."

"You won't be here on Friday?" Marie asked.

My father shook his head. "I've said my goodbyes, and I really must get back to my family. But I mean what I say about you all coming over – your children would love it there, Chris."

They all assured him they would make the effort. I caught Adam's questioning eye.

"I'll be here on Friday," I said.

"Good," was he all he said, but it warmed me nonetheless.

Before we left, Kate handed my father a parcel.

"Marsha's left really clear instructions about everything she wanted done – as you'd expect her to, of course – but she didn't say anything about these. So we all thought you should have them. They're the photographs she showed us the other night."

"The photos of Anna?" he asked, taking the parcel.

Kate nodded. "And all the early ones, of the two of you together."

For the first time that day my father appeared visibly moved. His stuttering words of thanks were covered by general farewells all round.

"Keep in touch this week," Marie said fiercely as she hugged me. "For God's sake put that phonecard in your mobile!"

"I will," I promised, managing a weak smile.

Adam hugged me and gave me a brotherly kiss to the top of my head, which made me want to weep as we climbed the steps to the wooden gate – for everything else which now appeared to be over; not just Marsha's passing. Then we were on the road out of Tremorden, followed by a wintry sun that really had no right to be shining brightly in a blue afternoon sky.

We were both quiet for much of the journey back to London, until the pain in my stomach could only be eased by talking about Marsha and re-visiting the events of the weekend.

"Kate was so devoted to her, she couldn't have had better nursing. I only hope, like Adam said, that Kate doesn't take any guilt on board for not being there when Marsha actually died."

"'Mmm," was all my father said. He was slumped in the passenger seat, his hands thrust into the pockets of his coat as if he was cold, even though the car heater was on. He was probably feeling the effects of the brandy from the night before, but I had to carry on.

"It's strange how it worked out in the end. Marsha dying when we were all together. She admitted to me recently that she was a control freak. She's probably chuckling somewhere at how even she couldn't have pre-guessed it happening like this. Thank goodness you turned up when you did ..."

I was glancing across at him from time to time as I spoke. Suddenly something in his expression sent a surge of comprehension through my body. We were just approaching a motorway exit to I didn't know where, but I swung the car into the inside lane and, with a screech of brakes, shot up the exit slope, over the roundabout at the top and pulled into a lay-by.

"It was planned, wasn't it?" I gasped. "Marsha planned it and you helped her!"

He'd sat up straight as we careered off the motorway. Now he said, "Is there somewhere around here we could get a drink, do you think?"

"*Tell me,*" I insisted. "You helped Marsha to kill herself ... or ..." – my voice rose in horror – "*you ended her life for her!*"

"Does it matter, the exact manner of her death?" he asked, his voice an oasis of calm against my shrill accusations. "Isn't it sufficient to know that her suffering is over and she wasn't faced with any further indignities?"

"*But if you killed her, it's against the law, no matter how ill she was!*" I cried, his calmness only serving to make me more anguished. "If anyone found out you could be prosecuted!"

He gave a great sigh. "I didn't kill Marsha. But she *had* decided that she didn't want to carry on living any more." He looked around again in the gathering gloom of late afternoon. "I really wish there was somewhere we could go, to talk about this properly."

"Well there isn't, so we can't. You'll have to tell me about it here."

I waited. Eventually he gave another sigh.

"Marsha had already decided some time ago that when she felt the time was right she was going to take charge of her fate. Despite Kate's diligence, she'd managed to accumulate a little stockpile of painkillers – usually by starting to take them as Kate left the room and then keeping one back. Anyway, she knew she had the means, she just wasn't completely sure of when or how – she was anxious that if she was found one morning, there should be no blame or suspicion attached to Kate, or anyone else for that matter."

"But how come she enlisted your help? She didn't even know you were coming down!"

"No, but she knew *you* were. And that meant that with a bit of luck all of her 'family' would be together – probably for the last time, because she knew what she had left was only likely to be weeks. So she'd already planned to end her life this weekend, after one final great get-together – it really was a 'farewell party', you see."

I could picture her, in the lonely reaches of the night, those interminable nights she'd referred to, deciding what she would do; accustoming herself to the prospect, so that she could carry it out unflinchingly.

"That was why she called the doctor out," he continued, "she was so anxious that there should be no blame attached to Kate or any question of a post-mortem. She knew that if she'd seen her doctor and he'd acknowledged her worsening condition then there would be no questions asked."

"And she told you all this? Told *you*, whom she hadn't seen for all those years? What if you'd blown the whistle on her plans?"

He gave a small dry smile. "You forget how well Marsha knew us all. By Friday night she and I had talked so much that she knew we were still on the same wavelength. She knew I wouldn't stop her. She just needed to tell someone, and she wouldn't have told any of you because she knew it would be too painful for you."

"So she asked you to help?"

He shook his head. "I didn't 'help'. But I offered to stay with her – until the end. She was scared, you see. Scared that at the last minute she wouldn't have the courage to go through with it alone. But she was equally scared of what the last few weeks might hold – the pain, the indignity – incontinence, loss of speech, loss of her faculties – she knew they were all possibilities and she couldn't bear it. And she wanted to release everyone from their responsibilities – she felt she had asked enough of those she loved."

Tears glistened on his cheeks. He took a deep, shuddering breath. I held his hand tightly. "You don't need to go on."

He didn't appear to have heard me. "It was the only thing I could do for her. After the way I'd let her down in the past ... all those wasted years. It was the only way I could make up for it. I couldn't leave her on her own again."

I rummaged in my bag for a tissue. Handing it to him. I could hear Marsha's voice, imploring me to speak to Marie: *'It has to be done tonight.'* No wonder she was so insistent.

I looked at my father with a new kind of respect. "You knew, all day Saturday. You knew she was going to die that night."

He nodded, more composed again. "That's why I stayed near her all day. And during the party I kept topping up her champagne glass when no-one was looking – Kate was concerned about her having too much to drink because of all the drugs she was taking, but that was precisely what she wanted, of course. Then, when you'd all said goodnight, she started on the tablets. It was very peaceful ... I just held her, talked to her ... until she fell asleep. And then she simply ... stopped."

"So she was already dead, when you came downstairs?"

"An expert might have been able to detect a faint pulse, but I couldn't. I was sure if I told Kate not to disturb her for a few hours then she would definitely be dead – but if something did go wrong with the plan, Kate wouldn't have been the last person with her – that was very important."

I didn't know what else to say. Snippets of conversation, my father's restlessness when we returned to the hotel, all fell into place.

"Are you ever going to tell the others?" I asked at last.

"No. That's why I want to go straight back to France – I wouldn't want to let anything slip at the funeral. I wish Kate could know that Marsha wasn't alone at the end, but I think it's better this way – and I promised Marsha."

We sat for a while longer in the warm cocoon of the car, in a nameless place, which was somehow comforting.

"I'm sorry I've now burdened you with the knowledge of what happened," he said after a while. "I hope you can understand."

"It's okay," I said automatically, then considered for a few moments. It really was okay.

'Since when have I ever done anything I didn't want to?' Marsha's voice was so clear in my mind she could have been sitting on the back seat. What should have been one last summer had stretched into a weary winter and she would have wanted to release everyone from what might, by now, be obligation.

It was shocking, nonetheless. Thoughts and images swirled through my brain. How did she cope with knowing it was to be her last day of life, even if it was by her own decision? How was she brave enough to swallow the pills, one after another? And how was my father able to watch and not put a hand out to stay her, in a last-minute pleading to hang on, even if only for a few more days?

I knew it was going to take an enormous broom to sweep all of this away, and even then it would stay in the back of my mind for a long, long time, pushing its way to the front in moments of despondency, just as the awfulness of Will leaving me had done an aeon ago, it now seemed to me.

But this time I would know that I wasn't on my own. Over in France there would be moments when my father would pause in what he was doing to relive those final hours, to reassure himself that it had been right from Marsha's point of view; and to seek comfort, I hoped, from Yvon when he was filled with doubt. Or, perhaps, to phone me, because I knew and would understand.

I leaned across to kiss my father's cheek. "I'm pleased you shared it with me. It's important." I straightened up, turning the key in the ignition. "And now I think it's time we both went home."

21.

"Allie!" – **"My God! You look** awful! You really have been ill, haven't you?" – "We tried to phone you but you weren't there. We thought Will must have whisked you away for a dirty weekend – but it's all right, we didn't tell the She-Devil anything." – "Then we knew he hadn't, 'cos he phoned here a few times – but we didn't tell her that, either."

Donna, Stace and Em had gathered round me as soon as I staggered into work on Monday morning. Fortunately, the 'She-Devil', Merrill, wasn't there yet.

"Why isn't she in?" I asked, to deflect the questions I knew were inevitable. "She's always here before us."

"Meeting with David," Donna said with a sniff. "Business meeting, *or so she says*."

It was a relief to be back at work, to see the office looking no different, and the girls chattering in the same old way. So much had happened that I felt like I'd been away for a month, not just a few days, and experienced a certain surprise that nothing had changed in my absence.

"So if you weren't away with Will, where have you been?" Stace asked. "Did you end up in hospital or something? – 'cos we'd have visited if we'd known," she added, to ensure that it was anxiety for my welfare that was driving the questions, not simply spurious curiosity.

"You look very pale," Em observed, and I could see *'abortion clinic'* in the significant looks that flashed between them.

I plonked myself down at my desk and began to sort through some of the paperwork sitting there.

"I'm fine, really," I said. But I knew that wasn't enough. I stopped fiddling with the pieces of paper and raised my eyes to their three pairs of expectant but, I had to admit, concerned ones.

"A ... friend from Cornwall turned up unexpectedly, to tell me that another friend was dying. So I went down to Cornwall to see her. Oh, and my father turned up unexpectedly as well – from France, which made things a bit more complicated, so he came to Cornwall too."

"Your Dad came all the way from France without telling you?" Em's eyes narrowed. "What did he want?"

Em's Dad lived in Walthamstow but regularly arrived unannounced at her mother's house when he was short of cash.

"He just wanted to see me. We hadn't been in touch for ages and he got worried," I replied, a feeling of warmth engulfing me at the thought of our loving farewells early that morning, compared with when he'd first arrived and I'd felt as suspicious as Emma.

Donna cleared her throat. "And, er, your friend, in Cornwall, did she ... is she ...?"

"She died. Saturday night. I'll be going back down there on Friday for her funeral," I said simply.

"Oh ... sorry," Donna said.

"Yeah ... sorry," Em echoed.

"Ooh, that's awful, when someone dies young like that," Stace said with a little shiver, moving away to her own desk as if a connection with death was like some infectious disease. I decided it was too complicated to explain anything about Marsha, so left the three of them with their assumptions.

They didn't know what else to say, so when Merrill came into the office a short while later it was to a subdued atmosphere and an unusual appearance of diligence.

"Ah, Allie, you're back!" she said, oblivious to Donna's surreptitious scrutiny to see if either her clothes or hair appeared disheveled. "Are you better? You still look a bit peaky."

"Stomach upset," I said promptly. "Probably what brought the migraine on – but I'm fine now, honestly."

"Good." She went through to her office (which didn't seem such a cubbyhole now that it was so tidy and organised), and didn't reappear before lunch.

"Probably sending *him* e-mails," Donna muttered.

"When did she start getting jealous of Merrill?" I asked Stace later, when Donna had flounced off to the ladies.

"Since last Thursday when it turns out it was David's birthday, which none of us knew, even though we've worked here for ages, but Merrill found out and gave him a card and, according to Donna, was all over him like a rash."

"So Will didn't know you were going to Cornwall, then?" Em

asked now that I had broken the ice again and it was clear they didn't have to talk in reverent tones just because my friend had died.

"There wasn't time to tell him," I said quickly, "and anyway, I didn't think it was any of his business."

"Oh, so your friend who died – it wasn't a friend of his as well, then – from when you were married?"

"No – no, it wasn't."

It was tempting to tell them the whole story, because I was desperate to get some of it off my chest, especially about Adam, but it was just too complicated, and I knew that if I started I'd get upset about everything all over again. I felt very lonely, though, with my father back in France, while Kate and Marie, who at least knew everything, would have too much else on their minds this week.

The feeling of isolation increased during the day, despite the reassuring ordinariness of the girls' chatter. So when the phone went in the afternoon I was almost pleased to hear Will's voice on the line.

"Allie! I've been trying all ways to get in touch with you! Where *have* you been? I thought you must have been deliberately avoiding me!"

"I've been away for a few days."

"Well, I gathered *that*. I came round on Friday, as we agreed, and you weren't there. One of the neighbours said you hadn't been about for a couple of days."

"There wasn't time to tell you. I had to go to Cornwall. To see a friend who was very ill."

"To Cornwall? With that Adam chap?"

A hard note had crept into his carefully modulated tones. There'd been no real concern in his voice up until then; no *'I had visions of you raped and murdered somewhere, are you all right?'* – which was why he didn't get an apology.

"No, I didn't go with Adam. I went with my father."

I could feel the girls' ears beginning to strain, especially when Adam's name came into the equation.

"Your father?" Will said. "But he's in France."

"Yes, he is now. Back in France. But he wasn't for the last few days. He was with me, in Cornwall."

"Oh, I see," he said, although he clearly didn't. "Well, can I come over tonight? I've got lots to talk to you about."

"No," I said, quickly, "don't come round. Goodness knows who might turn up on my doorstep if you do." *And the worst thing of all would be if it was Adam – which was probably wishful thinking, but ...* "Let's meet somewhere instead."

We settled on a pub restaurant in Croydon. I waited still for the query about my personal state of health, state of mind, whatever, but it wasn't forthcoming.

"My friend died, by the way," I said in the end, before putting the phone down abruptly.

I then made a series of quite pointless calls myself so that he couldn't call me back, quite unwittingly in the process managing to impress Merrill with my diligence, while also preventing the girls from asking the burning question: *'Who is Adam?'*

Will must have been jolted by my sudden end to his call, though, because he was Mister Solicitous when we met, taking my coat and ordering me a drink immediately.

"I'm sorry," he said when we were seated at our table, "I was so pleased that you were back that I didn't think to ask what had happened in Cornwall. It was a shame about your friend."

He'd always had this knack of wrong-footing me just when I was thinking the worst of him, I reflected. Anyone listening to him now, skilfully turning the conversation to happier topics, would have been impressed with his gentlemanly ways and no doubt wonder why I wasn't rushing back to him with open arms.

I realised with a jolt that he was saying something about a house. "It was amongst those details I brought over to you last week – but I don't expect you've had any opportunity to look at them. Anyway, it's still on the market, but we need to look at it as soon as possible, because I'm certain it will be snapped up ..."

'It's time to finish this,' Marsha had apparently said to my father when she'd decided to end her life. And it was time to finish this too, now.

Marsha. It hit me anew that I wouldn't ever see her again – in fact, if Adam and I didn't manage to make anything of our faltering relationship, which was how it appeared, I wouldn't see any of them after Friday. And if I said a final goodbye to Will I'd be alone, quite alone – again. But Marsha's voice was in my head, and suddenly there were tears blurring my vision.

I looked around wildly, trying to blink them away, not wanting Will to see my weakness. I needed to be strong to finish this. As strong as Marsha had been.

"I'm sorry," I mumbled, standing up quickly, "I need to go to the Ladies".

The place was huge and quite darkly lit, with different bars and eating areas on different floors. It took me a while to find the loo, but once there I shut myself inside a cubicle and let the tears flow, furious with myself that I should break down here, of all places, but helpless to do much about it, my tear ducts having apparently developed a will of their own.

I'd just passed the sobbing stage and reached the shuddering stage when two girls came into the cloakroom, evidently catching up on a bit of girly gossip as they fixed their faces. I stayed very quiet, wishing they would go so that I could splash water on my face and repair some of the damage.

"So I'd had enough in the end," the one girl was saying, "all the lying and cheating. There were always other women. And then when I found out that the business was going down the pan and there was no money, I decided enough was enough. I'm worth more than that, I told myself. So I got out while I could. He tried to get me back, but I wasn't having any of it ..."

Now that sounded strong. That was how I needed to be.

"Shame," the other girl was saying, "'cos he seemed really nice."

"Well, you know what they say – if he did it to his wife *with* you, he'll do it *to* you, the skunk!"

"You just can't tell, can you? I know when I first met your Will I thought ..."

Will?? – I straightened up, wiped a tissue round my face and opened the door, heading for the nearest washbasin. I had to get out of there.

"God, you made me jump!" the first girl said. "I didn't know anyone was in there!"

"Sorry," I mumbled, concentrating on washing my hands as if it was an obsessive ritual.

"Are you all right?" she asked kindly.

I lifted my head and our eyes met in the mirror above the basin. She was tall and blonde and leggy, with thrusting boobs in a tight Lycra top. I was small, dark and blotchy.

"I'm fine," I answered, looking at her steadily even though my face was streaked with mascara.

She had the grace to blanch rather horribly, and we stared at each other a moment longer. Her voice cracked a little. "Sure?"

I nodded, wiping away the mascara remnants. I didn't care any more if I looked a sight. I squared my shoulders; I could finish it now. "Quite sure," I said. "*I'm* worth more, too."

Ignoring her friend's mystified face, I turned on my heel and made a dignified exit.

Will was studying the menu when I returned and only looked up fleetingly. Luckily it was too dark to see my face clearly. "Was there a queue?" he asked. "You've been ages. This food looks good by the way – I hope you're feeling hungry?"

"Not really," I said. "In fact, I don't think I want anything to eat at all."

Something in my tone made him look up at me properly, inquiringly.

"Put the menu down for a minute, Will. I want to tell you something."

He did as he was told, but opened his mouth to speak. I could feel Marsha on my shoulder and put up my hand to stop him.

"I don't want to go on with this – with any of it. It was wrong to think that we could get back together again – we can't."

"But everything was fine – we've been getting on so well! What's brought this on?"

"I just don't love you any more, Will. I thought I did. All the time we were apart I thought I loved you – but it was what I'd wanted our marriage to be that I was still in love with, not the reality. We're not right for each other, and if we get back together we'll make each other unhappy again."

It was a noble speech, every bit as noble as the speeches he'd made to me when he first came back. I was quite moved by it.

Will, though, was not. His face darkened. "Look, Allie, I told you how I felt when I was with Lauren – how I realised what you meant to me, and I've tried to prove it to you every day since. I thought you were beginning to feel the same. If this is anything to do with that character who turned up last week, let me tell you ..."

"It's nothing to do with Adam!" I said fiercely. "This is *me*, Allie, making decisions for myself! I know that might be hard for you to understand, seeing as you made all of them when we were together, and I was stupid enough to let you, but I'm a different person, now! I'm my *own* person! This is *my* choice."

I could feel Marsha applauding me. *'Look at you,'* I could hear her saying, *'starting to take charge of your life!'* Perhaps, finally, I was.

Will changed his tone to wheedling. "You've had a difficult week. You're upset, I can see that. Why don't I give you some space for a few days, time to think ... think about how I love you ... think about saving our marriage—"

I stood up. "Okay. You just don't get it, do you? Try this then. You're a lying, cheating, self-absorbed bastard, which is not the sort of person I want to spend the rest of my life with!"

Breathe.

"I'm going now," I went on more sweetly, "but I don't want you to come with me. And I don't want you to call me any more. In fact, it's better if we don't see each other again – ever." I tossed my head in the direction of the noisier parts of the pub. "There are lots of girls up there – go and try your luck with one of them."

I picked up my coat and swept out of the pub, willing myself not to falter in any way. I could sense Marsha still on my shoulder. This time, she was chuckling.

The phone was ringing as I entered the flat. I rushed to pick it up and tried not to sound disappointed when it was Marie, ringing to confirm the time of the funeral.

"How is everyone?" I asked.

"It's just Kate and me for now. The lads all left this morning, so that they can come back down for Friday. It feels okay at the moment, though, because there's so much to do, and we're both feeling absolutely shattered. Early night for both of us, I think, then we'll see how things look in the morning."

We talked for a few more minutes, but I didn't say anything about Will because I knew it would lead to a discussion of Adam, and, for the moment, I didn't want that. I was still taking charge.

The house details Will had referred to were still on the coffee table. The house was a little semi in Sidcup. *Sidcup?* Where on earth was that? There was a definite sense of pleasure in consigning them to the bin. Then I followed Marie's example and had an early night, hoping that a good sleep would repair the swollen eyes and blotchy skin. I was suddenly so deeply tired that I didn't, couldn't, think of anyone else any more.

"Hallo darling, we're back! Oh, you do look pale now that your tan's gone – are you overdoing things? I don't know why you have to traipse half-way across London just for some temping job …"

It was early the next evening and my mother, closely trailed by Philip and a strong whiff of Chanel, had just swept into my flat all on one breath.

"I only look pale because your tan looks so wonderful," I replied with a smile. "Welcome home, both of you! It's good to have you back!"

And I actually meant it, I realised as I gave Juliet a lingering hug in response to her air-kiss, before deciding to give a surprised Philip a hug as well. "Did you have a great time?"

"Darling, we did!" Juliet breathed as she arranged herself on the sofa. I noticed a secretive little smile pass between the two of them as Philip sat beside her.

"We've got something to tell you!" she announced, whipping off the glove of her left hand and waving her fingers at me. "Philip and I are engaged!"

Three diamonds winked up at me, so large that if they had been given by anyone else but Philip and worn by anyone else but Juliet I would have suspected they were zircon.

"Isn't it wonderful!" Juliet exclaimed, and, not sure whether she was referring to the engagement itself or the ring, I quickly agreed that yes, it was.

"I'm really pleased for both of you," I said. "When's the happy day?"

"That's for my husband-to-be to decide," Juliet turned to Philip so coyly that I had to stop myself from laughing. Did he know how many times she'd been round the block? – Or how many blocks, for that matter!

Philip cleared his throat, to assure himself that his vocal chords still worked, I suspected. "I'd ... we'd –" *did he really return the coy look?* – "like it to be as soon as possible. I know people might think we've only known each other for a short while, but we go back a long way – it would be silly to waste any more time." His face became very serious. "But it's important – to both of us – that we have your blessing."

"Of course you do! Two consenting adults – it's really nothing to do with me, as long as you're both happy!"

"Oh, we are," he assured me, taking Juliet's hand. "Very happy."

He was nice, I decided, a very nice man. How did Juliet do it? Three decent men had been willing to marry her, and countless others had been kept on a string over the years. There must have been something in her genes which she hadn't passed on to me.

"We're not sure whether it will be Claridges or the Ritz," Juliet was saying. "It all depends on Joan Collins."

"Joan Collins?" I repeated, impressed. "Is she going to be a guest?"

"No darling, don't be silly. I need to check where she had her last 'do' – because one wouldn't want to choose the same place."

Oh! No, of course one wouldn't. Now that really was silly of me.

"So," she said when we had disposed of the wedding chat, "what have you been up to while we've been away?" Her eyes swept the room for evidence of wild living, or, at the least, a *soupçon* of excitement.

"Oh, this and that. Umm ... Will got back in touch – you remember he'd been trying to get hold of me? Well, he wanted to stop the divorce, try being married again, but ..."

"Will?" Juliet squealed. "Wanted you back?" *(The note of incredulity here nearly made me retract my earlier statement that I was pleased to see her.)* "But why? What had happened? What did you say?"

Philip tapped her lightly on her elegantly covered thigh. "Let her tell us in her own good time, darling," and to my amazement my mother shut up. Perhaps it would be third time lucky after all.

"I said no. I'm over him now. There can't be any going back. I don't love him any more."

"But—"

Philip gave Juliet an almost imperceptible nudge.

"Well, I'm sure you've done the right thing, darling," Juliet managed. Which was obviously a struggle for her, because she'd always been very fond of Will.

"Oh ... and Dad came to visit me last week," I said brightly to fill the slight pause in the conversation.

"Ian? Here?" she exclaimed, looking round again in case he was still lurking in the background. "Don't tell me – he turned up without any warning."

"Yes, he did actually. Said he'd been worrying about me because of a phone call he'd had from you ..."

She had the grace to look a little uncomfortable. "Yes, well, I was concerned about you when you went missing ... and I thought it was time he shouldered some of the worry. I didn't think he'd simply arrive out of the blue, but of course, he always was so dreadfully impulsive ..."

"Well I'm glad he did," I interrupted before she got into full *'you know what your father's like'* mode. "We spent a few days together and cleared a lot of things up."

We'd both agreed not to mention Cornwall to Juliet unless it was absolutely necessary.

"Good," Philip said firmly. "It's important for children to get on with their parents, whatever their ages. And their prospective step-parents for that matter," he went on, beaming at me. "So won't you join us for dinner this evening, a little celebration?"

I smiled back, but regretfully. "I'd love to, but I'm afraid I can't tonight. I've already made plans."

As soon as we'd settled on lunch the following Sunday instead, they left – "So that you'll have plenty of time to get ready for whatever it is you have on tonight," Juliet said archly, because I hadn't told her what it was.

This was mainly, of course, because I wasn't exactly sure what those plans would be myself. But seeing Juliet and Philip sitting there so happily, and aware that they could have enjoyed that sort of happiness for the last twenty-odd years if everyone involved hadn't ended up marrying the wrong person or whatever, made me determined to take charge again. All I had done so far was sit about and wait for Adam to get in touch with me, and feel sorry for myself if he didn't. Now was the time to do something about it.

I still had his mobile number, but I'd memorised it anyway, so, without giving myself time to back-track, I quickly dialled it.

"Adam Palmer."

"Adam, it's Allie. Are you in tonight?"

"Er ... yes ... yes, I am – I was going to call you ... Are you all right?"

"I'm fine. Adam, where do you live?"

"Shepherd's Bush – I told you ..."

"Yes, but where exactly?"

He gave me the address, and the directions from the tube station.

"Good. Are you going to be there all evening?"

"Well, it looks like I might be now ... I was going to suggest I come round to see you. There's something urgent I need to tell you about—"

"I'm coming round to you. Like you said at Marsha's, we need to talk."

"All right ..." His voice was careful, as though I was someone who might do something violent if they weren't humoured. "Do you want me to meet you at the tube station? My place is a bit hard to find."

"No, don't worry, I'll be able to find it. And if not, I've put the phonecard in my mobile. I'll be about an hour."

All the way there, I told myself that this must be finished too – so much so, that when a man opposite me in the tube smiled encouragingly I realised my lips had been moving to the words in my head. I scowled at him to show that I wasn't issuing any sort of invitation, which made him sufficiently discomfited to pick up a discarded newspaper and bury his head in it.

I went back to my mental deliberations. I'd finished my relationship with Will; now I had to find the words for Adam. I would simply tell him everything that had happened with me and Will, and he would have to make his mind up himself. If he didn't want me, okay. It would break my heart, but that had been broken before and I knew now that it could eventually heal. But at least I would know, and the rest of my life would not be blighted by confusion and lost opportunities like that of both my parents and Marsha.

Once outside the tube station I set off boldly in what I considered to be the right direction, from what Adam had told me, but of course I didn't really have a clue. I was determined not to phone him, though, so I asked about six different people – two of whom seemed to have even less idea of where they were than I did, one who turned out to be an Albanian refugee or something, and another whose educational development seemed to have stopped before he reached the lesson on right-from-left.

Eventually I found it, in the middle of a long terrace of lofty old townhouses which looked romantic at night but probably rather down-at-heel by daylight. My courage stayed with me right up until I heard Adam's voice crackle over the entryphone: "Hi, come on up. I'm right at the top."

I made my way up the seemingly endless staircase, feeling for Marsha on my shoulder, but she wasn't there. This time, I was completely on my own.

Adam was waiting for me at the top, leaning over the banister.

"Sorry about the climb," he said lightly. "There's oxygen up here if you need it."

But it wasn't just the stairs making me breathless. It had something to do with the thumping of my heart as well.

He led me through a tiny hallway into what was just one long room. At one end were sofas and chairs in front of a large curtained window, in the middle stood a kitchen island, and at the far end a table and chairs graced another even larger window which would probably overlook most of the rooftops of Shepherd's Bush. Now, though, it was just a mass of twinkling lights against an inky backdrop, like some sort of global Christmas decoration. Through a French door to the side of the window there seemed to be a small glass conservatory which looked as if it is was suspended in the night sky.

The room was painted a pale creamy yellow and had a sanded and polished floor; it was so minimalist that it made my flat look positively cluttered, yet somehow it still managed to look warm and inviting.

"I told you it was a broom cupboard," Adam said. He pointed along the room: "Living area, cooking area, eating area, work area through there –" he pointed to the funny little conservatory room – "bedroom and bathroom through there," pointing this time to a door next to the conservatory.

"It's lovely," I said breathily, wishing immediately that I'd thought of a less dull adjective. There was a pause.

"It must be very light in daytime," I continued, to breach the gap.

"It is. And quiet, because it's so high up."

Another pause. *Say something,* I told myself, *tell him why you're here ...*

But this time he filled the gap.

"It suits me – I'm not here a great deal. But I feel very comfortable when I am."

I nodded. He nodded at my nodding. This was awful. Since when had it been hard to talk to Adam?

"Here – let me take your coat," he said suddenly, moving forward as I, pleased to have something to do, hurriedly undid the buttons, dropping my handbag on the floor in my haste so that all the contents spilled out. We knelt together to retrieve the bits of paper and old shopping receipts and tissues with pieces of fluff on them. I resolved, too late of course, to tidy out my bag more often, just like one tidies the house immediately after unexpected visitors who found you in a mess have left.

"This reminds me of that first evening in Tremorden," Adam said, solemnly handing me a twopence piece and a faded Smartie which I stupidly returned to my bag because I couldn't see a bin anywhere.

"It's an evening I'd rather forget, "I said. "Oh – except for meeting you all of course – I wouldn't want to forget that – I just meant ..."

I groaned inwardly. What had happened to taking control? This was so much harder than dealing with Will.

I was still holding my coat, my scarf and my handbag all in one big jumble. "Let me take them," Adam said, carrying them over to one of the chairs, disentangling them as he went.

He looked tired and drawn, I noticed, making me ache to hold him and soothe the lines away from his face. Suddenly I felt strong again.

"Adam—"

"Allie, there's something I have to explain." He'd turned round swiftly, as if reaching some sort of decision at the same time as me. He took my hands and drew me down onto a dining chair, pulling another one directly opposite, so that he could look straight into my face. He was still holding my hands, and already I felt warmed.

"I'm going to tell you all of this, even though you might not like what you're hearing, but just remember that I'm telling you because I care about you."

Waves of heat ran up and down my spine. Here it was. The rejection. I could tell from the tone of voice. The next line was probably going to be: *'It's nothing to do with you, it's me,'* which always means the opposite.

"You can't go back to Will," he said emphatically.

Waves of relief ran all through my body this time.

"But I'm—" Before I could get any further he stopped me.

"When I took his mobile back, I checked through some of the numbers on it first. One of them was Lauren's – so I made a note of it. Then, when I got to his place he gave me all this guff about you and him getting back together again because you've realised that you're soul mates and I'd better back off, etcetera etcetera ..."

"I know, but—"

Adam held up his hand. "No, let me finish – this isn't easy, so I've got to say it all in one go. I met Lauren the next day, Allie – by which time you were on your way to Cornwall. She told me that she'd left Will because he was nearly bankrupt – he'd overstretched himself on the business, owed a lot of money on his flat, and had turned into the boyfriend from hell because of it. Allie, she told me that the only reason Will was trying to get back with you was to prevent the cost of the divorce and make some money from selling both your flat and his. I'm sorry ... but I thought you should know."

"I do know."

"*What?* You know that he's a total prick and you're still considering going back to him?"

The distress on his face made my insides contract and I knew I'd never stop loving him, even if he wanted me no longer, despite what I'd been telling myself all the way there.

"I'm not going back to Will," I said emphatically. "I'm not going back to him for all sorts of reasons – the main one being that I don't love him. But I've met Lauren too."

"You have? When"

"Last night, in a pub where I'd already arranged to meet Will to tell him it was over. She was in the Ladies talking to a friend, and I heard all I needed to."

"Oh. I see."

He let go of my hands and dropped his own into his lap.

"No, Adam, you don't see. Not properly." *Come on Marsha, this is where I need you! This is going to be the most important speech I've ever made in my life.*

I took his hands back in mine before taking a deep breath.

"Right up until I came to Cornwall in the summer I'd thought I was still in love with Will. I spent useless hours imagining what I would do if he came back to me. After the summer – after I was quite convinced that I'd messed up any chance I had with you – Will came back into my life, saying all the things I'd dreamed of him saying. I was intrigued, and I almost fell for it. *Almost,* but not quite. Because there was something missing."

Adam's tawny eyes were boring into mine with such an intensity that I almost looked away. But I knew I had to make him believe me.

"When we met on Westminster Bridge that day, I'd been trying to decide what to do. But as soon as I saw you again I knew what it was that was missing. Will didn't really care about me, the *real* me, because he'd never properly discovered who I was. But you *knew.* Right from the start, you'd known me so much more – and I was so truly happy to be with you again, that Will became an insignificance. I could see that I'd been clutching at straws to even contemplate that I could be happy with him again."

"You don't have to say any more ..." Adam said, wincing at my pain. Well, wincing at *his* pain if I'm really truthful, because I was gripping his hands so tightly that my fingernails were digging into his palms. But I was on a roll now; he had to hear everything I'd come to say.

"By the evening I was convinced that you and I were going to be able to make a go of things, but then Will turned up – so sure of himself, and so convincing; and I hadn't even mentioned him to you, so I knew you'd be thinking that I was some sort of two-timing slapper. And then my father turned up, so there wasn't time to speak to you; and then we were back in Cornwall – and there was Marsha – and I wanted to tell you that I loved you – but I couldn't because ... because ... and if you don't want to be with me in the end, then that's fine, but at least you'll have heard the truth and our lives won't be all mixed up like my parents', and Marsha ... and ..."

My voice had almost reached a pitch that only a dog would be able to hear, and held a distinct wobble. I bit down hard on my lip. *I was not going to cry, I was not going to ...*

But then Adam was pulling me to my feet and slowly, oh so slowly and deliberately, he held my face between his hands. He kissed the tears from the edges of my eyes, before placing his lips on mine. And slowly and deliberately his kiss built up into the most passionate moment I had ever experienced.

There was no need for any more words. Explanations over.

Later, much later, when I'd eventually had time to notice that lying back on his bed you could study the night sky through the skylight immediately above, Adam said: "The only thing I don't understand is the Smartie. I thought you'd have been much more of an M&M girl."

22.

Okay ... So when I started all this I might have sworn to anyone who would listen that I wasn't looking for a man to share my life with again, but I suppose in the end that's what we're all looking for, isn't it, if we're completely honest? Someone with whom we can endure this strange journey and satisfy our physical and emotional needs? I mean, you only have to look at Juliet and her role-model Joan Collins to see hope repeatedly triumphing over experience.

I have to admit that Adam's declaration of life-long devotion – which he made later that night, in case you're wondering – was everything I wanted to hear. Even so, I wasn't so wrapped up in the romance of it all not to register that there were still going to be one or two ordeals to get through before we could stroll off into the sunset.

Marsha's funeral, for one, which was immensely moving, especially when we saw just how many people turned up because she'd played a special part in their lives at one time or another. It was also entertaining in parts, as you'd expect, since Marsha had pre-planned the whole thing; for example, when the very sincere and orthodox vicar had to struggle through a reading from *Abelard and Heloise* which suggested that we loved the god in one another if we had trouble with belief in the Man himself – which struck a distinctly sacrilegious note.

But it wasn't just her funeral of course. There was going to be a lot of grieving to get through, especially for Adam, before the sun was going to shine on us again. But her 'family' pledged to stay together come what may, and, again, she'd pre-empted this by making a complicated bequest of her house for all five of them to share for many summers to come.

Already, though, there were signs of life continuing to move us forward. Not just me and Adam, but Simon and Marie too.

She had agreed to return to Simon's place for a few weeks, 'to see how things go'.

"I don't know whether it will work out," she whispered to me, "but I've got to try. I do really love him ... I'll let you know what happens."

"You'd better," I whispered back fiercely.

So, later that afternoon, as we stood on the rocks below Marsha's house looking out across the water, where Marsha's spirit now floated free, we both knew it was time to go.

"Ready for home?" Adam asked.

I smiled, and linked my arm confidently through his.

"Okay."

THE END

ABOUT THE AUTHOR

Julie McGowan has had over forty short stories and features published both nationally and internationally, and is an ardent playwright for the Welsh theatre. She has won numerous writing competitions over the years, as well as penning various features, a newspaper column, and a local annual town guide. Well known in her home town of Usk, Monmouthshire, for her work in the community, Julie runs a young people's drama workshop, *Stageright,* as well as a full theatrical group, performing variety shows and witty pantomimes to sell-out crowds every year. She also co-runs *Is It?,* a theatre company which tours secondary schools in Wales with productions covering health and social issues. And her talents don't stop there – Julie is also a pianist, though she claims to be extremely rusty nowadays!

Born in Blaenavon, Julie left Wales for Kent at the age of 12. She trained as a nurse at Guy's Hospital, London, and then as a Health Visitor in Durham, living there for 4 years after her marriage to husband Peter. The couple now have four adult children, and have lived in Surrey, Lincolnshire, and Hertford-shire before returning to Wales 15 years ago. Julie has had a wide variety of jobs, including teaching piano, and serving as Town Clerk in Usk.

Just One More Summer is Julie's second book – see details of *The Mountains Between* overleaf – and she is working on her third, *Don't Pass Me By.*

Visit Julie's web site at www.juliemcgowan.co.uk, or email her at julie@juliemcgowan.co.uk

Also by Julie McGowan:

The Mountains Between

ISBN: 978-0-9555283-3-0

- *"Intensely moving."*
- *"Funny, tender, utterly fascinating."*
- *"Wales gleams brilliantly through the dust of farmland and coalfield, mountain and valley, heartache and delight. You can almost taste it!"*

Order it from any good book store, or visit Sunpenny Publishing at www.sunpenny.com

Blaenavon and Abergavenny surge to life in this vibrant, haunting, joyful masterpiece, a celebration of the Welsh people in the 1920s to '40s. "The Mountains Between" is a saga of two families and their communities – farmers and miners, villagers and warriors, singers and mourners, in a smorgasbord that keeps the pages in perpetual motion. It tells the story of a little girl growing up on a farm, fighting to keep her balance in the face of an unbalanced mother and the deepest heart-blows a child can bear. It's the story of a Big Pit mining family who suffered an unspeakable tragedy. And it's a story about two young people who could have and should have found each other much sooner, but their valleys were separated by the mountains and never the twain, in those days, would meet.

It's a war story; a love story; a hate story. But more than all this, it's the story of a chunk of Wales's lifetime slashed like a scar on a mountainside - about the people of Wales, the people of the mountains and the valleys who formed the beating heart of that country.

This book is the story of their essence.